THE
DELTA

Also by Tony Park

Far Horizon
Zambezi
African Sky
Safari
Silent Predator
Ivory

Part of the Pride (with Kevin Richardson)
War Dogs (with Shane Bryant)

THE
DELTA

TONY PARK

St. Martin's Press ☙ New York

THE DELTA. Copyright © 2010 by Tony Park. All rights reserved. Printed in the United States of America. For information, address St. Martin's Press, 175 Fifth Avenue, New York, NY 10010.

www.stmartins.com

Designed by *Omar Chapa*

Cartographic art by Laurie Whiddon, Map Illustrations

The Library of Congress Cataloging-in-Publication Data is available upon request.

ISBN 978-1-250-05558-3 (hardcover)
ISBN 978-1-4668-5890-9 (e-book)

St. Martin's Press books may be purchased for educational, business, or promotional use. For information on bulk purchases, please contact Macmillan Corporate and Premium Sales Department at 1-800-221-7945, extension 5442, or write specialmarkets@macmillan.com.

First published in 2010 by Pan Macmillan Australia Pty Limited

First U.S. Edition: October 2014

10 9 8 7 6 5 4 3 2 1

For Nicola

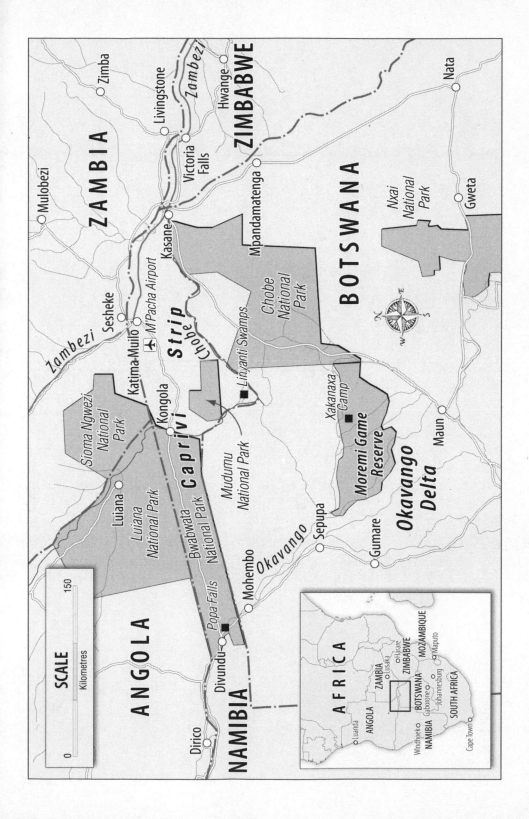

THE
DELTA

1

Africa was dying of thirst before her eyes. To keep herself awake, and alert, she watched the birds and the trees through the scope, but it was a depressing view.

Ficus sycamorus, the sycamore fig, on the bank of the river, still green, defying the drought, but for how much longer? It was a watercourse in name only, now nothing more than a sandy red scar through the tanned, dry skin of Africa.

Ziziphus . . . Ziziphus what? She couldn't remember the second part of the Latin name. Buffalo thorn, in English, but she knew it better by the Afrikaans nickname, *wag-'n-bietje*. It was called wait-a-bit because that's what you had to do if you brushed against it: stop and take your time to free yourself of its wicked little barbs. They got under your skin and poisoned you—like Africa. *Ziziphus mucronata*, that was it. Stirling would have been proud of her, although Stirling knew all the Latin names by heart.

She blinked away a drop of sweat, not wanting to risk even the movement of her hand to wipe it from her eyes. The sun was overhead and while the net covering the hide gave her some shade and concealment, it didn't keep the heat out. So well hidden was she that the cheetah hadn't seen her.

The sighting had made her heart pound. It was rare enough to see one in the Moremi Game Reserve or a national park. Who would have thought that in the barren farmlands of Zimbabwe she would see one slinking along the dirt verge of the main road at five in the morning? The cat's coat had shone like spun gold in the first low rays of the sun, the black dots seemed to dazzle her as she studied the cheetah through her binoculars. Later, once the sun was completely up, she saw a pair of steenbok and wondered if the cheetah had been on their scent. Why not cheetahs? she asked herself now that she thought about it. The lands as far as she could see, from left to right and out to the far horizon, had once hosted crops and cattle but were now returning to bush, the scrubby *wag-'n-bietje* reclaiming the earth and providing food and shade for browsers like the little steenbok antelope that took their name from the brick-red color of their coat.

Cheetah struggled in national parks and game reserves, Stirling had told her long ago as they spent an hour one school holiday watching a mother and four cubs perched on a termite mound at the far end of the Xakanaxa air strip.

"Ironically," he had begun, lapsing easily into the David Attenborough accent that always made her smile, "the cheetah is most at risk within the protection of a reserve. Here she will face danger at every turn; her life, and the lives of her cubs under daily threat from hyena, lion and wild dog."

It stood to reason, then, that cheetah could fare well in a place like Zimbabwe. With the bushveld reclaiming the commercial farms that had been abandoned by the so-called veterans of the liberation war who had taken them from the white farmers years ago, wildlife was slowly coming back. It was unlikely there would be lion in the area—perhaps the odd hyena—so if a cheetah had four cubs then all would have a good chance of survival. How odd, she thought, that something good might come of such a tragic chain of events.

The cheetah hadn't noticed her, although she'd been no more than two hundred meters from the road's edge. That was good. The cat had a sprinter's build, with long skinny legs, narrow hips and a deep chest that held the heart of a hunter. Its long tail twitched and swished as it walked along the gravel verge of the road. Here and there it stopped to scent-mark its territory, with a squirt of urine against a tree or kilometer peg. She watched it for half an hour until it crossed the bridge and carried on over the rise.

"Good luck," she had whispered. One predator to another.

Sonja lowered the binoculars and slowly rolled her shoulders, keeping the blood flowing with an economy of movement. She turned her feet, one at a time, and clenched and unclenched first her calves and then her thighs. She had prepared and moved into the hide after dark, at nine the previous evening, and once she was in place she had moved from the spot where she now lay only twice, to pee. Glancing down at her watch she saw it had been fourteen hours. She would wait as long as it took.

Three days was the longest time she had lain in a hide, but that was in training. It had been cold. No, bloody freezing. And wet, the misting rain collecting on the plastic leaves of the camouflage net and dribbling down on her head, to run down the back of her neck. Three days of peeing in the same patch of dirt and crapping in a plastic bag and wrapping it in tinfoil. They had never let her do it for real, in the field, which had angered her and the other two girls on the course.

Kigelia Africana. Sausage tree. Stirling would have said she was picking the easy ones, which was true. She heard a hum.

She swung the binoculars slowly westward. She had sited herself on the north side of a bend in the main road that ran between Bulawayo and Victoria Falls, facing southward, so that the sun would pass behind her on its arching journey from dawn to dusk. It meant she wouldn't be staring into the sun, and there was less risk of the light reflecting from her powerful Steiner binoculars, or the scope.

She saw the car coming from the west and took a breath, stilling herself. It was only the fourth vehicle she had seen all morning. Crippling fuel shortages did wonders for traffic control. It was moving fast, down the middle of the road, its tires straddling the broken white center line. That was a good sign.

As she focused she saw it was a Mercedes; white, with blue, gold and yellow strips running from stem to stern. Zimbabwe Republic Police. Its lights were flashing and she reckoned, judging by the seconds she counted from the first kilometer peg to the second, that it was clocking about a hundred and fifty.

He was coming.

"The convoy," Martin had said during the briefing, "is always preceded by two speeding police cars, who maintain visual distance between each other. Their job is to warn oncoming motorists to get off the road. Everyone who lives in Zimbabwe knows that when they see a patrol car screaming down the middle of the highway they must pull over immediately."

"What about tourists, or people who don't know what's going on?" Sonja had asked him.

Martin had nodded, dragged quickly on his Benson and Hedges and exhaled. Sonja's mouth had almost watered from the craving. "If the second car sees an oncoming vehicle still on the road he flashes his lights and drives toward, it, forcing it off the road. If all is clear—and other vehicles have pulled over—he lets the next car in the convoy know that it is safe to proceed."

The police car flashed past her and she looked west again. The second police car was traveling at the same speed and she focused through its windscreen. She caught a glimpse of the occupants, one smiling and nodding at something the other had said.

Her hand moved to the transmitter and she flicked the safety cover off the switch. The second car passed over the low concrete bridge, over the dry riverbed, and she imagined the stories the officers inside the vehicle—both vehicles—would tell for the rest of their lives about how narrowly they had avoided death.

She knew she shouldn't have looked at the men's faces. To personalize the targets—to give them an imagined identity—did no good at all. It was easier when they were further away, but the nature of this job meant she had to get close enough to see the men's faces, and to read them.

Sonja heard the combined drone of more engines and the whine of rubber on hot tar. The noise reminded her of an approaching swarm of African bees. She counted the vehicles with her naked eye as they came into sight. There was another police pursuit car; then three limousines—two black Mercs and a same-colored BMW, all armor-plated according to Martin. Behind the limos was yet another cop car, followed by an army *bakkie*, a pickup with a section of ten paratroopers in the open back. They would be armed, she knew already, with a mix of AK-47s, two RPD belt-fed light machine-guns, and at least one RPG 7 anti-armor weapon. Last in the convoy was a military ambulance.

Sonja pushed a button and the concrete bridge erupted in a cloud of smoke and debris. A split second later she heard the boom, and then felt the shock wave wash over her. The dry yellow grass around her was smoothed for an instant by the hot wind.

Rubber screamed at her from the valley, but at the speed he was traveling there was no way the policeman in the third Mercedes Kompressor could stop in time. The car shot into the smoking void where the bridge had once been and nosedived into the sand.

Twisting, buckling metal screeched in Sonja's ears, but she blocked out the sights and sounds as she moved her cramped body into a sitting position. She hefted the Javelin antitank guided-missile launcher onto her shoulder, pressed her eyes to the rubber cups and stared at the screen of the Command Launch Unit, or CLU for short. The drivers of the three limousines had all managed to avoid following the police car into the riverbed or rear-ending each other and were stopped at odd angles on the road at the end of snaking black skids of burned rubber. Gearboxes whined and a horn hooted as the drivers tried to straighten and reverse. Sonja shifted herself until the army *bakkie* was centered and bracketed by the aiming marks on the screen. The vehicle's driver had slewed to the left to avoid slamming into the rear of the police car in front. He was stopped now and the stunned soldiers in the back were rousing themselves. A couple had already jumped clear and were dropping to their bellies, taking up firing positions. The men seemed better trained than Martin had briefed her to expect. Using her thumb Sonja toggled the switch until "top attack" was illuminated. She braced herself for the launch and squeezed the trigger.

There was a loud click as the first of the projectile's two motors ignited. The missile left its tube like a thoroughbred leaping from its gate. Sonja's body was rocked and she squeezed her eyes shut to avoid being blindsighted by the ignition of the second-stage motor. The tail of the missile, she knew, would be dropping slowly, about five meters in front of her, but the whoosh she heard told her the main motor had just kicked in. When she opened her eyes again she saw a flying comet of furiously burning exhaust as the missile arced high into the sky then began its downward trajectory.

Javelin is a fire-and-forget weapon and she knew the missile would chase the army pick-up, even if the driver had restarted his engine and begun moving again. She didn't stop to watch the hit—there was no time. She was already removing the spent missile tube and fitting another to the CLU. As she locked it in place she heard the detonation of the warhead. When she surveyed the scene again it was through the monochrome of the screen. It helped, she knew, not to be able to see the blood as she selected another target.

She only had three missiles. Her plan had been to take out the *bakkie* so that its burning wreck would bottle the limousines between it and the destroyed bridge. The road was sunk in an earthen cutting at this point, which was why she had chosen it, so that none of the cars could turn off and escape into the thornbush-studded grasslands. But, by training, instinct or accident, the *bakkie* driver had pulled onto the verge, leaving enough room for the vehicles in front to reverse back past it.

The *bakkie* was ablaze. She moved the sights to the ambulance, which had been lagging a few hundred meters behind the convoy. She had wanted to spare it, so as to at least give a chance of survival to the soldiers and policemen she had already hurt. However, it now looked as though she would have to take it out.

On the screen she saw another vehicle moving. The police car that had been in front of the *bakkie* was reversing at speed. The noise had come when the driver pulled on his handbrake and swung his wheel. It was a classic counter-ambush move and well executed. The police driver was getting the hell out of there. That was odd.

The policeman floored his accelerator and headed west, but smoke from the burning pick-up was drifting across the road. As he swerved around the wreck he plowed head on into the ambulance. Sonja winced at the sound of the impact. The cop's eagerness to run away had done her job for her.

She shifted the CLU to the left and surveyed the three limousines.

Pop, pop, pop. She heard the tinny reports of AK-47s firing, though she felt no air displaced around her. Way off to her left was a tall knob-thorn tree, *Acacia nigrescens*, and to her right were the crumbling remains of a mud hut, which she imagined might once have been occupied by party faithful or war veterans who had staked a claim on the overgrown farm where she hid. She had dug her hide in open country, using the long golden grass to conceal herself from the road, and a camouflage net laced with the same to hide her from the air in the unlikely event there was a helicopter shadowing the convoy. Sonja banked on the fact that the paratroopers would direct their fire at the tree or the ruins, as these were the most obvious firing positions.

However, when one of the RPDs next opened up, the machine-gunner randomly raked the open ground, rather than aiming for specific landmarks.

Geysers of red earth erupted in front of her, but she maintained her watch on the limousines. A door opened in the lead Merc and a driver in a suit got out and ran from the car, away from her, scrambling up over the earthen bank at the side of the road to disappear into the grass and scrubby thorn trees beyond. Nothing would make him wait a bit.

The second Mercedes began to reverse and, despite the blaring warning of a horn from the BMW, rammed the car behind him. The two drivers then got out and after a moment's yelling they followed the lead of the first man and abandoned their vehicles.

"Shit," Sonja said.

She scanned right again. An officer was standing, with stupid courage, in the open, shouting orders at his men. One of the RPD gunners was climbing up the embankment, moving in her direction. A fire team of three men ran down the road, away from the carnage, and then crossed. They were going to try and outflank her.

There was no other movement from the three limos. She put the Javelin down and snatched up her binoculars. Although the windows were all heavily tinted, the drivers' doors of all three cars were open. She took a split second to scan each of them.

"Fuckers."

Sonja took an M26 fragmentation grenade from one of the pouches on the front of her combat vest and pulled the pin. She lifted the remaining spare Javelin tube and laid the grenade underneath it, the weight of the missile keeping the grenade lever down. It was a crude booby trap but she hoped some inexperienced soldier would be unable to resist the temptation of lifting the expensive anti-armor weapon. Awkwardly, she slung the third missile and CLU over her shoulder and snatched up her M4 assault rifle. She crawled through the long grass as machine-gun bullets cracked and thumped through the air over her head.

She had sited her hide just below the brow of a hill and once over the other side she half ran, half stumbled down the grassy slope. At the bottom of the shallow valley, on the far side of the same dry river the bridge had crossed before she blew it up, was her Land Rover, parked under a sausage tree. The vehicle was an old sandy-colored 110, the precursor of the Defender. It was rated one of the best offroad vehicles in the world and she prayed it lived up to its reputation.

Sonja opened the driver's door, reached in and started the engine.

Major Kenneth Sibanda reached forward and tapped the pilot of the Russian-made Hind helicopter gunship on the shoulder. "Down there, Land Rover!"

The smoke from the burning *bakkie* had been a beacon to them and Sibanda had radioed to the lead aircraft of the three Alouettes that he was going to investigate.

After a pause, the pilot of the Alouette radioed back, "The Comrade President wishes you good luck, and good hunting."

Sibanda had smiled to himself. It was an honor to be serving the president, the hero of the revolutionary war, even if his leader knew nothing of Sibanda's audacious plan. His heart soared to know the man was safe, on his way to Zimbabwe House in Harare. The day was turning out perfectly. The assassination "plot" had been foiled and the Comrade President would address the state-owned media that afternoon, explaining how the Movement for Democratic Change had been implicated in an attempt to kill him in order to illegitimately seize power in Zimbabwe. The assassin, the president would announce, pending the successful completion of the last part of the elaborate plan Sibanda had formulated, would have been wounded by security forces, but would confess, on his deathbed, that he had been paid by an MDC middleman to ambush the presidential motorcade. The president would also announce that the Criminal Intelligence Organization, or CIO, to which Sibanda belonged, had uncovered the plot and had advised the president to fly from Victoria Falls to Harare instead of drive. The president would cement his position, and that of his ZANU-PF party, as the rightful leader of the nation, while the MDC, who were in reality lackeys of the British neo-colonialists, would be undermined. The CIO, and Sibanda, would be hailed as heroes.

The president was an old man, near the end of his life, and Sibanda and a small group of other veterans of the liberation war serving in the military and politburo were concerned about what the future would hold for the party and themselves when the unthinkable happened and the great man passed away. Their plan, now being so flawlessly executed, would cast the opposition as international pariahs for years to come.

"What are our orders, Major?"

"Destroy the vehicle."

The pilot hesitated. "Surely, sir, you want to try and take the assassin alive? Perhaps some warning shots or . . ."

"Destroy the vehicle." The story about the assassin confessing, about it being a man rather than a woman, was all part of Sibanda's plan.

"Yes, sir."

The avionics and weaponry on board the Hind were not sophisticated—they dated from the early 1980s—but they were nonetheless deadly. In the swiveling turret under the gunner, who sat in front of and below the pilot, was a multi-barreled rotating 12.7-millimeter machine-gun, and under the stubby wings on either side of the gunship were air-to-ground rockets housed in pods.

"Pilot to gunner, select guns and destroy the Land Rover," the pilot said.

"Roger," replied the gunner, "selecting guns."

The gunner walked the rounds onto the Land Rover and Sibanda's heart pounded as he saw the fat projectiles strike home, ripping open the aluminum roof of the four-by-four like a tin opener.

"It is a strong vehicle, Major," the pilot said as their shadow passed over the truck, which, despite a cloud of steam gushing from a hole in the bonnet, was still bouncing slowly but surely across the open grassy plain.

"Use the rockets. Obliterate it."

"Yes, sir. Gunner, you heard the man," the pilot said.

"Selecting rockets."

The pilot banked the Hind into a sweeping turn and came up behind the Land Rover again. With no visible or briefed ground-to-air threat, he cut his airspeed and brought the helicopter down, until he was no more than 30 meters above ground level. At this height and speed, and from a distance of no more than two hundred meters from the target, there was little chance of the gunner missing.

"Firing now."

The first pair of rockets left their pods and scribed two trails of white smoke across the sky. One landed to the left of the vehicle and the other detonated just behind the moving target. For a moment, the truck was obscured in a cloud of earth, stones and smoke.

"It's hit," the pilot said, "but still moving. Gunner, fire another salvo."

The vehicle was crabbing badly, its right rear tire shredded by the blast.

Sibanda had to admit a grudging respect for the assassin. If it was him, though, he would have tried to escape on foot.

Two more rockets rushed away from the Hind and this time the gunner's aim was true. One of the projectiles smashed its way through the glass of the rear door of the Land Rover and detonated inside it. The vehicle plowed to a halt, ablaze and smoking.

"Set me down," Sibanda said to the pilot. "I need to check what's left of the body."

The Javelin was an anti-armor weapon and had not been designed to take out an aircraft, but Sonja saw no reason not to give it a try, especially as the pilot was now bringing the Hind gunship down to land.

The laser range finder reading on the screen put the helicopter at twelve hundred and forty-three meters from her, well within the missile's killing range.

She had planned for a number of different eventualities, but not the presence of a helicopter gunship. She'd needed a sizeable, convincing and moving target to take the helicopter's attention away from her, which was why she had set the Land Rover's hand throttle to about four kilometers per hour, tied the steering wheel in place and then jumped out of the moving vehicle.

Had the gunner and pilot not been concentrating so intently on the four-by-four they might have spotted the lone figure, or the flattened path she had left. But like typical men they had been too intent on finding something to blow up.

A fire had started in the grass, ignited by burning fuel from the vehicle. Smoke, combined with dust and grass thrown up by the chopper's down-wash, had temporarily obscured it from view. This wasn't a problem, however, as the Javelin also boasted an infrared detection function, designed literally to see through the fog of war. Sonja selected IR on the screen and the glowing image of the Hind, lit up by the heat of its exhaust, materialized from the gloom in front of her eyes. She selected top attack. Even if it missed the body of the machine the warhead would take the Hind down through its spinning rotors.

"*Fambai Zvakanaka*, you bastards," she whispered, bidding the crew goodbye in Shona as she squeezed the trigger.

Kenneth Sibanda had slid open the door of the small cargo compartment in the rear of the Hind and was sitting in the hatch, his legs dangling outside and ready to jump to the ground as soon as the wheels met terra firma. The helicopter bucked.

He still had his headphones on and heard the pilot shout, "Missile inbound!"

Sibanda looked over his shoulder and saw the smoky track of the weapon, arcing up into the sky. The grass was no more than four meters below him. He ripped the headset off and launched himself out into space.

The Hind started to rise above him as Sibanda hit the ground and executed a parachute landing fall, his feet and knees together and his elbows tucked in beside his body. He rolled as he landed, spreading the impact down one side of his body, and moving clear of the shadow of the helicopter. At that instant the missile screamed down from heaven and smashed its way through a rotor blade, then the metal cowling and into the screaming turbine engine.

Sibanda didn't spare the dying machine a second glance as he pulled himself to his feet and ran.

Pieces of rotor blades, panels and a human limb sailed past him as the Hind exploded and crashed.

The ground on which he ran felt hot through the soles of his shoes, and the grass was black here, already consumed by the fire which the rocket attack on the truck had started. He stumbled toward the now charred hulk of the Land Rover. Its driver's side door had been blown open by the force of the explosion. Sibanda drew the Tokarev pistol from the canvas holster on his belt. He wanted to empty the magazine into the body of the would-be assassin before he reloaded and went looking for whoever had fired the anti-aircraft missile.

Sibanda raised his right hand as he walked and curled his finger around the trigger.

"Empty," he said out loud, as his eye line followed the barrel of his weapon, sweeping the inside of the burned vehicle. Moving closer he saw a partially burned and melted strand of nylon rope dangling from the steering wheel, and the other end of the severed cord hanging from the brake pedal. It had been lashed. He swore in Shona and looked around him, suddenly feeling very exposed.

Sonja was up and running before the missile had hit its target. Whether it brought down the helicopter or not, she had to get moving.

"Fucking setup," she breathed as she returned her attention to the uneven ground in front of her.

The Javelin was much lighter now that her last remaining projectile was gone, but she couldn't dump the CLU and empty tube just yet. It dug painfully into her back and kidneys with each jolting step, but she ignored the discomfort, as she had been trained to do so many years earlier by the SAS instructors.

She held the M4 out in front of her, safety off, and set to semiautomatic. She raised the butt to her shoulder as she approached the pile of branches that covered the Yamaha trail bike. She slowed and circled the hiding place, but saw no sign of any recent approach or departure.

Sonja slung her rifle across her chest, cleared the branches away, climbed on the motorcycle and kick-started it to life. Releasing the clutch she powered off through the grass, savoring the feel of the breeze and turning her mind to the situation at hand. At the same time she kept a wary eye out for ant-bear holes and other hazards in front of her.

The Zimbabwean Air Force, to the best of her recollection, had only two serviceable Hind helicopter gunships, of which just one was regularly in service. Both were based in Harare, on the air base that adjoined the international airport. With the country plagued by critical shortages of petrol, diesel and aviation fuel, nothing drove or flew without a very good reason these days. She had been told during her briefing on the country that the air force's aging MiG 21 fighter jets were grounded as there was not enough fuel for them to fly from Thornhill Air Base at Gweru in the center of the country to Beitbridge on the South African border and back again. How had this helicopter miraculously appeared, then, just minutes after her attack on the convoy?

The president was not in any of the three armored saloon cars, of that she was sure. The fact that the military escort ignored the limousines, and that only the drivers had run from each car, confirmed her theory. The men in that convoy—or at least those doing the driving—knew they were decoys, even if they suspected the president was sitting in one of the other cars. Each had acted to save himself, with no thought for any passengers. It was she who had been ambushed that day, not the president.

Sonja crested a hill, both wheels airborne for a second. She pulled on the brakes once she was halfway down the reverse slope and stopped next to a mound of gray earth that rose to a peak nearly twice her height. It was a termite mound and, judging by the hole in its side, a disused one. Animals

such as cheetah, hyena and ant-bears made their homes in abandoned termite mounds. She dismounted and put the bike on its stand. Without stopping to see if anything was living inside, Sonja unslung the Javelin from her
back and tossed it inside the natural cavern. Too bad, she thought, if the
Zimbabwean police or army discovered the launcher now. If her suspicions
were right, they probably knew all about her and her weaponry already. She
walked back up the hill, stooping as she approached the brow, then dropped
to her knees and crawled through the grass.

She took the binoculars from the pouch in her vest and scanned the
horizon. The twin pyres that marked the graves of the Land Rover and helicopter seemed a long way off, but Sonja knew the gap could be closed in
seconds if her pursuers had access to another helicopter.

"Think," she ordered herself.

Exfiltration from this godforsaken country was always going to be
the hardest part of the mission. Even if all had gone according to plan, the
assassination of a president was news that spread fast. Borders would be sealed
in hours, if not minutes, and all westerners—even women—would come in
for extra attention from the police, army and customs and immigration officials.

Being female was an advantage, and clearly part of Martin Steele's reason for choosing her for this mission. A lone western man might attract the
attention of police, but she had passed through several roadblocks in Zimbabwe, easily playing the part of a German nurse. Only once did she have to
show her forged letter of introduction from a German development fund.

Sonja pulled the satellite phone from a pouch on her combat vest. She
dialed Martin's number. He would be waiting at Francistown Airport, in
Botswana, a few hundred kilometers from where she was crouching in the
grass.

"Sorted?" he asked.

"No. It's turned to shit here. We've been compromised. There was no
package and there was a surprise waiting for me."

"A surprise?"

"A fucking Hind gunship."

"Oh."

"Oh, indeed."

"Where are you? Should I come get you?"

The grass airstrip, their prearranged meeting place, was on an abandoned farm, about fifty kilometers from where she was, as the crow flew. She could be there in less than an hour, even if she drove cross-country, rather than on the secondary road that linked the property to the main Bulawayo Road. Every fiber of her being wanted to say "yes, please come get me." She looked down at her left hand. It was shaking, as the adrenaline began to subside.

"No. Does your contact know about the pick-up location?"

There was a pause on the other end of the line.

"Shit," she said. "Then that does it. I'll come by road."

"Which crossing?"

Sonja thought for a moment. "Not over the phone. I'll call you when I get there. Got to run."

She put the phone away and lifted the bike's seat. From the cavity made for a helmet she extracted a rolled-up nylon hiking rucksack. She slid her M4 into the pack and put it on her back. Also in the helmet well were two more hand grenades, which she put in pouches in her vest.

Sonja lowered the seat, got back on and kicked the bike into life again. She revved the throttle hard and rode down the hill, around its base and onto the main road. Speed was of the essence now.

The wind whipped her ponytail behind her as she rode. She watched the speedometer needle climb to a hundred and twenty kilometers an hour. It was good to be moving again. Outside of Victoria Falls was a police checkpoint and veterinary control post. If someone asked to look in her backpack there would be blood spilled. Her vest resembled a photographer's and she was counting on the novelty of being a white woman on a motorcycle being enough for her to distract the police on duty.

"Where are you going?" the male constable asked her when she pulled up.

"The Falls. It's hot today, isn't it?"

"Ah, yes, it is very hot."

"You are from South Africa?" he asked her.

"I am from Germany."

"Ah, that is very far. What have you brought me from Germany?" He craned his head theatrically to look at her backpack.

"Goodwill and a sunny disposition."

The policeman laughed and waved her through. She had been afraid the roadblock would have been alerted of the event happening not eighty kilometers distant, but this was Zimbabwe and few things worked here, least of all communications.

She raced past the Zambezi Lager billboard welcoming her to Victoria Falls, and turned left before entering the tourist town, following the sign to the border post with Botswana at Kazungula. This distance was about seventy kilometers—most of it through the Zambezi National Park, which ran along the river of the same name, upstream from the magnificent waterfalls. There was little traffic on the road and she overtook only a solitary overland tour truck, a converted lorry full of backpackers. The tour vehicles tended to avoid Zimbabwe these days, because of food and fuel shortages, but there were enough attractions in the country still to tempt the odd group of hardier tourists. The view of the Falls was better from the Zimbabwean side than across the chasm from the Zambian side.

She rode hard, not even slowing to watch a bull elephant feeding by the side of the road. A sign said *Kazungula twenty kilometers*. Sonja dared to hope. She looked over her shoulder at the disappearing blue blob of the truck. The sky seemed clear.

Ahead, the midday sun was sucking waves of heat haze from the black tar as she approached the crest of a hill. As she approached the peak she saw a dark shape shimmering through the curtain of hot air. Instinctively she pulled on the brakes, slowing her speed to eighty. She didn't want a head-on with a truck passing a slower vehicle.

The helicopter materialized in front of her, hovering just above the road. It was an Alouette and it had obviously been waiting for her, on the other side of the hill. How long had it been watching her?

The road was in a cutting, with steep banks on either side. It was, ironically, the same type of terrain she had chosen to ambush the convoy. Her enemy had turned her own strategy against her. Behind her was the overland truck, slowly gaining. If she turned she might bring harm into its way.

A man leaned out of the open cargo hatch and Sonja gunned the throttle as she saw an AK-47 barrel.

Rounds ricocheted and slapped into the tarmac on either side of her as she drove straight at the hovering helicopter. She couldn't reach the M4 in her pack and her nine-millimeter Glock 17 pistol was stuffed inside her vest. While keeping her right hand on the throttle, she unfastened one of her vest pouches and pulled out a grenade. Lifting it to her mouth she pulled out the pin with her teeth. It was a lot harder than it looked in the old war movies, especially when riding a bike. She spat the pin out; Lee Marvin, eat your heart out. The Alouette descended and it looked like the pilot was going to land on the road.

Sonja relaxed her grip on the grenade and rolled it in her palm, allowing the spring-loaded safety lever to fly clear. She had somewhere between five and seven seconds before it detonated, but she kept it in her hand. As the helicopter came down it turned broadside on, to make a better roadblock and to give the uniformed gunner in the back a clearer shot at her. He opened fire again and Sonja veered off the road. The motorcycle tipped and went into a skid in the dirt. She came off and slid through the gravel, following close behind the bike. Above and beyond the scraping of her skin on the unforgiving ground she felt the burning lance and jarring smack of a bullet hitting her right thigh.

The pilot turned the machine to get a better view.

Sonja came to rest near the bike, her khaki trousers and long-sleeved shirt torn and blood pumping from her leg. She released the fingers of her left hand, as unobtrusively as she could, and flicked the grenade away from her. As she did so she rolled through the dirt until she was pressed hard up against the motorcycle.

"What's that?" the pilot yelled into his intercom.

"Grenade!" Sibanda pulled the trigger on the AK, emptying his magazine into the motorcycle as the pilot hauled on his controls and fought to bring the Alouette back up into the sky.

The orb exploded and the machine rocked and bucked.

"Put her down! Land this bloody thing!" Sibanda ordered.

"No way."

The pilot had been diverted from the president's flight to collect Sibanda, but he lacked the aggression and bravery of the deceased gunship captain. The young man had initially refused to land on the road for "safety reasons" until Sibanda had waved the barrel of his AK-47 in the man's general direction. He would see the pilot court-martialed after this was all over.

It was too high for him to jump to the road and he thumped the hatch frame in frustration. "Do as I tell you!" he barked into the intercom.

"Major, I am in control of this aircraft," the pilot said back. "We have taken shrapnel damage and there is now a civilian vehicle on the road below. I am not going to land."

"Then come around, damn you. I want to see if she is still alive."

The pilot flew straight and level for a few more seconds, away from the scene of the explosion, ostensibly studying his instruments and experimenting with the controls to satisfy himself there was no serious damage. Sibanda knew the protocols were a mask for cowardice. "Now, Lieutenant!"

The pilot looked back at the rifle pointed at him and pushed the stick over. Sibanda tossed the empty AK-47 on the floor of the helicopter. He had neglected to take a spare magazine from the dead soldier's body by the *bakkie*. He still had his Tokarev, though, and he drew the pistol. It was a fitting weapon to administer the *coup de grâce*. He leaned out of the hatch as the pilot cautiously circled the crashed motorcycle.

Below them, a big blue tour truck headed for the border. Sibanda had seen it slow, but the driver was wisely continuing on past the cycle.

"Where is she?" Sibanda asked out loud. He could see the fallen trail bike, but no sign of the woman.

"She?" said the pilot.

Sibanda ignored the question. "Follow that truck. She must have jumped on board somehow. Can you radio the border post at Kazungula?"

"I'll try." The pilot fiddled with a knob and spoke into his headset microphone. "Ah, it is not working, Major."

Sibanda wanted to shoot the man, but as he didn't know how to fly, that wasn't an option. "Fly me to the border, now, you idiot!"

"Sir."

They circled the site of the crashed motorbike once more, but there was no sign of the assassin. The pilot lowered the nose and proceeded along the black ribbon of tar that sliced through the dry mopane bushveld of the national park. A herd of a dozen kudu took fright at their low passage and bolted across the road, their white tails curled protectively over their rumps as they jumped high to avoid the unseen threat.

The Alouette started vibrating, the tremor growing in a matter of seconds from a hum to a shudder. "What's that?" Sibanda asked.

"Oil pressure is dropping." The pilot tapped a gauge. "I'm putting her down before the engine seizes."

"Mother of God!"

Sibanda was out of the aircraft as the wheels touched the ground. If he didn't get away from that bloody pilot he would kill him, and he was in enough trouble already this day. His dreams of glory were turning into a waking nightmare. There would be no promotion, no more land, no spot on the politburo, and no money if this woman got away and exposed them. To make matters worse, he had deliberately not informed the police or border authorities of the bogus assassination plot. A vehicle was coming toward them, an aging red *bakkie* with a trailing cloud of black diesel smoke. As the vehicle approached Sibanda walked into the middle of the road and drew his pistol.

The driver was wide-eyed as Sibanda barked, "Get out!"

Speechless with fear, the thin man in blue workman's overalls did as ordered. Sibanda saw the four empty two-hundred-liter drums in the back. The man was on a fuel run to Botswana to bring back diesel or petrol for the black market. "I am commandeering this vehicle."

The citizen nodded dumbly; the sight of the helicopter in the middle of the road and uniformed men silenced any protest. Sibanda got in, rammed the gearstick into first and sped off. As he crashed through the gears and floored the accelerator, the best he could manage from the worn-out diesel engine was seventy-five.

•   •   •

The tourists were still in shock as their guide and driver, Mike Williams, pulled up at the customs and immigration office at Kazungula. He climbed down from the cab of the overland truck and shook his head. "I'm getting too old for this shit." He took a deep breath to calm himself. "Passports everyone. Now!"

It was odd, he thought, how easily he slipped back into army officer mode when he needed to. Someone had let off a grenade in front of them and a Zimbabwean Air Force helicopter had very nearly crashed on top of them. He'd thought he'd had his fill of danger on the road. Outstretched hands passed him the group's travel documents. They seemed as keen as he to put Zimbabwe in the rear-view mirror.

"*Kanjane shamwari*," Mike said to the immigration man, whom he knew by sight. He shook hands with the man and passed the stack of passports under the barred grille.

"*Kanjane.* You are in a hurry today?"

Mike coughed. "First beer's waiting for me at the safari lodge."

The man smiled and began checking, then thumping each passport with his stamp. "Have a safe journey."

"I sincerely hope so, mate."

On the Botswana side of the border-crossing the customs and immigration people made each of the passengers present themself so their passports could be checked. The group of Australians all knew each other—teachers, parents and senior students from a school in Coffs Harbor—and he'd taken them all the way to Kawalazi in Malawi, to visit a school they were sponsoring. Mike ran a hand through his close-cropped gray hair, then lit a cigarette while he waited outside at the back of the truck. The last of the teachers filed out and Mike ground out his smoke before he was halfway through. On the ground behind the vehicle he saw fresh wet spots. He made a mental note to check for oil leaks when they stopped, but the truck's dodgy gearbox was the least of his concerns at the moment. "Right! Let's make tracks."

"Stop!"

Mike turned. An African man in army uniform was ducking under the red-and-white-striped boom gate on the Zimbabwean side of the short stretch of no-man's-land—no more than a hundred meters—between the two border posts. A few of the teachers were gathered in a knot by the truck, watching the man.

"Maggie, Lisa, Claudia . . . get on the truck, quick." The three women started to board.

"What does that man want with . . ." began another.

"Don't worry about him—get on board the bloody truck. Now!"

Mike started the engine as the last two teachers were hauling on the chain to raise the steps. He was moving before the door closed and a girl shrieked from the rear cab as she lost her balance and fell against another student in the aisle between the seats.

He heard shots fired and saw, in his wing mirror, the Botswana customs and immigration people running from their office, then doubling back inside. He didn't know bureaucrats could move that fast. A Botswana Defense Force soldier in camouflage fatigues was pulling on the zipper of his trousers as he stumbled from the blue-painted toilet block behind the border post.

Mike changed up to second gear as he rounded a bend and gratefully put the diplomatic fracas going on behind him out of sight. The big truck lurched and slowed as he worked the gearstick, which gave Sonja Kurtz the chance she'd been praying for, to let go of the chassis and drop to the hot tar of the road. When the vehicle passed over her she rolled into the white powdery sand on the roadside, got up, brushed herself off, then fainted.

2

Sam wiped his brow and replaced the wide-brimmed bush hat with the faux leopard skin puggaree on his head. "Out here, in the African bush, there's no shortage of things that can kill you, and while they don't cause nearly as many deaths as the humble mosquito or the lumbering hippo, these three-hundred-pound pussy cats are . . ."

"Kilograms," Stirling said.

"Cut!" Cheryl-Ann screeched. "Stirling, please don't interrupt when we're filming, you know it puts Sam off his game."

"Well, an adult male lion weighs up to three hundred *kilograms*, not pounds."

"Well, we use pounds in the States, Stirling." Cheryl-Ann stood with her hands on her hips.

"Well then, at a conversion rate of two point two he should say six hundred and sixty pounds. It's a big difference."

"Stirling, I'm sure we all appreciate your expert guidance, but can we keep it to off-camera, please. Sam is the star of this . . ."

Sam held up a hand. "It's OK, Cheryl-Ann. Thanks, Stirling. I really appreciate you picking up the mistake. Let's do it again."

Sam heard Stirling mutter something under his breath as the safari guide picked up a yellowed stalk of grass and bit down on it. He was sure Stirling didn't like him, despite his efforts to make small talk and befriend him around the camp fire the past two nights. Sam knew that Stirling thought he had no right and no qualifications to be making a television documentary about the Okavango Delta. What, Stirling must have wondered, was "Coyote" Sam Chapman doing in Africa? Sam asked himself the same question, and came up with the same answer. He was here for the money. He sighed, took off his stupid hat, wiped his forehead again, took another look at the fake fur band and tossed it away.

"Sam, what are you doing?" Cheryl-Ann asked. "Gerry, get the hat."

Gerry, the sound recordist, got up and picked up the hat from the long grass, treading gingerly as he did so. They had all, except Stirling, been freaked out by the sight of the cobra that had slithered from under Ray's camera bag that morning. It wasn't Gerry's job to pick up after a petulant star, but Cheryl-Ann was the executive producer and when she was riled, as she was today, it was a brave man who said no to her.

"I don't want the hat," Sam said to Gerry when he offered it.

"*Sam*," Cheryl-Ann said in her schoolmarm voice, "put the hat on. It's important for continuity, and for your image."

Sam looked at Stirling and saw the guide rolling his eyes. "I wouldn't wear a Stetson with a coyote skin on it in Wyoming, Cheryl-Ann, so why should I wear some big bwana hat with a dead cat on it in Africa?"

"Aaargh!" Cheryl-Ann threw her production notes down on the ground and stalked past the camera crew until her nose was inches from Sam's square chin. "Listen to me," she said in a hoarse whisper, "you may be the *next big thing* in wildlife documentaries, Mister Coyote Sam Chapman, but this is *my* film and *I* call the shots here. The channel sent me because I know my stuff and I don't need you, or some copper-bangle-wearing out-of-Africa safari guide telling me how to make this documentary. If I tell you to wear the fucking hat, then you wear the fucking hat. Understood?"

He looked at the ground, and the stupid hat. It was all a sham anyway, so what difference did it make if they dressed him as someone he wasn't? He might be the star of the series of six documentaries for the Wildlife World Channel, but Cheryl-Ann was right. He was the talking head, the *talent*, nothing more than a reasonably well-known face. "OK."

"Excuse me?"

"OK," he said to her, louder, and picked up the hat.

"All right, people, we've got a documentary to make and a schedule to keep to. That includes you, mister." She raised her voice to attract Stirling Smith's attention.

"Yes, *ma'am*," Stirling drawled in a poor imitation of an American accent. "What can I do for you all?"

"Lions."

They were on foot, the open-top Land Rover game-viewing vehicle parked out of shot, and while Sam had been talking about lions as part of the script and pointing theatrically away, there were actually no big cats in the vicinity—at least none they had seen. The idea was to film him on foot and then cut to some footage of a male lion—once they saw one.

"I'll find you a lion. Sure as nuts, don't worry about that."

"That's what you said yesterday, and we still haven't seen anything bigger than a sherbal."

"Serval."

"Whatever."

Stirling shrugged. "Lions have feet. They walk. I can't tell you where they are every minute of the day, but there are three prides in our concession and we have a general idea where they are likely to be. I'll find you some just now. One of our other guides, Metsi, is out looking for one of the prides as we speak."

There was an arrogance about the man, Sam thought, and it was becoming clear that he had little fondness for Americans, which was a shame. Stirling might be blinded by stereotypes, but in his defense, Cheryl-Ann was giving him no reason to open his eyes.

Besides, Sam thought, Stirling ought to be grateful that they were making a documentary about the Okavango River and the delta of the same name. Wildlife World, a US-based cable TV channel that made and showed documentaries about nature and the environment, had helped raise awareness about endangered species and ecosystems around the world. Also, the lodge Stirling managed would get a few mentions, so the program would be good for business.

"Stirling, we need some water," Cheryl-Ann chirped.

"There's drinking water in the cooler box, in the back of the Land Rover," the guide said, spitting out his grass stalk. "Must I fetch it for you?"

"No, Stirling, I'm talking about water to film—for the documentary." She left off the word "duh," though Sam could clearly hear it was implied. He was glad Cheryl-Ann was picking on someone else for the moment. It gave him a chance to breathe. "This is supposed to be a film about the Okavango *River* and the wetlands, after all."

"We're a little short on H2O at the moment, I'm afraid. It's called climate change, and politics. Perhaps you want to put that in your documentary, or is that a bit much for your audience to absorb in between commercial breaks and getting their TV dinners out of the microwave?"

Cheryl-Ann scoffed, "No one eats TV dinners anymore, and we don't have commercial breaks during our programs. And, for your information, this documentary *is* going to be talking about the dam being constructed on the Okavango River."

"You are?" His tone softened. "That's great, Cheryl-Ann. If you can help tell the world about the impact the dam is going to have—is already having—then that might help our case. God knows, the Botswana government hasn't been able to achieve anything." Stirling snapped his fingers. "Hey, I just remembered. We've got a meeting of the Okavango Delta Defense Committee in a few days. It's a group of local safari operators, land owners and conservationists who are opposed to the dam. They'll be at Xakanaxa while Sam's out doing his survival segment. You could meet with them and we could tell you what we've been doing to lobby the UN and politicians in Angola and Namibia."

"We don't get involved in politics at Wildlife World," said Cheryl-Ann, parroting company policy. "We're playing it straight down the line. There's been a lot of hype already around the world about the so-called threat to the Okavango Delta, but we're also going to show the need for water in parts of Namibia."

"What? *So-called* threat? Don't you understand how serious a threat that dam poses for this ecosystem?"

"Like I said, it's going to be balanced. We've got experts from the Namibian government showing us around and giving us a guided tour of the dam site and the drought-affected areas of their country."

Stirling shook his head and turned away, walking back to the Land Rover. "Propaganda."

Sam could see the situation was spiraling out of control. Cheryl-Ann Daffen had a fearsome reputation at Wildlife World for never backing down and always coming home with the goods. She'd won two Emmys for best documentary, and one for best producer, and her film on the African fish eagle had been nominated for an Oscar. Sam knew he should consider himself lucky to be working with such a professional, but the woman had an uncanny knack for pissing off everyone she met. "Um, guys. We're losing the morning light and we've still got a lot to do."

Both Cheryl-Ann and Stirling looked at him like he was an annoyance. Sam sighed.

"I'll show you your lion, and your water," Stirling said.

Stirling Smith's knuckles were white as he gripped the warm steering wheel of the Land Rover. He selected low range and diff lock as they entered a patch of deep white Kalahari sand and gunned the engine. He felt the rear of the game viewer slide and allowed himself a small grin as he heard Cheryl-Ann's alarmed call from the back seat.

The woman was intolerable and the man, "Coyote Sam," a ridiculous parody of a wildlife researcher. The man supposedly had a PhD, but he was a fish out of water here in the delta. The analogy was a good one. He pictured the tall, impossibly handsome American flapping hopelessly around in the mud, slowly cooking under the African sun like a stranded barbel.

The Wildlife World film crew had been foisted upon him by the head office in South Africa. The TV people had been comped—provided complimentary accommodation, meals and drinks—by the marketing department, who hoped the exposure from the film they were making about the Okavango would revitalize bookings. The safari business was still trying to recover from the Global Financial Crisis, and an increasing number of

media reports about the decreasing stream of water to the Okavango Delta
was causing many potential overseas visitors to Botswana to choose Kenya
or Tanzania for their African holidays. The dam wall upstream in Namibia
had recently been completed and, as far as Stirling could see, this coupled
with the effect of an extended drought had served a death sentence on the
delta and the precious Moremi Game Reserve.

"This area we're passing through," he called back over his shoulder as
the Land Rover plowed on noisily through the deep sand, "should be underwater. Even in past drought years it's never been this dry."

"You're saying that's because of the dam?" Sam asked.

Coyote Sam. TV star, chick magnet and boy genius, Stirling thought.
"Who knows?" he answered honestly. "The Namibian government claimed
that flows to the delta would be reduced by no more than 1.5 percent, but
that was based on so-called *normal* rainfall periods. There's no doubt the
dam has exacerbated the drought problem and this area is short a hell of a
lot more than 1.5 percent of its usual flow."

Stirling drove on through the dry sand and bush. As if the Americans
weren't annoying enough, Stirling was also worried that Coyote Sam seemed
to have been flirting with his girlfriend, Tracey Hawthorne, over dinner the
previous evening. Tracey was seventeen years younger than Stirling and just
the thought of her firm, slender young body was enough to make him stir.
Chapman had talked to her all night and Tracey had doted on him, fetching
him coffee and insisting he try an Amarula Cream liqueur after they'd had
dessert. Tracey had first come to the lodge as a guest with her parents, and
on the third night of that stay Stirling had succumbed to her increasingly
unsubtle advances. Stirling had had sex with many female guests at the various lodges where he had worked in Moremi, but since returning to Xakanaxa
as the manager he'd made a point to avoid the advances of amorous clients.
"Khaki Fever" was a well-documented malaise in Africa, where visitors fell
for their handsome safari guides. Some lodges banned it and others turned a
blind eye to it, and as a manager Stirling knew he needed to lead by example.

That was until Tracey arrived. Her peaches and cream complexion
camouflaged a voracious sexual appetite that bordered on predatory. What

Tracey wanted, Tracey got, and once she had set her sights on Stirling his resistance had crumbled. At the end of her first trip she'd promised to return and he'd said he would be glad to have her come visit. He'd thought it was just a fling, but three months later Tracey had returned. A month later he'd managed to find her a job as an assistant food and beverage manager, and she had moved into his tent.

"Stirling?" Cheryl-Ann squawked.

"Sorry, couldn't hear you over the engine. What was that?"

"I said, are we going to see any water today?"

"Coming right up, ma'am."

There was still water at camp, in front of the luxury safari tents where the film crew was billeted, but even in the main channel the level was down lower than Stirling had ever seen it. Cheryl-Ann had ordered animals drinking from a river, and that was hard to film at camp, where the shores and river islands were choked with pampas grass that stood taller than a man.

"Here you go." Stirling switched off the engine and reached for his binoculars.

"I don't see any water," Cheryl-Ann said.

In front of them was a seemingly dry waterhole, about the length and half the width of a football field. "Look there."

"Where, Stirling?" Sam asked, scanning the gray surface. "It just looks like mud to me."

"Mostly mud, with a little ground water still seeping up underneath. This should be a foot deep in water at least at this time of year. Check the movement, in the middle."

"I see it," Sam said.

"Where?" asked Gerry.

"It's like a moving island. What *is* that?" Sam asked.

"Hippo. He's had to bury himself in the mud to protect himself from the sun. He has to stay like that all day, until he can come out in the cool of night to graze. That hippo has moved here from the pan where he usually lives, which is ten kilometers away. He may make it to the river, but hippos are very territorial animals and the pods in the main channel might not like him coming onto their turf. He'll most likely die before the next rains."

Wa-hoo, something called.

"What was that?" Cheryl-Ann asked.

"Baboon," Stirling said without looking over. Moments later, a troop of primates, about forty in all, crossed the open sandy ground where elephants had trampled or eaten the grass and other vegetation that once fringed the waters.

Stirling raised his binoculars. "They're desperate to drink here. It's dangerous."

"I don't see any predators nearby," Ray, the cameraman, said from the back of the truck.

"Get your camera out and start filming, Ray," Stirling said.

"Hey," Cheryl-Ann said, "Ray films when I tell him to and not..."

"Quickly," Sam said, watching the baboons intently. "Something else just moved out there."

Gerry was already climbing down from the Land Rover, helping Ray by setting up the tripod. He plugged his microphone cable in as Ray started recording.

The column of baboons was headed by a large male who paced up and down the sludgy edge of the pan looking for the cleanest spot from which to drink. Through the observers' binoculars it all looked unpalatable, even for animals, but the primate lowered his doglike snout to the ooze and started lapping. Soon the rest of his troop had fanned out on either side of them and began tentatively sucking up what moisture they could.

"Check," Stirling whispered.

"Hey," said Sam, "it's a..."

Stirling felt the vehicle rock as the ear-piercing shriek made Cheryl-Ann start in her seat. The crocodile, like the hippo, had been buried to the point of near invisibility in the mud of the waterhole. He knew the spot other animals would still consider clean enough to drink from and had positioned himself accordingly. The crocodile had launched himself from the ooze and locked his jaws around the leg of a young baboon.

The infant wailed hysterically and scrambled in the mud and dirt with its tiny hands as the croc started reversing back into the ooze. The male baboon gave his warning bark again and the rest of the troop fled screaming from the waterhole, but the leader stayed. He waded through thick slime to where the youngster still yelped and thrashed.

"Please tell me you're getting this," Cheryl-Ann whispered.

Ray had his eye pressed to the rubber cup of the camera's viewfinder. He raised a thumb over his head as the male baboon grasped the juvenile's hand and began tugging.

"Sam, start talking. Make me cry," Cheryl-Ann said.

Sam climbed down from the Land Rover and crouched beside Ray and Gerry, his face near the microphone. He took a deep breath, closed his eyes and thought for a few seconds. Stirling looked at the crew and shook his head.

"Here in the Okavango Delta the drama of life and death is played out every day. Sometimes it's not pretty to watch, but that's the way the circle of life turns. Family ties are strong in a baboon troop and this dominant male will risk his own life to try and save his offspring . . ."

Sam paused as the young baboon's wails punctuated his monologue. Half-a-dozen other members of the troop had stopped their flight and turned back. They clustered around their leader and, grunting and barking, also tried to grab hold of the hapless youngster.

"Baboons," Sam continued, "will chase off a leopard or cheetah if they discover one of the cats in their territory, but can their fearless devotion to their offspring defeat a predator that has had little need to evolve since prehistoric times?"

One of the baboons had jumped on the crocodile's back, but the reptile, who had exposed two meters of body length with still more hidden in the muck, shook the primate off with a flick of its tail. The dominant male baboon gave a whoop of what seemed like grief and frustration as the croc tore his baby from his grasp.

"What we've witnessed here," Sam continued, ad-libbing, "may well be more than the death of a single creature. It may be the beginning of the end of this once green wildlife Eden, which at this time of year should be criss-crossed with clear water channels and rivulets, where animals like that tiny baboon might otherwise have drunk in safety."

Stirling frowned. The woman was the bitch from hell, but the himbo, Coyote Sam, might just be smart enough to take some advice.

"Sam, don't pre-empt the end of the documentary before we've already begun shooting it," Cheryl-Ann said. "We don't know for sure this river's going to dry up."

"Beautiful stuff, man," Ray said quietly.

"How was your game drive, Sam? Did you get lots of lovely video?" Tracey Hawthorne's khaki shorts were so short they might better have been classed as swimwear, or underwear, Sam thought as he eased his sweaty body down from the Land Rover.

"Sweet."

Tracey giggled. "Brunch will be served soon, but you must tell me all about your morning before I let you go freshen up."

"I could use a shower first."

"Dip in the pool would be better. I've just been in. It's divine." Tracey glanced downward and folded her arms in front of her chest demurely, appearing to have just noticed that her wet bikini was showing through her white tank top.

Sam had noticed the wet patches, and her nipples, though he had tried hard not to stare at them, or at the tiny jewel in her bellybutton when her top rode up. "I don't have my trunks on."

"Nonsense. You're in Africa now. Jump in with your cargo shorts on."

Stirling tramped up the wooden ramp that led to the thatched reception area at Xakanaxa Camp. "Sam says he needs a shower, Tracey. Leave the poor man alone."

Sam turned. The camp manager and head guide had given him shit all morning. "You know, Tracey, I might just take you up on that idea of a swim, on one condition."

"What's that, Mr. Chapman?"

"That you join me for a quick dip, Miss Hawthorne."

Tracey looked at her watch. "Well, I *am* on duty, but brunch isn't on for another fifteen minutes. I'm game if you are."

Another Land Rover with two other tourists on board, a German couple Sam had posed for pictures with and signed autographs for the previous evening, pulled up at reception. Sam saw Stirling glare at him, then turn and walk over to the newly arrived game-viewing vehicle. Someone had to greet the returning guests and Sam imagined it was Tracey's job. Sam began unbuttoning his bush shirt as he followed Tracey's hypnotic hips across the sandy courtyard that separated reception from the common area of the lodge. Spread out along the banks of the main channel of the Khwai River were the dining area, with a long heavy wooden table where all meals were taken communally, a lounge area with coffee tables and deep, worn leather lounges, a self-service bar and, at the far right hand end, a small plunge pool, no bigger in circumference than a circular waterbed.

Sam unlaced and pulled off his hiking boots and socks while Tracey, on the opposite side of the pool, slipped off her rubber flip-flops and pulled the damp tank top over her head. As he shrugged off his shirt she unzipped her shorts and let them fall to the ground. She kicked them off with a pointed toe and smiled at him.

She stood on the opposite side of the pool to him wearing a white bikini that dazzled against the pale buttery tan of her skin. "I was nearly dry. Now you're going to get me all wet again, Coyote Sam."

3

Sonja woke up feeling like she'd spent a week in the kickboxing ring. It hurt even to open her eyelids, so she closed them again, carefully.

She reached up and found a wall, made of plastic or fiberglass, less than a meter above her head. When she kicked her feet out her toe stubbed something. She blinked a couple of times. It was gloomy, though she was aware of weak light above her. She craned her head back and saw a dull glow behind a translucent blue window. Her right arm ached in the crook of her elbow and when she touched it with her left hand she felt the tube. She grabbed it and ripped the long needle from her arm, gasping with shock. She was inside something—a vehicle, her brain slowly transmitted back to her. She had to escape. She rolled painfully onto her side, but when she tried to sit up she felt nauseous and banged her head on the roof. Cursing, she swung her legs over the side of the bed and tried to stand, but her right leg buckled under her.

An onslaught of light blinded her as she dropped painfully to one knee. She crumpled, but then felt herself caught by strong arms.

"Steady, steady, girl."

Sonja swallowed hard, forcing back the bile.

"Back into bed with you, young—"

"Outside," she gagged. "I need some fresh air."

"OK, OK, let me help you. I'm not here to hurt you."

She stiffened in his arms. The accent was from another world, another time in her life, and it frightened her. Soothing as the tone was, the off-kilter vowels with their jagged edges were from Ireland. Northern Ireland. Ulster.

"What . . . what do you want with me?"

"Sit. Sit yerself down."

Sonja shook her head but did as she was told. She lowered herself and found she was sitting on the floor of a Land Cruiser, at its split rear doors, with her legs out on a set of fold-down stairs. The sun was adding to her pain and she raised a hand to her eyes.

"I'd just gone to the gents. You've been out of it all night, and most of yesterday afternoon. Lost a lot of blood, you did."

Sonja looked up at the man. He had his back to the morning sun, and its rays shone through his wild, unbrushed gray hair like a halo, preventing her from seeing his face.

"You should lie down again."

She shook her head.

"Over here then." He took her arm and placed it over his shoulder and around his neck and supported her as she stood.

She was too shaky to resist. Panic rose in her chest as she suffered the soldier's special nightmare of suddenly realizing she was unarmed. "Where's my . . . my stuff?"

He snorted back a laugh. "You'll be talking about your M4 and your Glock, I suppose? Safely hidden away, along with the spare ammo and the fragmentation grenade. You're the most heavily armed backpacker I've ever come across."

She let him lead her to a padded camping chair, low slung and covered in green canvas. It was a safari lounger and he lowered her into it carefully. She looked around at the thick tangle of bush and vines that separated this camp site from the others around it. Through the natural camouflage she noticed bell tents and open-sided tour vehicles. A fish eagle called nearby, the piercing, high-pitched rise and fall telling her there was water nearby.

"Tea?"

She nodded. He crouched in front of her and prodded and blew a mound of white coals into flame. On a *braai* grid above the fire was a battered black kettle. "Where are we? Botswana?"

He nodded. "Kasane. This place is called the Chobe Safari Lodge. We're not far from where you collapsed, on the side of the road. I found you near the border. Did you come from Zimbabwe?"

Her mouth was dry. She licked her lips and started to speak, but as the fog slowly cleared from her brain she closed her mouth.

"I don't need to know," he smiled.

He was about twenty years older than she, nearly sixty, she reckoned. His body was lean under his tight T-shirt and his arms sinewy but muscled. He had blue eyes that glittered when he looked at her, but even when he smiled his mouth had that hard set she'd seen in so many men. It was as if they could never bring themselves to show true joy, because each time they tried, some memory or other returned, unbidden and unwelcome.

She touched the bandage around her right thigh and saw the red spots. "My leg . . . what happened to it?"

"Through and through. If I'm not mistaken, a 7:62; the AK-47 being the preferred weapon of most shooters in this part of the world. I've seen worse wounds, but like I said, you lost a fair bit of a blood. Also, one side of you is covered in abrasions."

"The bike . . ."

"Makes sense. I've also seen those types of grazes before." He prodded the fire, whose flames were now licking the old teapot. "I had a 1969 Triumph Bonneville when I was a wee bit younger and I came off that thing more than once. I also plucked a few fragments of metal out of your side. You wouldn't have been anywhere near a grenade explosion on your holiday, I suppose?"

She ignored the raised eyebrows. "My stuff . . ."

"Aye, we'll get to that soon enough. But you might consider a thank you, first. I kept that IV drip of saline for emergencies. You seemed to qualify as one."

"Thank you."

He nodded. Steam hissed from the kettle and he poured darkly stewed tea into two enameled metal mugs. "NATO standard?"

She nodded. "Please."

"Aha!"

Sonja frowned theatrically. "Oh dear. You got me. Or was it the assault rifle and the grenade that gave me away?"

"Well, I was in the intelligence corps for quite a few years before I retired. Tactical questioning of prisoners was one of my fortes, if I do say so myself."

"Very intelligent."

He ignored the sarcasm and heaped two teaspoons of sugar into each mug and poured in generous dollops of long-life Steri-milk. He handed her one. Two sugars and milk—NATO standard, in British Army slang, had told him she had a military background, but not much more.

He blew on his tea and took a tentative sip. "BBC World Service is carrying news this morning of a failed attempt on the life of the President of Zimbabwe. Seemed it happened not far from here, just across the border near Victoria Falls. The big man always likes to say the Americans and British are out to get him, and the so-called assassin apparently used a US military antitank weapon to attack the presidential convoy. Bit like using a sledgehammer to crack a walnut, I would have thought."

She said nothing.

"Of course," the gray-haired man continued, "the radio didn't say the Zimbabwean police and army were looking for a woman."

He waited for her reply, but none came. "It's Kurtz, isn't it, if I'm not mistaken?"

She sipped some more tea.

"Susie, Suzette . . . something equally German if I remember correctly. I was at Aldershot when they flew you back from Ulster for the board of inquiry. You won't remember me, though."

Sonja was grateful for him picking her up out of the dirt, but she was suspicious of his prying and the fact he was from Northern Ireland, and she really needed to put some distance between them. He was fucking with her, and she was in no mood for games.

"Sonja! Yes, that's it. I thought it was you, even before you woke. You haven't aged much in, what, eighteen years?"

That made her smile. "Something like that." She closed her eyes as she took another sip. It was a lifetime ago; someone else's life. A pied kingfisher squeaked nearby. She knew this place, though the campground was better organized than the last time she and Stirling had stayed here. Simply being back in Botswana made her think of him.

"Stirling, I love you, too, but I want to see the world. I want to do something with my life."

He'd tried to be cool, busying himself by putting another worm on the end of his hook, then casting it out into the Khwai River with a practiced flick of his wrist. "Stay," he'd quietly pleaded as he reeled in the slack, watching the river's surface, unable to look her in the eye.

He'd suggested that she become a safari guide, but although she knew the bush almost as well as he, except for trees, which she found boring, she hated pandering to the needs of the tourists. Her dad, Hans, had been the manager of Xakanaxa Camp, until his drinking had become too much for the owners. Her mother had less patience and had gone back to England while Hans still muddled on, but Sonja had lingered, unwilling to abandon the old man, or Africa. In time, she'd become keen to do both. After losing his job at the camp her father had stayed in Maun, lost to his wife and daughter as surely as if he'd died. Perhaps he had.

"You know I can't handle the foreigners." When she went into the bush she liked to go alone, or with Stirling. It was hard to describe. For her, going to the bush was like going to church was for her mother. She went into a kind of trance sometimes and felt as close as she ever would to believing, not in the existence of a supreme being, but in a sense of order and completeness in this otherwise fragmented world.

"What about going to 'varsity?" Stirling had persisted. "Your marks were good enough. You could become a zoologist—get a gig as a researcher back here in the Delta. We could be together forever."

"*Ag*, I couldn't stand another four years of schooling. I'd go crazy. I've got to *do* something, not read about it."

She had seen the genuine pleading in his eyes. Why couldn't she love him as much as he loved her? If he truly loved her then he must realize that she needed to do this, to see more of the world. She loved Botswana, and the Okavango swamps and the bush and the wildlife, but if she couldn't be a researcher, a safari guide, a lodge manager, or a cook—cooking was one thing she was totally useless at—then what would she do with her life in Africa? Become the wife of one of the above? That wasn't enough for Sonja.

"You fucking bitch," her father had screamed at her when she told him she was leaving. "Just like your fucking mother. That stuck-up, cheating English whore has poisoned you!"

"Papa, no." He had abused her verbally a couple of times in recent months when very drunk, and though he had never physically hurt her the words sliced like a panga.

"Fuck her, and fuck you!" He'd tossed the empty Jägermeister schnapps bottle at her, but she was sober and easily dodged it.

At eighteen she was as tall as he. She had a swimmer's build, lithe and with good upper-body strength and a toned tummy from endless crunches. Living in the confines of a safari camp she had learned to exercise when and how she could, so weights and sit-ups were part of her daily routine. At boarding school she had swum five kilometers a day to escape the soul-crushing boredom of being in Cape Town, so far from Botswana and the delta, and had won interschool championships.

"Stop it, Papa, you're drunk." She had grabbed the arm he raised and turned it, behind his back, pinning him there. Stirling had taught her the move as self-defense.

"Oww. OK, OK, let me go," her father protested.

When she released him he turned, his face crimson with anger, and slapped her, back-handed across the face. She reeled from the blow, which pushed her against the canvas wall of the permanent safari tent in which they lived. Standing, she glared at him, rubbed her jaw, and walked out on him. For good.

"Sonja! Wait . . ."

But it was too late. He had crossed the line and while she had tended to take her father's side in some of the arguments he'd had with her mother, now she would forgive him nothing. Her mother had retained her British citizenship. Sonja had already applied for and been granted right of abode in the United Kingdom.

She scrawled a quick goodbye letter to Stirling, who was out on a game drive working toward his guiding qualification, got in her father's old Land Rover and drove it to Maun. The old bastard could retrieve it himself, she thought. She caught a bus to Gaborone and her mother wired her the money for a flight to London. England was a shock to her senses but even in the dead of winter the knife-edge chill of the outdoors was still more appealing to her than the overheated fug of a job indoors. To her mother's horror Sonja joined the British Army.

The British girls who reported to the Women's Royal Army Corps recruit training barracks at Queen Elizabeth Park at Guildford, in Surrey, were a mixed bunch, but many of them struck Sonja as coarse and foul-mouthed. Sonja may have grown up wild in the African bush, a barefoot kid who knew more about elephants than human beings, but it wasn't until basic training that she realized how good her manners were and how sheltered her life had been until then.

Unlike most of her fellow recruits she found the physical training a breeze and excelled at weapons handling.

"Too bad they won't let you in the infantry," said the male sergeant, a former Special Air Service man named Jones, who took her and the other girls in her section for weapons lessons.

Some of the instructors were even more chauvinistic than the hunters and safari guides she'd grown up with, but Sergeant Jones was patient and encouraging around the women, some of whom had never held a firearm before, let alone fired one.

While some of the other girls fell by the wayside Sonja excelled at basic training and was named the student of merit, the top recruit, at the end of her course. From the limited choices available to women at the time she applied for posting to the Royal Corps of Signals. She'd briefly considered military intelligence—even though everyone joked that was an oxymoron—but when she made inquiries she found she might well end up spending her days cooped up indoors staring at aerial photographs through a magnifying glass.

Unlike most of the girls on her course she'd learned to use radios for communication from an early age. She had a confidence born of living in a war zone and growing up in the African bush, and her only regret was that as a trainee signalman she spent too much time in the classroom and not enough out in the field. She passed the course with flying colors and was posted to a signals unit at Aldershot, home of the Parachute Regiment.

With peace talks on again it seemed the conflict in Northern Ireland between the Irish Republican Army and the Protestants loyal to the British Crown was winding down, although the paratroopers Sonja met were about to deploy to the troubled province of Ulster, so things weren't over yet.

As the months progressed Sonja grew bored of life in barracks. There was precious little travel involved, save for one exercise in Germany where she thought she would die of the cold. She spent much of her time typing signals on a telex machine and making tea for senior NCOs and officers. Her first full winter in England was depressing, her mood matching the dull gray of the skies. She missed Stirling and wrote to him every week. When she telephoned him in Botswana he begged her to come back. It wasn't, she explained, as if she could just quit with two weeks' notice, and while she was tempted for a brief moment to pack it in and go AWOL she forced herself to be strong.

"Kurtz," the female lieutenant said, looking up from her desk.

Sonja saluted. "Ma'am." She'd wondered what she had done wrong when the sergeant major had told her to report to the troop commander's office.

"At ease. How are you settling in, Sonja?"

"Fine, ma'am."

"You're South African?"

It was a common mistake. "Born in South-West Africa—Namibia they call it now—ma'am, and raised mostly in Botswana. British citizen now, though, ma'am."

"I see. Your NCOs tell me you're a fine soldier, Kurtz, with potential to go a long way."

"Thank you, ma'am." Sonja had no idea where this was heading. "Is something wrong, ma'am?"

The officer looked up and smiled. "No, not at all, Sonja. A signal has come through seeking females to volunteer for special duties. All very mysterious, but there's an emphasis in the requirements for physical fitness. If I hadn't done my knee in last month playing squash I might be tempted to volunteer myself. I've also had a signal from a Captain Steele from the Special Air Service Regiment drawing my attention to you in the context of this request. Seems a sergeant . . ." the officer rechecked the printout in front of her, "Jones spoke highly of you after your recruit course."

Sonja felt proud, excited and nervous all at once. Her troop commander told her to think carefully before making any rash decision. Bluntly, she told Sonja she did not want to lose her, but the mysterious message offered Sonja the ray of sunshine she had been hoping for during the interminable gloom of the British winter.

"Here're the coordinates for the next checkpoint," Sergeant Jones said, cupping his hands around the small blue flame of a portable gas cooker as the rain pelted the canvas that sheltered him. Jones, it turned out, had been transferred back to his beloved SAS, but then reassigned to a special forces training role.

Sonja looked at the piece of soggy paper and memorized the grid reference before she handed it back to Jones. From a clear plastic envelope she pulled out her map of this cold and rain-swept part of Wales, the Brecon Beacons mountains, and located the next checkpoint. The smell of the instant soup brewing over the cooker in a tin cup made her stomach rumble. Jones heard it and simply rolled his eyeballs. Sonja was soaked to the skin and her teeth were chattering. Her feet were blistered after walking fifteen miles in wet socks and boots and the skin on her back felt raw from where the pack loaded with bricks and a sandbag had chafed her.

"Right. Fuck off, Kurtz," Sergeant Jones said, stirring his soup.

For two weeks Sonja's mind, body and soul had been hammered and bent to within an inch of breaking in a series of increasingly grueling tests of her stamina and basic military skills in the bleak mountain landscape. There had been lessons on unfamiliar weapons, navigation tests—like this one—and mile after mile of walking and running through the wilderness. The recruits were referred to by surname only regardless of rank. The training was a great leveler and already three-quarters of the hundred men and women who volunteered for special duty had been RTU'd—returned to their unit.

Sonja checked the luminous dial on her watch. It was three in the morning and she had been without sleep for more than twenty-four hours. Walking out of the tent, back into the rain, she lifted the compass from its lanyard around her neck and took a bearing.

"Kurtz?" Jones called from the comparative luxury of his tent, the canvas walls snapping in the merciless wind.

Sonja looked back at him, blinking away the rain. The man winked at her.

Northern Ireland mirrored her experience so far in the army; an exciting, and at times scary, headlong rush into unending tedium. Sonja had passed her selection course and had been transferred to 16 Intelligence Company, which had started life as an intelligence detachment in Ulster, and since then had been known simply, and obscurely, as the Det.

The Det's core business was surveillance of IRA personnel and locations. Forward-thinking for its time, in the late eighties and nineties the Det had pioneered the use of women in a special operations role. In staunchly republican villages and neighborhoods the presence of unknown, hulking single men on surveillance was a giveaway. Female soldiers and officers had been trained in surveillance and photography. Posing as wives or girlfriends they had helped male operatives blend in on the streets of Londonderry and in the rural villages of South Armagh, and had driven vehicles dropping men off at concealed "hides" in the green fields of the county and townhouses of the city's republican strongholds.

Once more, Sonja found herself frustrated. Women in the Det were barred from the more dangerous missions and the best they could hope to be was "handbags" for male surveillance operatives. Women were banned from spending time in the concealed observation posts or hides, for the bizarre reason that if they were having their period they might give away their position to sniffer dogs. Sonja had seen or heard of no evidence whatsoever of the IRA using canines for this purpose. The Det sailed close to the wind in any case, for while women could be a useful extra layer of cover for the men, females were still technically prohibited from taking part in combat roles. While Sonja carried a nine-millimeter pistol with her, and had a Heckler and Koch machine pistol under the seat of the car she drove when dropping off and collecting male operatives, the weapons were strictly for use as a last-ditch means of self-defense if she was ever compromised.

Things changed the day two schoolteachers, friends from different sides of the religious divide, decided to pioneer a project in which children from their respective communities would come together for joint field trips. Some outspoken parents—Catholic and Protestant—made a show of keeping their eight-year-olds home from school, but the majority of mothers and fathers were happy for the children to mix with each other. There were peace talks on at the time, brokered by the Americans, and the school excursions gained prominence in the press as a sign that things might be slowly changing in the troubled province.

The Provisional IRA and Sinn Fein were quick to deny any involvement in the setting up of the two-hundred-kilogram culvert bomb that exploded as the bus carrying forty boys and girls from warring religions, and their well-meaning teachers, passed over it. Eighteen small bodies were pulled from the twisted wreckage, and the site reduced even paramedics and firemen hardened by years of warfare to tears.

"Right, people, gloves are off," Captain Martin Steele told the packed briefing room of grim-looking soldiers in civilian clothes. Sonja, like many of the men, smoked during the briefing. Smoking was a means of killing time and, though she hated to admit it, a means of finding some common ground with some of the more Neanderthal of the men, who still weren't convinced of the value of women in undercover work. She, like the two other girls in the Det, June and Mary, a captain and a lance corporal, thought Captain Steele was a dish. June and Sonja had been on the same course and remembered the SAS officer as the senior staff instructor. He had returned to Ireland shortly after them and acted as a liaison between the elite regiment and the intelligence people of the Det.

"This man," Steele pressed a remote connected by cable to a slide projector, "Daniel Byrne, is believed to be the so-called True IRA's quartermaster. We believe he's the bastard who sourced the Semtex that was used to kill those innocent little children and one of the teachers. We know precious little about the splinter group, but we do know that Byrne was disenchanted with the Provisional IRA and their part in the peace talks. We—that is, you—are going to follow and keep watch on Byrne for every second of his miserable life from now on. He's going to lead us to the rest of these animals, including their leader. One thing we know about Byrne is that like a lot of these paddies he likes a drink and a party, so be prepared for plenty of pub time."

Steele's last remark raised a few half-hearted laughs, but there was no doubting the seriousness of the task at hand.

When Steele paused and looked around the room Sonja felt that the gaze of the blue-eyed man with the wavy jet-black hair rested on her. "Be careful. Very careful. Byrne will have been trained in countersurveillance and he'll be looking for you while you're looking for him. Byrne and his ilk have been shunned by the Provos. They're mad dogs, operating on the extreme edge, alone and with no care for life or humanity."

Sonja had been paired with Sergeant Bruce Jones. The SAS man had been assigned to the Det, supposedly to boost numbers. Sonja wondered if the presence of the extra special forces soldiers on the surveillance teams was more about being in position to deliver a killing blow, if the opportunity arose, than manpower.

The world had been outraged by the chillingly casual admission by the True IRA of their actions, and the public and press across the water in the rest of Britain was baying for blood.

"Lost eyeball," Bruce said into the microphone concealed in the sleeve of his bomber jacket. "He's gone into the pub. Following him in."

Sonja pulled the Ford Escort into the pub's car park and stopped at the far end of a row of cars, away from Byrne's battered van. He was a plumber by trade and the stick-on sign advertised *satisfaction guaranteed*. Tell that to the bereaved families of the children and their pretty young Catholic teacher, Sonja thought, as she switched off the engine.

"Right, let's get a drink, shall we?" Bruce made it sound like they were on a date and she admired his cool.

Sonja's heart was pounding as she followed him into the smoky pub and she felt like every eye was on them. The pub was not a known republican watering hole—Byrne was too clever to use those—but nonetheless Sonja felt she couldn't be more conspicuous as a British soldier unless she had a Union Jack tattooed on her forehead.

To Sonja's horror, Byrne, who had made straight for the bar, looked past Bruce and smiled at her as they moved past him. Sonja looked away as Jones appeared to ignore the Irishman and headed for a booth at the far end of the crowded pub. It was nothing, she told herself. The bar's clientele was mostly men, although there was a trio of young office girls sitting at one table. Perhaps Byrne just had an eye for anything in tight jeans. Sonja wore a hooded sweat jacket that was baggy enough to conceal the nine mil clipped high on her waist, but when she sat she felt it dig into the small of her back and she wondered if Byrne habitually scanned every person he saw for signs of a weapon.

"We'll wait till he's left the bar and I'll go get us some drinks," Bruce said under his breath as they slid into opposite sides of the booth. "Then . . . bloody hell."

"What is it?" Sonja's eyes widened at the groan that emanated from the sergeant who suddenly looked very pale.

"You didn't have the kebab at lunchtime, did you?"

She shook her head. "I had the hot chips, remember."

He winced as he nodded. "My bloody guts feel like they're going to explode. Jesus Christ. We've got eyeball on the top X-ray in the province and I'm about to shit myself." Bruce lowered his hand to his belly.

"Go. I'll be fine. I'll get the drinks while you're in the bathroom," she said.

He started to protest, then clamped his jaw shut as another cramp forced him to double over at the table. "OK. I'll just be gone for a minute."

Sonja shifted in her seat and forced herself to relax as she watched Jones disappear into the men's room. She ran a hand through her hair, got up and went to the bar.

"Soda water and . . ." she tried to think what Bruce would want. They were undercover, but was it a good idea for him to be drinking beer or spirits if he was ill?

"Make up your mind, love," the elderly barman said.

"Sure, and you can't be entering a fine establishment like the Hen and be drinking soda water."

Sonja turned. She smiled to try and disguise the chill that ran down her spine, the likes of which she hadn't felt since she'd been confronted by a Mozambican spitting cobra for the first time in her life. It was Byrne, standing behind her, nursing a pint of Guinness. "Um, soda water and a Coca-Cola, please," she said to the barman.

"*Coca-Cola?*" Byrne said, mimicking her accent poorly. "You sound like you're a way from home. I would have picked you as a couple from across the water, but not that much water."

Sonja fished in her wallet for the money, frantically wondering what to say. If he thought they were "from across the water," did that mean Byrne had already suspected the strangers in the bar were British agents? "*Ja*, I'm a long way from my 'ome," she said, laying on a thick Afrikaans accent.

"South Africa?" Byrne prodded.

"Namibia, though it was called South-West Africa when I was born."

"Sure, and it's a shame when someone takes over your country, isn't it?"

Sonja smiled. "*Ja.* The bloody British and the South Africans took it from my grandfather's people in 1915. Before that we were German. Where I grew up we spoke Afrikaans and German. It was confusing."

"You don't say. Well, what brings you to Ireland? This part of the country's not usually recommended in the guidebooks. Most foreigners are too scared to visit Ulster."

Sonja shrugged. "I grew up in a war zone. I used to load my pa's rifle for him and my mom had an Uzi she used to carry with her when she took us kids to school."

"Beautiful and a killer to boot, eh?"

Sonja tried to look for Sergeant Jones over Byrne's shoulder, wondering how she was going to get herself out of this mess. "Don't joke. I shot a man when I was fourteen."

Byrne raised his eyebrows.

"I didn't kill him—at least I don't think I did. The newspapers made a big thing of it at the time. It was a nice propaganda victory against the SWAPO terrorists, even if we couldn't hope to win the shooting war."

"SWAPO?" Byrne sipped his drink. "South-West African People's Organization if I remember my limited African history. I would have said freedom fighters rather than terrorists."

Sonja shrugged. "Terrorists when they're shooting at *you*. Besides, if a firefighter fights fire, then what does a freedom fighter fight?"

Byrne laughed. "Fair point, but you essentially had a colonial power, the Germans, subjugating the local people and then the South Africans taking over after that. You can understand the African people fighting to take control of their homeland."

"I was born there, too, but we were the minority, and the minority can never win, can they?" Sonja raised her eyebrows.

Byrne looked around the bar without moving his head. "It doesn't mean we can't try."

"You're talking about Northern Ireland?" She lowered her voice. "The IRA?"

"Now what gave you that idea?"

"Minority, majority. I've read enough about this place to know the British have no place here trying to enforce a system that disadvantaged Catholics for years."

"And what truck does a Namibian have with the British?"

"My mom's side are Afrikaners—my dad's German. My maternal great-grandmother died of cholera in a British concentration camp in South

Africa during the Anglo-Boer War, leaving four children, two of whom later died as a result of malnutrition. My pa's people were interned during both the world wars, although I had an uncle who evaded detention and used to cache supplies for U-boats on the Atlantic Coast."

"Skeletons in the cupboard on the Skeleton Coast, eh?"

She smiled and sipped her drink. "You know a lot about Africa, for an Irishman."

"You know a lot about the problems here, for an African. I think your friend's coming. He's been a while in the bog and doesn't look too grand, now, does he? Who is he?"

"That's a forward question."

"I'm a forward man where a pretty girl's involved."

Sonja glanced at Bruce, weaving his way toward them. "He's nothing. I was hitchhiking. He picked me up and offered me a lift."

"Sure, and that's a bit dangerous, isn't it? Going into a pub with a stranger who's just picked you up?"

Sonja stirred her drink with her finger, making the ice cubes rattle on the glass, then licked her fingertip. "Nothing wrong with a little danger now and again, is there?"

"Sorry?" she said, aware the older man sitting by the camp fire had said something else. A hippo grunted out in the Chobe River.

"I said I'm Chipchase, Sydney Chipchase. You looked like you were in another world for a few seconds there, staring into yer tea. Were you?"

"Interesting name," Sonja said, attempting to change the subject.

"My father was a sailor in the Royal Navy. Served in the Pacific and liked Sydney when he stopped there on leave."

"I meant Chipchase."

He smiled and shrugged, as though he'd heard it all before. "You were distracted. What's on your mind? Zimbabwe—or maybe Northern Ireland?"

"You seem to know all about me, Sydney. Whatever you heard about me, in Ulster, was true, and you likely haven't heard the half of what went wrong." She clasped the tin mug tight, feeling the burn. She didn't want to be reminded of the pain, nor of Daniel Byrne. "What are you going to do? Turn me into the police?"

Chipchase shook his head. "I don't live in the past anymore. I left the army, hit the bottle for a while longer, then found sobriety and the Lord, around about the same time. I'm a traveling missionary here in Africa, distributing Bibles and religious textbooks to remote schools and missions. I don't condone the path you seem to be on, but I won't surrender you to the squalor of an African jail. You'll have to find the right path for you, but you'll be safer for a wee while if you let me take care of that leg of yours."

She drained her tea. "Don't think I'm not grateful. If the police had found me before you I'd be in trouble."

"Like as not you'd be dead of blood loss."

She shrugged. "I had a sat phone with me."

Chipchase nodded. "There's a storage locker under the bed in the camper. I put all your kit there. Your rifle and pistol are in there. Best leave them for the moment if you don't want to attract undue attention around the camp ground."

Sonja set the empty mug down on his fold-out table and climbed gingerly back into the Land Cruiser. She opened the locker and found her bag and vest. She checked the M4—there were still rounds in the magazine—and slipped her nine mil into the waistband of her pants, which Chipchase had turned into shorts to get to the bullet wound in her leg. The phone's casing was cracked and the battery cover had come loose. There were wires hanging out of it. When she went outside she held it up to the Irishman.

He raised his palms. "Wasn't me. Here," he said reaching into his shirt pocket, "you can use my mobile phone. Dial overseas if you wish."

"Thanks." She left the camp site with a nod to his generosity and wandered down to the water's edge, by the thatch-roofed Sedudu Bar. She stopped by a sign that said *Beware of crocodiles* and dialed a mobile phone number in the UK.

"Hello?"

"Emma?"

"Oh. It's you," her daughter said.

"Hello, my girl. It's nice to hear your voice." And it was, after what she'd been through in Zimbabwe. Sonja did what she did for Emma—to ensure her only child wanted for nothing in life. She knew she'd missed too much of Emma's life, as a trade-off, but at least Emma had, until recently, been safe and happy in the care of her grandmother when Sonja had been away. There were things Sonja liked—loved—about her work, but she tried hard not to dwell on them.

"Whatever."

Sonja drew a breath and tried to remain positive. "How's school?"

"How do you think? I hate it and can't wait for it to be over. Situation normal, all fucked-up. SNAFU. Isn't that what you say in the army?"

"Not my army." Sonja knew Emma was simply trying to provoke a re- action with her swearing. "University will be much more fun and it's just a few short months away. You're too clever for your teachers. How are you going with your pre-law subjects?" Sonja prayed the pause on the end of the line meant Emma was continuing to do well, and that she might, reluctantly, show some pride in her academic achievements. She loved that her daughter was so bright—gifted according to her teachers—and took some solace from the fact that the things she did to earn a living would pay for Emma to become a lawyer. Sonja told herself the disciplinary incidents at school were a natural part of Emma's intellect and strong personality—a tendency to challenge convention, rather than warning signs of delinquency. She was a teenager. She'd get over it.

"We were studying human rights law. We discussed Iraq and Afghani- stan and torture . . . rendition, that kind of stuff. It made me ashamed, like, to think you'd been part of it."

Sonja gritted her teeth. "How's your friend . . . Gemma, isn't it? She seemed nice when I met her at the last parents' day."

"It's Jemima. And she's a slag. I hate her. Look, Mum, don't pretend like you know or even care about my friends. You don't. You're not part of my life anymore."

Sonja put her fingers against her temple. She'd nearly been killed and, while she wasn't looking for sympathy from her daughter, she found it frustrating that she couldn't even tell her what she'd been up to—even if she could, Emma would disapprove. She hated, too, the way Emma used words such as "like" to dumb herself down.

"Where are you anyway?" Emma yawned.

"Botswana."

"All right for some. It's fucking dire here. Cold and raining."

Sonja saw the opening. Perhaps she could console herself with some small talk about the weather. "It's lovely here. The sky's clear and it's a beautiful warm day. Perhaps one day . . ."

"I have to go. Perhaps one day you'll give up your bloody bodyguarding or whatever it is you do when you're away and, like, really take an interest in my life for a change. At least Gran used to know who my friends were, but then again she did come and visit me on weekends in this jail."

"Emma, I . . ."

"Or maybe it'll be just like Gran all over again. I might die and you might miss the funeral. Wouldn't that be sad?"

"Emma . . ."

The line went dead.

Sonja stared out over the wide expanse of the Chobe River, which glittered blindingly in the midday sun. It was the reflection, she told herself, and the fact that she had been cooped up inside the stifling darkness of the campervan for so long, that made her screw up her eyes and push her palm against each of them, in turn.

4

Sam felt toes sliding up the inside of his right calf, and he was fairly sure they weren't Stirling's. Two men had tried to hit on him at parties since he'd become a household name in the States, but mostly it was women, an uncomfortable number of whom, like Tracey Hawthorne, were already in relationships.

He coughed, hoping Tracey would take the hint and ease off. Instead, he felt her toenail trace a path to his knee and along his thigh. She had long legs, that Tracey, as he'd seen in the pool.

Sam had known from a previous dip that the plunge pool was overchlorinated, so when he dived in he had kept his eyes shut and his hands out, so he could feel for the wall. Tracey had slid into the water and positioned herself so that he swam into her. His palm had connected with her hipbone and she had fallen backward in the water as he'd surfaced.

"You must think me a pushover, Sam," she'd giggled.

Stirling and Sam were seated diagonally opposite each other, in the center of the long dining table, with other guests and the members of the film crew on either side of them. Every now and then Stirling would lean over to Tracey, who was seated next to him, directly opposite Sam, and draw her into his conversation. At the precise moment that Tracey's dainty, manicured toes found Sam's crotch, Stirling laid a proprietary hand on her shoulder as he recounted a story about her and a python. Sam grimaced and Tracey winked as Stirling carried on talking.

Shit, Sam thought. A beautiful, sexy young woman was coming on to him and he knew he couldn't do anything about it. Sam knew from past experience that any of the dozen retirees and well-heeled guests from New York, Texas, Florida and London around the table wouldn't have a second thought about emailing a gossip magazine or Fleet Street if they caught a whiff of a celebrity involved in a scandal abroad.

His on-again, off-again relationship with Rebecca Lloyd, a Hollywood starlet who presented part-time on Wildlife World, had come to an end when footage of her kissing a Baldwin on a beach in Bermuda had aired on *ET.* In truth, the relationship was dead by then as for the third time, despite her protestations that she had given up, Sam had found a line of white powder in their hotel room in Denver. He'd offered to help her stay off drugs, but she'd told him she didn't need him. Apparently it was the truth.

But a Baldwin? That still hurt.

"Cheryl-Ann," Stirling said, "have you thought about my offer to meet with the Delta Defense Committee when they get here? We've hired a public relations guy from Jo'burg. He could be good material for an interview about the negative effects of the dam."

Cheryl-Ann dabbed her mouth with a serviette. "I don't think a PR flak is going to be your best spokesman, and in any case it's really not the sort of thing we could use in our program . . . but I'll think about it."

Stirling seemed about to try his pitch again, but one of the African safari guides came to the table and whispered something in his ear. Stirling excused himself from the table and pushed back his chair. "I just have to check the generator, ladies and gents. Back soon." He walked into the night, followed by the guide.

"We've got an early start tomorrow, don't we, Ray?" Sam said.

The cameraman had been focusing intently on the words and the breasts of a divorcee from Houston at the far end of the table. "We do? I mean, sure, we do, but, hey Sam, it's still early yet."

"Well, I just don't want you getting sick in the helicopter like last time, is all," Sam said.

Ray sighed. "You go, if you like."

"Oh, Sam, please stay and tell us another story about trapping coyotes," said the divorcee. Perhaps, Sam wondered, she wanted to be freed from Ray's halitosis as much as he did Tracey's roaming foot.

"You need someone to escort you back to your tent, in case of dangerous animals," Tracey said across the table.

"That's right," Sam said, relieved to feel Tracey's foot slip out of his lap. "Let's go, Ray."

"But . . ."

"No, it's fine, Ray," Tracey said, smiling brightly. "You stay here and finish your dessert . . . have an Amarula. I'll be happy to show Sam back to his tent."

Sam looked over his shoulder and out into the gloom behind the deck, but there was no sign of Stirling, who was presumably still off checking the generator.

Tracey grabbed the torch, with its heavy rechargeable battery slung underneath. She switched it on and shone it out into the darkness. She wasn't looking for lions or leopards, but for Stirling. There was still no sign of him. The adrenaline and desire was burning her from the inside out.

"OK, Sam?"

She saw the reluctance on his face as he glanced one more time at the cameraman. Sleazy Ray with his bad breath who had already hit on Tracey, suggesting she come back to his tent for champagne the night before, was busy staring at the American woman's cleavage.

She wondered if Sam was shy, or if he was genuinely principled and avoiding her because he thought she belonged to Stirling. Tracey liked Stirling—loved him maybe—but she wasn't owned by any man. Whether bashful or high-minded, the more Sam tried to resist her, the more his unwillingness excited her. Both Stirling and Sam were handsome men, but the TV star had something over the safari guide. Both were big men in their fields—alpha males—but Sam's territory was the whole world. Women adored him and men wanted to be him. Tracey just wanted him. She hoped to god he wasn't gay, although he was pretty enough.

"This way," she said. "Come on," she added in a whisper once they were away from the riverside deck, "I won't bite. Not unless you want me too, of course."

"Tracey . . ."

"Shush."

"No, really, I just want to—"

"No, shut up, Sam. For real. I heard something out there." She shone the powerful beam into the bush, away from the river. "There, see?"

He had been behind her and as he moved alongside and crouched a little he was within range of her, at last. "There . . ."

"I don't see a thing."

She held the torch out with one hand and rested a hand on his shoulder, as if guiding his gaze to the point she was looking at. As he lowered his head she looked into his gorgeous brown eyes and, as he stared intently at nothing at all she slid the pointed tip of her tongue into his ear.

"Tracey!"

"What's wrong? Are you gay, Sam?"

"No, I am not gay. Was there anything dangerous out there, really?"

She smiled, but left her hand on his shoulder. "There's nothing out here except me, Sam, and I am danger with a capital D."

"That you are." He brushed her hand off his shoulder, but she moved in for the kill, pressing her body against his. Despite his protests she felt the bulge of his erection against her belly. She dropped her hand and traced it through his khakis.

"Tracey . . ."

She heard the waver in his voice. It was what she was waiting for. Men. They were all the same. Bad. Even the good ones. It was what she loved most about them. She switched the torch off and led him behind the thick girth of a massive mopane tree.

"Tracey, no . . ."

She silenced him with her tongue, probing his mouth, which still tasted of red wine. Her fingers found his zip and before he could move his hips in one last pretense of resistance, she wrapped her hand around his shaft, surprised and even more aroused by the fact he wasn't wearing underpants. He groaned, and she knew she had won.

Tracey threw back her head and was rewarded with the heat of his breath on her neck, followed by his lips. The head of his cock was already slick and she massaged the slippery fluid into his thickening hardness. She couldn't close her hand around him.

She felt his hand under her tank top now, taking one of her nipples between his first two fingers and rubbing the thumb over the trapped tip. She shuddered and pressed herself closer to him, drawing his prick to her, feeling its heat scald her belly.

Then he let go of her breast and placed a palm gently but firmly on her chest. "No." He exhaled deeply.

"Enough, Sam," she hissed. "I know you're a good guy, OK. It's why I want to fuck you."

"Tracey, no . . ."

She stood up on her toes and clasped her arms around his neck. She heaved with all her might and climbed up onto him. Reflexively, as she knew he would, he embraced her in those thickly muscled arms of his to stop her from falling, and she wrapped her legs around him. She could feel his hard, wet penis pushing into her and she moved against it. "Now, Sam. Fuck me, Coyote Sam."

Stirling heard the rustling in the bush. There was no sign of light from a torch.

"Shit," he said to himself. He should never have left the table; but what basis was there for a relationship if he couldn't leave the woman he loved in the company of another man, no matter how famous and supposedly good-looking he was? He thought the American looked like a *moffie* with his fake tan and his capped teeth and his body builder's physique. He'd heard all gays worked out in gyms. Still, the way Chapman was carrying on around Tracey— and she around him—gave him little hope that Coyote Sam preferred men.

The beam of Stirling's torch was blocked by the big mopane between tents three and four, but whatever was out there in the bush was just on the other side of the tree. By the amount of noise it was making it was probably a porcupine or a honey badger, snuffling about in the carpet of dead leaves.

"No!"

Stirling stopped and cocked his ear. That was Tracey.

"No, Sam," Tracey said, "I won't take . . ."

It was all Stirling needed to hear. As he rounded the bulk of the old tree he already had the heavy flashlight raised in his right hand and as he took in the sight—Sam Chapman with his fly undone and his erect penis in his hand, and Tracey, one breast exposed, backed against the mopane—he swung the torch hard into the American's right temple. Coyote Sam fell to the ground, out cold.

Tracey started sobbing, and Stirling took her in his arms and she buried her face in his safari shirt. "It's all right, baby. Bastard. I should get my gun and shoot him."

Sam laid his aching head against the warm perspex of the helicopter's window and watched, gratefully, as Xakanaxa Camp disappeared below him. He'd be happy if he never saw the place again, especially crazy Stirling and his psychotic nymphomaniac girlfriend.

"Don't worry." Cheryl-Ann's nasal voice sent a new blast of stereophonic pain through the earphones of the headset he wore. "The makeup covers the bruise and there's no way it will show on camera. We'll just have to reapply the foundation before you film the pieces to camera, especially if you've been sweating."

Don't worry? Was she serious? And did she think a purple bruise on his face was all he was concerned about? Tracey was gone by the time Sam had regained consciousness to find the safari guide standing over him, fists clenched. Sam had rubbed his head and risen groggily to his feet.

"I can explain . . ."

"Like fuck you can, pretty boy." Stirling's next blow connected with Sam's chin and sent him sprawling again. Still dizzy, and in no mood to prolong his own personal agony, Sam didn't fight back. "Get up, you fucking snake."

Cheryl-Ann had arrived then, and for once Sam had been glad to see her. Dressed in her shorty pajamas she had bravely put herself between the two men and pushed Stirling away. "Cool it, buster!"

Back in Cheryl-Ann's luxuriously appointed safari tent, Sam had explained it all to her.

"I knew it," Cheryl-Ann said. "That little bimbo was coming on to you from the moment we arrived. I could see it and you could see it too, so you shouldn't have let her get you alone."

Sam had groaned in pain and self-pity.

"No use crying over it, though. We'll talk money to them tomorrow. The network will settle out of court."

"What?" Sam was outraged. "She came on to me, Cheryl-Ann. You just said yourself . . ."

"I know what I said, but what's Tracey going to do? Is she going to tell her big *bwana* boyfriend that she was trying to jump you, or is she going to say that Mister Hollywood Big Shot tried to leopard stalk her in the dark while she was escorting him home? If she's got half a brain she'll already be thinking about selling her story to the tabloids, and that kind of PR we definitely do not need."

"You talk like it's a forgone conclusion, that everyone would believe her."

She'd stared at him like a schoolteacher despairing at the dumbest kid in class.

"Relax," Cheryl-Ann said into the helicopter's radio headset. "I'll sit them both down, individually, when we get back to camp and talk turkey. I'll find out what Tracey wants and we'll negotiate. Don't worry your pretty bruised head about it, Coyote Sam."

"Don't call me that." He stared out the window. On the flight into Xakanaxa the spiderweb of channels and game paths through the alternating patches of dry dusty bush and emerald green islands of reeds and grasses had mesmerized him. Now he just wanted to go home to the States. The wildlife paradise passing below him did nothing to lift his mood.

A herd of a hundred or more buffalo stampeded at the sound of the descending helicopter. Ray was busy filming through the opening where the pilot had removed the co-pilot's door, as the bulky black animals sent up silvery splashes of water. Here, at least, Sam registered numbly, there was water. While the buffalo looked like overgrown cows from above he knew from his research that hunters called them "black death." Cape Buffalo were one of the most dangerous animals a human could encounter on foot in the

African bush. Them and jealous safari guides, he thought ruefully. He squeezed the bridge of his nose and thought he'd prefer to take on one of those buffalo than see Stirling again.

"Ready when you guys are," Gerry said.

Cheryl-Ann nudged Sam in the ribs and he looked back into the interior of the helicopter. Gerry was recording the audio direct from the helicopter's intercom system and Ray had swung in his seat so that now he was filming Sam's face.

Sam forced a smile, looked out the window again, then back to the camera. "Below me is the untamed wilderness of the Okavango Delta, a wildlife garden of Eden; yet this is a paradise where death awaits the unsuspecting visitor at every turn."

He paused and took a breath. He felt queasy from the Scotch he'd downed in his tent to ease the pain of Stirling's blows and the shame of what had happened. He was paying for it now.

"You OK?" Cheryl-Ann asked, impatience plain on her face. "You look a little green."

"Yeah, I'm good."

"Keep rolling, Ray."

Sam's Adam's apple bobbed as he swallowed hard. "I'll be living down there, in the African bush for the next three days, all on my own, with enough food and water for one day. I'll be using the survival skills taught to me by the original occupants of this part of Botswana, the Khoisan people, also known as the Bushmen. If I haven't been paying attention, then it might be goodnight, for good, from me, Coyote Sam."

"Good job," Cheryl-Ann said into his headphones.

"Yeah right. Cornball crap and you know it."

"We can always reshoot it on the ground. Now, you sure you're all set for the next three days?"

"No." He wasn't sure at all. It had sounded like fun, back in the States, when he and his agent had pitched the idea for a program that combined wildlife documentary with reality show. Sam had spent plenty of time on his own in the Rockies and on the windswept prairies of Utah and Wyoming in search of coyotes, and while he knew enough to keep himself alive in a snow-storm, he was suddenly far from sure he could survive in the swamps of Botswana, where the predators were a lot bigger and more numerous than even the mountain lion he'd once encountered on foot.

He'd had a four-hour session on finding food in the African bush with a San guide just outside the town of Maun, where they'd acclimatized for a day after flying to Botswana from South Africa. On arrival at Xakanaxa, they'd filmed Stirling briefing Sam on the basics of staying safe around lion, leopard, buffalo and elephant—basically it amounted to staying cool, staying quiet, not wandering far from his camp, and keeping his tent zipped up and a fire burning at night. If he came across a dangerous animal on foot, the cardinal rule was to stand still, and avoid the natural urge to run away. Stirling had reassured him, kind of, by telling him that even tourists camped in unfenced sites in and on the edges of the Moremi Game Reserve and incidents with dangerous game were very rare. Cheryl-Ann, Stirling and the rest of the crew would be on standby if anything did go wrong—Stirling to defuse the situation and Ray and Gerry to film the action. The chartered helicopter would be waiting near Xakanaxa and they could get to him within fifteen minutes of a call, the pilot had assured him. How long, he wondered, did it take a lion to eat a man, and how long would Stirling take getting dressed, loading his gun and strolling to the chopper after what had happened with Tracey?

"You'll be fine," Cheryl-Ann chirped. "You're Coyote Sam, remember. You tamed the Aussie outback, so Africa will be a piece of cake."

"Right."

He watched a herd of elephant slow its pace to turn their heads and look up at them. The risks were greater here than in the outback and a big star wouldn't have agreed to actually camp out in the middle of Africa all alone, even with a helicopter on standby to rescue him. But Sam wasn't a big enough star. He shook his head.

"Just remember to keep the video camera going, Sam," Ray laughed. "Get some shots of the chopper leaving you all alone out there, surrounded by lions and leopards and hyenas."

"Stop teasing, Ray." Cheryl-Ann placed a hand on Sam's arm in an unusual gesture of sympathy. "Relax, it'll be OK. But like Ray says, if you think you're getting into serious trouble, just make sure you hit the record button."

Sam looked at her to see if she was joking, but all he saw was ice in her eyes. The helicopter settled into knee-length dry yellow grass and Ray unbuckled himself and jumped out to stand a short distance away with his camera on his shoulder. When Ray raised his thumb Sam climbed out of the aircraft. Gerry passed out his tent, bedroll, backpack, a five-liter plastic bottle of drinking water, camera bag, machete, a handheld radio and a satellite phone. "Good luck, Sam!" The sound man, at least, seemed genuine.

He finished piling up his gear and walked, bent at the waist, across to Cheryl-Ann's window, from where she was beckoning to him.

"There are going to be a couple of surprises thrown your way. Just go with the flow and keep the camera rolling, OK?"

He nodded, still feeling dejected. His spirits only sank deeper when he fished the handy cam from its pack and started videoing as Ray climbed back into the helicopter and the pilot took her up into the clear blue sky.

He switched the camera off to conserve the battery as soon as the helicopter was out of sight. He'd record some corny line, such as "Be seeing you guys . . . I hope," when his mood improved. Right now all he wanted to do was sleep off the booze and the events of the previous night.

Sam trudged fifty meters through the grass to a brick-red termite mound and climbed to the top of the earthen insect city, which was taller than he was. From there he scanned the surrounding area. A herd of impala, grazing in a far-off tree line, saw him. The lyre-horned male barked a warning call to his harem of dainty females and they leaped away. There was nothing deadly in sight so he climbed down. Sweat started to pour from him with each step he took in the midday sun. Shelter, as always, was his first priority, so he unrolled the tent.

In the first episode of the *Coyote Sam's World Survival* series, "Danger Down Under," he'd had to build his temporary home out of sticks and bark, the way an Australian Aboriginal national parks ranger had shown him. In the outback, the greatest danger came from snakes but he had been relatively safe from even them by stringing his mosquito net up and tucking it under his bedroll. Here in Africa, with the very real possibility of lions, hyenas and leopards prowling around his camp site, hard-arse Cheryl-Ann had relented and allowed him a tent. Sam unrolled the simple dome-shaped structure of sturdy green canvas and slotted together the two metal poles that would support it.

He wondered what the obligatory "surprises" would be this time. In Australia, the box of matches he had been allowed to bring had been substituted at the last minute with a packet in which all of the incendiary heads had been carefully snipped off. He'd had to make fire using a pointed stick rubbed against a soft piece of wood and to his—and his viewers'—surprise he'd been able to do so, after two days of trying. His hands had been rubbed raw until they bled, which Cheryl-Ann said had made great TV.

Of course, the surprises weren't always bad. On his third and last day in the outback he had been waiting impatiently to be airlifted back to the luxury resort at Uluru where the rest of the crew was staying. Instead of the sound of a helicopter he had picked up the noise of a car horn blaring somewhere in the distance. Reluctantly, he had taken the camera in hand and set off in the direction of the incessant noise.

Slogging through the thick red sand had sapped the last of his strength. He'd eaten nothing but grubs and lizards for three days and his stomach had protested vociferously at the physical effort. When he came within sight of the vehicle his heart sank. It was an aging, rusted four-wheel-drive camper. A young man with long blond dreadlocks was alternating between blowing the truck's horn and returning to the rear of the vehicle, which was bogged to the axles in sand. With no shovel, the man was furiously trying to scoop loose sand away from the stuck tires.

"I have become stuck!" the man called out to him in a German accent.

Sam dutifully started filming, then turned the camera on himself. "One of the first rules of survival in the outback is don't travel without the correct gear."

As he approached the stranded motorist the man dropped to his knees.

"Thank you, thank you," he cried. "I have no water and I am thinking I am going to die out here in the outback."

"One of the other rules," Sam told the camera, "is that if you see a fellow traveler in trouble, always stop and see if you can assist."

At that moment, the rear doors of the camper swung open. A beautiful tall red-haired Australian girl dressed in denim shorts, a white T-shirt and a chef's hat climbed from the truck, carrying a covered silver platter. He recalled her immediately—one of the cooks from the resort who had asked him for his autograph after he'd sent his compliments to the kitchen. From further up the sandy road, emerging from behind a red anthill not dissimilar from the one he had just climbed, came the crew. The survival exercise was over and the redhead lifted the lid on a mouthwatering dinner of freshwater crayfish. The German actor shook his hand and reached inside the Land Cruiser for a dew-frosted beer.

Sam wondered now if there would be a happy ending to this survival program, or if Stirling would be waiting for him with a gun at Xakanaxa Camp. Unbidden, an image of the Australian girl's milk-white skin below her tan line, on either side of a trimmed strip of red hair, filled his mind. "Stop it," he told himself out loud.

As he clipped the canvas dome to the second tent pole he swore. He tossed the pole on the ground and unclipped the other one. "Fucking Coyote Sam's World Survival, my ass."

He had forgotten to set up the camera on its tripod. If he finished the three days without some vision of him setting up his tent then Cheryl-Ann would make him do it all over again.

Uh-roo, Uh-roo.

"Hear that?" Sam said as loud as he dared, looking into the lens of the camera on its tripod. "That's the King of Beasts, the African lion. They call on dusk, signaling the members of their pride to come together . . . for the hunt. I just hope it's me on the menu . . . aw, fuck it."

He started his monologue once more, leaning closer to the camera as he said the last line again. "I just hope it's *not* me on the menu for tonight."

Fortunately, the box of matches in his backpack had not been tampered with and he was able to light a fire in a modest pile of dead wood he'd been able to scrounge without venturing too far from his camp site. This part of the documentary was being filmed in a privately managed concession outside the Moremi Game Reserve, on the southern fringe of the reserve.

"I wouldn't be allowed out at night by myself inside the game reserve, on the other side of the river, or to light a fire like I've just done, in the middle of nowhere. But these flames will keep the lions away—so the theory goes."

"Poor bugger. He didn't look too happy," said John Little, the New Zealand pilot of the helicopter as they lifted away from the lone man on the ground. Little was the antithesis of his name; he was tall and broad-shouldered and very easy on the eye, Cheryl-Ann thought.

"He'll be fine," Cheryl-Ann said. "He's done this sort of thing before."

"Better him than me," John said. "If the lions don't get him the crocs will. Fancy taking the scenic route back to Xakanaxa?"

"Sure," Cheryl-Ann said. She could play the hard arse until the cows came home—she had to be tough to get along in the cut-throat world of television—but in truth she was dreading the confrontation with Stirling and Tracey. This had all the elements of a class-A fuck-up. Most stars she knew screwed around when on tour, but she'd believed Sam up until now when he'd said that he only went for single girls. What had he been thinking going off into the dark with Tracey?

"Nice giraffe down there," John said, pointing off to the right.

"Really?" She had a shot list a mile long to get through in the next three days so she and Ray and Gerry would not be sitting on their backsides while Coyote Sam lazed around his camp site, starving. "Light's pretty good now. Let's get some giraffe shots, Ray."

"Yes, ma'am," replied the cameraman.

"Can you take us lower?"

"Not a problem. You're the guys with the greenbacks," John grinned.

Cheryl-Ann felt her stomach lurch as the Kiwi—she liked the sound of that—brought the chopper around the giraffes in a wide arc, losing altitude as he set them up for the shot, with the sun behind them. He was professional and courteous, and had obviously worked with film crews and professional photographers before. Plus, he had a nice arse in those shorts.

"Nice," she said into her microphone.

"Thanks," John said, glancing back over his shoulder at her again. "Shit!"

A warning siren blared loudly above the background hum of the engines, filling the helicopter's passengers with instant fear.

"What's that?" Cheryl-Ann asked.

Little ignored them, his fingers roving across the panel in front of him. "Mayday, mayday, mayday . . ."

Sam checked his watch for the fourth time in twelve minutes. It was still three minutes to go until seven o'clock. It wasn't that he was scared of the lion—it still sounded a long way off—but the hyena seemed much closer.

Woooo-ooooop, it called again. Another replied. Sam stoked the fire and tossed on another undersized piece of wood. The bundle he had collected had diminished quickly, as much of it was rotten, reduced to the weight of cardboard by termites. He doubted there would be enough to keep the fire going all night. Tomorrow he would have to look for a log, and remember to check for snakes. Stirling had stopped the Land Rover on the first day beside a fallen tree and they had all wondered what he was looking at, until the rock python raised its huge head and tested the air with its tongue. "We often stop here for sundowners and some of the tourists sit on that tree," he'd said, not attempting to hide his patronizing tone.

Sam unzipped the tent, which he had kept closed since he erected it, in case anything wanted to slither or crawl inside. He knew that during the night he should keep the flap zipped closed, no matter how hot it got, or what he heard going on outside. He checked his watch again, sighed, then pressed the record button on the camera.

"As long as I stay zipped inside my tent tonight I *should* be OK." He could see his face in the flip-out LED screen, which was reversible so that he could check his image while the camera recorded. The camera had a night-vision function and his features were captured in atmospheric but slightly blurry lime-green light. "That's a hyena you can hear in the distance, and they've been known to rip into tents if they smell food inside. Luckily," he laughed for effect, "my crew hasn't left me any food to eat, so I should be safe from the hyenas. As for those lions you heard earlier, they hunt by sight and sound, much the same way as your house cat does. If they see something moving, they'll investigate and pounce on it. However, they don't have great depth perception so when they see my tent, the theory is they'll think it's a solid object, like an anthill or a rock. If I unzip and stick my head out to take a peek at them, they might just jump on me, like a cat pouncing on a mouse. Difference is, these cats can weigh in at around six hundred pounds. Now I know how a mouse feels."

He switched off the camera and checked his watch. He wondered if his monologues would look as lame on TV as they sounded to him now. One thing about Cheryl-Ann, she had a good eye for editing and timing. She'd make him look good, even if she made him feel like shit for the rest of the trip. It was finally seven o'clock. He rummaged in his rucksack for the satellite phone and slipped it out of its black nylon case. Cheryl-Ann's number was pre-set, so he scrolled down and pressed send.

The phone rang.

Outside the lion called and was answered by another. Great, Sam thought, stereophonic death.

The phone rang.

"Come on," he said, checking his watch.

"*The service you are calling is not responding. Please try again later,*" a transcontinental-accented female voice echoed from the other end of the line.

Having drinks by the river, he presumed. He wondered what the mood was like between Cheryl-Ann and Stirling and Tracey. Perhaps they were locked in a heated debate right now about whether to hang, draw or quarter him. Sam dialed the number again.

He drummed his fingers on the plastic-coated floor of the tent while he waited for Cheryl-Ann to answer. Nothing.

5

Sonja clapped her hands. "Shoo!" she commanded the trio of tan-colored mangy African dogs. The heavily pregnant warthog didn't pause to acknowledge her intervention, and continued snuffling in the overturned rubbish bin as she had been when the dogs were nipping at her hindquarters.

"*Eish*, you must be eating for four or five, my girl," Sonja said to the grunting, farting creature as she passed it.

Sonja walked on, through the dusty car park of the small shopping center near the entrance to the Chobe Safari Lodge. Chipchase had done a good job of cleaning and stitching the holes in her thigh. The skin was pink, there was no blood, and while her leg still ached she had been well enough to walk on it by the second day. She still hadn't confirmed to him that it was she who had tried to assassinate the President of Zimbabwe, although she hadn't denied it and he had stopped probing her for more information for the time being.

She wanted to buy some food for the road, and to cook a meal for him in part payment for his kindness. Also, despite his offering her the use of his laptop and mobile phone to check emails, she wanted to do that in privacy, from an anonymous computer.

Near the Choppies supermarket was a *bureau de change* with half a dozen Internet computers. "Fifteen pula fifteen minutes," the bored African woman behind the counter said to her. Sonja sat down on a buckled plastic chair and opened the browser. She went to her Hotmail account and logged in as sallytraveling. Apart from the usual spam there was one message from steeleman1043@yahoo.

Where are you? read the subject line of the email. She clicked on it and the full message was equally brief and to the point. *No answer on your satphone. Advise locstat asap. Too bad about the job, but I have another. M.*

"Too bad?" she said out loud. An African man two terminals down looked at her and she smiled an apology. She wasn't sure she wanted her locstat—her location—posted anywhere on the Internet. She doubted the Zimbabwean CIO possessed state-of-the-art cyber-monitoring equipment, but perhaps they had friends in North Korea or China who did. She hit the reply button and typed: *Satphone US. I'm heading for home. You know where to find me.*

Her satellite phone really was useless, as it had been squashed at some point during her escape. She had bought a cheap phone and a prepaid SIM card at an Indian shop in Kasane on her walk the day before, but she couldn't risk giving that to Martin, as it would be easily traceable.

Sonja looked over her shoulder to make sure she was still alone in the *bureau de change* and logged into her Channel Islands bank account. True to his word—and she had no reason to doubt him—Martin had deposited her share of the first payment for the Zimbabwean job. It was some small comfort that she had received a reasonable payment for nearly losing her life. No matter what her daughter thought of her as a mother, Emma would inherit enough to see her way through university, plus a very tidy nest egg. Sonja gave a small nod of satisfaction as she double-checked the balance and closed out of her account and logged off. If she'd lived in England for every second of Emma's childhood they would have barely scraped by. Standing, she painfully stretched her injured leg, then paid the girl behind the steel grille. Her work had its risks, she thought as she walked out into the sun and toward the supermarket, but she might have died from the inside out if she hadn't fallen in with Martin after the army.

The Choppies supermarket hadn't been there when she'd last stayed at the safari lodge with Stirling. It was a sign of progress, an indicator that Botswana really was doing well. If you could afford to shop in air-conditioned comfort and buy fruit from the Cape and seafood from Mozambique, then your government was doing something right. She ordered a kilogram of fillet steak at the butchery counter and bought some ice cream for dessert. She paid cash for the food, not wanting to leave a paper trail by using a credit card, and stopped in at the liquor store for a bottle of South African red—a nice Alto Rouge—a six-pack of St. Louis beer, and a copy of the *Daily News.*

Sonja walked back into the Safari Lodge, through reception and along the edge of the verandah that took in a spectacular view of the Chobe River, whose shiny, still surface was broken here and there by grassy emerald islands, in turn punctuated with the dark dots of grazing buffalo and elephant. Waiters doted on tourists lounging around the swimming pool and children splashed in the clear waters. Not a hundred kilometers away was a country where people starved and died of cholera. That was Africa, Sonja thought.

When she got back to the camp site she shooed a pair of vervet monkeys off Chipchase's camping table. She heard snoring from inside the campervan and wondered how the man could sleep in the mobile coffin in the heat of the day. She'd slept in his hammock, a mosquito net suspended above her from a tree, soothed to slumber by the grunt of the hippos in the Chobe and glimpses of stars through the riverine bush canopy above her.

She eased herself into the safari lounger, grateful to take the weight off her leg, but pleasingly achey from the walk. She couldn't afford to lose muscle tone, even if it hurt a bit during the recovery. Sonja took another big gulp of her fast-warming beer and opened the newspaper.

BDF, POLICE HELP SEARCH FOR ZIM ASSASSIN shouted the headline. She frowned as she read.

The Botswana president said that while he had not always agreed with his Zimbabwean counterpart's policies and politics there was no excuse for someone to try and kill a head of state.

Sonja snorted. For years the dinner-party conversation around the world had been "Why hasn't someone simply killed him?"

Police sources said a description of the alleged assassin had been circulated to them and the Botswana Defense Force, although the identikit picture would not be released to the media.

"Not surprising," Sonja said softly. However, the news that the president had nearly been offed by a woman would be too salacious to be kept quiet for too long. It would make traveling harder for her, but not impossible.

Page three of the *Daily News* lead with a story sourced from the Botswana president's spokesman admitting a lack of progress in talks with the Namibian and Angolan governments to increase flows from the recently completed dam on the Okavango River. Diplomatic efforts to stop the dam being built had failed and the governments that had part funded the project were pointing to the severe drought as the reason why the impact on the Okavango Delta was so far more drastic than had been predicted. The final stage of the project, the newspaper reported, would soon be completed once the hydro-electric power station associated with the project was commissioned.

Sonja turned her head when she heard the creak of the Land Cruiser's rear springs. The rear cargo door opened and Sydney Chipchase poked his head out.

"Afternoon. Or is it still morning?" he said, blinking.

"Too much Bushmills last night?" They had both stayed up late and Sonja had enjoyed blotting out the events of the recent and distant past for a few hours. The stories they'd told had been funny ones, from their army days, and she'd told him a little, very little, of her time growing up in Botswana.

Sydney looked over Sonja's shoulder at the newspaper article about the dam. "What do you think about that?"

Sonja shrugged. "I know people need electricity, but I can't help thinking there's more to this than meets the eye. Mines need lots of water. This dam could destroy the Okavango Delta for what? So some more people can get satellite TV and some politicians can line their pockets with kickbacks from the companies that will really benefit from damming the river."

Chipchase nodded. "I visit the construction site often, to minister to the workers and their families. It's provided a lot of employment for a poor region in these tough financial times." He helped himself to one of the beers still in the plastic bag on the table. "I've got to leave tomorrow, Sonja. I'm heading south to Francistown. Can I give you a lift?"

"You know the cops will be looking for me at the roadblocks."

Chipchase nodded. "They'll be looking for a solo woman, not a missionary couple."

She laughed. "I don't know if I can play the part of a God-botherer's wife."

"You played the part of an IRA sympathizer."

She knew she shouldn't rise to his bait, but she couldn't help herself. There had been too many whispers, too much speculative bullshit after she'd returned from Northern Ireland. "I was told to get close to the quartermaster who supplied the explosives for the school bus bombing. I did that."

Sydney lowered himself into his camp chair and took a sip of his beer. "And Martin Steele hung you out to dry."

She didn't like him making suppositions about Martin either. Chipchase was an intelligence officer who fought his war from behind a desk. "We pushed the boundaries, yes . . . even for the Det."

"The word was you slept with Byrne. Is that true?"

"That's none of your fucking business, Sydney."

He nodded. "Aye. You're right. I'm interested, though, from a professional and historical point of view. You were probably closer to the fighting in Northern Ireland than any military woman ever was. Didn't you feel Steele was using you, as a woman?"

Sonja shook her head. "Why do men have to paint us as victims or, worse, as helpless pawns? I got close to Byrne, yes, and I found out that his brother was the brains behind the bus bombing."

"The ends justified the means?"

"Get your mind out of the gutter, Sydney. It was war, and I fought it the way I thought it needed to be fought."

"He was a killer, Sonja—as guilty as his brother was. He supplied the explosives and he must have known what they were going to be used for."

Chipchase could never understand what had gone on between her and Danny Byrne, or between Danny and his brother. "I was able to get close to Danny because I knew where he was coming from. He was a guy who'd grown up in a war, on the side of the minority that thought it could never win. He grew up in an environment where killing made you a man, and where those who carried guns were seen as peacemakers and patriots. I grew up in the same world. That's how I got to him."

"And that," Sydney said, pausing to drink some more beer, "is how you set him up to be assassinated by the SAS."

6

The road from Kazungula to Francistown was one of the most boring in Africa, and only the potholes provided a distraction from the dull brown bush and dry yellow grass that flanked the shimmering river of tar that stretched endlessly into the distance.

Chipchase played AC/DC on his iPod, fed through the Land Cruiser's radio speakers. When "Highway to Hell" blasted forth Sonja told him she thought it an odd choice for a missionary.

"It reminds me of my good old days as a sinner and gives me a reference point for how far I've traveled."

She smiled, but she had too much on her mind and small talk wasn't her forte. She was heading for a confrontation. The safest place for her to hide was at Xakanaxa, and that would mean seeing Stirling. Chipchase's gentle but persistent questioning about her days in the army had brought back memories she'd fought for a long time to suppress. She knew that the more she thought about the events in Northern Ireland, the quicker she would reopen that particular wound. Would seeing Stirling again heal her, or kill what was left of her soul for good? A month earlier, while still in the UK, she had succumbed, over a couple of glasses of wine, to a simmering urge to look for Stirling on Facebook. She'd found him and been quietly ecstatic to see his status was listed as "single." It had taken all her self-control not to message him or try to add him as a friend. She'd known she would soon be headed for Africa and she had wanted to surprise him, rather than give him the option of an easy rejection via the Internet. She couldn't quite decide whether her strategy smacked of bravery or idiocy.

"Sydney, stop!"

Chipchase put on the breaks and veered off onto the dirt strip. The road's surface had improved between the turn-off to Elephant Springs camp and Nata, the next fuel stop. "There's nothing here. Do you need to go to the loo?"

Sonja shook her head and pointed to the figure ahead of them, taking form out of the shimmering heat haze, the horizontally shifting bands slowly coalescing into one outline. It was, as she had spotted long before the aging Chipchase, a man on a horse.

She got out and opened the back of the campervan, retrieving her pack, which contained food and water and a compact camping gas stove she'd bought in Kasane. It also held her M4, broken down into its component pieces, and spare magazines. She moved the nine mil from the front of her shorts to the rear of her waistband and stretched her tank top over the pistol grip.

Sonja hoisted her pack onto her shoulders and walked to the driver's side window. "Sydney, I can't thank you enough, but please take this." As she shook his hand she palmed some green bills to him.

"I won't take money from you, Sonja." He thrust the cash back at her.

"If you don't want it then do some good with it. You're a missionary, for fuck's sake, you must know a worthy cause somewhere."

He smiled down at her from the cab and reached his hand out to shake hers again. Instead, she rose on her toes and kissed him on the cheek. She was rewarded with a brick-red blush on his weathered old face.

"I'm sorry, Sonja, if it seemed like I was prying about . . . well, you know, about the old days."

She shook her head. "I didn't want to talk or even think about it and haven't for years, except in my nightmares. I don't know if it helped, but I do know I've had enough of the past. I've got enough problems in the near future to keep me going."

"Aye, well if you feel the need to go after any other African despots then my advice is . . ."

"Read the Bible?"

"Better intelligence and a .fifty-caliber sniper rifle with a decent scope."

She smiled and waved as the Land Cruiser was swallowed by the heat haze. The clip-clop of the hooves was close enough to hear now, and she stood in the middle of the road waiting for the man to arrive. She'd need to conserve her depleted energy.

The man was in far better shape than the horse that bore him. He wore a ten-gallon cowboy hat made out of zebra-print fabric, and a single-breasted charcoal gray business suit, old and frayed, but clean and pressed. The same went for the blue business shirt with white cuffs and collar. The uppers of his black leather shoes, though as clean as the Kalahari sand would allow, were peeling up from the soles. When he stopped in front of her she saw tightly frizzed patches of gray hair beneath the deep shade of the hat. If she was a tourist she would have wondered what an old African man in a suit and cowboy hat was doing riding slowly down the Nata to Kasane road in the middle of the day in one-hundred-seven-degree heat, but she wasn't a tourist.

"*Dumela*," she said in Tswana, lingering over the middle syllable. "*Le kae?*"

"*Ke teng, wena o kae?*"

"I, too, am fine, thank you," Sonja answered in Tswana. In addition to English, from her mother, and German, from her father, she spoke Ovambo, from the maid who had nursed her until she was ten, and Tswana from Stirling and the staff kids at Xakanaxa. If the old man was curious as to what a white woman was doing wandering the empty highway by herself, then he knew better than to be so rude as to ask. "I would like to buy your horse," she said to the man.

He shook his head. "If I sell you this horse, then I would have to walk, and I do not wish to walk to where I am going. Thank you, but no thank you."

"With what I will give you, you can buy a motor car."

"I have no need of such a thing. Besides," he looked around him from his position above her, "where would I buy the petrol?"

"I will give you three thousand pula," she said, reaching into the pocket of her shorts. Pula, the currency of Botswana, meant rain in English. She'd offered him close to five hundred US dollars, but the man shook his head. "Four thousand?"

"Not for ten. This horse is not for sale. He is my prized possession."

Beneath the cracked saddle she saw the outline of ribs and the fuzzy coat that spoke of malnourishment and disease. The horse shook its head in a futile attempt to chase the flies away and looked down at her through rheumy eyes.

"Twelve."

The cowboy shook his head and clicked his tongue. He was serious about not selling.

Sonja sighed. She'd hoped it wouldn't come to this. She reached behind her and pulled out her pistol. Leveling it up to his startled face she said, in English. "Get off the fucking horse."

The old man moistened his lips with his tongue and looked behind him. There was no one. She could see him weighing his options, wondering if he could outrun her. They both knew the horse wouldn't get far at a gallop, but still he didn't move.

Sonja fired. The tired horse tried to rear up but, with the weight of the African on its back, barely managed a buck. The man was on the ground, his feet raising puffs of dust, before she had time to readjust her aim. He brushed imaginary specs from his jacket and tossed away the reins. "I will call the police!"

"I'm sure you will. And be sure and tell them I gave you this." She threw the rolled wad of twelve thousand pula at his feet, "which is more than you deserve for the way you've treated this poor excuse of an animal."

Sonja wheeled the horse and headed east, toward Zimbabwe.

Fark, fark, faaaark! The screeching of the bird roused Sam from his dozing. He sat upright in the tent and looked around its gloomy green interior. He was disappointed to discover the events of the past eighteen hours had not been a nightmare.

He'd found it hard to sleep, not only because of the dueling whooping and grunting of the hyena and lion, and the snuffling of something snooping in the grass around his camp fire and tent, but because he was worried about Cheryl-Ann and the camera crew.

Cheryl-Ann had told him to expect surprises, and to keep the camera rolling, but never before had they broken the routine of the morning and evening calls on the satellite phone. It was a safety precaution.

He checked his watch. He'd set the alarm for six a.m., but had woken half an hour earlier. He pushed the send button anyway. "Fuck." It was the out-of-contact recorded message again. "This can't be happening."

He cursed himself for not writing down the number of Xakanaxa Lodge and for not spending more time learning about the satellite phone and the service they used. If he had, he might know the number to call for directory assistance.

"The office!" He wasn't good at remembering phone numbers—never had been—but he knew the number for the Wildlife World Channel's production office in Los Angeles. He calculated the time difference and punched in the digits. It was just after eight-thirty in the evening in LA, but the switch was manned late as there was almost always someone working well into the night on post production. The phone started ringing. "Come on, come on, please be working late . . ." He would ask whoever answered to track down Tom, Cheryl-Ann's personal assistant, and get him to call back with the number for Xakanaxa, and to call them to find out what was going on. No doubt there had been some easily explainable misunderstanding somewhere along the way.

As an afterthought, he leaned over to push "record" on the tripod-mounted camera. As he was clipping on the lapel microphone with one hand he lowered the phone, but still heard the female voice.

"Good evening, this is Wildlife World, Stacey speaking, how may I direct your call?" It was Stacey, one of the receptionists.

Sam sat upright and in doing so snagged the microphone cable. The camera crashed into his lap. "Shit! Hello . . . hello?"

"Excuse me?" said the receptionist.

"Stacey, it's . . ."

There was an echo on the line and Stacey cut across him. "Hello . . . yes, this is Stacey. Who is calling, please?"

"Stacey, Stacey, listen to me, it's Sam Chapman here . . ."

"No, sir, I'm sorry, this is a bad line, but Sam Chapman is not here. If you'd like to contact him I can give you the address of his official website and you can click on the contact options there to—"

"No, no, no! It's Sam Chapman HERE! Stacey, I need you to—"

"Sorry, who did you say it is?"

"Aaaaaargh." Sam heard a series of beeps and quickly glanced at the phone's screen. "Listen," he yelled. "This is Sam Chapman. I'm in Africa. Something is wrong. I need you to get a message to Tom Cartman ASAP!"

"Mr. Chapman, is that really you?"

Sam swallowed a quick breath. "Yes, Stacey."

"Oh my god! I'll put you through right away. Just hold on, sir."

Sam wished he hadn't been put on hold, and wondered what Tom was doing working back so late. With his workaholic boss Cheryl-Ann away in Africa he should have been keeping regular hours for a change.

Beep, beep, beep.

"No!"

Sam had left the phone on all night, in case Cheryl-Ann tried calling him. Their standard procedure in the past had been to keep the satellite phones switched off, to conserve batteries in the field. If for some reason they couldn't make contact at the appointed hours, usually six p.m. and six a.m., then they would switch on again every half hour afterward, for five minutes. Sam had done that, until midnight, when he decided he needed to try to get some sleep. He'd left the phone on, reasoning the battery would last through the night. The call was obviously chewing battery power.

The low-battery warning beeped again. "Come *on*."

While he waited he busied himself righting the fallen camera and re-attaching his microphone. "This is seriously not funny. I'm stranded in the African bush with no contact with my producer and now my satellite phone battery is going flat while I listen to a computer-generated version of a Barry Manilow song."

"Sam?"

"Tom. What the hell is going on, man? I've been trying to call Cheryl-Ann and she's not picking up. I need the number for—"

"Sam, are you OK?"

"Me? I'm stuck in the African bush surrounded by man-eating animals and poisonous snakes, but other than that I'm just peachy. Do you know why Cheryl-Ann isn't answering her goddamned phone, Tom?"

"Sam . . . oh my god," Tom sniffed. "Cheryl-Ann's . . ."

Bee-eep.

"Cheryl-Ann's what?"

Sam looked at the darkened screen of the phone and screamed again in frustration. He ferreted through the black nylon carry bag, but couldn't find a spare battery. He couldn't recall ever seeing—or needing—one.

He ran a hand through his hair and over his stubbled jaw while he thought. It was probably all a setup, he told himself. If they wanted raw emotion—good TV—they would get it. Was sniffling Tom back in L.A. in on the act as well? Could Cheryl-Ann be that conniving, that manipulative, to get Stacey on reception—normally so efficient and prompt at fielding calls—and Tom to start crying in order to rattle his cage?

Yes.

Sam composed himself and looked at his image in the small LED screen to the right of the lens. "It's at times like these—when you realize you're in a jam, with no communications, and no food—that you wished you'd paid more attention to TV programs like *Coyote Sam's World Survival*. We'll be back after the break with some tips about how to save yourself when your phone battery goes dead . . ."

He switched off the camera and exhaled. At least Cheryl-Ann and the guys would get a laugh out of his station break announcement, even if they didn't use it. He sucked a deep breath. He'd show them. No matter how disorientated and scared he was right now, he wouldn't show fear or panic on camera.

Sam unzipped the tent and crawled outside, stretching to ease away the cramp of sleeping on the foam camping mattress. At forty-two, he wasn't getting any younger. He remembered nights sleeping on the floor of his pup tent on the prairie, with nothing except a thin high-density foam camping mat between him and the ground, when he was a college student working on his thesis. He couldn't even afford a decent sleeping bag in those days, but now he earned six figures for being the face of a range of expensive camping equipment. Much of the stuff wouldn't last a weekend in Yosemite, let alone the Okavango swamps of Botswana. He thought about those good days, and the bad ones beforehand, when he was in juvie. He'd imagined leading a quiet life of solitude in the mountains and prairies, dedicated to the study of his beloved coyotes. He'd loved the fun ride of his early years in television, but now he wondered if any of it had really mattered. His ratings were slumping and the survival series was a last roll of the dice. Perhaps he'd been heading for a fall all along.

The fire was out, and so was his stock of wood. Sam crouched and placed his hand over the ash and felt a faint aura of warmth. He looked around him and snatched up some dry stalks of yellowed grass. Placing them on the coals he blew them to life. "All right!" he said out loud as the grass blossomed into flame. He looked around but there was nothing else to throw on the flames, which quickly died.

"Shiiit."

He still had some matches, so it wasn't a total disaster. He'd do the blowing-on-embers trick again for the camera, even if he had to reshoot it tomorrow.

Tomorrow. It seemed a long way off. He scanned the sky, hoping to spot the spec of a hovering helicopter, briefly fantasizing that he was being filmed by some long-range military-type image intensifier, that his every word was being recorded by hidden microphones. Instead, he saw a sun whose ember-red color would soon ignite to scorching gold. His stomach rumbled. He needed to pee.

Sam walked ten meters from the tent, as far as he dared for the moment, and unzipped. He looked around him as he urinated, but a rustle in the dead leaves and long grass in front of him made him clench.

"Holy crap!" The dark serpentine tail slithered away from him. He jumped back and his bladder released again, splashing his leg. "Goddamn!"

He was pleased the camera wasn't rolling now, catching him pissing on his pants, Sam zipped up, picked up a dead branch and snapped off the ends to create a short fork. He'd caught snakes as a kid and although this one had startled him, he wasn't going to let some reptile scare the pants off him. He'd eaten snake in Malaysia and while he hadn't agreed it tasted like chicken, it was edible. He wanted to get through this whole episode without killing anything in the concession, but his stomach was telling him berries and insects might not be enough.

Sam crept forward, watching where he put his boots to avoid snapping twigs. He paused and listened. He heard, then saw, the movement in the grass. It was impossible to film the hunt, but he'd re-create it later, then cut to a nice shot of skinned snake roasting on the coals. Involuntarily, his mouth started to water.

"Gotcha!" He lunged and planted the prongs of the stick in the ground. Trapped between them however, was not a snake, but a lizard as long as his arm and as thick, at the widest part of its belly, as his calf. "Leguan," he said, identifying its sandy background color and gray-green camouflage stripes. It twisted and flicked against the stick that imprisoned it. It was a slow mover, searching for ground-nesting birds' eggs and carrion. Sam looked down on the poor tormented thrashing reptile and, though he imagined it would be edible, he didn't have it in him to kill the creature. He lifted the stick and took a step back. The lizard scampered off.

"Shoot," he said. He knew that a key ingredient of the survival show was him killing something and eating it. He'd had some ethical troubles with it during filming of the first show, but Cheryl-Ann had told him outright—the only way she knew how to communicate—that people out there in TV land, no matter how squeamish some of them might pretend to be, wanted blood.

"It's the same as on the news," she'd said. "If it bleeds, it leads. Ditto for us in the ratings."

Sam fossicked in the bush for more firewood, gingerly probing each fallen branch with the toe of his boot before picking it up, in case one of Stirling's pet pythons was hiding underneath.

A branch snapped somewhere close by.

Sam stopped and cocked his head. "Hallelujah," he breathed, looking heavenwards. The cavalry was on its way, hacking through the bush to come get him—hopefully with an attractive female chef riding shotgun and carrying breakfast. He dropped the termite-ridden bough he'd picked up and wiped his hands on his shorts as he walked toward the sound. Peering ahead he tried, as Stirling had advised him, to look *through* the trees, not at them.

The splintering of wood was almost as loud as gunfire now, but still he could see nothing of his rescuers. Was this one of his surprises? God, he hoped so. If Cheryl-Ann had been trying to put him off balance she had succeeded in spades.

"Hey!" he called out. "Over here."

The noise stopped, and so did Sam, realizing he had probably just done something monumentally stupid. He heard a rumbling noise, like his own stomach, though amplified a hundred times.

Now he saw the movement. A gray sail flapped slowly in the nonexistent breeze and a shadowy bulk eclipsed the sunlight filtering through the trees. Sam started to walk backward, slowly. How could he not have seen them? A trunk curled and rose like a periscope, seeking him out. Was he downwind or upwind of them? He couldn't feel a breath of wind, but the elephants had heard him and now they were intent on finding him.

The matriarch—he remembered from what Stirling had said that the big one in the lead with the squared-off forehead would be a female and the greatest danger—shook her head. The dust surrounded her like an ominous rain cloud. He kept moving, faster now, though still not looking where he was going. She watched him through a beady eye and rocked her left front foot backward and forward, a gesture of irritation. He fell.

Sam cursed, silently, and slithered backward, using heels and elbows to propel himself. He'd fallen over the nylon guy rope of his own tent. He rolled sideways and in through the open door. As he zipped it shut he wondered what else he could do wrong today. At the rate his luck was holding out he would be lucky if there wasn't an Egyptian cobra under his sleeping bag by now.

The elephant approached. Sam lay in the bottom of his tent, in the middle of nowhere. "May as well go out an Emmy winner." He switched on the camera and waited to die.

7

Stirling snatched up the vibrating mobile phone, cutting off the ringtone, a woodland kingfisher's call, which seemed absurdly frivolous given the magnitude of the disaster unfolding around him.

"Stirling, it's Wayne from Mack Air, howzit?"

How did he think it was? Stirling had spent a sleepless night making and taking calls to and from the United States about the missing production crew. That morning an aerial search of the concessions to the south of the Moremi Game Reserve had finally found the charred and twisted wreckage of the helicopter that had been carrying the Americans. The initial report had come from the pilot of a light plane who had spotted the smoking wreckage and someone waving a shirt to attract his attention. There was nowhere near the crash site for the fixed-wing aircraft to land, so another helicopter had been scrambled from Maun Airport.

"Give me the news, Wayne."

"The rescue helo landed fifteen minutes ago. John Little, the pilot, is in a bad way—he's in a coma and quite badly burned. One of the American guys, Ray, the cameraman, has a broken arm and the other one . . ."

"Gerry."

"Right, Gerry, is a bit bruised and probably has concussion. The woman . . . sheesh, that woman. She's threatening to sue everyone in Maun and wanted us to fly her back out to the bush this afternoon. She's already found herself a replacement cameraman. Man, she's a piece of work that one."

"Tell me about it. What about their star, Sam Chapman?"

"Not on board. They'd dropped him somewhere in the bush and we've still got three aircraft out searching for him."

"Why?" Stirling asked. "Didn't they have a GPS coordinate or grid reference where they left him?"

"GPS was left in the chopper when they all evacuated and it was burned to a crisp. Cheryl-Ann's given us a description of the area, and we know it was in the hunting concession on the edge of the game reserve. The researchers down there know the general area where he was dumped and they're sending out vehicles to look for him. Sam has a sat phone, but Cheryl-Ann's was destroyed in the crash as well."

Stirling shook his head. He felt bad for the pilot and now he had something else to worry about when it came to Sam Chapman. He felt an attack of guilt when he recalled thinking to himself that he hoped something happened to the TV star during his "survival" filming. "Where are they all now?"

"In the Maun hospital. We offered to call MARS and have them evacked to Jo'burg, but Cheryl-Ann insisted they all stay local so they can get back to work as soon as possible."

"Thanks Wayne. Do me a favor; call me and give me a heads up when Typhoon Cheryl-Ann is headed my way."

"Will do. Bye."

Stirling put the phone in his pocket and turned at the sound of footsteps on the wooden floorboards outside the camp office. Tracey stood there, chewing on the fingernail of her right index finger.

"Any news?"

He relayed Wayne's update. "Chapman's out there in the bush somewhere, all alone. He's an expert in survival, according to the commercials on DSTV, so he should be fine for a night or two until they find him."

Tracey's lower lip started trembling. "Oh, Stirling, I feel just terrible about all this. About what happened between you and Sam, I . . . I just . . ."

As angry as he was with the American, Stirling couldn't rid himself of the nagging suspicion that Tracey had not been completely innocent. If it turned out that Chapman had tried to force himself on Tracey, then the man would wish he had been on board the helicopter and died. But Tracey was young and she might simply have been mildly infatuated with the Coyote man and his star status. The question was, had Chapman taken advantage of her naive adulation, or had Tracey gone after him?

She started crying and he pushed the suspicions aside. He closed the gap between them and wrapped his arms around her. "Hush, my babe. Everything will be all right. You've had a rough couple of days." He kissed the salty tears from her eyes.

Tracey buried her head in the wiry hairs above the V of his shirt and spoke into his chest through muffled sobs. "I feel awful. Maybe I led him on just a teeny bit..."

"No, babe. If that bastard can't tell the difference between your friendly personality and a come-on, I'll teach him when I see him."

"Don't... please don't hurt him, Stirling."

He lifted her chin with his finger. "Tracey, is there something you need to tell me?"

She bit her lip and shook her head. "Can't we just forget all about it? I *love* you Stirling, and only you."

"I still want to break every bone in his body. Slowly."

Tracey smiled through her tears. "It was just one of those things. Perhaps we'd both had a bit too much to drink, but I just need to know that you still love me, Stirling."

"I do, babe. Of course I do."

"I'm so glad, Stirling." She placed her head back down on his chest. "The lodge needs the business, right?"

He nodded, reluctantly. It was true that the documentary shoot would be good PR for the camp at a time when business was slowing, so if there was a way to get past the incident with Chapman—and that was up to Tracey—then they might be able to salvage something from the mess of the last few days. He couldn't stay mad at the beautiful, sexy young woman in his arms. Perhaps he was partly to blame for Tracey's behavior around the lantern-jawed pretty boy. "Do I pay enough attention to you, Tracey?"

"Of course you do, my big, tough safari guide. Sometimes it's hard for me, though, being stuck out here in the bush away from everything."

"I understand, my babe. Maybe we can get away down south to Jozi or the Cape after we get rid of the Yanks."

"That would be *lekker*, Stirling," she said into his chest. "Also, maybe you want to come take a look on the computer. I just found the most *divine* gold bracelet on eBay. Come, see!"

For a moment, Sonja thought she was lost.

She checked her GPS and saw that she was thirty-one kilometers southeast of Xakanaxa as the crow flew. It was where she thought she was, but the countryside here was alien to her.

Where there should have been a channel of cool, clear water there was just a cratered pathway of dried black mud. Elephants had sucked and trampled the last of the moisture from this place, leaving nothing but the deep imprints of their circular feet, which had set like fossilized dinosaur footprints. Occasionally, in past years of very severe drought, this distant offshoot of the Okavango had dwindled to little more than a meter wide, yet it had always flowed, right through the dry season, providing a transfusion of life to the game that usually roamed here until the rains came again.

She looked around. Not an animal in sight. At this time of year, in early October, there should have been zebra, waterbuck, impala, kudu and warthog queuing for their ration of water, tentatively sniffing the air and looking around them for evidence of predators.

Sonja scanned the tree line. It wasn't lions keeping the other game away from this badly healed scar on the earth's surface, it was men. "The dam," she said. In between assignments she caught up with news via the Internet and she'd read reports of doom and gloom from various environmental groups about the damming of the Okavango and the impact it was creating already, despite having only recently been completed. Although the waters of the delta flowed in her own blood and the place was the home of her soul, she had been skeptical initially about the impact the dam would have.

Perhaps she'd been fighting on the side of greedy and corrupt governments and taking tainted money from oil and mining companies to fight
their clandestine fights for too long. She'd believed the spin doctors from
the Namibian and Angolan governments who assured the world the dam
would have no lasting impact on flows in the delta's game reserve, no detri-
mental effects on man or beast. Sonja was Namibian-born, after all, and she
couldn't begrudge the poor people of the country their right to clean water
and electricity.

She shook her head. Perhaps this unseasonal lack of water was just
an anomaly, caused by some other natural event. The Okavango Delta sat on
a major geological fault between two tectonic plates deep below her feet.
Earth tremors were common, although the thick cushion of Kalahari sand
masked the presence of all but the most severe. Sonja did remember a waterhole, a favorite place for her and her father to go game viewing, drying up,
overnight.

"Earthquake, my girl," her father had explained when she had asked
where the water had gone.

"Did the ground open up and swallow it, Pa?"

"It just shifted a little, like this," he held out his hand, palm down, and
waggled it slightly, "and this water has drained away, somewhere else."

"*Ag*, shame," she had said. "The poor animals, where will they drink?"

"God gives as he takes, Sonja. Somewhere nearby some other animals
are now drinking water where yesterday there was none. Good things can
come from bad in nature, if not in the life of humans." At the time she'd
wondered at his last remark. As an adult she could replay that little vignette
and spot the clues, the signs she had missed as a child. When her father
looked away from her, out over the dry expanse where the water had been, he
was not ignoring her or avoiding her questions, he was remembering something he'd done, probably someone he had wronged. The Americans had
coined a term for it in Vietnam—the "thousand-yard stare." The eyes of a
man fixed on nothing, but seeing things too terrible to speak of. She'd seen
it in the eyes of pimply-faced soldiers, barely out of their teens, on the streets
of Baghdad, and in the Blackhawk pilots flying over the dusty nothingness
and pitiless mountains of Afghanistan.

Sonja and her tired old horse, that she had named Black Beauty even though the mare was a mangy chestnut brown, had crossed many channels that only flowed with water after the summer rains, and she had thought nothing of finding them dry, but what she saw here was not normal. "There should be water here, old girl," she said to the horse. "Sorry. You'll have to plod on a bit further." Sonja smoothed the horse's flank and stilled the snorted protest.

She had spared the horse as much as she could. After leaving the main road and the old man in his zebra-skin cowboy hat, she had deliberately headed the wrong way: east, toward Zimbabwe. Once she was deep into the bush, out of the man's sight, she had wheeled the horse to the right and carried on south for a kilometer before crossing the road again and heading west, toward the delta.

Finding the horseman where she had was fortuitous for she was not far short of the cut line which ran west from the main Kasane to Nata road, into the delta. The cut line was an extension of the cleared area that ran along the southern border of the Moremi Game Reserve, where a veterinary fence separated wild animals from domestic cattle.

The vet fences were a controversial feature of the modern-day Botswana landscape. Crisscrossing the country, they were erected to cordon off sections of the country from buffalo, which can carry foot and mouth disease, in order to comply with European Union regulations regarding meat exports. Sonja knew from her youth that some of the fences, such as the one bordering the Moremi Game Reserve, were useful, as they also stopped cattle and humans from straying into wildlife areas. Others, such as the Kuke fence that cut across central Botswana and the northern border of the Central Kalahari Game Reserve, had been an ecological disaster. The Kuke fence had stopped seasonal migrations of animals from the south to the north. During years of particularly bad drought, like in the 1980s, an estimated 300,000 wildebeests, 260,000 hartebeests and 60,000 zebras died because the fence stopped them reaching water.

The horse had responded immediately to Sonja's tender touch. Her guess that it had not been well treated by its previous owner was confirmed

not only by the ticks and fleas in the mare's coat, but also by the presence of
a stone under a poorly fitted shoe. Sonja used her Leatherman's pliers to
pull out the nails and remove all four shoes. She filed down the hooves and
left them unshod as she knew the horse could easily handle the bush without shoes. In a quiet corner of a cattle farm she found a dip with water still
in it and coaxed Black Beauty in. Once in, the mare enjoyed herself. Later,
Sonja risked stopping at a cluster of cattlemen's huts and at the village store—a
hut selling odds and ends—she was able to buy some Sunlight soap, a few car-
rots and some mealies. Beauty relished the food treats, and with directions
from the teenage girl running the shop Sonja was able to find her way to a
nearby waterhole.

The water was far from pristine, but it was free of the chemicals in the
cattle dip and Sonja could join the horse in the water. Sonja made sure the
dressing on her leg was well sealed, then stripped off. The horse tossed her
head in pure joy as Sonja massaged her flanks with the soap. Sonja laughed
as the mare splashed her and nudged her until she fell. It was almost like
being a kid again, but the ache in her leg reminded her they had a long way
to go until they were both out of danger.

Her route took her through empty, dry country to the north of Nxai
Pan National Park and the south of Chobe National Park, with its huge
herds of elephants and the healthy prides of lions that preyed on them. Even
though she was outside these parks, she knew there could still be lions in the
area, so each evening she made a boma of *wag-'n-bietje* to keep Beauty safe
while she grazed.

They were up before the dawn; Sonja, stiff-legged, bathing the puckered bullet wounds and changing her dressing, and Black Beauty neighing
and protesting against the saddle, although Sonja knew it was just for show.
The horse had bounced back quickly and they made between fifty and sixty
kilometers per day. Sonja walked for an hour at a time, to spell the horse and
keep the muscles in her injured leg working. It was a hot, at times uncomfortable, journey but they were making progress.

Occasionally she saw game; a lone oryx, a small herd of zebra and some
far-off springbok. Sonja had long since finished the last of the bottled water

from her pack. When they came to a waterhole, Sonja would watch it for a while, then walk the muddy banks to check for the drag marks of crocodiles. Once satisfied the water was safe she would let Beauty drink and then scoop water in a canvas filter bag shaped like a pointy-toed sock. The stitching at the bottom of the bag trapped the coarse particles of mud and other muck from the water, which Sonja later boiled in a tin billy over a fire in order to purify it.

Sonja pushed thoughts of frosted cans of Coke and chilled glasses of Cape sauvignon blanc from her mind. When she rode she sat side-saddle with her injured leg crossed over the good one and removed the dressing to let the sun and air aid with the healing. There was no infection, which was good, though she kept taking the antibiotics Chipchase had given her.

Sonja thought about her phone conversation with Emma. She hoped that despite her daughter's teenage angst she was keeping up with her studies and continuing to do well. Emma was the one good thing left in her life, even if the cheeky little cow hated her. Sonja felt guilty, as usual, about not spending enough time with Emma, yet ironically she knew that she was usually at her most content when she was alone, like now. This was no holiday, but she found herself calmed by the long ride. Sonja thought about the three men in her life to whom she'd been closest. It was probably a good thing Martin had had a wandering eye and an off-and-on gambling problem, though Sonja couldn't help but remember his prowess as a lover. She'd not had better since the time they'd spent together. Also, she thought Martin would have made a good dad for Emma. The pair still got on well whenever they met. After Chipchase's probing there was no way to keep Danny Byrne's handsome, boyish face out of the shadows at the edges of her memory, but she mentally eased him back into the gloom with thoughts of the future. She wondered what Stirling looked like now, after so long, and felt her anxiety and excitement rise in her chest as she allowed herself to think about their coming meeting.

Sonja walked toward the setting sun, with Beauty following contentedly in her footsteps. The moon was rising behind her, its pumpkin orange a pale yet stunning reflection of the sun's crimson. The country here was flat, open grasslands, tinderbox dry and begging for the water that might now never come.

Her arms and legs were brick red from the sun, and the evening cool, when it finally came, was like a reunion with a long-lost friend. Sonja spared the batteries in the GPS and navigated by the stars. As darkness descended the sky lit up and it was easy to believe she and her horse were the only two living things on the planet. When at last fatigue overtook her, she tethered the horse and rolled out her sleeping bag. She was almost too tired to make a fire, but she knew if she did not boil the water she had collected that day then she would have nothing to drink when the sun relaunched its offensive on them in the morning.

Routine, she thought. Roll out bed, make fire. Boil water, decant. Eat, not because she was hungry, but because she had to. Clean and oil rifle, clean and oil pistol. It was like being in the army again. Routine, routine, routine. The orderliness, the mundaneness of it all gave a sense of personal control and discipline to a life that would otherwise be one of pure chaos.

Sonja chewed a stick of biltong and washed it down with lukewarm water while she watched the fire—African television they called it here—and waited for the billy to boil.

The flames were mesmerizing and they took her back to Danny Byrne's living room in his cottage in Northern Ireland, where the pair of them had sat naked, wrapped in a blanket, and gazed at the glowing coals in his hearth. What had she done, and why had she done it; she had asked herself that over and over. It was impossible to extinguish the memory, or forget the guilty warmth that had radiated out from within her.

After that first meeting in the pub she'd been surprised when Martin ordered her to try and get closer to Byrne. She'd half expected a bollocking for getting into a conversation with the terrorist, instead of just keeping him in view. She'd been too excited by the added responsibility to think there was anything seedy about Martin's strategy. The surveillance teams stayed on Byrne and a "chance" meeting on a footpath had been orchestrated. Byrne had asked her out for a drink. It had all been so easy. Dinner followed the next night. Martin went through the motions of warning her not to become enamored by Byrne's charms, but he had also praised her after he and Jones had snapped pictures of Danny kissing her outside the bistro. The more she got to know Danny, and his beliefs and his politics, the more she became convinced that while he might have been a middleman for explosives distribution, he could never knowingly be involved in the deaths of women and children. She could tell there was something bothering Danny, though, and that he needed to unburden himself. It was just a matter of time.

The heat from the fireplace had dried the tears on Danny's cheeks almost as quickly as they fell, as he finally confessed his part in the bombing of the school bus—he had indeed sourced explosives, though had not known the final target—and the remorse and fear he felt when he thought of the man who had planned the operation and planted the bomb.

Sonja had held him to her breast, then kissed away the dried salt.

"I'm pig sick of it, Sonja. I want out. I want to run away, far, from this place forever. But I'm scared. Will you come with me?"

She'd nodded and kissed his hair as she cradled his head. "Scared of who, Danny?"

"My brother."

"It was him?"

"Yes." He'd looked up into her eyes and she'd seen the reflected flames burning in his. She wondered if he'd be forever damned, like his brother. For a moment she wanted to believe that hell really existed, for Patrick Byrne's sake. She couldn't hate Danny, though.

Because she thought she might love him.

8

Vic-torrrrrr, vic-torrrrr the little brownish colored bird called.

It was driving Sam crazy. "Shut *up!*" He tossed a green branch he'd stripped from a nearby tree on the pathetic fire in front of his tent and it started smoking. He was too dejected to go in search of more dead wood. Two days and still no contact. He'd eked out the last of the two energy bars that Cheryl-Ann had allowed him to carry, and his stomach was no longer rumbling, it was crying.

Vic-torrrrrr, vic-torrrrr.

Earlier that morning, as he'd sat on his sleeping bag taking stock of his meager supplies, elephants had surrounded his tent. At first he thought they were trying to break through the canvas with the tips of their tusks when he'd heard the scratching on the fabric. In fact, they were feeding on seed pods from the branches above his tent and as they shook the branches the pods were raining down on the tent. It had been a nerve-racking forty minutes as the great beasts gingerly moved around his tent. He heard the whole tree shake at one point and put his hand over his mouth to stop from sneezing as their ceaseless browsing and shuffling enveloped the tent in a mini dust cloud. He could smell their rich mildewy odor through the mosquito gauze and hear them communicating with each other via deep rumbling belly growls that echoed the churning of his own hollow insides.

He had risked unzipping the tent flap just enough to squeeze the camera lens through and been rewarded with some amazing vision looking up into the pink mouths of the creatures as they daintily popped pods into them. When a trunk had snaked down to inspect the shiny lens he'd hastily pulled it in, but he knew it had been worth the risk. Cheryl-Ann would be pleased, if he ever saw her again.

Sam's imagination, fired by his hunger, had constructed more and more elaborate reasons for the complete lack of contact from his production team. It was either a clever ploy to make him fall back on his rudimentary knowledge of survival in the wild—and produce some great TV at his expense—or something had gone terribly wrong.

At what point, he wondered, should he set off in search of help? In Australia the Aboriginal people he'd worked with had told him stories of German tourists who had died in the desert because they had left their stricken four-by-fours to find help on foot. Inevitably, the search parties found the stranded trucks and the dried-up remains of the occupants a few kilometers away.

How long, he wondered, could he last on foot in the African bush? He knew that despite the heat he would be better walking by day and sleeping by night, making a fire to keep lions, leopards and hyenas at bay. However, and this was a big stumbling block, he really didn't know which way to walk. He cursed himself, Cheryl-Ann and Stirling for not giving him a map. What harm could a goddamn map have done to the program? He knew that the hunting concession was on the southern border of the Moremi Game Reserve and that somewhere to the south and east of where he was he would strike the road that led from the town of Maun to the South Gate entrance of the reserve. But he had no idea how far away that road was or how far north Xakanaxa Camp was.

He'd hoped to hear the sound of gunfire, from a hunting party, and make for it, but the bush had stayed eerily silent. Except for that fucking bird.

Vic-torrrrrr, vic-torrrrr it cooed on cue.

He looked up at the tree. Why was this little bird with the whitish underparts and spots on its cheeks hanging around him? It fluttered, occasionally, from branch to branch as if it was taunting him deliberately or trying to get his attention.

"My attention!"

The hunger had slowed him mentally as well as physically, but now he suddenly remembered what the old bushman guide had told him. Sam was no ornithologist, so he'd found it hard to keep up when the man had reeled off names of birds he might encounter, but the story about this one had surprised him.

He craned his neck. "You're a freaking honeyguide, aren't you?"

Vic-torrrrrr, vic-torrrrr.

"Victor." It was the distinctive call of the greater honeyguide. "Stay right there, little guy. I'm with you."

Sam grabbed the camera and tripod from inside the tent, as well as his daypack containing a half-empty water bottle—the last of his ration—his poncho, matches, binoculars, bush hat and first-aid kit. He'd tied his US Air Force survival knife, the kind immortalized by Sylvester Stallone in the first *Rambo* movie, to a stripped sapling, fashioning a makeshift spear. He set the camera up and angled the lens upward, focusing on the bird. He hit record.

"African legend has it that this little bird, the greater honeyguide, deliberately attracts the attention of honey badgers and even human beings to help it feed on honey from wild beehives. This dude has been pestering me all morning and I've only just worked out that he's been trying to get me to come and give him a hand at finding breakfast. Like him, I could use some food, so let's find out if this bush story is true. I'm counting on it."

Sam turned off the camera and laid the tripod over his left shoulder. He picked up his spear as the bird took off, and followed it, stumbling as he tried to keep sight of it.

A herd of impala took flight when they saw him, and bounded high in the air, rear legs kicking out horizontally. He tried to keep a lookout for dangerous game at the same time as following the bird. Every now and then he lost sight of it, but it would call, reassuringly, and he would find it again.

A trio of giraffes peered down at him from behind a crop of thorn trees, their long faces moving in unison as they studied the strange creature stumbling and jogging after the bird.

Sam felt jazzed. He was excited and a little nervous as he walked, but pleased to be doing something instead of squatting outside his tent wondering what had gone wrong, and generally feeling miserable for himself. Cheryl-Ann had told him to be ready for a surprise. Some surprise! He'd show her . . . he'd show Stirling . . . he'd show the whole goddamned world. He was Coyote Sam, survival expert and outdoorsman. "Freakin' A."

Sam was feeling light-headed and his mouth was parched by the time he caught up with the bird. The honeyguide was hovering beside a tree and when it came to rest on a branch it was silent for the first time that morning. Sam stopped, set down the camera and shrugged off his pack. He took a moment to admire the natural paradise the bird had led him to.

He'd sensed they were heading toward water as the bush had become progressively thicker and slightly greener. Around the camp site the colors had been khaki and gold, but stretched out before him now, from his vantage point at the edge of the tree line, was a wide floodplain, perhaps a kilometer across, carpeted in a rich covering of emerald green.

Meandering through the middle of the open area was a glittering serpent of water. He wanted to rush to it and immerse his sweat and dust-streaked stinking body in it; to gulp until he was too full to move. But that would have to wait. He was light-headed with hunger and the plain was dotted with animals. Hundreds of them.

He counted fifty or more zebra in loose herds of eight to ten queuing for their turn to drink. A herd of elephants munched in the shade of the trees on the far side of the plain. He saw the tiny babies in their midst and knew the herd should be given a wide berth. The same went for the four old male buffalo that wallowed in the mud and reeds at the edge of the river.

Sam looked up again and saw the honeyguide was still sitting silently in the same branch. He approached the towering mopane tree cautiously. Craning his head he heard the hive before he saw it. The bees buzzed busily in and out of a hollow in the trunk. The cavity, which looked large enough for him to get his upper body inside, was almost four meters above the ground, but he'd been climbing trees since he was six years old.

The Khoisan bushman had said his people smoked wild bees out of their hives by burning elephant dung. Sam didn't have to look far to find some. The trunk of the tree that held the hive was worn smooth from elephants rubbing themselves against it, and piles of their dried, yellow-brown droppings were everywhere. He inspected a couple of samples, settling on a stack that seemed not fresh, but not completely dried out. "The smokier the better, I guess," he said to himself.

He positioned the camera and held a softball-sized lump up to the lens. "This stuff has many uses. When you light it," he placed the clod down and struck a match, "the smoke can be used to keep mosquitoes at bay." He bent over and blew on the flame until the aromatic smoke began wafting around his face. "And if you breathe it in, it's supposed to cure a headache or a hangover. As my producer and camera crew haven't left me any food, let alone booze, I can assure you I'm not hung over. But I *am* hungry, so I'm going to use this stuff to send those bees up there on their way."

He stoked the dung fire at the base of the tree and the bees above him increased the volume and pitch of their buzzing. They weren't happy. Sam selected the largest chunk of dung, which was big enough for him to hold with one hand without burning himself. He angled the camera up a little more and started climbing the tree, one handed, with the smoking mass in his other hand.

The bees seemed to be calming and he noticed many of them were already drifting away from the hole in the tree. Awkwardly, he hoisted himself higher, grabbing onto a branch with his free hand and pulling. All those early mornings in the gym were paying off, and not just because his agent said he needed to look buffed on TV. His feet found purchase on a thick bough and he was able to reach the entrance to the hive, holding the smoking dung in front of him as more bees took flight. He swallowed, hoping nothing else was living in the cavity, and reached in. He raised himself up a little more, on his toes, and could see the prize—football-sized chunks of wild honeycomb oozing with sweet golden honey. His mouth watered. He reached in and started breaking off lumps of the treasure and tossing them down to the ground. "A little dirt won't kill me, and I'll probably eat it anyway, I'm so hungry," he said for the camera's benefit.

Glutinous honey oozed between his sticky fingers and smeared the tree as he shimmied down and jumped the last couple of meters to land dramatically in front of the camera. He held up a piece of honeycomb to the lens and sank his teeth into it.

"Mmmmm. Oh, my, that tastes . . . *great*." He licked his lips. "It's got a kind of acrid, raw taste to it, and the same scent as the leaves of this big old mopane tree where it came from. It's not like honey from a supermarket. It's stronger, wilder, but damn, it's good!"

He stopped talking and continued to gorge himself on the sticky, chewy delight, for the viewers' benefit and his own.

"What I'm doing now," he said as he broke two of the larger remaining chunks of the honeycomb in half, "is leaving a little something for my avian friend up there. We've just proved one legend right—the one about honeyguides leading not only animals, but also humans to beehives. The other legend I recall about this bird is that if he leads you to a hive and you don't share with him, then the next time he sees you, or another human being, he'll lead you into a trap, such as a lion or a leopard, or a Mozambican spitting cobra. Here you go, little guy." Sam set the offering down on a fallen log and stepped back. Using his palm—his fingers were a mess—he panned the camera around until it was focused on the log and the pile of dripping honeycomb. Within seconds the honeyguide had left its perch and alighted on the makeshift altar, where he proceeded to peck away at his reward.

"Man." Sam stood and watched the bird. He felt an incredible rush, partly from the honey in his empty stomach, and partly because he'd just witnessed the manifestation of a symbiotic relationship between man and a wild creature. He also felt pretty damned proud of himself for truly starting to survive in the African bush on his own merits. With the camera still rolling he raised his makeshift spear in a sticky hand high above his head and shouted, "Yeah!"

Then he heard the buzzing. He looked up. "Oh shit!"

Sonja saw the smoke and dismounted. "Hush, girl," she whispered to the whinnying horse. "I'm just going to leave you here for a bit." She tethered

Black Beauty to a tree, patted her reassuringly on the neck, and untied her daypack from the back of the saddle. She took out the M4, slotted in a thirty-round magazine and yanked back on the cocking handle.

She was trespassing and unless the local community had changed the lease on the land she was crossing it was probably still a hunting concession. Smoke meant fire and a narrow column of gray rising into the blue sky in otherwise unburned bushveld meant a camp. It could be hunters, wildlife researchers, Botswana Wildlife Rangers or even poachers. None of them would be particularly happy to see a lone woman on a horse crossing their turf.

The extendable metal butt of the rifle was in her shoulder and her finger resting outside the trigger guard. She scanned the bush from right to left. She had learned in the army that because westerners learn to read left to right they normally scan their surroundings in the same way. Forcing herself to do the opposite made her eyes work slower and ensure she missed little.

Sonja moved in an arc, off to her right, so that she stayed downwind of the pillar of smoke. She smelled man. Sweat, urine, toothpaste. No food.

She paused to unhook a thorn from her bush shirt. Every step was placed carefully, slowly, ensuring she avoided dry twigs and piles of leaves. A flock of guinea fowl cluck-clucked nearby, but weren't alarmed by her presence. A gray *lourie* warned her to *go-away, go-away*. Her curiosity wouldn't let her.

The smoke was strong in her nostrils now and she dropped to her belly and leopard-crawled forward. She saw the green canvas dome tent. It looked new. It could belong to anyone, but poachers were rarely so well equipped. Sonja lay still and watched the camp site for ten minutes, listening for snoring or other sounds that would indicate there was someone inside the tent. She heard nothing. Slowly, she got to her feet and moved closer.

The camp site was empty. Inside the tent she found a satellite phone—definitely not poachers—and an expensive sleeping bag. The make was foreign, not South African. It smelled of unwashed male, with a lingering hint of aftershave or cologne. Not local. She circled the tent looking for spoor. She found his footprints—expensive hiking boots with deep new tread, but no tire tracks. Odd. If there had been food in the tent she would have taken it, but there was none. Sonja knelt and took a closer look at the man's trail.

It was fresh, the broken stems of grass still bent, not having had time to spring back. She wondered how he had got here, whether he had walked in.

She decided to leave the horse where she was and track the mystery man. He'd left a trail a blind woman could follow, so it was easy for her to keep careful watch on the bush ahead of her. He was carrying a tripod with him—the three indentations plain in the dust whenever he stopped to rest. A bird spotter? There were no particularly rare species in this part of the delta. Wildlife photographer? If so, how did he get here—by parachute?

She followed the man's tracks and a short time later she smelled old smoke again. Sonja recognized the sweet, earthy natural incense—elephant dung. She and Stirling had recovered from enough teenage binge-drinking nights that way for her to remember the smell. She stopped short of a large mopane tree when she heard the buzzing of angry African bees. She'd been stung on the cheek once and for two days it had felt as though she'd been kicked by a donkey.

"Aargh!"

Sonja raised her rifle instinctively as she sought out the source of the cry. It was human. She moved forward quickly, with all her senses ratcheted up a notch. The trees gave way to a verdant floodplain slashed by a river. The Gomoti. She knew it by its location, though not by its size. This was a trickle compared to the river she remembered from her youth. She heard the groan of pain or distress again and peered through the 1.5 times magnifier of the sight on top of the rifle. She saw movement on the river's bank. It corresponded with the sound, but barely looked human. If he was in the river, he was in trouble. She ran forward, the tip of the M4's barrel up and leading the way as she crossed the open ground.

A zebra stallion snorted and his harem of females wheeled and galloped away from their approach to the river, raising dust clouds with their pounding hooves. The matriarch of an elephant family on the far bank raised her trunk at the mix of new scents. A pair of Egyptian geese honked in panic and took off as Sonja's feet sloshed through the mud.

The creature looked up at her, white eyes blinking from black mud. "Help," it croaked.

Sonja paused and, seeing no sign of a weapon, slung her rifle over her shoulder. The black ooze reached above the tops of her boots, slowing her progress. She saw the outstretched hand. The man coughed and spat, trying to get to his hands and knees, but slipping.

The mud was foul here, stinking of animal shit and dotted with algae. The water was a sickly bright lime green in places, fringed with a wicked-looking red. Out of habits learned as a child she scanned the river left and right.

"Help me." He reached out for her. "Bees . . ."

She slogged closer and took his hand, hauling on it.

"Thank you." He coughed again as he thrust his free hand into the goop to steady himself. "Are you . . ."

She let go of his hand and he fell again, face first.

He coughed and spluttered. "Holy shit, what did you do that for?"

The noise of four gunshots silenced his protests. Sonja saw at least two hit home and the water a meter behind the struggling, cursing man's right boot started boiling.

"Fuck, fuck, fuck, fuck!" He scrabbled forward on all fours, through the mud, past where she stood, legs apart, braced, smoke curling from the muzzle of the M4, her gaze still fixed on the slowly settling ripples. "What the hell was that in aid of?"

"Flatdog." She let the rifle dangle by her side from its sling, the barrel comfortingly warm against the bare skin of her thigh. If there was one creature she didn't mind seeing dead, it was one of these prehistoric beasts. Man was fair game to a flatdog, and vice versa.

"A what?"

"Crocodile." She reached down again and dragged him to his feet.

She wiped her hand on her shorts; it was sticky and gooey, and not just from the mud. She sniffed her fingers. "You were after the honey in the beehive?"

"How did you know?"

"Elephant dung smoke; the way they were buzzing when I passed the tree. The way you buried yourself in animal shit and mud to escape them."

He made a futile attempt to wipe the worst of the muck from his clothes and skin but winced when he wiped his eyes and drove more mud into them.

"Here." She handed him her water bottle. "Just a little. For your eyes."

He followed her back to dry land, onto the grass, sluicing his face as he went. He stopped and she turned when she no longer heard his feet scuffing the dry grass.

"Wait a minute . . ."

She looked at him. White shone in the black face as his mouth broke into a wide, almost idiotic grin.

"Wait just a freaking minute! Ha ha!" He broke into laughter and started doing an impromptu jig on the spot. "Woo-hoo! Yes, yes, yes, yes, yes!"

Sonja was confused. She moved a hand slowly to the plastic pistol grip of the M4 and took a step backward.

"You've been watching me all along, haven't you?"

She shook her head. "I just got here, man. And lucky I did. Who are you?"

"Who am I?" He started laughing again. "Oh, lady, this is rich. But save it. This is great. We really have to get this on camera. Wait. We *are* on camera, aren't we?"

Sonja licked her lips. The man was mad.

"Ray? Gerry? Cheryl-Ann? Come on out, guys," he bellowed. He started spinning around, searching the trees on either side of the river. He cupped his filthy hands on either side of his mouth. "Where aaaaare you? Come out, come out wherever you are. You got me, guys. Let's talk."

"Talk about what?" she asked.

"Oh, come *on*. I get it. This is the surprise. Goddamn, you had me going there for a while. Please, please, please tell me you got me running into the river. I got stung, like, three times, but I'm not mad. You guys had me worried for a while but . . ."

She held up her free hand, palm out to him. "Mister, calm down. I don't know what you're talking about. I think we need to get you some more water." She turned and started walking back to the tree line, lengthening her stride to keep the distance between them. Shit. She shouldn't have followed his tracks in the first place. She could have given him a wide berth. Now what was she going to do? She couldn't leave a madman to die in the bush.

"OK," he said, running a sticky hand through hair gelled with mud and honey. "I get it. Still need to play along. Just tell me, on the QT if you like, are we being filmed now? Just so I know whether or not to set the handy cam up again."

She stopped and looked at him. His eyes were wide and intent. He believed the questions he was asking were sane. True madness. "No, mister, we are not being filmed. I can confirm that." He started walking toward her. "Keep your distance."

"*Keep your distance?* Who are you supposed to be? Sheena of the freaking African Jungle or something? Ha ha." He lowered his voice. "Or is it, 'Hasta la vista, baby?' Doesn't matter. It's your gig—your character. I'm getting the camera. Stay right there."

She took another pace back as he passed her. Beside the tree, on its side, was a video camera mounted on a tripod. He unclipped the camera from the head and raised it.

"No!"

"What do you mean, no? You're the surprise guest star. Say something to the folks back home."

"No!" In the army, working with special forces, there had been a blanket ban on operatives in the Det being photographed or filmed by the media. As a mercenary she guarded her privacy and anonymity just as fiercely. She raised her palm and pressed it against the lens as he closed on her.

"OK. Very good for the opening shot, but let's get serious now." He cleared his throat. "So, who are you, mystery gal of the bush?"

"I said, no filming." She grabbed the lens and pushed the camera, ramming it back into his chest.

"Hey, take it easy. There's reality TV and there's reality, OK?" He raised the camera again. "So, who are . . ."

Sonja slapped the camera, hard enough to make him fumble and almost drop it. While he was cursing she swung her M4 up and across her body. She didn't point it at him, but he seemed to get the message.

"Hey, hey . . . OK, no camera until you've done your makeup. I get it. I've gotta say, though, I think you might have overdone it a bit on the method acting, Lara Croft."

She took a step back from him, her rifle still held up and ready. "Who are you?"

He looked around him again. "OK. I get it, I get it." He cleared his throat again, and laughed loudly.

"Drink the rest of that water. I think you might have heat stroke. You're not making sense, mister . . ."

"Chapman. Coyote Sam to my friends and gun-toting saviors." He winked.

Dehydration and heatstroke—she was sure of it. "I found your tent."

He drank the rest of the bottle of warm water in one long gulp then wiped his lips, leaving a smear of mud and honey. "Uh-huh. And don't tell me . . . you used your excellent tracking skills to find me here and save me from the *crocodile*. Incidentally, that was a nice touch. Are they blanks in that rifle?"

"I think I need to get you back to your tent. Throw me the empty water bottle. Wait here."

He saluted her and tossed the bottle. "Yes, ma'am!"

Sam sat in the shade of a tree—not the one with the bees—and watched the woman walk back out to the river. She held her assault rifle in her right hand, by its pistol grip, and the empty plastic water bottle in her left. She waded out through the mud into the river, which was only knee deep. When she reached midstream she looked up and down the watercourse then bent to fill the bottle.

Sam righted the camera on its tripod and started recording. He kept the device at arm's length, so that if she looked back at him she wouldn't see him staring into the viewfinder. He could see the LED screen from where he sat and when her back was to him he zoomed in on her.

She was a looker. No makeup, and he couldn't help but notice as she bent over that atop her nicely shaped legs was an equally perfect arse. He scanned the surrounding bush, the far tree line, and even the air, looking for the camera team. If they were here they were well hidden. Maybe she had a concealed camera on her and she was filming him.

He had to hand it to Cheryl-Ann; this surprise was almost the best yet. Up until now the red-headed chef in the outback had taken the cake. In fact, he remembered chocolate torte in the well of her belly button. This one was different though—she was a hard-body and not a willowy waif like the Aussie girl. She straightened and started wading back toward him. She was fit. She had broad shoulders and a narrow waist, but her hips were still wide enough to give a hint of hourglass. Her auburn hair was pulled back in a ponytail. It was functional, but he bet she'd look great with it teased out. Like her legs, her arms were sculpted. This girl worked out, and then some. As she came closer, he saw that her eyes were green. The way she moved, and those eyes, reminded him of a cat. He'd only seen footage of lionesses—not one in the wild yet—but that's what she reminded him of. Powerful, predatory, pitiless. She could eat him alive—if she played her cards right.

He pressed the stop button on the camera then called: "I'm all yours. Take me to your leader." He winced and reached back between his shoulder blades. "Oww."

"Bee sting?"

He nodded. "I think so. I can't reach it."

She drew a short-bladed skinning knife from a pouch on her belt.

"Whoa there, cowgirl."

"Relax. Sit still."

She moved behind him and he did as he was told. He felt her fingertips on the nape of his neck and the collar of his T-shirt stretching against his Adam's apple as she searched. He shivered. Her touch was firm and cool, like gunmetal. He shuddered again as he felt the razor's edge of the blade touch his skin.

"I said, be still."

"OK. You're not going to dig it out, are you?"

She ignored him and he felt the edge of the blade sliding across his skin as she brushed toward the stinger and, he imagined, shaved bare any hairs that might have sprouted since his last waxing.

She pushed his head forward with her free hand, her fingers burying themselves in his hair. Man, he thought, this is hot. He really hoped someone was recording all this from afar. He could smell her. He felt himself start to stir. In his peripheral vision he caught a glimpse of the tan-colored dressing stuck on her thigh. "Did you hurt yourself? Oww!"

"Still," she commanded again. "Yes. There, it's out. It'll hurt for a day or so."

He rolled his neck and shoulder muscles. "You're telling me." Free to turn his head he saw the blood spotting the sticking plaster on her leg. "What did you do to yourself?"

"Cut myself shaving."

"What did you use, your skinning knife?"

"Come, crazy man."

He almost said, "Whenever you say the word," but the gun made him think twice. It also made him nervous. The closest he'd ever come to shooting something—anything—was a tranquilizer dart into a coyote's rump. "Can you put that thing away?"

"No. Get up."

He sighed and dragged himself up, wiping his sticky hands on the grass as he did so. All that did was coat them in fine sand. "Can I go wash in the river?"

"The blood from the croc I shot will bring the others—and maybe lion and hyena. We should go now. I've got more water with my horse."

Her horse? This just got wilder and wilder. A cowgirl in Africa. "Giddyup," he said in his best Kramer voice. She walked off in silence, and he followed.

"So," he called to her back, "what do I call you? Jungle Jane?"

She ignored him.

"OK, OK. I'll just play my part as the out-of-depth star then . . . But we do have food, right? Surely Cheryl-Ann . . ."

She stopped and turned, her right hand still gripping the business end of the rifle. She raised the barrel a fraction. It was enough to stop him in his tracks. "I said I'd get you more water when we get to my horse."

He chewed his lip. This didn't make much sense. If this starlet was bucking for an Oscar she was wasting her time on Wildlife World. He didn't recognize her, but suspected she might be reasonably well known in South Africa, even if he couldn't place her.

"I found your tent," she continued, "but no sign of a vehicle. There aren't any of your tracks, either—except to the beehive. What did you do, come by helicopter?"

"You know it, sweetheart."

"Don't call me sweetheart. Are you some kind of filmmaker?"

Sam tried to run a hand through his hair, but it had solidified. "Look, Jane of the Jungle, for the record, and for whoever, however, this is being filmed," he cleared his throat again, "boy, am I glad you showed up. Lead on, I'm ready for the next scene, and a decent meal."

She remained silent, staring at him down the barrel of her rifle.

"Oh, come *on*. Enough, already. Shit, I'm fucking filthy, I'm fucking hungry, I've been stung by a bee, and I was *supposedly* almost eaten by a fucking crocodile." He raised his fists to the sky and threw back his head. "WHAT MORE DO YOU FUCKING WANT, CHERYL-ANN?"

He screwed his eyes shut tight, hoping, praying that when he opened them Cheryl-Ann and the crew would emerge from behind that big old leadwood tree in front of them with an ice bucket full of Perrier and Budweiser. What were they trying to do, break him? Turn him mad for the sake of ratings? "For Christ's sake, this is Wildlife World, not the Military Channel, and . . ."

He felt his right wrist gripped and pulled behind him. "Hey!" He spun around, trying to see her, but she sidestepped faster than a rattler striking. "Ouch!" She wound his arm back up into the small of his back and forced him to double forward. When he clawed back at her with his free hand she grabbed it. He heard a zip and felt his wrists being drawn together. "What the fuck is that?"

"Snap ties. I need to restrain you until you start talking sense."

"OK, that's it! You are so fucking fired, lady. This prank has gone far enough and you can tell . . ."

The last thing he felt was her fingers digging into the skin behind his collarbone, at the base of his neck.

He was heavy. Not fat—far from it—just a big build, and when his shirt rode up she saw the carefully sculpted abs that could only be purchased in a gym. And no chest hair. She shook her head. Gratefully, she lowered him to the grass, in the afternoon shade cast by his dome tent.

His breathing was steady. The effects of the hold she'd applied to the pressure point would wear off shortly. She'd carried him the two hundred meters to his camp site over her shoulder, in a fireman's carry, her right hand still gripping her weapon. It reminded her of special forces training, but she forced the memory from her mind. She drew her knife and cut the ties that bound his wrists behind his back. She'd overdone it a bit, as the skin was red and his hands were cool. She massaged the life back into them, but used a new tie to bind them in front of his body, though looser than the first.

She fetched a dirty, smelly T-shirt from his tent and moistened it with water. She cleaned his face. He was a good-looking madman, she would give him that. He had thick, black wavy hair that reminded her of an actor— one of the two guys from the Pearl Harbor movie. She couldn't remember the man's name. She didn't have much time for TV in her job, except for the twenty-four-hour news channels, which were always reporting on some war or other.

When she checked the white T-shirt she saw a skin-colored stain in amidst the black silty Okavango mud and the amber of the wild honey. She sniffed it, then wiped a finger over his forehead and checked it. "Makeup?"

He blinked, then groaned. She rocked back on her haunches as he tried to sit up.

"What? Where . . . You!"

She raised a palm, not touching him, but when he saw his wrists were tied again he lay back, closed his eyes and screamed.

"Hush. Listen to me, mister. I don't know who you think I am, or even if you know who you are, but I have no idea who you are or what you are doing here and that is not from some script or some movie or some television show. Now, tell me who you are, for real, and how you got here."

He looked into her eyes and she could tell he wasn't insane—just frightened. When he told her his story she shook her head at the absurdity of it all, but it explained what he was doing here alone in the bush, covered in mud and makeup and toting a video camera.

"*Fok*" was all she could say.

"Does that mean what I think it means?" he asked.

She leaned forward and cut the plastic cable tie between his wrists. "Yes, in Afrikaans."

"So, you know who I am. Who are you?"

The lie came quickly to her lips. Always base it on truth, Steele had drummed into her. "I'm a professional hunter."

He stared back at her for a few seconds, not moving, lying back in the grass. "I just told you the truth, so please do me the same courtesy."

"It is the truth. I come out here on the concession in my spare time to go horse riding and game viewing and to shoot my quota for the pot. You do know you're on a hunting concession, don't you? There are people with *guns* here. It's not a smart place to be filming." The other thing Steele taught her was that when your cover was challenged go on the attack. Turn the tables on the questioner.

He shook his head. "If you worked on this concession you'd know we've been planning this film shoot for three months. You'd also know there are no hunts scheduled this week because we've made a block booking and *we've* bought the quota to shoot what *we* need for the pot to make this documentary. You're not who you say you are. What's your name?"

She bit the inside of her lower lip. Stay on the offensive, she told herself. "Sonja. You're in a bad way. Do you think something's happened to the rest of your film crew? You said you tried contacting them by sat phone and got nothing. I can't believe they'd cut off your emergency comms, can you?" Sonja saw the turmoil behind his eyes.

"I'm worried, yes."

"Do you want to get back to Xakanaxa Camp, to check on your people, find out what's happened? Surely they don't want you going crazy out here for the sake of a TV program?"

He made a face. "Cheryl-Ann—the producer—would say the verdict was out on that one until the ratings came in."

She shook her head. "It's up to you. I'll leave you some biltong and some drinking water if you want to continue your survival program, or you can come with me. I'm going to Xakanaxa." She stood and slung her rifle over her shoulder.

"You are? I thought you said you were based here on the hunting concession."

She shrugged. "I've got an old friend there I've been meaning to visit for some time. I'm going. Are you coming with or not?"

He looked around his meager camp site, and at the useless satellite phone. "Let me write a note, in case someone comes looking for me. I'll leave the tent and stuff here."

"Good idea. I don't want to overburden my horse."

He chewed biltong as they walked, talking with his mouth full. Like most Americans she'd met he liked the sound of his own voice and talked in complete sentences. She used words like ammunition—sparingly and for effect.

When they came to the horse she asked him if he wanted to ride for a while. He was still hungry and she didn't know how fit he was. Heavily muscled soldiers sometimes had the least stamina, in her experience. "I'll walk," he said. "How's your leg? Perhaps it would be best if you rode for a while."

She shook her head, then slung both their hiking packs over the saddle and set off, leading Black Beauty. Her stride was long and measured and he had to run a little to catch up, before he got into her rhythm.

"How long do you think it will take us to reach Xakanaxa?"

"A day. Day and a half if you keep stopping."

He looked sullen, but at least he was quiet for a few minutes.

"Why would anyone need an automatic assault rifle to go hunting?" he asked, eyeing off her military-style weapon.

He wasn't going to shut up. She knew most people liked talking about themselves. She'd acted the part of a journalist to infiltrate a west African country as a member of the advance party of a coup and had been surprised just how easy it was to get people to open up to her. It was generally the ones who protested initially that they didn't want to be photographed or interviewed who ended up doing most of the talking.

"Tell me more about you," she said, not looking back over her shoulder.

"Aw, you don't want to hear all about me."

She knew the modesty was false, so she held her tongue. A trio of scimitar-billed wood hoopoes was laughing and chattering as they tapped away at the bark of a mopane tree. They reminded her of the unceasing chatter of tourists on a game-viewing vehicle. He would talk. Americans loved to talk.

"You really haven't heard of me, have you?"

The arrogance of the man was fitting nicely into the stereotype she had conceived for him.

"I'm sorry, that sounded so arrogant, didn't it? Don't say anything. Well, about me. About a hundred years ago I was doing my PhD, working in the field in Montana, studying coyotes. The coyotes in the area I was studying had a reputation for killing lambs on sheep farms. We found out that this only happened when the dominant pair of coyotes in the area had produced pups and this overlapped with the lambing season. We figured if we could change their reproductive cycles, by administering or getting them to ingest contraceptives, we could lessen the problem. As part of my research I started working on a system to get the coyote females on the pill."

Sonja wasn't interested at all, but she was prepared to let him talk if it meant he stopped asking her questions.

"They're incredibly smart animals and not easily fooled or trapped. Did you know, the Native Americans call the coyote the 'trickster'? I guess not, huh. A friend of mine, another researcher, trapped one once and as she was getting the animal out of the underground cage she looked around and saw she was being watched by half a dozen other coyotes. The next day she came back to check her traps and saw they'd all been dug up, exposed by the coyotes that had been watching her, with not a single animal trapped. Amazing, huh?"

Sonja's eyes never stopped sweeping left and right as they walked. The long, brittle golden grass could easily hide a predator. The M4 was slung loose over her right shoulder, and she held Black Beauty's reins in her left hand.

"Amazing," he repeated. "Well, I started leaving out meat—benign baits—and eventually the coyotes realized there was no danger of them being caught or dying and they kept coming and eating. Eventually we dosed them with contraceptive and the problem of sheep attacks dropped off. A local TV station found out about my research from the university's PR department and ran a story on me. Part of my other research was trapping coyotes—I used to fire a net over them from a helicopter. Pretty exciting stuff. At least, it made for some good TV. They got me to do a lot of talking and I was able to use the program to correct some misconceptions people have about coyotes being scavengers or cold-hearted killers. Wildlife World saw the program and the rest, as they say, is history."

Sonja stopped. There wasn't a breath of wind, but the tips of the grass had just rippled a hundred meters ahead of them. About twice that distance away, off to her right, a herd of about twenty impala was grazing in the open. He stopped behind her and washed down his partly digested biltong with a swig of her water.

"History that has now landed me in this shit," he continued with a half-chuckle.

She raised a hand and he knew better than to keep talking. Sonja pointed to the long grass, where she'd seen the movement. "Cheetah," she whispered.

The impala ram barked a short, sharp warning call and the rest of the herd, all of his females, started running. The cheetah showed itself, then shot across the vlei. The cat used its long tail like a rudder as it turned to follow the herd, anticipating the male's evasive maneuver, and gaining on the impalas.

Sam held his hand to his brow to shade his eyes from the glare of the afternoon sun. "They saw him coming a mile off."

Sonja nodded. "That's his strategy. Look. One of the impalas is lagging behind the others. That's what he was waiting for."

The cat drew on every reserve of energy as it made straight for the slowest animal in the herd. Long legs stretched and its nonretractable claws dug into the dirt and grass like a sprinter's running spikes, propelling it forward, a blurred missile of gold and black fur. It reached out and hooked the flagging impala's rump with a wickedly curved dew claw. The impala stumbled and the pair of them, predator and prey, disappeared in a cloud of grass stalks and dust.

Sonja handed him the reins of the horse and unslung her rifle. "Stay here. Look after her."

"Excuse me? You're not going over there, are you?"

She walked off in the direction where they'd seen the impala brought down.

"Hey! Are you *crazy*? Sonja! Come back!"

She strode through the knee-high grass toward the kill. The mournful braying soon stopped as the cheetah clamped its jaws around the impala's neck. She knew it was killing the impala by suffocation, the same as a leopard would, to stifle the dying noises that might bring lions or hyenas to the carcass. The cheetah was built for speed, not for fighting, and would have no hope defending its prize from a larger predator.

"Hah!" Sonja waved her hand and the rifle high over her head as she advanced. "Hah!"

"Sonja! Come back!"

The cheetah looked up at her, over the red-brown neck of the impala, fixing her with angry red eyes.

"*Voetsek!*" She slapped the side of the rifle's curved magazine with the palm of her free hand. "Yah!"

The cheetah snapped its tail in annoyance and released its jaws from the impala. The impala was dead, and the cheetah was reluctant to surrender its kill to anyone or anything. The cat bared its teeth, then chirped its incongruous birdlike call in annoyance.

Sonja showed no fear. She had never heard of a cheetah killing an adult human, but she supposed there was always a first time. This was a battle of wills, but the odds were on her side. Nevertheless, her heart was thumping and she yelled again, louder, as she came to within ten meters of the cat. "Fight or flight; you choose." Her finger slipped through the trigger guard of the M4 and she flipped the safety catch off with her thumb. She didn't want to shoot, not even to scare the cheetah away, in case she attracted the attention of any trackers out looking for Sam. It would be easier for her to deposit him at Xakanaxa rather than explain her illegal presence in the concession to a stranger. "Hah!"

The cheetah rose and backed away from the kill, annoyance plain in its snarling jaws and glowering eyes.

"Thank you," Sonja said. She dropped to one knee and drew her knife. Keeping a close watch on the cheetah she lay her rifle down in the grass next to her, well within reach, and began hacking away at one still-warm leg.

The horse whinnied behind her and she looked around to see Sam, in the saddle, looking down at her. "You're crazy."

"Keep an eye on him." She nodded toward the cheetah as she sawed through sinew and cartilage. "There, that should do us nicely for dinner." She stood, the severed haunch dripping blood into the grass and her hands smeared red. She wiped the knife on the fur of the dead animal and stepped back. "All yours, my friend," she said to the cheetah.

"I've never seen anything so foolhardy in my life," he said from his lofty perch. "You could have been killed."

She thought about the number of times in her life that she could have—should have—been killed and couldn't help smiling.

9

"I think fashion and shopping are best left to the ladies. Sabrina, how would you like to take on the role of choosing the colors and lettering for our 'demolish the dam' T-shirts?" Bernard Trench said from the head of the table.

Stirling glanced at Sabrina Frost and saw the scowl color her face in the candlelight. Trench had a justifiable reputation for being a lecherous, sexist, chauvinistic bore. He'd told Stirling after the last meeting that he thought Sabrina, a staunch environmentalist and president of the Southern African branch of the international group GreenAction, was a lesbian. Stirling suspected this was based on her rejecting Trench's ham-fisted advances and her desire to be referred to as Ms. rather than Miss in committee meeting minutes. As bedfellows they didn't come any stranger.

"I didn't join this committee to be the ladies' auxiliary or bake cakes or shop for T-shirts, Bernard. But, all right, I suppose I can get one of my volunteers to look into it."

The meeting of the Okavango Delta Defense Committee was dragging into its third hour and Stirling knew that Sabrina wasn't the only one frustrated that the pace and agenda of the meeting reflected perfectly on their campaign against the dam upriver. They had been too slow to action and now they were tinkering at the edges of the issue talking about T-shirts when the dam had already been built. In a way he was pleased Cheryl-Ann wasn't here to see how fractured and impotent the committee was.

The Xakanaxa catering and waiting staff had been dismissed and the eighteen lodge owners, managers, consultants and activists pushed aside the remains of their desserts or set down their drinks as Trench cleared his throat. They might not all like him—indeed some, such as Sabrina, probably loathed him—but the sheer physical bulk of him, topped with his massive, bearded cannonball-bald head commanded attention, if not respect. Trench was a florid-faced Englishman who spent half the year on his wildlife properties dotted across southern Africa and half in the Cayman Islands tending to his offshore investments. His passion for young African women was surpassed only by his zeal for the conservation of Africa's wildlife. Rumor had it that no fewer than four of his female staff at Hippo Island, his luxury lodge in the Moremi Game Reserve, had been paid to drop sexual harassment charges.

"Item thirteen," Trench put down his agenda and raised a hand to his mouth in a failed attempt to muffle a burp, "public relations and lobbying. I'll now hand you over to Sheldon, our PR *expert* from Johannesburg. Sheldon?"

Stirling felt for the young man with the steel-rimmed glasses and pallid complexion. Stirling had offered to take the consultant out on a game drive that afternoon—he'd wanted a bit of time in the bush to get his own head in order before the meeting—but Sheldon had complained of a headache, brought on, he said, by the heat. Stirling had made him drink a liter of water, but he'd still spent the afternoon in his tent.

"Thank you, Bernard." Sheldon opened a folder in front of him and paused to swat away a moth with his linen serviette. "We still have a number of avenues to approach in our lobbying of the Namibian government and the United Nations—"

Trench smacked the table with an open palm. "Enough of the spin, Sheldon. Facts. Give us the facts. What was the outcome of the meeting at the UN?"

Trench knew the answer, as did the rest of them, but he wasn't going to let Sheldon off the hook.

"As you may have seen on the news last week, the Namibian government delivered a very emotive and very slick presentation to the UN's environmental commission—"

"Their PR company did a better job than ours," said Jan Nel, the Afrikaner manager of another lodge. His sun- and tobacco-weathered face showed no sympathy for the city boy. "Himba babies with distended bellies . . . pah! It's their own damn fault half their people are starving, not the weather's."

Sheldon grasped for a lifeline. "We know that the Namibian government spent a small fortune hiring one of New York's best PR companies."

"You want more money, Sheldon?" Trench interrupted. "I don't think so."

Sheldon opened his mouth to speak, but Trench silenced him with a wave of his stubby fingers. "Thank you. There will be no more money for PowerPoint presentations and taking politicians to dinner in New York, Sheldon." He looked at the faces around the table. "The world sees this issue—thanks to the Namibians' fast-talking spin doctors—as about people versus animals. We know," he looked up and down the table, "that lodges such as ours and local businesses that serve us employ thousands of Africans who might otherwise starve. But we're fighting a losing battle trying to convince people half a world away that saving animals and the environment is also about protecting people."

Stirling nodded, but like the rest of them around the table he'd seen and heard it all before. He also had other things to worry about, such as the still-missing American TV star and the injured and impatient film crew who were due back at Xakanaxa tomorrow, with a replacement cameraman. A search aircraft had spotted Sam Chapman's tent in the bush but the ground party the pilot directed to the site had found that the American had left. *I'm doing fine and walking to Xakanaxa Camp. I have a guide with me who knows the area*, Chapman had written in a note, which had been relayed by satellite phone to Stirling by the searchers. Chapman had also left an estimated time of arrival—this evening or tomorrow morning, but Stirling cursed the American's stupidity. As a so-called survival "expert" he should have known the best thing to do was to stay at his camp. Stirling wanted to get this meeting over with and as secretary of the committee he needed to ensure they stuck to their agenda. Bernard had another consultant to introduce later, an Englishman by the name of Martin Steele, who sat quietly at the far end of the table.

"Bernard, excuse me," Stirling said, tapping his printout of the agenda. "Perhaps we could hear Sabrina's report now."

Trench exhaled and Stirling could smell the wine two places away down the table. "Good idea."

Sabrina Frost was a few years older than Stirling, somewhere in her mid-forties, with steel gray hair cut short. She wore jeans and a black T-shirt. No makeup and no jewelry, save for three piercings in her right ear. She was tall, nearly six foot, and she towered over the portly Trench. He could see why some men might think she was gay, but Sabrina always sat next to him at the meetings and somehow her left leg always seemed to end up touching his right. It could have been that she was unaware she was invading his space, or that he was reading too much into the gesture, but Stirling didn't think she was a lesbian at all. Perhaps bi.

"We've got the report from our environmental consultants and there's some interesting stuff in it," she said. Trench stifled a yawn, but Sabrina ignored him. "The agronomist—that's a soil doctor, Bernard," there were laughs around the table, "makes a compelling case in relation to siltation."

"Fascinating," Trench said.

"It is. As well as depriving the delta's ecosystem of water, the dam's also going to prevent the carriage of silt from the upper reaches of the Kabango in Angola into Botswana. The silt carried by the Okavango is important for the support not only of indigenous plants and grasses, but also for farming on the Botswana side of the border. The report also concludes that so much silt is carried by the river that the dam will eventually fill up with it and become useless."

"How long would it take for that to happen?" Stirling asked

Sabrina looked at him, then at her notes and shrugged. "Thirty years? Fifty? By then Moremi and the rest of the Okavango Delta will be nothing but Kalahari sand and animal bones."

"It does give us some new ammunition, though," Sheldon interrupted.

Trench silenced him with a glare. "We won't win this fight with inches of paper or wads of money thrown at public relations firms. Sabrina, we should all read it in full and discuss further when we next convene. Now I'm afraid I must ask you to leave us, Sheldon," he directed with an aggressive nod toward the young man. "You're not required for the final session of tonight's meeting."

Red-faced, the young man stood and nodded. His chair protested on the wooden decking as he backed out. Stirling felt sorry for Sheldon, but couldn't deny that the hundred thousand dollars the lodges had pooled for the PR campaign had achieved nothing. The dam wall was complete and the Namibian government would soon commission the hydro-electric power generator. It would be a brave government or world body that turned off the water and electricity to poor African villagers in need of both, particularly in the middle of a crippling drought. Stirling looked around the table at the committee. By no means was the overweight, bullying Trench representative of the other lodge owners. However, they were all relatively wealthy white people who were, it was sad but true to say, more concerned about profits and animals than mothers and babies.

The group fell into an expectant silence, broken only by the receding muffle of Sheldon's trainers on the walkway, and the croak of a frog from the shallows below the viewing deck. Far away, a hyena whooped its eerie night call.

"Lady and gentlemen, I'm sure you're all wondering who the tall, dark stranger at the far end of the table is." Heads turned to the man, whose name, Steele, suited him, Stirling thought. "Martin Steele is a *consultant* of a different breed to Sheldon. You may have heard of his company and, if you have, he will need little introduction or time to explain what skills he brings to our table. But I will start by asking him to tell us a little about the business he founded, Corporate Solutions."

Jan Nel whistled low. Stirling felt Sabrina's left hand on his thigh. He glanced at her and saw her disbelief, impossible to hide in her wide eyes. She wasn't touching him because she wanted him. She was scared.

Martin Steele stood and the frog stopped croaking. He was silent for a moment as his eyes swept his audience. "Mercenaries, hired killers, gunslingers, murderers, war criminals, vultures, assassins. I've heard all of these terms and more to describe my company, my people and myself, but I can assure you all that the people of Corporate Solutions are none of these . . ."

Steele paused and Stirling stared at him, recalling the name that had been linked to half a dozen conflicts and coups—failed and successful—on the continent in the past two decades. The company had faced allegations of atrocities in Nigeria, links to diamond smuggling in Sierra Leone and civilian deaths in Angola in the old days. Corporate Solutions needed a PR company more than the Okavango Delta Defense Committee did, Stirling thought.

"... unless you want us to be."

Several of the men around the table laughed at the joke. Sabrina moved her hand off Stirling's leg and muttered, "Oh my god."

Steele held his hands up for silence. "Seriously, people, it may or may not be that you have exhausted your diplomatic options to have this dam decommissioned. That is not for me to decide."

There was silence around the table.

"There is a concrete wall across the Okavango, upriver, in Namibia's Caprivi Strip. Your legal challenges and protests may carry on for years, but that dam is filling up and your time—the Okavango Delta's time—is running out. Forgive an old soldier if I stick to habits of a lifetime. I would like to begin my briefing with an outline of the situation, as I see it, and then follow on with the details of my offer and proposal to you. I would ask, please, that you leave questions to the end."

Sabrina shifted in her chair and for a moment Stirling thought she was going to slide it back and walk out. She looked at him and he shrugged. He wanted to hear what Steele had to say. The Englishman stared at her and she held his gaze for as long as she could—perhaps ten seconds—then reached for her water glass.

"Very well. Situation. Despite your best efforts, and those of other conservationists and the Botswana government, the dam is substantially complete. Given the ongoing drought in this part of Africa it will take longer than expected for the new dam to reach capacity and, as a flow-on effect, the poor rains predicted for the next wet season will exacerbate the impact on users downstream, such as yourselves. Botswana is the only country that will be adversely affected by the dam and its government has run true to form by being diplomatic, nonconfrontational and peaceful. The wildlife in Botswana will suffer, migration patterns will change and people will lose their jobs.

"There is a third political force in this debate—the Caprivi Liberation Army, or CLA for short. There has been one armed attempt already to disrupt work on the dam, an ill-fated attack carried out by the CLA."

Stirling and others around the table nodded. The Okavango River passed through the Caprivi Strip region of Namibia and the dam was sited upstream of Popa Falls near the town of Divundu, at the western end of the disputed territory. The Caprivi Strip was a historical anomaly, a narrow, four-hundred-and-forty-kilometer corridor of land ceded by the British to Germany when they were carving up colonial Africa. Its proclamation was rooted in a mix of deceit and ignorance. Germany had claimed South-West Africa yet wanted access to the Indian Ocean on the eastern coast for trade purposes. The British "gave" Germany the strip to link Namibia to the Zambezi River, which flowed into the Indian Ocean. What the British didn't yet know, or weren't telling the Germans, was that not far from where the Caprivi Strip ended the Zambezi was interrupted by the mighty Victoria Falls, making trade by riverboat from South-West Africa to the Indian Ocean an impossibility.

The corridor of seasonally flooded land bordering the Kavango, Chobe, Linyanti and Zambezi rivers bore nothing in common with the rest of Namibia, which was a mostly barren land of scorching deserts and wild sandy coastline shrouded in chilling Atlantic mists.

Ethnically, the people of the Caprivi were Lozi in the main, with closer ties to tribes in Zambia to the east, rather than the Ovambo, Himba, Nama, Damara and Herero people who populated the rest of Namibia. The Caprivians were fiercely independent and had never considered themselves part of Namibia. They viewed the dam on the Okavango as an example of the Namibian government taking resources they considered belonged to the local people and using them to benefit other tribes far away, as well as future water-dependent diamond mines whose profits the Caprivians believed they would never share.

"A year ago, two hundred members of the CLA stormed the Okavango

Dam construction site, expecting to sweep through and plant explosive charges on the walls of the temporary coffer dam, constructed to divert waters so work could commence on the main wall," Steele said, reminding them of facts they already knew. "Instead of finding only local laborers and some German and Namibian engineers, the CLA came up against a Namibian Defense Force infantry battalion of roughly five hundred men, lying in prepared ambush positions. There was clearly a rat in the ranks of the CLA and the attack cost the lives of seventy-two of its members, with a further thirty captured. The detainees are still languishing in jail and awaiting trial. As I understand it, after the attack the remnants of the CLA conducted an internal purge and four of its members were quietly dealt with."

"Dealt with?" Sabrina whispered to Stirling. "Is this guy for real?"

"Very real, madam," Steele said from the far end of the table.

Sabrina gulped her water.

"But getting back to the situation. There exists, to this day, a strong desire by the indigenous people of the Caprivi Strip to govern themselves. Despite the setback at the dam the CLA maintains a small cadre of highly trained soldiers ready to fight and, if needs be, die for their cause. And we have a dam, consisting of a substantial amount of concrete. Not as easy to destroy as a coffer dam, but not impossible, either."

One of the lodge owners raised a hand.

"With your indulgence, questions at the end, please." The man nodded. "Now, to the mission."

Steele picked up a glass of water and sipped from it. He set it down and leaned on the table, supporting his muscular upper body on his fists as he closed the gap between himself and his audience.

"Mission. Destroy the dam on the Okavango River and bring about a simultaneous regime change in the Caprivi Strip, installing a new, self-governing administration which will be opposed to any future dam on the river in perpetuity. I say again—"

Sabrina stood up. "This is crazy. I don't want to hear another word."

Steele ignored the outburst. "That, Ms. Frost, gentlemen, is the end of my presentation. There is no point in me going into the execution, administration and logistics, and command and communications aspects of the plan

I have developed, unless you are all on board. I'll hand you back to your chairman now."

Sabrina resumed her seat and Trench studied the faces of every person at the table. "Questions?"

"Questions?" Stirling said to himself. Bloody hell, he thought, it was hard to know where to start. "I've got one. You reminded us all that the Caprivi Liberation Army has already had one try at destroying the dam and failed. Security at the dam site remains tight. How can you hope to get in again?"

Trench looked at Steele, who nodded, and said, "As I've just said, I'm not going to go into details until I have your support—and, quite frankly, your money."

The muttered laughs and snorts were more a release of tension than genuine mirth. Steele continued. "However, the CLA's strategy was flawed last time around. They thought that by blowing up the dam they would get their people to rise up spontaneously along the length and breadth of the Caprivi Strip. In effect, they put all their eggs—or bullets—in one basket. The strategy I have in mind is different."

Sabrina raised her hand, and Steele nodded. "I've been to the dam site recently, as part of a protest blockade. Stirling's right. The security is tight as a drum. We couldn't get within five kilometers of the wall. We were stopped by police and army checkpoints."

"I have a plan in mind to get past the security," Steele said. "But I stress again the strategy I'm proposing is not just about the dam. If we blow the wall and the Namibian government still holds sway over the region then it will simply be repaired or rebuilt in time. We don't want just a hole in a wall."

"No, you want a war," Sabrina said.

Steele shook his head and met her glare. "I want justice, for a people denied it."

"Rubbish," Sabrina said. "You want blood and money."

Trench raised a hand. "Hear Martin out, Sabrina. The Caprivians do have a legitimate claim on their land, which has been denied by their government for decades."

Steele stood again. "In 1964 a pro-independence group based in the Caprivi Strip, the Caprivian African National Union—CANU—made up of Lozi-speaking peoples signed an alliance with the Ovambo-dominated South-West African People's Organization, SWAPO, to combine forces in the fight against the whites in South-West Africa. It was a marriage of convenience, which made military sense at the time. The South African military would be fighting on two fronts—SWAPO guerillas, supplied from and based in Angola, and CANU's forces, now aligned with SWAPO, but with safe havens to the east in Zambia. CANU and its successors have always claimed that the agreement between CANU and SWAPO stated that once independence was gained from the whites a referendum on self-determination and self-government would be held in Caprivi. According to CANU, SWAPO later reneged on the deal."

"Yes," Sabrina interjected, "but SWAPO says CANU gave up such ambitions when the deal was signed in 1964."

Steele shrugged. "It's academic. There are people who are prepared to take up arms and fight for the establishment of a Caprivian homeland. Linguistically, ethnically, culturally, this has always been a separate part of Africa. Even the German colonial administrators of South-West Africa lost interest in the Caprivi Strip once they realized they couldn't sail down the Zambezi River to the Indian Ocean. For much of its history it was administered by the British from here in Botswana. It wasn't until the mid twentieth century that the South Africans even bothered to build a road linking the Caprivi to the rest of South-West Africa. These people want nothing more than to be able to determine their own future. They are people of the river, people to whom the waters of the Okavango, the Chobe and the Zambezi are sacred. The Caprivians will never dam your river."

"It's not actually ours," Stirling said. "It belongs to all the countries it traverses."

Steele thumped the table. "Exactly! Yet why should Angola and Namibia be able to rob water from the people and from the wildlife of Botswana? The Botswana government will continue to protest but they will never go to war over water."

"They're too sensible," Sabrina said.

Nel lit another cigarette and coughed. "I know some Lozi. They're good, honest, hard-working people. They feel robbed, disillusioned. They think the world has ignored them and left them hanging out to dry and I believe there is truth to that. If things hadn't been so bad in Zimbabwe all these past years then the UN might have paid more attention to the Caprivians."

Steele took up the thread. "There are more than eight thousand Caprivians living as political refugees in Botswana. Many of those people want to return home and are prepared to fight for the right to do so."

"Yes," Sabrina conceded, "I'm sure that's all true, but starting a war to save a river? Is it worth it?"

Steele shrugged and sat down. "That's not for me to decide. It's for you. The Caprivians are ready to fight to seize their homeland, but they need weapons and ammunition—especially the heavy stuff, such as rocket-propelled grenades, mortars and explosives. They need money."

Sabrina shook her head and looked to Trench. "What I don't get, Bernard, is why I'm here at all. I don't have money to contribute to this operation. I'm from an environmental organization. I seriously hope you don't expect me to go back to head office and ask for a donation. The moms and pops in Sydney, Ontario, San Francisco and Cape Town who support us would have a collective heart attack if they thought their donations were going to fund a *coup* organized by mercenaries."

Steele took a sip of water. "Ms. Frost, your organization chases and boards Japanese whaling ships—technically acts of piracy. Your members chain themselves to shipments of spent nuclear fuels and sabotage bulldozers clearing Amazonian rain forests."

"That's different to warfare, where innocents will be killed."

"My point, Ms. Frost, is that your people are prepared to risk their lives for a cause. The Lozi who live in exile in Botswana are ready and willing to risk their lives for their homeland, and to save the river that means as much, if not more, to them than it does to you. Will you deny them that?"

"What is it, exactly, you want from me, from my group?"

Trench cleared his voice. "Legitimacy."

10

Sonja used her knife to carve the seared flesh from the leg of impala and handed a strip to Sam.

His mouth watered as he held the greasy piece of meat in his hand while he waited for her to cut her portion. He felt helpless around her. The least he could do was mind his manners and wait for her before eating— even if he was starving. His stomach rumbled in anticipation.

"Enjoy," she said.

The meat was drier than he expected, and quite bland, but he wolfed down his sliver while Sonja was still taking her time over her portion. He didn't want to appear greedy, but wasn't sure what the protocol was for eating a hunk of meat stolen from a cheetah and roasted over open coals. The leg sat on a flat rock Sonja had placed on the coals as a kind of warming and carving surface.

"May I?" he asked, pointing at her knife.

She looked at him while she chewed and said nothing. He reached for the knife gingerly. The blade didn't reflect the glow from the coals as it was coated with a matt black finish. Only the very edges showed silver, where she had been sharpening it. Judging by the way it glided through the well-cooked meat he reckoned he could shave with it. As he cut himself a ragged slice of meat, he found that despite its sharpness the knife was difficult to carve with,. It had a T-shaped handle that normally sat in the palm of the hand, with the second and third fingers either side of the shaped shank. It wasn't a knife for skinning buck or whittling sticks to roast marshmallows with over the camp fire. It was a weapon for stabbing. For killing. He placed the knife back down on the rock carefully next to the joint of meat, and retreated back to his side of the fire clutching the slippery meat in his fingers like a wild man.

As he ate, Sonja glanced at him occasionally, as if to satisfy herself that he was in his place. Other than that she gazed out into the night.

From a nearby tree he heard a high-pitched *brrrr brrr* at regular intervals. "Is that an owl?"

She finished chewing her mouthful and swallowed. "Scops."

He nodded. Another Scops owl called from a different tree, maybe fifty meters away. At least the birds had something to talk about.

His sense of being out of his depth and deep in the shit had magnified with each passing hour. He'd been unable to get more than a few words from the woman all afternoon, after the incident with the cheetah. Since realizing he wasn't being set up by Cheryl-Ann and that something had gone wrong somewhere along the line he'd decided he had no option but to trust Sonja. Even so, he sensed the little she'd told him about herself and why she was out here in the middle of nowhere contained precious little truth. It was bad enough that he was making a documentary about an environment he knew nothing about, and even worse that when he was put to the test, for real, he had very nearly died. If this brooding, heavily armed stranger hadn't come along when she did, his body might never have been found.

"Forgive me," he said.

She glanced across the fire at him and raised her eyebrows.

"I guess I should say thank you. For saving my life, I mean. If you hadn't come along I would have just lain there in the mud waiting for the bees to go, and by that time the crocodile would have got hold of me and eaten me. What a way to go, huh? The survival expert who flunked out." He laughed at his own joke. Lame. Talking to this woman was like walking on hot coals—theoretically possible but likely to cause pain.

She carved another slice of meat, for herself, and began chewing it.

"What does your tattoo mean? I saw all those letters and numbers while we were walking. Is it a code or something?" He reached for the knife again.

Sonja swallowed her food. "It's a place."

"Oh, OK. I get it. Like a GPS waypoint. That small 'o' is a degree symbol, right?"

She looked at him like he was a moron.

"Where is it, the place on your arm?"

She looked out into the darkness again.

"Is it home?"

Good Lord, did the man never shut up? If she answered his banal questions it encouraged him to ask more. If she stayed silent he kept on at her until she said something. It was worse than the resistance-to-interrogation course the SAS had put her through before her deployment to Northern Ireland.

"I wish I knew where home was," he said, picking at the gristly leftovers still clinging to the white bone. "Time was, I thought I was pretty grounded. I thought I'd grow old in Montana, maybe working for the state in animal management or conservation, or the national parks for twenty or thirty years. I thought maybe I'd go back to college to teach. There'd be a wife and some kids and a nice house, a piece of land outside of town. The American dream, right?"

She unscrewed the lid of the plastic water bottle and took a sip. The American dream? Working as a military contractor she'd seen it die in the faces of too many idealistic young marines and soldiers in Iraq and Afghanistan. Her dream had died in Northern Ireland, with the flash and the bang of the stun grenades; the shouted commands; the tear gas; the thud of nine-millimeter bullets tearing into timber, plaster and flesh.

She held a hand over the coals to see if there was enough heat in them to boil some water. It wasn't nearly warm enough.

"Have you ever found yourself at the wrong place at the wrong time of your life?" Sam asked.

She looked at the American. "Yes," she said, before remembering to stay silent. She stood and winced. The bullet wound was healing well and didn't hurt too much during the day, but when she sat for too long, and after sleeping, her leg became stiff.

"You look like you're in pain. Are you OK?" he asked.

He was like a puppy, always seeking attention.

"Pain is just weakness leaving the body."

He laughed out loud, the peals echoing off the trees. He wiped his eyes. "Wait a minute, you're serious? Where did you learn that, the drill sergeant's guide to holistic healing and alternative medicine?"

She felt her cheeks color. She'd been around soldiers too long. But who was this pampered TV wanker to make fun of her?

"Pain is not *weakness leaving the body*, it's just pain. It's your body's way of telling you to take it easy, to rest up."

When and where exactly was she going to "rest up"? she wondered. They had another twelve hours of walking and riding to reach Xakanaxa and precious little food and water. The best hope for them was to reach the camp as soon as possible, but it didn't seem worth the time or breath to explain it to him. She took her sleeping bag out of her pack and rolled it out on the ground, then laid her M4 on the down-filled nylon. From her daypack she took a compact mosquito net out of its bag and slotted the short, three-piece spreader pole into the loops at the top. She tied it to a low branch of the mopane under which she had made the cooking fire and tucked the white netting under her bag. She dragged two more logs onto the fire and stood by it until they caught, sending an offering of sparks to the stars above. She looked up—the sky was clear as far as she could see. No rain on the way and it was already two weeks past Botswana Independence Day, 30 September. For as long as she had lived in the Okavango swamps it had always rained either on or a day or two on either side of Independence Day. Not a drop had fallen here, though, and the last three wet seasons had been terribly dry.

"Where should I sleep?"

She didn't bother answering him. Sonja knelt and lifted the hem of her mosquito net and slid underneath. She lay on her back and rested her head on her pack. She wished she had a cigarette. On the other side of the fire Sam cursed as he tripped over a tree root. She tried to block his fumblings and babble out of her mind by thinking about Stirling.

How had he aged? Was he seeing someone and hadn't had time to up-date his Facebook profile? Was he still happy managing the camp and living his life in contented isolation from the rest of the world? Would he take her back? The way she had treated Stirling had been a mistake; she saw that now in hindsight. But was it an error she could rectify?

As she listened to the rustling and faint curses of the American settling under his mosquito net she thought about what it would be like to live in the camp again, with Stirling, but this time as a couple, perhaps even as husband and wife. She wished she had made this trip years ago, and in different cir-cumstances. She knew that by leaving it so long it would be even harder re-connecting with Stirling and that he may not want to have anything to do with her. There was Emma to think of as well. She wondered if Stirling had found out about her, or even cared that she had a child. God, she thought, she really had left this homecoming too long. She started to feel silly and embarrassed that she was even bothering to daydream that she might be able to pick up again with a boy she'd known so long ago. Yet something was pulling her back to the Delta. The smart thing would have been to get to an airport and fly out of Africa, yet here she was traipsing back to the only place and the only person she had ever associated with a life of innocence and honesty.

She sought out the stars through the close weave of the mosquito net. Bats squeaked like a rusty gate somewhere in the distance. She wished she could travel back in time. Her child should have been Stirling's, and could have been his, if she hadn't been so opinionated, so stubborn, so restless. She was coming back to the Delta because she knew, like a territorial animal, that this was where she belonged. She'd known it nineteen years ago when she'd gotten the stupid tattoo on her arm that this was where her home was. So why had she been so determined to leave it? What was wrong with her?

Ambition? That was part of it. Certainly none of the job choices on offer to her at the time she left were appealing to her. But what had she done with herself? She hadn't become a doctor or a vet or a nurse or even a bloody secretary. Her drive, her *ambition*, her past and her pride had taken her to war and taught her to kill.

Was it the excitement? Don't go there, she told herself. Don't admit the highs—stick with the lows. The depression was easier to understand, easier to live with than the jazz. How could she explain to herself, let alone anyone who hadn't been through it, the rush from heart to brain to fingertips and toes that came from being under fire; firing back, surviving and winning? It was terrifying, just how intense the feeling was. But it didn't outweigh the regret. The realization, deep in the dark of night, that the person who died, no matter how bad they were, how much she disagreed with their cause, left a mother or a father or a sister or a brother or a wife or a girlfriend or a husband or a boyfriend. Or all of the above. And there was her fear for Emma, that she would be left alone.

When Emma was growing up Sonja had at least had the comfort of knowing that her mother, Emma's grandmother, was there in case something happened. More often than not it was her mother that took Sonja's place at parent days, recitals, sports days and awards nights. Her mother had been killed just six months earlier, in a hit-and-run accident. Sonja had been in Dubai, working a two-month contract as a personal protection officer for the wife of an oil sheikh who had received threats to kidnap her children. Sonja's flight had been turned around because a warning light had appeared on the captain's console and she'd had to spend an extra night in Dubai. The funeral had gone ahead without her and she'd returned to England to cuttingly snide abuse from Emma and the frowning disapproval of her mother's friends. She'd grieved for her mother the only way she knew how—in private, with a couple of bottles of wine.

Sonja saw, after the funeral, the woman her daughter was becoming. Emma was very bright academically—the top of her class when she chose to be. There was also a strong streak of independence that had landed her in trouble more than once when she'd spoken back to her teachers. There had been incidents with drinking in the dorms, too, made worse by the fact that Emma had been a ringleader. As saddened as she must have been by her grandmother's death, Emma had been able to rein in her grief around Sonja and treat her with crushing disdain.

Emma knew part of what Sonja did for a living—the close personal protection work. Bodyguarding was easy to explain, even though it was the safest and least rewarding of the tasks she had undertaken for Martin Steele. Sonja knew she probably shouldn't have agreed to the Zimbabwean job, but the money was good and the job itself had been the biggest challenge of her professional life. Assassination was dirty stuff—black ops as governments called it—but if it had come off and the president had been killed, well . . . Pity it had gone tits up, she thought.

Before leaving for Africa she had changed her will and Martin had agreed to take on the role of Emma's legal guardian, until she turned eighteen, if something should happen to Sonja. Whether or not he was her real father, Emma liked and respected Martin and he was the closest thing she had ever had to a dad. Emma was headstrong and nearly an adult, but Sonja feared she was still young enough to go horribly off the rails without someone else to guide her for a couple more years. With her grandmother gone Emma would be alone in the world if Sonja was killed.

Sonja hadn't ever been afraid of being alone and she had certainly been happy enough for some time without a man in her life. She could outshoot, outswear, outdrink and outdrive most of the men she'd met in the army and as a mercenary. She'd raised a child virtually on her own and she was financially independent. Materially or even physically, she didn't *need* a man. It was laughably easy for her to get sex on the occasions her hormones told her she needed it. It was occasionally enjoyable, though invariably unrewarding. So why, she asked herself, did she think it was so important to connect with Stirling again?

Was it her version of what Sam had called the American dream? Did she, deep down, want to be part of a family in the traditional sense—husband and wife and child, with maybe another child before it was too late for her? She thought about it. Maybe.

Was she still in love with Stirling? Had she ever loved him? She'd been *in love* with him when they were both seventeen going on eighteen, although not enough for her to stay put and marry him. Would she still feel the same or even a fraction of the physical and emotional attraction to him when she saw him again?

Or was it, perhaps, the place, rather than the person that she loved more? Perhaps. Her version of the dream didn't include a mansion in Sandton or a cottage in the Cotswolds or even a game farm in Namibia. She rubbed the tattoo on her arm.

She just wanted to go home.

11

Sam slapped himself in the face. A mosquito was inside his net and had been buzzing around his ears for what seemed like an hour. He was hot, but had zipped himself into his sleeping bag partly to protect the rest of his body from the insect, and partly because he remembered the sight of the python sliding its way into the hollow log.

His left side ached from contact with the one rock he hadn't cleared from the ground under his mat. He rolled over. In his tent he'd had a thick, high-density foam camping mattress covered with green rip-stop canvas. He hadn't thought it too luxurious on those first two nights but now it lived in his memory alongside the five top luxury hotel beds he'd ever slept on. Sonja had not let him bring it with them because it was too bulky to strap to her old nag.

The ridiculously named Black Beauty neighed nervously from the shadows beyond the fire. Stirling coughed as a breath of wind blew smoke into his net. Maybe he should have stayed in his tent, he thought, and waited for someone to come find him. The weird, wired, toned creature sleeping silently beyond the low flames may have saved his life after the episode with the bees, but she might yet get him killed out here in the bush with nothing but a nylon net between him and Africa's super-predators.

The mosquito let him know he'd missed by landing on the tip of his left ear and buzzing. He swatted again. "Goddamn."

Then he heard the growl.

It was deep, low and continuous and it sounded almost like purring. It was as if someone had put his mum's house cat in front of a speaker, connected a massive amplifier and turned the treble to zero and the bass to full. He felt it in his chest. He swallowed hard and slowly lifted his head.

Sam looked around but saw nothing. The horse made another sound, higher pitched, and he heard its hooves shuffling in the dry grass. Sam saw something moving. He turned to the left and glimpsed the shadow of a flick of a tail cast briefly against the pale bark of the tree. The noise was still there.

"Sonja," he called softly.

"Quiet."

"But . . ."

"Lion. Stay still, and quiet. Under your net. Don't move."

Stay still? He pulled the sleeping bag up to his chin and took a breath. When he started to feel light-headed he remembered to breathe again. Quietly. He thought it might have left, but then he heard a galloping sound. Had the horse snapped its tether?

The horse whinnied in pain.

Sam sat up and looked around him. The horse was thrashing, causing leaves and seed pods to rain down from the branches of the tree to which it was tied. There was a ripping sound and a deep, guttural growling.

Sonja's mosquito net twitched as she shrugged out from under it. She stood there, bare arms and legs glowing bronze in the reflected firelight, the ugly, squat assault rifle in her hands. She grasped the cocking handle and pulled it back viciously, letting the working parts fly forward with a menacing rattle.

"*Voetsek!*" she screamed into the blackness but the lion or lions were not nearly as easily scared as the panting cheetah.

What happened to stay still and quiet? Sam wondered. He watched Sonja stride away from the fire into the darkness, her rifle up and ready. "Sonja!"

She ignored him and pointed the barrel skywards.

Bang, bang. Sam flinched with each shot. He saw her again, momentarily illuminated by the lightning flashes from the rifle's muzzle. The growling and tearing ceased, replaced by a snarled challenge.

Sonja fired again.

"Oh, Jesus," Sam said. He lifted the hem of his mosquito net, then had second thoughts, so he set it down again. He peered into the darkness but saw nothing. The horse was whinnying but its noises were fainter and he heard Sonja speaking soothing words. At least she was still alive. He lifted the net again, took a deep breath and got up, wearing only his boxer shorts. He looked around for a weapon and grabbed the end of a dead branch whose tip was in the fire. He hefted the improvised torch and walked into the nothingness.

He found her, kneeling in the dark. The horse was on its side, writhing in the grass. He ran the flame the length of its body and saw white bone showing through a rip on its right hind leg. Far worse, though, were the ghastly wounds at its throat, which bubbled and frothed with blood.

Sonja stood, pointed the rifle at the horse's thrashing head and pulled the trigger.

Sam flinched again.

She stood there, just staring down at the horse, which was at peace now.

"The lions?"

"Lioness," she said. "Just one. She was . . ."

Sam held up the flaming end of the log. Sonja held her rifle loose in one hand now and wiped her eyes with the back of the other.

"Are you OK?"

She turned and stared at him. "Of course I'm OK."

He said nothing, and looked down at the horse to avoid her glare. "Um . . . sorry."

She looked down at her hands and seemed to see the blood on them for the first time. "I'm fine. It was just a horse." She rubbed them on her shorts three, four, five times. "The lioness was on her own, which probably means she's got cubs somewhere close by. They leave the pride to give birth and return once the cubs can look after themselves. She'll be dangerous. We should get back to the fire. Stoke it up."

He nodded and they walked back to the relative safety of the flames. Sam busied himself dragging more logs onto the fire until it was blazing again, sparks shooting high into the clear night sky.

Sonja fetched her bedroll and dragged it to the same side of the fire as his. She laid it out between the bonfire and his mosquito net and sat down. She flicked the safety catch on the M4 to safe and laid it down on her sleeping bag, then sat down. "She'll come back to finish off the horse. If she's well fed she'll leave us alone, but females with young are unpredictable, aggressive. I'll keep watch."

"Let me—"

She silenced him with those green, feline eyes. "Get some sleep."

"You really think I can sleep after all that? After discovering there's an unpredictable aggressive lone female nearby?"

That made her smile, reluctantly, and he grinned back at her.

"Adrenaline's a funny drug. You feel pumped, jazzed now, but you'll be unconscious in twenty minutes' time. The low's as incredible as the high."

"You sound like you know." He didn't know where to sit and couldn't go back to his bed right now, whatever she said, so he stood with his back to the flames, looking out into the night.

Her silence was a challenge to him. He didn't know why. Maybe he wanted her to stop treating him like an encumbrance or a stupid child. She stared into the flames. Beyond the ring of light cast by the fire he thought he heard movement in the bushes. No way could he go lie down now, whether she was keeping guard or not.

"You were crying before."

She snapped her head around and looked at him like he'd just hit her.

"It's all right, you know. I was taught that it's not a bad thing, to let your emotions show. It's harder, supposedly, for a guy, but it's therapeutic. It took me a while to learn."

"To learn?" She shook her head.

"Yes. It never came natural to me. I was never a crier as a kid, except for the time I broke my leg. I didn't even cry when . . . when a good friend of mine passed away. But I learned."

She picked up a stick and poked the fire. "You Americans. You live in a society in which men are taught to cry." She shook her head at the absurdity of it. "In Africa there is so much sorrow people gave up crying long ago. In Zimbabwe, just across the border, children are starving, yet *you* have a generation that is being told to eat less in case they die of obesity."

Finally, he'd got her talking, and she turned out to be just another American hater. He wished he hadn't bothered. "You Africans . . ."

She looked back at him.

"White, black or brown, you can't help but screw up one of the most beautiful continents on earth. You think you've got a monopoly on sorrow? Well, if you do it's because every time the ball passes from one team to another you can't wait to stick a knife in it."

"An odd analogy."

He clenched his fists. "Fuck it up, is what I mean, excuse my language."

She laughed. "You're excused, but please go on."

"We have enough bad shit to deal with in America, too, believe it or not. At least our government is accountable to its people. Here—in Africa—whichever tribe is in power does its best to rob the rest of the country blind and, if it can get away with it, maybe kill off a few thousand of the opposition at the same time."

"Botswana's not like that," she said.

"Sure, maybe not as bad as the Afrikaners when they ruled South Africa, or the Shona in Zimbabwe, or the Hutus and Tutsis in Rwanda, but they've moved Khoisan people off their homelands to dig new diamond mines."

"You know a lot about Africa for someone who's been here a week."

He presumed she was being sarcastic, but didn't want to give her the satisfaction of acknowledging it. "I read. What do you know about America? About Americans?"

She opened her mouth as if she was going to say something, then shut it. She seemed tempted to carry on with the argument, but another emotion or thought stilled her. She took a deep breath through her nostrils and when she spoke her voice was calm and low. "It's late. Get some sleep."

He paced out to the darkness then back to the fire. "I told you, I can't sleep. Also, for the first time we were damn close there to actually having a conversation. It turned into an argument, but started because we were talking about crying."

She glared at him, saying nothing.

Once upon a time he'd been happy to sit on the prairie or in hides and watch and listen and take notes. When he was observing his coyotes in the wild, just them and him and the big sky and wide open plains, he truly felt like the happiest man in the world. He felt that was the way he should be; the reason why he had been put on earth, to form a link between humans and this misunderstood, maligned but amazing mammal. Now all he did was talk for a living. Talk shit.

They stared each other down. He knew that if he said a word right now she might never speak to him again. He didn't want that.

She looked away, back to the fire. "I don't like seeing animals die."

He laughed.

She looked up at him, anger flaring in her eyes. "What? I tell you something about myself—admittedly to shut you up, to end your incessant questioning—and you *laugh* at me?"

"You must be tired." He squatted and placed his ten fingertips on the ground to steady himself. "Either that or you're a terrible liar. You told me you were a professional hunter yesterday, and now you tell me you cry when see an animal die?"

She unzipped her sleeping bag and slid into it, still wearing her boots. "You're right, I'm tired. If you're not going to sleep, then you can take first watch. Don't touch my rifle and wake me if you get too scared."

The noise of a vehicle engine woke her. She sat upright, all senses alert instantly. The sun was breaching the dark tree line, a crescent of red beginning its morning chore of redecorating the landscape. She checked her watch. Four hours, maybe five? It was a long sleep for her.

Sam was standing, looking out toward the noise. "Morning. I only just heard it." He took three steps in the direction of the noise.

She grabbed the M4 and got to her feet. "Sam, stop." He looked back at her. "The lioness, remember? She's over that way. Stay put. The smoke will bring them."

The growl of the diesel was getting louder and she heard the snap of small trees being broken and the splintering crunch of fallen branches and dried leaves beneath off-road tires.

Sam held his hand to his eyes to shield them from the brightness of a spotlight.

"*Coo-eee!*" cried a voice over the engine noise.

Sonja smiled, slung her M4 and cupped hands either side of her mouth. "John Lemon!"

The white Land Cruiser came into view and shifted its aim, destroying a few more saplings as it trundled over the uneven ground toward them. There was a black African man sitting on the roof. He smiled broadly and waved.

"Watch out for the lioness!"

The African man pointed over his shoulder, from the direction they had just come. "The *mafazi* is gone now, Miss Sonja."

She took another look at the tracker. "Elliott!" She ran to the vehicle, which stopped in front of her. "Oh my god! How are you?"

"I am fine, missy."

John opened the door and climbed down. He was four inches shorter than Sonja and she would once have teased him about the sweat-stained foam rubber pillow on the driver's seat, but not today.

"Bloody hell, are you who I think you are? Sonja bloody Kurtz? Well I'll be buggered." He stood on his toes to kiss her cheek.

"John bloody Lemon. I never thought I'd be so glad to see you. I can't believe you're still here after all this time."

He held her at arm's length. "Time, tide and the painted dog wait for no man. But I know what you mean, the time's flown. You were, what, eighteen when you left?"

She nodded.

The Australian whistled. "Stirling was mad to let you go. You're even more beautiful than when you left."

She punched him in the heart and he grasped his chest theatrically. "And you're still a lecherous sexist pig. I've missed you, John."

There was a cough behind her.

"Aha, beneath all that dirt and grime that looks like the missing, almost late, Mr. Sam Chapman. Is that right, mate?"

Sam nodded.

"Pleased to meet you." John stepped around her and shook Sam's hand. The American had thirty centimeters on him, easy.

"Likewise. You must be the cavalry?"

John laughed. "Yup. We've been looking for you, Sam. G'day, I'm John Lemon."

"John, it's great to see you, but if you're looking for me then hopefully you know what the hell is going on. Do you know what happened to the rest of my crew?"

John paused by the Land Cruiser. "The helicopter, Sam . . . it crashed."

"What?"

"Pilot's badly burned, but he'll live. Poor guy. Little's a good bloke, for a Kiwi. Your mob's all right, though I heard one of them has got a broken arm or leg or something. The others are probably back at Xakanaxa by now."

"Jesus." Sam leaned against the truck as he tried to compose himself. "Thank you, anyway, for coming along. You're Australian?"

"As the late, great Steve Irwin. I was kind of hoping I'd be the one to find you. I'm a fan of your work, Sam. Be an honor to buy you a beer once we get back to civilization, if you're not too busy."

"Well thanks, but the beers are on me."

"Can we stop the love-in and get moving?" Sonja said.

Sam asked John what an Australian was doing in Africa as they gathered their things and, with the help of old Elliott, the gray-haired scout who had worked on the wild dog research team as long as John had, loaded the Land Cruiser.

"Been researching painted dogs—that's the new warm and fuzzy term for the old African wild dog—since this girlie Sonja was still at school. You been to Africa before, Sam?"

"Nope."

"Didn't think so. I've seen all your shows on satellite telly and don't remember you doing one over here. Anyhow, beware of Africa, mate. Once she bites you or gets under your skin you might find yourself coming back here, for good. I couldn't see myself going back to Oz full-time. And besides, I reckon I'd get bored researching kangaroos or wombats."

"How long did you say you've been here?"

"Me? Twenty years, give or take. I heard your mob was in the area filming and I was hoping to meet you, but we were told that once you'd finished your survival filming you'd be off to Namibia. Is that right?"

Sam nodded. "That was the plan, but I've got no idea what's going to happen now."

"Elliott, can you get these guys some water out of the fridge, please?"

The tracker nodded and opened the side door of the heavily modified Land Cruiser. He reached inside and pulled two bottles of cold water from a humming Engel car refrigerator mounted behind the driver's seat.

Sonja unscrewed the cap and downed the crystal clear water in two long gulps. After the purified but muddy swamp water she'd been surviving on it was like nectar. She wiped her mouth with the back of her hand. "How did you find us?"

"We've been searching the bush looking for Sam for a couple of days. They found his tent from the air and Elliott and I got there late yesterday. We found his note and tracked you for a while late yesterday afternoon and we made camp when it got dark. Didn't like the idea of driving round the bush in the middle of the night in case I put a stump through the sump or a branch through the radiator. The note said Sam was with a guide, but when Elliott told me there was a man, a woman and horse walking through the bush, I was pretty surprised. Who'd have guessed the mystery sheila would be our Sonja?"

"I'm glad you showed up when you did. It would have been a long walk to camp from here." Sonja told John about her horse and they just stood there for a few moments looking at each other, both replaying a stream of memories.

"Your dad . . ." John began.

She shook her head. "I'm not interested, John."

"Fair enough. Anyhow, let's get you two loaded and back to base. What about your gear, Sam? Do you want to go back for your tent and stuff, or would you rather have a hot shower and a cold beer?"

"A beer sounds better, John. Besides, I really want to catch up with the rest of the team and see how they are."

John climbed up to take his place behind the wheel, but didn't make it into his seat before Sonja grabbed the slab of foam rubber and pretended to fluff it up for him. He scowled at her, but couldn't hold it. She sat in the front passenger seat. Most of the roof of the Land Cruiser had been cut away to make a viewing hatch and the inside edges were heavily upholstered with canvas-covered rubber. Sam stood in the open observation area behind Sonja and John. Elliott resumed his place sitting on a padded bench seat that ran along the leading edge of a roof rack.

Sonja looked out the Land Cruiser's window and saw the vultures in the tree above the remains of the horse. She squeezed her eyes shut and fought back the prickling tears before they showed. Get a grip, she told herself.

How many men had she killed? Maybe the SWAPO terrorist in the South-West when she was a kid—maybe not. The *Koevoet* team that did the follow-up said there was a blood trail and that judging by the amount he wouldn't have survived, but who knew? The next one there was no doubt of. She forced him from her mind. There were the two RUF men in the jungle of Sierra Leone; the Afghan; and the female suicide bomber in Baghdad. The Americans had wanted to give her a medal for that one. It didn't matter if it was a woman or man, it had never seemed to affect her.

She didn't cry, though she did have nightmares occasionally. In between jobs a few years' back she'd been to a shrink and he'd told her she was probably suffering post-traumatic stress disorder, and that the degree might increase or lessen as years went by, depending on her future career choices. She'd made her decision, though, when she woke in the back of Chipchase's campervan in Kasane. This was it. She was through with the mercenary game once and for all.

When she saw the big lappet-faced vulture leave the tree and touch down in the grass, wings spread wide like a grotesque angel of death, she wanted to cry again. Why on earth would the death of a half-starved animal past its prime make her want to bawl, while the death of a human had little effect on her? How fucked up, how evil had she become since she'd left Stirling? She shook her head.

"I said, how was Iraq?"

"What?" She looked at John, who had returned his eyes to the bush in front of him. He wrenched the steering wheel to avoid an aardvark hole.

"Iraq? That's where I heard you were."

She glanced behind them and saw Sam's caramel brown legs. She wondered idly if his tan was sprayed on. His head and shoulders were sticking out of the hatch as he watched for game. Sonja nodded toward the American and mouthed "Shush" to John.

The Australian nodded. "Secret women's business, eh?" He winked. "Mum's the word. So, what is it that you do . . . officially?"

"I've told Sam I'm a professional hunter," she said softly.

John laughed. "A hunter with a 5:56-millimeter assault rifle? That's rich. I remember you crying when your dad had to shoot a hyena that had become a problem in camp. OK, professional hunter it is."

"I'll tell you all about it later."

John navigated them back into the parallel deep ruts in the sand that passed for a road through the concession. The Australian had to slow to a near crawl and engage low-range four-wheel drive in some stretches, but it was still faster than bashing through the bush, and certainly quicker than walking.

She looked out over the open grassland. It was beautiful country, even if it was too dry. They passed the big dry pan and four female kudu took flight at the growl of the engine. She loved the way their short white fluffy tails curled over their rumps as they leaped. A cheeky vervet monkey peered at her and blinked when she raised her eyebrows at it.

"I think my sterling rescue effort calls for a liquid celebration," John said. He jabbed a thumb over his shoulder.

Sonja reached around the back of the driver's seat and undid the catch on the Engel fridge's lid. "Beer?"

"Is the Pope a German?"

She grabbed two bottles of Windhoek Lager and handed one to the driver, then craned her head out of the passenger side window. "Elliott?"

"Coke, please missy." She passed the can to the tracker, via Sam. "How about you?"

"Um, it's a little early for beer. Do you have any Diet Coke, John?"

The Australian laughed and shook his head. "You're in Africa, mate, not New York. Give him a beer, Sonja, and hold the twist of lime."

She handed a Windhoek to Sam, who nodded his thanks.

"Stirling'll be pleased to see you, I expect. Pleased, but surprised."

"What do you mean by that?" Sonja asked.

"Best you just wait and see."

With the welcome breeze in his face it was difficult for Sam to hear what John and Sonja were talking about below him. Although it was none of his business, his ears pricked when he heard the word "Iraq."

He wondered, still, exactly what Sonja did and what she was doing riding about the African bush with a military rifle in her hand and a bullet wound in her leg. He could tell, by the lull in their conversation, that Sonja had told John to be quiet.

All the same it was amazing for him to see how different Sonja was around people she knew. She'd been bubbly and talkative and joshing with the Australian. Perhaps he'd see more of this other side of her when they arrived at Xakanaxa, where she'd said she had a friend.

The cold beer was disappearing fast and he was feeling euphoric now that he knew where he was going and what he was doing again. The view was great from the open top of the vehicle and he marveled at the sight of a herd of elephant as they trundled slowly across the road in front of the Land Cruiser. John had stopped to give them right of way. He wished he had his camera, but then wondered if the documentary was even salvageable. He wondered how Cheryl-Ann and the guys were after their ordeal. His time in the bush had been no picnic, but it wasn't on the same scale as being involved in a helicopter crash.

The Australian's mention of Stirling's name, however, gave him something else to worry about.

12

Stirling was standing outside reception at Xakanaxa Camp when he saw the painted dog research vehicle coming up the sand road. Elliott, the wild dog team's chief scout, waved from the roof, his grin wide. No doubt he and John Lemon thought Stirling would be relieved, but he had very mixed emotions about the return of the missing Sam Chapman.

The camp was groaning with people at the moment, adding to his stress levels. If all had gone according to plan the American television crew would have been leaving this morning, but instead they were all arriving after their unplanned absences.

Stirling clenched and unclenched his hands. It had been a difficult few days for him, what with tracking the search-and-rescue plan; the bombshell dropped by the mercenary, Steele, over dinner the previous night; and Tracey's tearful confession that she may have led Chapman on.

He and Tracey had made up last night, with her swearing her love for him and earning his forgiveness well into the small hours of the morning. She'd pouted when he'd returned to the tent, after eleven—late for a man who had to be up before dawn each morning—and asked him what had been so secret about the committee meeting that had prevented her from attending.

"Just politics, babe," he'd said.

Stirling had initially felt bad about passing on Bernard's request that

only committee members attend the dinner, seeing no reason why his partner should be left out. But after hearing what Steele proposed, and the chorus of support from the members that reached a crescendo by the time the
port and cigars had come out, he was glad she hadn't been there. Even
Sabrina Frost had come around in the end.

It was surreal. What had begun as a lobbying and public relations campaign had progressed to a virtual military coup which, if successful, would
see the formation of a new country, or at least gain a greater measure of
sovereignty for the people of the Caprivi Strip. He shook his head. Madness.

John had radioed Xakanaxa two hours earlier, reporting that he had
found Chapman and that the American had been rescued by a stranger who
would need accommodating at the camp.

"I'm full, John, over," Stirling had replied.

"You'll make room for this person, trust me, over," the Aussie had said.

"John, I repeat, there is no room at the inn, over."

"There will be, John, out."

Stirling saw that as well as Elliott, John and Chapman, who was riding
in the back of the cruiser like a dog, with his head sticking out the hatch and
tongue lolling, there was a fourth person in the vehicle. He had his bush hat
pulled down low over his eyes. Stirling sighed. He had no idea where he would
put this stranger. He walked down the wooden ramp as the Cruiser pulled
to a halt.

"G'day," John said, climbing down from the driver's seat. "Special delivery. Two guests, but no tip required. All in a day's work."

Stirling nodded to Sam, who lifted his hand in greeting as he opened the
side door of the four-wheel drive. As soon as the stranger in front opened
the passenger door he saw it was a woman, with shapely legs capped by ragged,
cut-off shorts. He walked around the truck's protruding front bumper bar.

"Hello, I'm—"

She flipped up the brim of her hat and smiled. "I know who you are."

His jaw dropped. He couldn't speak. Pricks of light glittered at the
periphery of his vision.

"Don't you recognize me after all this time?"

He managed to lift his hands, opening his arms. He was so totally taken off guard he didn't have time to register the different emotions that tumbled and turned in his mind.

Sonja closed the gap between them and wrapped her arms around his waist and hugged him tight. "Oh, Stirling," she said, her voice muffled by his chest, "it's so good to see you again."

"I . . ." He hugged her and then gently placed his hands on her shoulders, moving her away so he could look at her. She stared up at him. "Sonja."

She nodded. "*Ja*. It's me."

He tried to think of what to say. Behind him he heard the slap of sandals on the wooden decking. "Hello John, hiya Elliott. Sam."

Tracey stood beside him in the sand. "Hello," she said to Sonja. "I'm Tracey Hawthorne. Looks like you two know each other."

Stirling let go of Sonja. Sam hovered by the Land Cruiser. Stirling would deal with him later, but how was he to handle this meeting? "Um . . . Tracey, this is . . ."

"Sonja Kurtz. I used to live here. When I was a kid. When Stirling and I were younger."

The two women shook hands.

Stirling's mouth felt dry "Tracey is—"

"Stirling's significant other, I suppose you'd call me," she said, wrapping both of her hands around his left bicep. "You must tell me all about what he was like as a boy. I bet he was naughty!" Tracey rose up on her tiptoes and kissed him on the cheek.

He felt his face color. "Sonja, I had no idea . . . I'm . . ."

Sonja took a step back from them and forced a smile. "Stirling, I hate to impose, but I was hoping you might have a staff tent or somewhere I could kip for a couple of days."

He ran a hand through his hair, but Tracey clung firmly to his other arm. "Of course. No problem. John told me he had someone who needed somewhere to stay."

Tracey looked up at him. "We're awfully busy, Stirling. Perhaps in the staff compound?"

"That's fine by me," Sonja said.

Sam cleared his throat. "Excuse me. Stirling?"

Stirling looked at him, the memories of the night he had caught the American and Tracey rising like bile. "Sam?"

"I presume you have a safari tent for me to stay in?"

He presumed. The hide of the bloody man. Stirling swallowed his anger for now—though he fully intended to vent it later. "Yes, of course. I'll have someone show you to your suite in just a second, if—"

"No."

"No?"

"No. Sonja will be sleeping in my safari tent tonight—alone—and for the duration of my stay."

"That won't be necessary, Sam. Your booking has been arranged. You, Cheryl-Ann, Gerry and your replacement cameraman each have your own suites."

"I'll bunk in with Gerry. He won't mind. Sonja can have my tent. I insist on it."

"Sam, I'm fine," Sonja said.

He shook his head. "No, I won't hear of it. You'll stay in my suite and Wildlife World will be paying for all your meals, drinks and other incidentals."

Sonja looked at Stirling and all he could do was shrug.

"It's the least I can do after your friend here saved my life, Stirling," Sam said.

Stirling didn't like people taking control of his camp, but the American's offer did solve a problem. Sonja couldn't come and stay with him and Tracey, and the staff compound was actually full. The camera crew's replacement pilot also needed accommodation and had taken the last bed. Sonja would have been sleeping on a cot in someone else's hut. "Very well. Tracey, could you please show Sonja to tent eight?"

"Of course, *darl.*"

Bloody hell, Stirling thought. He wondered what he had just put in train as his new girlfriend led the first love of his life away. He cleared his throat. "Sam, if you've got a minute?"

"Sure." Chapman squared his shoulders as though girding himself for a fight.

"John, Elliott, thanks so much, guys. Please go through to the dining area. Brunch is being served, so help yourselves. On us."

"You ripper," John said, clapping a hand on Elliott's shoulder. "Come on, mate, let's get stuck in. It'll be better tucker than the research camp."

Once the other two were out of earshot, Stirling walked over to the Land Cruiser, where Sam was retrieving his daypack. "Cheryl-Ann, Gerry and the new man, Jim his name is, will be at brunch in a few minutes. Ray's in Maun hospital with a broken arm and is under observation for suspected concussion. Apparently Cheryl-Ann tried to sign him out, but the doctors wouldn't allow it."

Sam nodded. "Sounds like Cheryl-Ann." He put his pack down on the ground. "Look, Stirling, I just want to explain . . ."

Stirling took a step forward and stood toe to toe. They were of equal height and build. The American didn't flinch as their eyes met, like a couple of impala rams about to lock horns to establish their dominance. He dropped his voice. "Save your explanations. Tracey was in tears after you left. She seems to think she might have led you on, but I'm not so sure. If you're the sort of man who thinks that if a girl dresses in a certain way or is friendly to you then you can assault her, then I don't want you in my camp, no matter how rich or famous you are. Are we on the same channel, Mr. Chapman? Are we watching the same program, *Coyote* Sam?"

Stirling watched the other man for a reaction. He half hoped he'd raise his hand to him, or try to malign Tracey. He wanted so much to finish what he'd started and to plant his fist in the middle of that big, perfect, all-American pretty-boy face of his. Chapman opened his mouth and Stirling's fingers curled.

Sam moistened his lips with the tip of his tongue. "We are."

Stirling felt cheated, impotent. He wondered if he should *klap* Chapman just for the hell of it, to let his message sink in. The red mist cleared, though, just as it was about to overtake him. Something else in his brain reminded him of the conversation with Cheryl-Ann. The extra mentions of the camp's name, guaranteed in the program, and the glowing review on the Wildlife World website. He'd been furious at Cheryl-Ann, as well, but as much as he tried he couldn't dismiss what the producer had said to him at the close of their brief meeting that morning.

"And Stirling," she'd said, "speaking as a woman who's been around the block a couple of times and worked with some pretty big-name celebrities, keep an eye on your girlfriend. She's a star-fucker—a groupie."

Stirling turned his back on Chapman and hopefully on the whole damned mess. He started walking back up the ramp to reception. He had even more to occupy his mind now that Sonja had returned to Xakanaxa.

"I see you know Sonja," Sam said.

Stirling stopped and turned.

"She's a great girl. I wasn't exaggerating when I said she saved my life."

Stirling raised his right index finger and pointed at Chapman. "If you lay a finger on her, I'll kill you."

"Who, Sonja?"

"Yes." Stirling walked back up the ramp to reception.

"So tell me, Tracey, how long have you and Stirling been together?" Sonja tried as hard as she could to sound as though she was just being polite, making small talk.

"Let me see . . . three months, thirteen days and," she checked her watch, "forty-one minutes. I came here with my mom, from Johannesburg, as a guest, and the rest . . . well . . . the rest you can figure out for yourself."

She was skinny. And young. Too skinny. Too young. A Johannesburg *Kugel* from her painted toenails to her dyed blond hair. Sonja followed her pert young bum up the stairs. Water spattered the ground beside the tent and Sonja looked up to see where it was coming from. A sprinkler irrigation system had been set up on top of the roof and a constant trickle ran down over the waterproof fly sheet above the green canvas safari tent.

"Bush air-conditioning, Stirling calls it," Tracey said.

"It's new. Everything looks new." At the foot of the stairs leading up to the platform on which the tent sat was a welded steel sculpture of a leopard. The artist had captured the slinking cat's essence—a balance of strength and stealth.

Tracey nodded. "Yes, Stirling's put a lot of work into renovating and replacing things around the camp. The place had gone to rack and ruin under the previous manager. He was an alcoholic, apparently."

"He was my father."

"Oh, you're *that* Sonja. Sorry."

Cow, Sonja thought. She obviously knew exactly who she was. "Yes, that one."

The small deck in front of the safari tent was shaded by the roof's overhang and a mopane tree. The view looked out across a channel of the Khwai River, which was about four meters wide at this point and led to the Xakanaxa Lagoon. It was much narrower than Sonja remembered it. Tall pampas grass and reeds sprouted on the far side of the channel. A hippopotamus grunted somewhere nearby. Tracey unzipped the green mosquito mesh door and led the way into the suite, which Sonja had to admit looked beautiful.

Sonja dumped her bag on the fine cotton duvet. At the foot of the king-sized bed was a bedspread in leopard print. Looking around, she saw the room was trimmed with the same fabric. The leopard suite had a sexy, predatory feel about it, which she liked. She did not, however, like the girl, at all. "And what do you do here . . . ?"

"Tracey." She flicked a lock of straightened blond hair from her face. "I'm the catering manager."

"You tell the African chefs which dish to cook each night."

Tracey pursed her lips. "You're joking, right? It's a demanding job."

Sonja smiled and shrugged. "I lived here for several years. I know all the jobs—I did most of them when I was a teenager."

"That long ago? Well, brunch is ready when you are. You should freshen up. Seriously." Tracey wrinkled her nose.

Sonja bit back the retort as the waiflike creature walked out onto the deck and down the stairs, her tread as light as a rat's. She sat on the big soft bed and took off her hiking boots and socks. Unfortunately, the smug little bitch was right. The rest of her clothes she stripped as she walked to the rear of the tent and opened the wooden door which led to the open-air shower. She kicked her smelly clothes into a pile as she turned the hot tap on full. The gas hot water geyser kicked in with a *woomf* and Sonja's mind flashed back instantly to the exploding helicopter gunship. Would they find her here? She doubted it.

She was filthy. She looked at her fingernails, which were brown with the horse's blood. She felt a lump in her throat and swallowed hard. "Enough," she said out loud. She looked up into the trees to see if she could spot a pretty bird, or a squirrel or even a lizard. Something alive.

It was no good, the tears sprung from her eyes and her body started to shake with the sobs as something in her fucked-up brain forced her to replay the scene of the horse lying there, bleeding. She felt the M4 in her hands and saw the animal's head across the open sights. She felt the kick in her shoulder of the single round, saw the entry hole and heard the horse's final shudder. And then it was over.

She held her face under the scalding water, sluicing the tears away, and wondered if she would ever be normal. She unwrapped the plastic from a translucent bar of soap and scratched at it, filling her dirty nails so that when she squirted the nicely scented shampoo into her palm and started lathering and massaging her scalp her nails would be cleaned as well. Wincing, she peeled the dressing from her thigh. The wound was still puckered, but there was little blood oozing and the skin was a healthy pink. "Fucker." She wished she could have killed the man who shot her.

Short showers were part of barracks life and she was finished in less than three minutes.

Her only regret, as she toweled herself dry and turned on the complimentary hair dryer, was that she would have to get into her dirty clothes. She ran her fingers through her hair as she blasted it, but then she thought she heard someone calling. She turned off the dryer.

"Housekeeping! Madam? Sorry?"

Sonja took a cotton kimono from a hanger and belted it around her waist. When she stepped into the main part of the tent there was an African maid standing with a small pile of clothes in her hand. "Madam, these are for you."

Sonja shook her head. She didn't recognize the woman, who was in her late teens or early twenties. "Not mine. They must be for Mr. Chapman. Is it his laundry or something?"

The woman held a hand to her mouth to stifle a giggle. "No, madam, not *for* Mr. Chapman. *From* Mr. Chapman. He is saying that this is a gift, for you, madam."

"A gift?"

The maid smiled and placed the clothes down on the bed and turned to walk out. "Um . . . thank you." Sonja padded to the bed. On top of the clothes was a folded piece of paper. It was a note, handwritten on Xakanaxa stationery. *Hi Sonja. Please don't think me presumptuous but I noticed you didn't have much luggage. Feel free to return or exchange anything you don't like. Just wanted to say thanks for the last couple of days. Sam C.*

She reread it. It was predictably verbose. She sorted through the stack of clothes. There were two safari shirts, one short-sleeved in green and the other long-sleeved khaki, in two different sizes, although either would have fitted. She smiled. There were also two pairs of trousers—the kind with the removable lower legs that zipped off. This was tourist-only wear and normally she wouldn't be seen dead in them, but she had nothing else that was clean. She tried on both pairs of trousers but the second fit better so she left those on. The short-sleeved blouse was fine. Her sports bra was rank, so she left it off. Her breasts weren't huge, but she was proud that at thirty-eight years of age they were still pert enough for her to go without if she wasn't exercising.

She ran the brush through her damp hair and tied it back while she thought about the gift. No man had ever bought her clothes before. The selection would be limited in the Xakanaxa gift shop and she probably would have bought the exact same articles, so there was a practical sensibility about it. It wasn't as though he'd bought her lingerie or a cocktail dress. However, the fact that he'd even thought about her and her dilemma of what to wear to brunch was . . . what was the word? Sweet? It wasn't a word that filtered through to her world very often. "Weird," she said out loud. She giggled—something she hadn't done in quite a while.

Reluctantly she reached for her dirty socks and boots, then dropped them on the floor with a thud. "Fuck it." She unzipped the lower part of her new pants, turning them into shorts, and walked out of the tent, barefoot. She padded down the sandy pathway to the dining area feeling like a kid again.

13

Sam tried to remember his manners and not talk with his mouth full, but it was hard. The food was good and the buffet table was still groaning invitingly, but it seemed everyone wanted to hear everybody else's stories all at once.

He'd helped himself to bacon, both lamb and pork sausages, fried tomato, toast, mushrooms and ordered two fried eggs, sunny-side up, from the cheery African woman cooking the eggs to order. His plate was almost empty already, but he knew he still had room for more.

John Lemon was next to him at the long wooden dining table, now onto coffee, while Cheryl-Ann was seated opposite him. On one side of her was a sun-tanned square-jawed English guy called Steele, who said he worked in security, while on the other was another Australian, a thin guy in his thirties called Jim Rickards, who had an unfashionable ponytail and a big mouth.

"So have you done much wildlife filming, Jim?" Sam said in between mouthfuls of runny egg.

"Sure have. Been up in Chobe and Savuti the last month shooting lions—on video that is. Boom-boom."

Sam smiled politely. "Lucky that Cheryl-Ann found you."

"I reckon. I was at Maun in the Mack Air lounge waiting for a plane back to Jo'burg and a month of no work on the horizon, when hurricane Cheryl-Ann here," he nodded to the producer, "swept in like Katrina on steroids."

Cheryl-Ann chewed her food. Sam guessed that Cheryl-Ann wanted to slap the cocky cameraman, but was forcing herself to be tolerant in case he found out too soon what she was really like and decided to get back on the next plane to Maun. When he'd heard Ray was out of action he'd wondered whether the whole project would have to be shelved or, worse, canceled.

Cheryl-Ann swallowed. "It was a stressful time. I thought Ray might have just dislocated his arm or something, but it was a bad break—all round. We were lucky that Jim was passing through at the right time and right place."

"To tell you the truth," Rickards said, with toast crumbs spattering the table, "I've mostly done news in the past, but I love wildlife filming and really want to get into more of it. I'm stoked to be working with you, Sam, and I'm not pissing in your pocket."

"Excuse me?"

"Sucking up. Arse-licking . . . excuse my French."

Sam nodded.

Stirling sat at the head of the table, a perpetual frown on his face. Sam wondered if the hatchet really had been buried, or if Stirling was still holding it behind his back. Tracey sat next to him, on his right, two away from Sam. She hadn't acknowledged him since he'd arrived for brunch, and that was just fine by Sam. When he glanced at them he saw Tracey had reached out and laid her hand over Stirling's in a gesture of loyalty—or was that propriety? Everyone's eyes turned when Sonja said, "Good morning."

When she'd found him she'd looked like an Amazonian guerilla, her face streaked with a camouflage pattern of dust and dried perspiration, her cut-off shorts grimy from her hours on horseback and her tank top mottled with dirt and body salts. The M4 on her shoulder and the bloodstained dressing on her thigh were the perfect accessories and matched her hard-arsed stare.

Now, however, freshly showered, barefoot and unarmed she was a dif-

ferent person. She smiled—a little self-consciously and definitely for Stirling, Sam noted—and introductions were made.

Sam pushed back his chair. "Hello again." He stood and all of the
other men still seated at the table were embarrassed into following his gesture. Politeness cost nothing, Sam figured, and this woman was worthy of
his respect.

He had already forgotten the names of the other half-dozen people
either still at the table or taking their coffee further down the deck. Stirling
had said, when introducing them, that they were mostly other lodge owners
who had come to Xakanaxa the night before for a regular meeting about
tourism and land-use issues. It explained why no one had been out game
viewing this morning, as these guys, and the one woman in their midst, had
seen it all before. He remembered her name, Sabrina. She was an environmentalist and he wanted to talk to her before she left.

"Martin. Fancy seeing you here. What a surprise," Sonja said when
Steele remained standing after the others had sat down again.

"I could say the same thing," the Englishman said, "but I was fairly
sure you'd come home to roost."

"You two know each other?" Stirling said.

Genius, thought Sam, but he was just as intrigued as Stirling to find
out the connection between Steele and Sonja.

"Long story," Sonja said. "I'm sure Martin will tell you all about it, right
after he's told me what he's doing here in the middle of the Okavango Delta."

The midmorning sun caught the highlights in Sonja's auburn hair,
making it glow like polished copper. It was still a little damp, but that just
added to its metallic sheen. Sam wondered what it would be like to run his
fingers through the cool, damp softness. He glanced at Stirling and saw that
he was following her too, with his eyes, as she walked to the buffet and filled
a bowl with fruit salad.

"You hit the gift shop early, I see," Stirling said.

Sonja found an empty seat on the other side of Jim Rickards.

"No, I . . ." She looked across the table at Sam, who gave a sharp shake
of his head before Stirling could register. "I asked one of the maids if she

could wash some clothes for me later, because all I had was what I was wearing, and she rushed off and came back with these. Sweet, hey?"

"Nice threads," said Rickards, using the news as a chance to inspect her chest. "I'm James—my friends call me Jim, or Jimbob."

"Sonja. Mine call me Sonja."

"And where do you fit into this merry little menagerie here at Kakawhatever?"

"I'm just passing through," she said.

"Maybe, maybe not," said Martin Steele and the others at the table looked at him.

Cheryl-Ann wiped her mouth with her linen serviette. "Martin here was just telling me, Sam, that we should seriously consider taking some security with us on our trip into the Caprivi Strip."

Sam chewed his bacon, then swallowed. "Some?"

"Someone," Steele said. "Since the failed attack on the Okavango Dam the Namibian Army and police have been on high alert. My organization has been monitoring the situation in Caprivi and we believe there are still irregular forces of the Caprivi Liberation Army on the loose and active in the region."

"I'm sorry, Martin. Your organization?"

"Corporate Solutions."

"No shit." Jim Rickards nearly choked on a piece of sausage. He gulped a quick mouthful of orange juice and croaked: "The mercenary mob?"

Steele smiled and shook his head. "Security risk assessment consultants."

"Right," said Rickards. "War dogs. Cool."

"Think what you might, but I'd say a well-heeled, well-equipped film crew carrying, what . . . tens of thousands of dollars worth of gear . . ."

"Try hundreds, dude," Rickards interjected.

"Very well, hundreds of thousands of dollars worth of gear might be just the sort of target the guerillas in the Caprivi region are after. They're short of funds and they need to re-equip after their recent defeat. They haven't resorted to K and R yet, but . . . who knows?"

"K and R?" asked Gerry, who had so far been content to eat in silence.

"Kidnap and ransom," Steele provided.

"What do you think, Stirling? You know the area," Cheryl-Ann said.

Sam had been glancing at the lodge manager during the conversation. At first he thought Stirling would dismiss Steele's concerns. He'd noticed Stirling closing his eyes and, almost imperceptibly, shaking his head when Steele explained the possible threat. Was Steele just a sharp businessman who spotted a way to make a fast buck from a bunch of naive Americans?

"I think I can see where Martin's coming from."

Cheryl-Ann frowned. "What does that mean?"

"There's also the question of a guide—someone who knows the lie of the land, the local languages if needs be. Cheryl-Ann, you told me earlier that your helicopter pilot was going to double as your guide for the trip to Namibia."

She nodded. "That's right. We do have to find another, in a hurry. Stirling, I don't suppose you'd be interested?"

"Oh, I'm *so* sorry, Cheryl-Ann, but as soon as you all leave I've got back-to-back bookings for the next two weeks."

Interesting, thought Sam, as only a few days ago Stirling was bemoaning the state of business. Sam was relieved, though, because he didn't fancy the idea of spending any more time with the man than was necessary.

"Surely time's a factor as well, Cheryl-Ann?" Steele cooed.

She frowned again and nodded. "Yes, we're already way behind on the shooting of the survival scenes—we'll have to make that up on the road somewhere—and we've got to fly back to Maun, pick up our transportation and try and find a safari guide, all in the next two days."

Steele sipped some coffee and laid his cup down on its saucer. "It seems to me that the answer to all your problems is right here."

Sam looked up and down the table and his eyes, along with Steele's, came to rest on Sonja, who was staring back at the Englishman with a look that pleaded with him not to say . . .

"Sonja is just the right person for you and your team, Cheryl-Ann."

"Hey! Great idea. I didn't know you were a guide, Sonja," Sam said.

Before she could speak Steele pressed home his attack. "She is. A first-rate one at that. Knows the African bush like the back of her hand. Born in Namibia, grew up in Botswana, and speaks German, Ovambo, Afrikaans, Tswana and a smattering of Lozi, if I recall correctly."

"Not much at all," Sonja said. "And Martin, no, I don't—"

"What Sonja's saying is that she doesn't mind at all. You've heard from Sam what a fine job she did saving him from the jaws of hell. She'll be able to give you a wealth of ideas for your survival segment, as well as navigate you around the wilds of Namibia. She's also a qualified close personal protection operative. Bodyguard, that is."

Sam had forgotten his food. He leaned forward, elbows on the table. "I thought you were a professional hunter?"

Sonja glared at Steele. "Martin. Please . . ."

"Who do you work for, Sonja?" Sam asked.

"Sonja," Steele said, "works for me."

Damn him, Sonja thought as she looked out over the river and the gently swaying pampas grass. She slapped the wooden railing of the deck. "Fuck."

"The girl who left us all behind never used the F-word," Stirling said.

She turned and faced him. After Steele had offered her services, with as much subtlety and thought for her reaction as a pimp, she had excused herself from the table, saying, "Can we discuss this later, Martin?," and strode along the deck near the lounge area. She still loved Martin, in a platonic sort of a way, but he infuriated her sometimes with his Sandhurst officer's arrogance and his unflinching assumption that she would do as he commanded. What irked her more than anything was that he was usually right.

"I've changed, Stirling. There's lots you don't know about me. That's why I came back here, to talk to you."

"You did?"

"Stirling, I . . ." She was lost for words. How could she tell him why she was here when she wasn't a hundred percent sure herself, particularly since she'd arrived to find him shacked up with a poppy almost young enough to be his daughter. What should she say? "Stirling, I've come here to say you should ask me to marry you and we should live out our days with my seven-teen-year-old daughter—who I haven't told you about—happily ever after here in the swamps?"

". . . I was hoping we could spend some time together."

Stirling had brought a bread roll with him from the brunch table. He ripped off a chunk and tossed it over the railing into the water below the deck. Some bream appeared and began feeding. He stared out over the water. "I cried after you left, Sonja. Not very macho. Not very safari guide. There were women, a long time later, and quite a few before Tracey, but none of them lasted long. I suppose I was always waiting for you to come back, but it's been a hell of a long wait."

Sonja looked back, past the jackalberry tree that the new deck had been constructed around, to the dining area beyond. A few of the guests lingered there and she saw Tracey looking at her, and at Stirling. "Is it serious?"

"With Tracey? I think so. We've been together for three months. She's living with me here."

He *thinks* so. "She's very pretty."

"And young. I know what you're thinking."

"It's none of my business," Sonja said.

"I know why Steele has offered you to the Americans as a bodyguard," he said, changing the subject.

"Really? Then perhaps you can explain it to me."

He looked around. "You're a mercenary."

"Says who?"

Stirling shrugged. "Word gets around. Everyone knows you went off to join the army, but you left after only a year or two. You know how Maun feeds on gossip. Do you remember Heyn, the South African guide who drove his Land Rover through the wall of the Sports Bar that night we snuck in?"

She nodded, knowing what Stirling was going to say next. She recalled the night—they were both still underage—and, years later, meeting Heyn, the Afrikaner, in Kabul. He was working as a security contractor. The last person she expected to meet there was someone from the dusty safari town of Maun.

"He said he saw you in Afghanistan. That you were carrying an assault rifle and wearing body armor."

"I do close protection—bodyguarding—sometimes."

Stirling shook his head. "I think it's more than that. You show up here carrying a rifle and pistol, with a bandaged leg after sneaking onto a concession and into the game reserve like a poacher. I don't think you're a bodyguard, Sonja."

She looked down at the water. The snout and eyes of a crocodile broke the surface. "Hey! That's not Popcorn, is it?"

"Don't change the subject," Stirling said.

"Why not? It was OK for you to do so when I was asking about Tracey."

The crocodile was about two meters long. It propelled itself deftly through the shallow water and took a piece of bread in its mouth.

"Yes, it's Popcorn. He was just a baby when you left."

"*Ja.* I used to get mad at my old man feeding him popcorn when he was little. And now you're doing the same thing."

"Not me. I drop the bread in and he takes some, not to eat, but to use as bait. Watch him. He's clever."

Sonja stared intently at Popcorn, who submerged himself just below the surface, a piece of bread sticking out the tip of his snout. He kept himself stationary and after a short while the bolder of the fish began moving toward him, scenting the bait but unaware of the fisherman. A bream began nibbling and Popcorn struck, flicking his tail to propel himself forward like a torpedo. Water splashed as his jaws snapped shut and he disappeared into the depths of the river with the dying fish flapping in his mouth.

"He's clever," she agreed. "But you're still giving him an unfair advantage."

"I know. I'm worried about Steele and this mad plan of his."

Sonja didn't know what Stirling was talking about so she asked him to explain. Indecision creased Stirling's face. He took a deep breath and rested both hands on the railing. He exhaled and moved closer to Sonja, lowering his voice: "He's going to blow up the dam on the Okavango River."

"What?"

"And that's not all."

As he explained the plan to destroy the dam and foment an insurrection in the Caprivi Strip Sonja had to work hard to concentrate. The smell of his aftershave was competing with his words. He'd worn it the first day they made love—the first time she recalled him using aftershave. It was Old Spice. He told her later it was what he thought a man should wear, and he was still using the same brand. It was an outdated scent, something the hero in a Wilbur Smith book would have worn, but she would forever associate it with first-time sex, with love. It still did the trick.

"Thanks for letting me know," she said to him honestly. Martin had a flair for the dramatic when it came to handing out assignments and he didn't like to give his operatives too long to think before accepting a job.

"Surely he won't get you to blow up the dam while you're there with the Americans?"

She looked back at the dining table. Martin was talking to Cheryl-Ann and Sam, who was nodding his head enthusiastically. Tracey made no attempt to hide the fact that she was watching her and Stirling. "No. It'll be a CTR."

"Stop talking like a soldier, Sonja."

"Sorry. A close target reconnaissance. I've got to hand it to him, it's a good cover for me to go in with the TV crew. They're expected and they'll get unfettered access to the construction site." Very clever, she thought, looking down again at the water. Martin Steele was a canny predator as well. CTRs were one of her specialties. A woman could go places a man couldn't, and charm her way past officials. In the past she'd played the part of a nurse, a wildlife researcher and a teacher to scope out potential targets. She caught a flash of Tracey's orange T-shirt in her peripheral vision, then heard her sandals on the floorboards. "Can we talk, later, in private somewhere, Stirling? It's important."

He looked around and saw Tracey. "Not sure. It might be difficult."

Fuck, she thought again. After all these years he couldn't even spare her the time to talk.

Tracey took hold of Stirling's arm. "Babe, Bernard and the others are going to catch their flight. I thought you'd want to see them off."

Babe? Stirling looked at her and smiled an apology as his partner—or whatever Tracey wanted to call herself—led him away. Martin left the Americans and their new cameraman to discuss things among themselves, and walked over to join her at the railing.

"Crocodile," he said, looking down at Popcorn. "Nasty things, but ruthlessly efficient and devilishly cunning."

"Like you."

"Let me walk you back to your tent, we have things to discuss," Steele said.

"So I hear." They left the deck and took the sandy pathway. A female bushbuck looked up at them but, sensing they were no threat, carried on nibbling on some grass. Its coat was mangy and Sonja wondered if its condition was due to the drought.

"I should tell you what we're up to," Steele said.

"You're going to blow up the dam on the Okavango and start a civil war in Namibia."

Steele cleared his throat. "I do hope Stirling isn't going to tell *all* his old friends about our plans, otherwise I might have to kill him."

"I'm not interested," she said.

Steele laughed. "Why must we always go through this hard-to-get act, Sonja? The best thing you can do for your daughter is make more money, and I'm the only one who can give it to you. We both know that."

It irked her that he knew she'd been thinking about Emma. She shook her head as they walked. "The Zimbabwe job was a wake-up call for me, Martin. I nearly didn't make it out this time."

"You're still in shock. You've had close calls before. Besides, I think I know now what went wrong. We were double-crossed."

"That seems pretty bloody obvious. There was no one in the limos, Martin. They knew I'd be there. I was bait." She thought again of the crocodile luring its prey with the piece of bread.

He reached into the pocket of his chinos and pulled out a photograph. "Do you recognize this man?"

She took it and studied it. It was a covert surveillance photo of a black man wearing a business suit, leaning forward over what looked like a restaurant table, with his elbows on the white tablecloth and his hands clasped together. He was talking to another man and Sonja could tell by the haircut and the familiar broadness of the shoulders that the person with his back to the camera was Martin. The African man's head was shaved and he had a thin mustache that crawled along the top edge of his upper lip and looked out of place on his jowly face. "He was on the helicopter—both helicopters. The Hind I shot down, and later on the Alouette. He's the bastard who shot me. He was in uniform, though."

"Damn. It's no satisfaction being right."

"Who is he, and what the hell were you doing with him?"

"His name is Major Kenneth Sibanda. Zimbabwean Central Intelligence Organization."

"What the hell were you doing dealing with the CIO? Did he tell you he was a traitor?"

"No, he said he represented a splinter group of the main opposition party. After I heard your news I emailed a scan of this picture to a contact of mine at the British Embassy in Harare and asked if they knew who he was. They did."

She stopped on the pathway and placed her hands on her hips. "It might have helped if you'd checked him out in advance."

He brushed away her concerns with a wave of his hand. "Who with? I couldn't very well have gone to the embassy and said, 'Excuse me, chaps, do you know this fellow? He's paying me two million dollars to assassinate the president,' now, could I? I'm sorry, Sonja—and you know I don't say the S-word, ever."

She chewed her lower lip then started walking again. "So you're saying the Zimbabwean CIO promised you two million dollars to organize a bogus hit on the president in order to discredit the opposition and garner some sympathy for the old man?"

Steele nodded. "And I'm afraid their plan seems to have worked. The American government has issued a statement condemning political assassination, no matter how serious the grievances against a leader, and the UK government has had to deny strenuously it had anything to do with the 'plot.' The president is all over CNN and BBC World, claiming the moral high ground for the first time in decades."

"Those men . . ." She thought of the uniformed bodies she'd seen on the road beside the *bakkie* and the driver of the police car that had hurtled into the chasm left by the exploding bridge.

Martin placed a hand on her shoulder. "Their own government agency sacrificed them—killed them—not you, Sonja. Look on the bright side—at least you and I got to split the million-dollar down payment. The president might have bought himself a few weeks of good PR, but you and I didn't do too badly out of it either."

"Jesus, Martin, don't joke about it. I've had enough of killing."

They stopped at the path to her tent and Martin left his hand on her shoulder. "CTR, Sonja. That's all I want."

"Yeah, right. For now."

He smiled. "For now. You always were the smartest on the team. I want you to go to Namibia with the Yanks. They'll think you're their bodyguard, but Cheryl-Ann will tell the authorities at the dam that you're their substitute safari guide. I've told her the Namibian government would be suspicious if she said you were their bodyguard, as they're trying to downplay the threat to foreigners in the strip."

"There is no threat to foreigners," Sonja said.

"I know that and you know that, and the Namibian government knows that, but Cheryl-Ann and her Coyote boy don't. She's already loving the intrigue of it all, but of course she doesn't know your real mission. You know what I need—troop numbers, dispositions, a progress report on construction . . . a full recce."

"I told you, I'm not interested. I've had enough. I quit."

"Let me come into your tent so we can discuss this in private."

She shrugged his hand off her shoulder, though there was little fight and no malice in her gesture. She knew exactly what he wanted from her. There was a time when she'd succumbed to and taken solace in his smooth words and the touch of those strong hands. Life might have been simpler for her if she'd forgiven him his infidelity and gambling and taken him back to her bed. Emma would have had a father and she could have stayed at home and raised her daughter. She started walking toward her tent and as she did she knew it would never have worked out between them. She could never be happy as a housewife and stay-at-home mum and Martin, damn him, knew it.

"What are you going to do, Sonja? Stay here and play happy families with Stirling?"

She stopped and tried to fight the urge to turn around.

"Tracey might not be too happy about that. Stirling's the one you left behind when you joined the army, isn't he?"

She wouldn't let him bait her, wouldn't rise to his taunts.

"You're a beautiful woman, Sonja, but you ran out on your childhood sweetheart. Tracey is gorgeous, and she's got her hooks into him. Even me, a simple soldier, can see that. What did you think, that you could just show up unannounced and get Stirling to pick up where you left off—where you left him—twenty years ago?"

He had the hook into her. He didn't have to twist it so hard. "Bastard."

He laughed, and she grimaced as she looked over her shoulder. He pulled the cigarettes from his pocket, flipped the lid and drew one out with his long fingers. His electric lighter clicked and she smelled the smoke across the gulf between them. She clenched her fists, wanting the strength to fight the addiction, but craving it all the same.

"Does he know about Emma, Sonja?"

She looked ahead again, down the path toward the river that had been part of her life with Stirling all those years ago. Part of her wished she could turn back time, but she knew that back when she'd left this place, it was something that she'd needed to do. She left Martin and followed the path to her tent.

14

From the air she could see even more evidence of the river's strangulation, of the slow death of an ecosystem, but it was cold comfort to her, knowing there might be some good in the mission she was embarking on. Her life, her future, was as barren as the parched Kalahari sandveld passing below.

She leaned her head against the Perspex window of the Mack Air Gippsland Airvan, which had all the charm of a flying caravan. The noise and vibrations from the engine almost, but not quite, drowned out the sound of Cheryl-Ann heaving into a paper bag behind her, but they couldn't kill the smell. Sonja stared down at Africa below her, filtered gray through a haze created by far-off but ever-present fires. Traditionally, African farmers burned their lands to clear them before the rains came. But what if the rains didn't come? Ash and dust blanketed the countryside, the first symptoms of a slow painful demise.

Stick figure shadows gave away tiny giraffes on the ground and the elephants were dark ink blobs on dirty parchment. As they crossed the cut line that marked the southern border of Moremi there were more and more signs of human habitation. Long mekoros, traditional canoes made of hollowed sausage trees, lay encased in dried mud, waiting to be floated by the rains and water that might never come. Likewise, the woven reed walls that were laid by villagers to trap fish moving down the delta's tendrils now looked like cattle fences on some barren grassless farm.

Martin had done as his snide remark to her had implied. He'd told Stirling about Emma before she could get to him. In a way, she didn't mind too much, as it saved her from broaching the subject with Stirling.

"Why didn't you say something, about your daughter?" Stirling had said to her the previous day when she'd found him by the shallow-draft aluminum boats. He was supervising the loading of fuel and a cold-box full of drinks onto the craft. "Thanks, Paul," he said to the African guide, who stepped off the boat and retreated back to the deck, where a big black metal teapot was boiling on a brazier of hot coals. Paul would serve the guests—Cheryl-Ann and her crew in this case—tea, coffee and biscuits before their afternoon cruise on the river and out into the Xakanaxa lagoon.

"I didn't get the chance. Tracey whisked you away before I could tell you. I told you I wanted to talk to you in private."

"Tracey? Don't drag her into this, Sonja."

She flared, her limited stock of patience exhausted. "I'm not dragging anyone into this, Stirling. Who told you—Steele?"

"What if he did?"

She wanted to tell him the truth, as she saw it, that Steele was trying to drive a wedge between her and Stirling, so that he wouldn't want her to stay at Xakanaxa. How could she tell him all that without sounding paranoid?

"Stirling, please. Emma, my daughter, was . . ." She stopped herself before she said "an accident." "Unplanned. I've wanted to tell you about her since she was born. She was part of the reason, though, why I haven't come back before now."

"Who's the father?"

She took a deep breath. It was actually none of his business. "It's complicated."

"Jesus, Sonja, what did you get up to in the army?"

She resented him inferring she was some kind of slut. To many soldiers in the army women were either sluts or bitches. Sluts slept with everyone, while bitches slept with everyone except you. Sonja always knew it would be difficult, telling Stirling, but this whole scene was going pear-shaped. She ignored his remark. "I've told Steele that I'm not going to Namibia with the Americans. They can find their own guide and bodyguard."

"I'm pleased about that, at least," he said, dragging the boat a little further up on to the riverbank, then wiping his hands on his shorts. "I can't believe that the overwhelming majority of the defense committee's members voted to employ a bunch of mercenaries, Sonja. Even Sabrina Frost, the environmentalist, went along with Steele's hare-brained bloody scheme in the end. Starting a war is no way to save the Okavango. I'm going to try to get some of the other lodge owners to change their minds about the whole thing. It's crazy."

Frankly, right then she didn't care about the dam, the liberation of the Caprivi Strip, or how much money a bunch of rich foreign investors stood to lose if the river dried up for good. All she wanted to talk about was her and Stirling, but she couldn't find the words. Facing gunfire was easier.

"What will you do? Where will you go?" He stood in front of her, his hands on his hips, the distance between them as wide as an ocean.

"Um . . . I thought perhaps we could take it slow, catch up on old times. Talk about what we've been up to, and—"

"I know what you've been up to, Sonja. You're a mercenary and a single mom. Me, I'm still the same old Stirling, stuck out here in the middle of the bush. You got your adventure, and then some."

She gritted her teeth, chomping back the retort. He was acting like a spoiled child. She exhaled. Behind her she could hear the twang of the Australian cameraman's voice, followed by raucous laughter. Time. She needed more time. "I was hoping I could stay here for a couple of days."

The mournful cry of a fish eagle gave Stirling an excuse to look away from her, out over the forest of grass that almost choked the river. "I'm sorry, Sonja, we've got no room. Also, you know the camp rules. If you're not on staff then we have to organize payment of park entry fees et cetera."

"Well, put me on staff then. I'll clean the fucking tents for you if you want, Stirling."

He looked at her now, emboldened. "You didn't talk like that when you were younger and you didn't want to work here then. What changed you, Sonja?"

"Stirling!" They both turned and saw Tracey striding along the deck, waving. "Call for you, at reception. It's Bernard, following up on your meeting."

"Coming," he replied. He looked back at Sonja. "I'm sorry." He walked off.

Sonja could have sworn that Tracey was smiling at her, but she found herself surrounded by the film crew a moment later, as they started loading cameras, tripods, spare batteries and cases onto the boat.

Sam had invited her to accompany them on the cruise, but she figured she would be spending enough time with the television people over the coming week, so she declined. Stirling had rejected her and Tracey had made sure Sonja didn't get the opportunity to have another shot at winning back his affection. Sonja had called Emma from the camp and the monosyllabic responses she'd come to expect from her daughter reminded her, to her shame, that she had nowhere else in the world to go right then except where Martin Steele chose to send her. She'd sought out Steele and told him she would take the CTR job. At least he'd been kind enough not to say he knew she would come around.

She felt miserable and stupid. What right did she have to expect Stirling would open his arms, and his safari camp, to her? She'd returned to the only place in the world she could imagine herself living, long term, to find herself locked out—an unwanted guest. She'd gone back to her tent and started packing. Afterward, she'd gone to find old Amos, who had been the chef when she was a kid and was still working in the kitchen. He'd hugged her, dampening her bush shirt with his perspiration, but she hadn't minded. It was nice to be held by someone. He'd fixed her dinner early and she'd eaten it with him and his wife, Hope. She couldn't face Tracey's gloating or Stirling's aloofness over dinner.

Sam leaned around his seat on the aircraft. "OK?"

"Sure," she said. "Why wouldn't I be?" Sonja heard Cheryl-Ann dry-heaving into her airsickness bag behind her.

Sam was nearly yelling over the buzz and drone of the small aircraft. "You said you skipped dinner last night because you weren't well. Just wanted to see how you were, is all."

She nodded, remembering the lie. "Probably dehydration. I drank lots of water. Your face is red—it looks like you might peel from the sunburn."

He grinned. "I can always cover it with makeup."

Despite her misery and self-pity she smiled. He looked forward again. He was a harmless fool, she thought, a product of a society where people thought they were doing something for the environment by paying their monthly DSTV subscriptions and watching handsome lightweights wax on about endangered species. She forced her thoughts away from the harridan behind her and the himbo in front. Even though she had told Martin she was only going along for the CTR Sonja couldn't help but wonder how she would go about blowing up a dam and what the explosion and release of water would look like.

The engine note changed and she felt and heard things moving around her. They were starting their descent into Maun. The haze grew thicker as they entered the shroud of dust and smoke that always made the safari town just that little bit hotter and less comfortable than anywhere else in Botswana.

Brittle yellow grass flanked the shimmering ribbon of dark tar below. The turbulence increased as they met a final barrage of hot updrafts from the baking runway. Cheryl-Ann moaned. Sonja almost felt sorry for her. It had only been a half-hour flight, but the woman sounded like she was dying back there.

The Airvan's wheels kissed the tarmac; then, as though the surface was too hot to touch, it bounced once before settling. The pilot swung hard to starboard and hooked around into the taxiway. There were three other light airplanes queued for takeoff. Maun Airport only received and dispatched a couple of jet airliners a day—the Air Botswana Flights to and from Gaborone—but with its constant stream of light charter aircraft shuttling tourists in and out of the delta it could seem as busy as Heathrow or JFK in its own shabby little way.

On the ground, and without the rush of air from the small vents over their heads, the passengers started sweating as the temperature spiked inside the cabin during the short taxi.

"Oh my god, let me out of here!" Cheryl-Ann said.

Sonja breathed through her mouth to avoid the stench.

"Welcome to Maun," the pilot said, finally audible as he switched off the engine. "Mind how you go outside and wait for me before crossing the runway, please."

"Thanks," Sonja said, ignoring the pilot's proffered hand to help her down the steps from the rear hatch. Once she was on the tarmac she adjusted the Glock in the waistband of her pants, hidden under her shirt. She'd left her M4 behind with Martin as it would have been too difficult to conceal and she didn't expect to need it on her recce mission.

The smell of burning avgas and the silhouette of the drooping wings of the Air Botswana jet brought back memories of the Russian-made IL76 parked on the runway at Sierra Leone. She saw, again, the bodies being loaded for shipment back home to South Africa. There was no guard of honor, no national mourning, for dead mercenaries, and no welcome-home parade for the live ones. Just money, and always another war.

"Sonja, will you go get the four-by-four?"

Cheryl-Ann had recovered quickly from her bout of airsickness now that she was back on terra firma, though she was still pale and her words wafted a foul smell. Sonja knew she was wound tight because of Stirling's words, and Steele's conniving, but she suppressed the urge to tell Cheryl-Ann to fuck off, that she was not the woman's slave. For the time being, she was. "Of course. There's a cafe across the road from the entrance to the airport. It's called the Bon Arrivee. I'll see you there. Order me a double-shot espresso." She would do what was required to play the part of guide-cum-bodyguard, but she would also let Cheryl-Ann know she would not take any shit on the way.

"Deal. Jim, Gerry, get those cases loaded onto the trolley," she barked at the men. "You, stay away from that, it's valuable."

Sonja smiled as she saw the porter shake his head and turn his back on the Americans. The pilot ushered them across the runway, at a trot to avoid a Cessna hurrying past to make its departure slot. On the edge of the taxiway a white pilot strained as he single-handedly pushed his aircraft up to a fuel bowser. Sonja wondered how many people were diced by propellers here each year.

The terminal had grown in her absence, as had much of the town, judging by the sprawl she'd seen from the air on approach. The building was now two stories, brick, and bustling with people dressed in floppy safari hats and khaki ensembles. There was a menagerie of animal print scarves and puggarees and a jumble of languages in the stuffy room. The tourists reminded her of a herd of wildebeest. She was glad to break free of the crowd, and the film people, if only for a few minutes.

She walked across the road from the airport entrance gate to the blue-and-white painted Natlee shopping and office complex. As the TV crew's guide she was also doubling as their driver and Cheryl-Ann had told her the keys to the rented vehicle would be at the Mack Air office.

Sonja opened the office door and paused for a second, with eyes closed, to savor the chilled air. When she opened them, she saw a weathered face she remembered well. The blue eyes were framed by racoon white patches left by his sunglasses.

He stared at her, from over the shoulder of a woman sitting at a desk.

"Laurens?"

"Sonja? Is that you?"

She nodded. He walked around the desk, took her hand and kissed her cheek. He kept hold of her hand for a few seconds. "My god, you were just a girl last time I saw you."

"I was eighteen, *Oom* Laurens."

He laughed. "You don't have to call me uncle anymore."

"Why not, you're still old enough."

"You always were a cheeky girl. But, yes, we're all getting old. Hey, I saw your father about a month ago. Up country, way up to hell and gone, near Linyanti. I was taking some mining people up there—at least they said they were miners."

Laurens was Dutch, and had been in Maun for thirty years or more. He'd come, like so many young Europeans, Australians, New Zealanders and South Africans, to accrue hours as a bush pilot and had ended up staying. He still looked as fit and handsome as she remembered him. She'd had a tiny crush on *Oom* Laurens before she and Stirling had discovered each other. "We're not close, Laurens."

He nodded. "I know, but he's changed, Sonja."

"I don't care. Have you got a vehicle for me?"

She knew it would be like this, especially in Maun, where everyone knew everyone else's business. People knew her family's history the same way they knew who was sleeping with whose partner. Per capita, the white community boasted too many testosterone-charged alpha male hunters and safari guides, her mother used to say, as well as too many good-looking women, too much heat, and too much alcohol.

"He's off the booze. And he's got himself a good woman."

"It's a Land Rover, I believe, Laurens, booked under the name of Cheryl-Ann Daffen from Wildlife World. And there was nothing wrong with my mother."

He held up his palms in a show of apology. "My English . . . you know that's not what I mean. Your mother was too good for him—everyone knew that, except Hans. He's trying to make amends. For lots of things."

"I don't care." She was being as frosty as the office's air-conditioning and it finally sunk in.

"Very well. But it's *lekker* to see you again anyway, Sonja. Hannelie, do you have the keys to the Land Rover?"

The woman was a pretty, thin redhead, and Sonja guessed she was three or four years younger than her. Hannelie opened her desk drawer. Laurens put his hand on her shoulder.

"Thank you, my girl." He handed the keys to Sonja.

Sonja raised her eyebrows. Over Hannelie's head, Laurens smiled and winked. The old devil.

"Good luck with those TV people," Laurens said.

She opened the door and was met with a furnace blast of air. "Thanks, I think I'll need all the luck I can get."

Hannelie caught her eye before she walked out and held up an Afrikaans gossip magazine. "That *oke* Sam Chapman looks hot, hey, and according to this, he's dangerous, too."

Sonja closed the door and walked back to the desk. "Can I see?" There was a picture of Sam Chapman on the front cover, holding up his right hand as though he was shielding himself from the glare of the photographer's flash. Sonja mentally translated the Afrikaans into English. *Clean cut Sam's shame . . . star was jailed over friend's death.*

"I haven't finished reading the article, but it seems he was quite the *poephol* in his youth."

Sonja had no idea what the woman was talking about. "Can I take this?"

"I haven't finished reading it." Hannelie cast her green eyes up to Laurens.

"*Ag*, give it to her, doll, I'll buy you a new one."

The Bon Arrivee Cafe catered for tourists in transit and bush pilots in between flights or recovering from hangovers.

The decor and memorabilia were all aviation related. The walls were painted sky blue and cloud white, a cool contrast to the hazy gray skies and gritty airborne dust outside. There were pictures of airplanes old and new, and reproduction sepia-toned press clippings about Charles Lindbergh and the Hindenburg disaster. A Cessna's wings and ailerons hung over the brown wooden bar and scale models of jet airliners and military aircraft were gently buffeted in the turbulence of a fan that swirled the hot air from one end of the cafe to the other.

The smokers were outside under the shade of umbrellas advertising a mobile phone company. Sonja stopped to chat to a gray-haired man in shorts and white shirt, who had just paid his bill and was on the way out as she arrived. Sam watched her, and noticed the way she threw back her head when she laughed. She was wearing the safari shirt and shorts he'd bought for her. She looked good in them. Damn good.

A pretty waitress in an African print mini dress with pilot's epaulettes on her narrow shoulders asked Sonja if she would like something to drink, as she joined them at the table.

"I've *already* ordered for her," Cheryl-Ann told the girl. "Can we get served some time today, please, miss?"

The waitresses lifted her nose and lowered it in an approximation of a nod and sashayed slowly away.

"African time," Sonja said. "You'd better get used to it."

"People in this country are lazy," Cheryl-Ann said. "Everything takes ten times as long as it should."

Sonja shrugged. "By African standards, Botswana is a model democracy with low levels of unemployment. Its people are generally well off and the country has the best public health system on the continent. The local people here do things at their own pace."

"You make it sound like a virtue."

"It is what it is. You can't rush around at a hundred miles an hour in this heat," Sonja said.

Their coffees arrived and Sam blew on his latte. "Are you an apologist for Africa, Sonja?"

"No way. All I'm saying is that you can't assume that what goes in LA or New York goes in Maun, or even Gaborone or Johannesburg. The west has been trying to impose its ways, its values, its religion and its timetables on Africa for centuries, but it's made precious little progress in converting anyone."

"What about religion?"

Sonja nodded. "Most people in southern Africa would call themselves Christian, but many of those people would still visit their local *sangoma*—what you would call a witchdoctor—if they want to lay a curse on someone or have one lifted."

"What about the crime and corruption?" Sam asked. "I think I read somewhere that more people die in gun crimes in Johannesburg each year than are killed in Iraq."

"That's probably right, but you've just highlighted what's wrong with the developed world's perception of Africa."

He raised his eyebrows at her.

"You think," she went on after sipping her coffee, "of Africa as a 'place,' a single entity. Even one of your vice-presidential candidates thought the continent of Africa was a country."

"Embarrassing, but true," Cheryl-Ann said.

"South Africa and South Africans have no more in common with Kenya and the tribes who live there, than, say North Americans and Colombians. South Africa's problem is crime; Botswana's may be that its people lack the get-up-and-go needed to capitalize on their wealth; and a succession of Kenyan governments have squandered the country's natural wealth through corruption and mismanagement in the decades since independence. Zimbabwe showed what can go wrong—anywhere in the world—if one man and one party run a country for too long, and then do whatever it takes to maintain their grip on power. Tribalism rears its ugly head all over the continent—look at the genocide in Rwanda, for example."

"Lots of problems," Sam said. He was surprised to hear Sonja speak at length—but he'd obviously touched on a sore point.

"*Ja*, sure, but things such as accountability in government, effective crime control and even the acceptance of the need for a free and fair media weren't always a given in the west."

"So, basically, the whole world is fucked," said Jim, the Australian, grinning over his cappuccino.

Sonja ignored his comment. "South Africa has first world infrastructure, Botswana has peace and a stable government, Zimbabwe is the most fertile country in Africa, and Kenya and Tanzania have wildlife paradises foreigners will pay a fortune to see. There is hope for Africa, but the continent still needs time to develop—not only roads and power stations but ideals, such as justice, integrity, honesty and equality. It took you Americans a revolution, a civil war and the human rights movement to get to the stage where you can have a colored man in the Oval Office."

Sam leaned back in his bar stool and studied her. She looked away from them and sighed, as though she regretted wasting the breath and time it took to educate a bunch of spoiled foreigners. When she glanced back at him he saw her green eyes glowing, like a cat's, as if daring him to disagree with her. What she'd said, however, made perfect sense.

Sonja put down the rolled magazine she'd been carrying and nodded to the mountain of camera gear and their personal baggage, which had claimed an entire corner of the cafe. "We'd better get that lot loaded. We've got a long drive ahead of us."

Sam drained his latte and started to stand when he saw the cover of the magazine. He didn't understand the writing, but he recognized the photo of himself. Rather than hiding from the photographer, as the pose implied, he'd actually been brushing a fly away from his face when the picture was taken, but it had fit the story so perfectly that it had been syndicated around the world when the latest bit of gossip about him became public. He was sure the story was about him and David. He slumped back in his seat.

Sonja lowered her cup and saw his reaction. "I didn't know how famous you were. I haven't read it," she picked up the magazine and passed it across the table to him, "and I don't need to."

He shook his head. "Keep it. You might get a laugh out of it. If it's the same as the English language edition of that magazine," he recognized the masthead now, "then enough of it is true to make me glad we're filming in Africa right now and not London or LA where the paparazzi would be in overdrive."

She nodded. "I'll read it. They have stringers even in Africa, you know."

"I guess. But hopefully not where we're going."

"We're on our way to Namibia, the same country where Brad and Angelina thought they could have their baby in private." Sonja stood, then grabbed the handle of the closest black carrying case and started to lift it.

"I'll take that," said Rickards.

"I can lift it, even though I am a woman."

He moved to her and wrapped his fingers around hers, forcefully taking the weight of the case from her. She was close to elbowing him in the solar plexus when he said, "I'm sure you can bench press one-eighty, love, but it's my camera and nobody messes with it. OK?" He glared at her. She let go, but held his gaze defiantly.

They loaded the Land Rover and climbed aboard. It was a stretched version of the venerable Defender, the one-hundred-and-thirty-inch wheelbase version, with an extended passenger cab that gave a third row of seats. Cheryl-Ann took the front passenger seat, and Sam and Jim were in the middle row. Gerry didn't get the third bench to himself, however, as the filming equipment cases spilled over from the cargo area onto the seat next to him. Their personal backpacks, along with tents and camping gear, were all stored on a roof carrier, which Sonja secured under a cargo net made of stout nylon webbing.

Sonja was sweating freely by the time she started the turbo diesel engine.

Cheryl-Ann fiddled with the air-conditioning controls, but Sonja knew from past experience it wasn't worth the woman's time trying to coax anything more than a lukewarm breath from the vents. "Better to open your window."

Cheryl-Ann ignored her at first, but changed her mind before they had driven less than a kilometer, to the Spar supermarket. "OK," Sonja said, swiveling in her seat so the rest of them could hear her, "I understand you're eating in the restaurant at the camp where we're staying tonight, but if you want any food or drinks for the road, now is the time to get them. We've got about four hundred kilometers to drive and, short of an emergency, I'm not planning on stopping."

"*Jawol!*" Rickards needed no further prompting. He climbed out and the others filed after him.

Once the others had left Sonja got out of the Land Rover. She looked around to make sure no one was watching her and took the Glock from the cubby box between the two front seats and slipped it into the waistband of her shorts, in the small of her back. She pulled her bush shirt over the pistol and walked to a small tree and stood in its shade, watching the vehicle. She didn't even want to think how much the camera gear was worth, let alone whatever they had stored in their packs.

A dust devil tore down the street, sandblasting half a dozen young backpackers who had just climbed down from an overland tour truck. Sonja smiled as they pulled T-shirts over their faces and spat dirt. Welcome to Maun, she thought. A mangy donkey walked past and brayed with laughter.

"Good afternoon, madam," a voice said behind her.

She turned and checked her watch at the same time. It was five after twelve, though the African man wore no watch. He might have been forty, but he might also have been sixty. His breath reeked of beer and the whites of his eyes were yellowed.

"I am looking for a job, madam. I can be a gardener."

Sonja greeted him in Tswana, adding, "Sorry, I don't have a garden." She looked away from him, back at the Land Rover, in case he was the decoy.

Two new Land Cruiser Prados with blue-and-white Gauteng Province GP numberplates pulled up next to the Land Rover. The South African cars were festooned with every camping gadget in last year's Outdoor Warehouse Christmas catalog. Sonja was glad for the arrival of some competition for any thieves in the area.

"I do not speak Tswana," the man said in English, even though she had ceased looking at him. "South African people have trouble telling the difference between our peoples, but thank you for trying."

With the threat reduced and no suspects in sight Sonja turned and lowered her sunglasses. She hadn't paid enough attention to him first time around. He was too dark, too black, to be Tswana. He looked like he came from the hot humid river valleys to the north, not the sun-scorched wastes of the Kalahari. He was a few inches shorter than she and solidly built. "I'm not South African. Are you Lozi?"

"Sorry, madam. We are both quick to jump to conclusions. We are human. Yes, I am Lozi. I speak Lozi or English, but my German is very bad. Where are you from?"

It was a good question and Sonja knew she should not get into a conversation with a drunk. However, if he was Lozi he was probably from the Caprivi Strip, so given the job she was about to undertake her interest was piqued. She formed her answer carefully. "I was born in South-West Africa, but my family had to leave. We weren't welcome there anymore."

The man moistened his lips with his tongue, as he forced himself to concentrate through the fog of inebriation. "Then we are both far from home, madam. I, too, am from Namibia and was forced from my home by the Ovambo." He hawked and spat in the dust. "We have something in common."

"You're Caprivian."

"You know of our struggle? There are eight thousand of us, refugees, here in Botswana, madam. The world has forgotten us. They care only for Zimbabwe, not for my people. Do you need a gardener, madam?"

"I don't have a garden."

"I don't have a country. But if you have money, madam, I have not eaten for two days."

No, she thought, but you've drunk half a shebeen dry last night and now you need more hair from that dog that bit you. "I'll pay for information,

and what you spend your money on is your own business. The CLA—the
Caprivi Liberation Army. You know of them?"

Sonja was interested to find out for herself how keen the average
Caprivian was to fight for independence, particularly in the light of the disastrous setback at the dam construction site. A recce wasn't just about counting troops and guns, it was also about gauging the morale of the enemy—and
that of the friendlies.

"I am UDP."

The United Democratic Party, Sonja knew, was the political face of the
Caprivians' push for independence, supposedly with no direct links to the
military organization, the CLA. He averted his rheumy eyes from her. He was
lying. "I can get information on the UDP on the Internet, old man."

The man looked left and right, along the dust blown street. There was
no one in earshot. "I know the CLA."

"They failed in their attack on the dam upstream from Popa Falls. Why?"

He scanned the street again. "We . . . the CLA was betrayed."

The drink had produced the mistake. "You were there?"

He bent and lifted the right leg of his jeans. The scar on his calf was
ugly—puckered from poor stitching and slow healing. He let her see it then
lowered the hem again. She looked at his white trainers—they were spotless—
and his jeans, while old and holed at the knees, were clean. His button-up
shirt was pressed. He was unemployed and drunk, but he took care of his
appearance. "Yes, I was there. The Namibians were waiting for us. Many
of them. We made no noise, but they used their mortars to light . . . to
enlighten . . ."

"Illumination rounds, you mean?"

He nodded. "They knew the date, the time and the place of our attack.
Many of our men died."

"Was that the end of the CLA?"

He shook his head and met her eyes again, defiance cutting through the
glaze. "We are weakened, but we are not dead. There are younger men who
are . . . who will one day be ready."

"Are they in training now?"

"Who are you, madam?"

"I'm a safari guide with an interest in current affairs in the region."

The man smiled broadly. "The first safari guide I have seen who hides a Glock in the rear of her pants and the first woman I have met who knows what an illumination round is."

She turned the questioning back on him. "And you are the best turned-out drunken unemployed gardener I have ever seen."

He belched and put his hand over his mouth. "I am not drunk. Not yet, anyway, and to tell you the truth, I hate gardening."

"You were a soldier."

"I was a warrant officer in the Namibian Army, and I still *am* a soldier."

She knew it. "Why did you join their military?"

"To learn how to kill them."

Sonja reached into her pocket and discreetly counted out three hundred pula. He licked his lips again, and it was as though he could almost taste the booze. "What is your name?"

"Gideon, madam. Warrant Officer Gideon Sitali." He stiffened, as though coming to attention.

She held the money loose in her right hand, baiting him. "Who betrayed you, Gideon?"

He looked both ways again, always watchful. "I knew nearly every one of the men in the assault team personally. Nearly every one, that is. It's possible we were infiltrated, but unlikely. We are of the same blood, like family. However, two of the eleven men I was not one hundred percent sure of were missing after the attack."

"And the others?"

"Dead."

"Whose idea was it to go for the dam? Why not raid another police station, or a barracks?"

"The water is our lifeblood, madam. We are people of the rivers and the swamps. We always have been. The Ovambo have no more right to take our water than they have to take our freedom. The *mukuwa* said that destroying the dam would also give our cause more publicity around the world than attacking the police station at Katima Mulilo or Divundu."

Sonja didn't know the dialects of the Caprivi, but *mukuwa* was similar to *mukiwa*, the Shona word for white boy. "There was a white with you?"

Gideon nodded. "Two of them. They trained us. One of them had fought the Ovambo in the old days. Once the whites were our enemy—I fought for SWAPO during the liberation war—but today the enemy of my enemy is my friend."

"Could they have betrayed you?"

Gideon thought about the question for a couple of seconds. His broad forehead was beaded with sweat. "I don't see why. One of them was of your people, ex-*Koevoet* from your South-West Africa days. I cannot imagine the *boer* taking money from the Ovambo. The other was an Englishman. He stayed for a few days before the attack and gave us some final training."

"Could he have sold you out—betrayed you to the Namibians?"

"It is possible, but I can't imagine the Namibian government doing business with a white mercenary, either. They have their own spies and, in the past, we were able to detect them and . . . to send them on their way."

Sonja agreed with him, though anything was possible in Africa. She handed the money to him, which he accepted with a bow of his head. "Where will you go now, Gideon? Where do you stay?"

He shrugged. "I stay in Maun for now, but when my people are strong again myself and others will be called back to the swamps." He looked up the street again, but this time he was watching a swirling funnel of flying sand and grit coming toward them. "I hate this place. It is too dry. A man needs more than a body to live. He needs a soul, and the river is ours."

15

The sound of singing lured Sam from the camping ground at Drotsky's Camp. He'd been lying in the hammock, strung between two mighty trees, letting the suggestion of a late-afternoon breeze cool the sweat on his bare chest after finishing putting up the tents. He put down the field guide to African mammals he had been reading and pulled on his T-shirt.

A well-trodden, winding path led him through the thick riverine bush toward the main dining area, a wooden building with a thatched roof and a wide shady verandah overhanging the Okavango River.

He saw a flash of color through the leaves ahead, orange and bright and bobbing like some exotic African bird. When he emerged in a grassy clearing he saw it was a woman—several, in fact. A singing, dancing, clapping procession dressed in vivid printed dresses and turbans came into view. The lyrics were repetitive but harmonious and melodic. The voices filled the clearing and reverberated off the surrounding trees, which formed a natural auditorium.

Past them walked the newlyweds. Unlike the traditionally dressed guests the young African couple looked like they'd been plucked off the top of a wedding cake. The groom wore a tux made of a shiny gray material, with a burgundy cummerbund and matching bow tie. His shoes were the same color as his suit, and pointed. His bride's obvious natural beauty was eclipsed, rather than enhanced, by the folds of ivory satin and lace that engulfed her and the lacy parasol she gripped awkwardly. Her new husband hooked a white-gloved finger in his collar and ran it around, clearly chaffing.

The photographer, in a funereal black suit with mildew on the shoulders, organized them on the lawn into the most uncomfortable poses possible while the female chorus kept up their joyously monotonous lyrics.

Like Sam a few tourists had been drawn by the sounds of the wedding party and some of them filmed and beeped away with their digital cameras while the official photographer laboriously snapped, wound and manually focused his battered Nikon, oblivious to the increasingly pained looks of his melting subjects.

Sam loved the spectacle of it. Cheryl-Ann would probably have ordered Rickards to film it, but Sam thought that even the tourists' pocket digitals seemed intrusive. Here was Africa, he thought, as the groom was finally allowed to raise himself from his knee and haul his grateful bride to her feet. Traditional singing and blessings for a couple who had probably blown a couple of months' wages to dress like people out of a twenty-year-old American or British wedding magazine.

Rickards swiveled on his stool at the bar as the wedding party filed in; he waved and Sam moseyed over to join him. "Quite a spectacle, eh?"

"Yeah," Sam said. He ordered a Windhoek lager for himself and another Castle for Rickards.

"Whole clash of cultures thing makes for good vision. I've shot shitloads of that sort of cake and arse crap for docos in the past."

Sam took a sip of beer and wiped his mouth with the back of his hand. He stayed standing, even though Jim had pushed a chair out from the bar for him. He wouldn't have described what he'd seen as crap.

"Hey," Rickards said, pointing with the neck of his fresh beer bottle. "Here comes Robo-Barbie. Nice and salty—just how I like 'em."

"I'll have another of these," Sam said to the barman. "Excuse me, Jim." He took both bottles and left the bar.

"Assume attack formation, soldier." Rickards raised his Castle in a mock salute, then turned back to watch the cricket playing on a TV mounted above the bar.

Sonja stopped on a grassy spot by the river and pressed some buttons on her watch. She shook her head.

"Not a good time?"

She looked over her shoulder at him and brushed damp strands of hair from her forehead. Her green tank top was camouflaged with black blotches of perspiration and she wore short gray running shorts made of a stretch fabric. The word "ARMY" was printed in white, vertically, on the right thigh of her shorts. "Could have been better."

"Could be your leg," he said, pointing with a bottle at the dressing. It was fresh, but there was a small stain in its center. "Any more weakness leaving your body right now?"

She regarded him curiously. "It's not too bad. Are you going to drink both those beers yourself?"

He handed one to her and she took a long, deep swallow. He thought the smooth skin of her neck was incredibly sexy as she tilted back her head. "Nice view of the river," he said, to take his mind off other brewing thoughts.

"Nice breeze, too," she said, leading the way to the verandah, which skirted the dining area and reception room, where the wedding meal was in full swing.

The setting sun was turning the river into a flow of red lava. They found two chairs made of dark timber slats that were a lot more comfortable to sit in than they looked. She put her running shoes up on the railing and leaned her head back, taking another sip of beer.

"How far did you run?"

"Only five or six kilometers, toward the main road and back."

"Weren't you worried about wild animals?"

"There isn't the wildlife on this side of the delta that there is in Moremi and the concessions bordering it. Crocs and hippos in the river, for sure, and maybe the odd leopard in the riverine bush, but not much else."

"It's a shame the whole delta and the river can't be proclaimed a game reserve or national park."

Sonja drank some more lager and nodded. "I agree with you, but plenty of others don't. Botswana has a strong commercial farming sector and the panhandle is good agricultural land. Plus, there are the traditional land-holders to consider. Some of them, like Chief Moremi III back in 1963, saw there was money to be made by locking up parts of the delta and charging tourists and white hunters big bucks for access. Others are quite happy to keep hunting, fishing or running their goats and cows on the land."

He nodded. "I want to cover all that in the documentary—the competing land uses."

"They needn't be competing. Africa's a big bountiful continent, but we humans have made some terrible mistakes over the years in how we've used and abused her gifts."

"There's so much to learn."

"Yes," she agreed. "A lot to fit into a sixty-minute TV program."

"Hey, *two* sixty-minute programs. And don't forget my survival special—though we may have to reshoot some of that, minus the bits where you try to kill me. Not good for my tough-guy image."

She laughed, and he was grateful for it. "Hey, it's none of my business, but I kind of got the impression when we were headed for Xakanaxa that you were intending on staying at the camp."

Sonja looked out over the river, all trace of mirth gone from her face. "You're right, it's none of your business."

"I'm sorry," he said, meaning it. It seemed that every time he got this prickly creature close to being at ease with him he said something to make her curl up into a ball again. Screw it, he thought, sensing she was about to get up and leave. He had nothing to lose and a lot to gain. She was beautiful, even after a run and streaked with dust and sweat. "Stirling told me he'd kill me if I laid a hand on you."

Her eyes and mouth opened wide as she stared at him. "What? What the hell?"

Sam shrugged. "All I did was ask him how he knew you. Were you two close?"

She ignored him, obviously stunned by the revelation. She took another gulp of beer. "He . . . the fucking hide of that man. Aargh! How *dare* he say that to you and treat me like I didn't even exist."

"So, how do you know each other?"

She slumped into her chair and waved a hand in the air. "We were teenagers together. I thought I loved him and I thought he loved me, but I left, to . . . to go away."

As always, she was holding back more than she was telling, but he was interested to learn more of the connection between her and Stirling. "Stirling thought I was hitting on his girlfriend, Tracey, and he whacked me. See?"

She leaned closer to see the discoloration on his cheek. "Were you? Hitting on her?"

Sam shook his head. "It was a misunderstanding. I don't want to talk out of school, but Tracey, well she kind of . . ."

Sonja nodded. "Stirling's an idiot to fall for her."

"If Stirling's an idiot it's for not wanting to see you again."

She looked back at him and he couldn't read what she was thinking. "Thank you," she said at last, and he breathed a tiny sigh of relief.

Sam reached his hand across the arm of his chair to Sonja. "With all that's happened I haven't had a chance to say a proper thank you for saving my life in the bush, and getting me back to Xakanaxa safe and sound."

She shook his hand and smiled, and he felt his heart start to pound. "Thank you."

She held on to him and her grip was firm yet not manly. He didn't want to let go and waited for her to relax her hold on him. He looked into her eyes. He could see her chest heaving and wondered if she was still short of breath from her run.

"It was nothing. And thank you, seriously, for my clothes," she said, and pumped his hand up and down once, then let go.

Sam could still feel the burn of her on his fingers, like dry ice.

Sonja stood. "Thanks for the beer. I've got to go get some water now, and shower."

With that, she walked away. Sam relaxed in his chair and enjoyed the rest of his beer, and the sunset, alone but with a secret smile on his face.

The guests at the wedding feast started singing again and their joyous harmonies pricked at Sonja like an annoying mosquito. Like Sam's remarks about what Stirling had said to him at Xakanaxa. She couldn't believe how childish Stirling had been, falling for his two-timing poppy yet still thinking he had some proprietary claim on his old girlfriend. It was maddening.

A yellow-billed hornbill sailed past her, wings spread straight and wide, and landed in the fork of a tree. She paused and watched him deposit a bug through a small hole in what appeared to be the tree's trunk. She knew that it was a facade, a wall of mud covering a much larger hole, inside which resided the bird's mate and their chicks. The male had probably spent the whole day shuttling from the ground to the tree, catching insects for his wife and babies. The female would have plucked out all her feathers and used them to line the nest as the male had walled her in with lumps of wet clay. She and the chicks were safe inside from predators, but totally dependent on the male to keep them fed. Safety and security at what price? The ability to fly.

The other TV people seemed to have all gone to dinner when she returned to the camp site, which was just fine by her. Annoyingly, one of the men had ignored her warning about monkeys and baboons and left his tent flap open. She peeked inside and wrinkled her nose. It was Rickards's tent. An empty chip packet lay on his unrolled sleeping bag. Salt and crumbs covered the bag, but worse than that was a small turd, covered in bright green buzzing flies. As well as being expert thieves and wanton vandals, vervet monkeys liked to add insult to injury by leaving their small but disgusting calling cards. Sonja was tempted to leave the tent flap open, but she would hate it if a snake slid into Rickards's sleeping bag and bit him during the night. She paused to reconsider for a second, then smiled and zipped the tent closed. She left the monkey's dropping where it was—that would be enough of a reminder.

She unzipped her own tent and sat down on her mattress. A francolin strutted past her tent and squawked a few notes. The run hadn't cured her restlessness and if anything she felt more wound up after talking to Sam. She did fifty push-ups and a hundred sit-ups to try to stop thinking about men and how stupid they were. The additional exercise speeded up the effects of the beer she'd drunk, so she finished off the bottle of warm water from her pack.

Sonja saw the rolled magazine protruding from a pocket of the rucksack. She pulled it out, along with her Surefire torch, which she switched on. She flicked to the article about Sam. There was a picture of him with an attractive blonde starlet, whose name Sonja vaguely recognized, and another one of him, much younger. It was a police mug shot and he stared back at the cameraman with a mix of shock, sorrow and defiance. She'd seen that stunned expression on soldiers after a firefight.

STONED AND DRUNK CHAPMAN DID TIME OVER FRIEND'S DEATH.

Sonja folded back the cover of the magazine and read on.

Wildlife World presenter Sam Chapman's image as a clean-cut all-American boy has been shattered with the revelation the handsome star did time in a juvenile jail over the death of his best friend.

Chapman, aged seventeen at the time, stole a car with buddy David Rollins, also seventeen, and terrorized the streets of the quiet suburb in Butte, Montana, where they lived, on a high-speed drink- and drugs-fueled rampage.

Police sources in Montana this week confirmed reports in Entertainment Truth *magazine that Chapman lost control of the car and rolled it. Rollins, a high-school football hero, died instantly when the car came to rest against a streetlight pole.*

"I'm glad the truth is out, at last," said a still distraught Denise Rollins, the dead boy's mother. "Sam Chapman is living the life of a Hollywood star, but he robbed my David of his future. He killed my son and I will never forgive him."

Chapman was convicted of the manslaughter of his friend and drink-driving offenses, and sentenced to two years in the Pine Hills Youth Corrections Facility. He also pleaded guilty to possession of marijuana, which was found in the wrecked car.

Wildlife World, which produces Chapman's award-winning documentaries, refused to comment, as did the star's agent. Chapman is said to be filming in Botswana for a forthcoming series of specials for the cable TV company.

Staff at the University of Montana were stunned to learn of Chapman's checkered past, with one former academic colleague, who asked not to be named, saying Chapman was well respected before leaving academia to pursue a career in television.

A back-handed compliment, if ever she had heard one, Sonja thought as she lowered the magazine and leaned back against her pack. She'd thought Chapman just another perfect product of a soft, well-fed suburban life; a smart man who had capitalized on his good looks to find a shortcut to the American dream.

Chapman has had other contact with juvenile delinquents later in life, reportedly working as a volunteer at so-called brat camps where he teaches young inmates about survival in the wild. It's not known if he has ever shared his dark past with any of the kids he has worked with.

There were several pictures of Sam with the article. There was a shot of him administering a drug or taking a blood sample from a sleeping coyote; a frame taken in front of Ayers Rock, now known as Uluru, in the middle of Australia; and another one of him walking from the surf at a beach. He had a perfect set of abs. She remembered the feel of his warm skin on hers as she took his hand. Her face reddened when she remembered how she'd held on to it for too long.

It was dark by the time she grabbed her towel and a bar of soap and headed for the small ablution block in the campground. Inside the ladies she stepped into the shower cubicle and stripped. Sonja turned the hot tap on, but no water came out. The pipes juddered and groaned somewhere behind the wall. "Shit," she mouthed. She tried the cold and the same thing happened. She wrapped her towel around her and fastened it above her breasts and picked up her clothes.

Outside she paused at the door to the gents side of the block. The light was out and there was no sound from inside. She pushed the door open and peeked inside. The curtain to the single shower stall was half open, but she could see no one inside. There was no one else in the campground, so there was little chance of anyone disturbing her. She laid her clothes down on a bench and stepped further into the darkness.

Then she heard the breathing. It was deep, but rapid.

Next she smelled him, the strong rich odor of his body.

Shit! There was a man in there, behind the half-drawn curtain. Sonja bent to grab her things and only then noticed that hanging on the back of the door she'd just come in through were Sam's jeans and bush shirt.

Sonja took a step on tiptoe toward the door and reached for it, but recoiled as she saw movement in the half-light. Sam had turned and was leaning, with one hand up against the tile wall. She ducked backward so that she was concealed by the wall of the toilet cubicle, but she could just see around the edge of the partition. Sam's arm was moving.

She caught her breath and dared not take another in case he heard her. He was breathing louder now. She rested her cheek against the wall and watched him through one eye. As her eyes adjusted to the gloom she saw his hand, wrapped around his thick, engorged penis. She stared at it.

He worked his palm up high over the head, then squeezed as he slid it down his shaft. She could hear the slickness of his natural lubrication. Tearing her gaze from it she saw him lean his head back, his mouth half open as he breathed out.

The well-defined muscles in his back and shoulders glistened with perspiration as his hand and breathing increased their pace. He shifted again and moved his left hand from the wall to the shower tap. The water pattered on the plastic curtain and he replaced his hand on the wall. He'd shifted in the process so she could see more of him, though his back was to her now so she couldn't see his right hand or his cock.

Sonja felt the moisture seep from deep within her and her nipples strain against the weave of the towel. She swallowed and allowed herself a half-drawn breath. Her face was on fire, and she wanted to run for the door. And she wanted to run for the curtain and rip it to one side.

Sam raised himself up on to his toes, his beautifully chiseled backside clenching in the process. He threw his head back further and let out a gasp of relief as his whole body shuddered.

Sonja darted to the door of the block, slipped outside and ran, barefoot, through the campground to her tent. She hastily unzipped, threw her clothes inside and lay down on her mattress. Her heart was racing as she stretched out, but it threatened to explode from her chest as she came in the darkness.

Sonja braked to let a trio of male kudus cross the road. The middle antelope paused and stared at them for a second, then gave a toss of his long curved antlers and leaped away, his white tail curled protectively across his rump.

It wasn't a close call as she had cut her speed to eighty kilometers after they crossed the border into Namibia at Shakawe. Botswana, Namibia and South Africa were all part of a common customs zone, so there was no problem taking the vehicle across borders. Sonja held her breath while the African woman on the Botswana side scanned her passport, but the forgery was good—Steele maintained the best sources around the world—and the document passed inspection on both sides of the border. Sonja made a mental note of the Namibian Army *bakkie* parked behind the customs and immigration building, and the two soldiers who chatted to a cleaner leaning on her mop outside. The soldiers, in camouflage, were armed with AK-47s. It wasn't a large force, but nor was it common to see armed military men at a border post in this part of the world.

The country around Shakawe on the Botswana side was given over to commercial farming—crops and cattle—but as soon as they crossed the line into Namibia they were in wilderness, with brittle bone-dry bush on their flanks. It was why Sonja took it slowly, as there was little warning if an animal wanted to cross. A yellow-billed kite wheeled above them patrolling the road in search of roadkill.

"What's this place?" Sam asked from behind her.

"The Mahango Game Reserve. It's about thirty thousand hectares. The Okavango River is off to our right and beyond that is the beginning of the much larger Bwabwata National Park, which was called the West Caprivi Game Reserve when I was younger."

She watched him in the rear-view mirror, nodding at her explanation, then recalled the sight of him rising on his toes in the shower. She looked out the driver's side window in case Cheryl-Ann saw her blush. Sonja had

imagined him on her, in her, as she'd touched herself in the tent and wondered if it was her he'd been thinking of in the shower.

Sonja pushed the distracting thoughts from her mind. She'd play the
tour guide for the TV people, but her other job was to assess the landmarks
they passed from a military planner's point of view. The Mahango Game
Reserve extended north to within about twelve kilometers of Popa Falls,
near where the dam was being built. If Steele's force infiltrated Namibia
near Shakawe the reserve would provide cover for part of their journey, or
perhaps a hidden bush base where they could group and prepare for an assault. There would be Namibian Wildlife Authority rangers patrolling the
reserve, but not enough of them to pose a threat to a force of heavily armed
mercenaries. Sonja would have liked to have taken a boat up the Okavango
from Drotsky's Camp to the border, to see what kind of controls were in
place on the river itself, but there was no way to justify the trip.

"Big five country?" Gerry asked.

Sonja shook her head. "All the rhino were killed here decades ago, but
there are still lion, buffalo, elephant and leopard, plus occasional sightings
of wild dog and cheetah."

"Cool," said the sound man.

Rickards yawned and Sonja could smell the stale booze on his breath.
Cheryl-Ann sat in silence, watching the grays and browns of the thorny
bushveld pass her by. Sonja had arrived late for dinner, just as the others
were finishing, and ordered herself a snack from the bar. She didn't feel like
a confrontation with Cheryl-Ann and, besides, they were talking business,
planning the shoots for the next few days. She had half feared she might
stumble on Sam eating alone, or that he might make an excuse to stay back
in the restaurant with her, but he left with the others and nodded a polite
goodnight to her as she ate her burger and drank another two beers by herself to calm her pulse.

They had all breakfasted together early that morning and Sonja had
eyed the other woman off across the table. Polite and friendly, but a long way
from friends. That was fine by Sonja and she hoped it would be enough for
Cheryl-Ann.

"I phoned ahead," Cheryl-Ann said. "They definitely have cabins available for us tonight."

So there would be no fighting over tents. "Good."

Cheryl-Ann looked away from the scenery and across to Sonja. "Did you have trouble with the water in the shower block, Sonja?"

"Um . . . yes."

"I complained to reception, but they just told me to use the other block. It was way down the other end of the camp. That's really not good enough."

Sonja shrugged. "I just used the men's shower." She couldn't resist a glance in the rear-view mirror as she said it and when she looked up she saw Sam looking her way. It felt like his eyes were searching for hers and she shifted her gaze immediately.

"You're coming on the river cruise with us this afternoon, Sonja."

It was said as a statement rather than a question, but Sonja was pleased nonetheless. Cheryl-Ann would want her there to ensure they correctly identified any birds and mammals they saw during the filming, but Sonja wanted to do a recce of the stretch of river leading to the falls and the dam wall. If she hadn't been automatically included on the river cruise she would have asked to come along, or booked one for herself. The last option was the least desirable, though, as it might have aroused the TV crew's suspicions. "That'll be great, Cheryl-Ann. I never get sick of going out on the river," she said.

Ngepi Camp was a couple of kilometers off the main road, toward the river on a sandy but firm track that passed a village and some local people tending a few cows. The camp itself was on a sand island, though the tributary of the Okavango they passed over, via an earth and rock causeway, was dry. Sonja wondered when it had last flowed. She parked and walked into the reception building, which was open on three sides.

Cheryl-Ann bustled up to the bar, but Sonja hung back and looked around her. She'd heard about Ngepi, but never stayed here. The camp and its accommodation were pitched at new-age backpackers and free-wheeling overland travelers. It was fun and funky. Every sign around reception seemed to contain a joke and some of them were funny. Behind the bar was the obligatory collection of baseball caps and foreign currency bills stuck to a wall. Overhead was a poster of Che Guevara, and the Namibian flag hung from the rafters of the thatched roof. Sonja wandered past a fire pit surrounded by benches made from old sausage tree *mekoros*, and onto a wooden platform that jutted out over the river.

The river in front of Drotsky's had been divided into narrow channels by islands of pampas grass and papyrus. Here, further upriver and much closer to the dam, the river was wide and open, though judging by the pinkish brown back of a hippo that protruded above the water's surface, it was not all that deep. She could see the far shore, several hundred meters away, which was the beginning of the Bwabwata National Park. More country that was largely empty, except for animals.

A force traveling by boat might be able to conceal itself by taking a quiet channel downstream, but here all traffic was clearly visible from both sides of the river.

The Okavango was flowing quite fast, judging by the stems of grass and a plastic bag that motored past her. Beneath the platform was a swimming cage, about eight by eight meters, held afloat by old fuel drums and fringed with a rickety-looking wooden walkway. The cage was to protect swimmers from wildlife. Hippo, it was often said, killed more people than any other animal in Africa, but Sonja knew crocodiles were responsible for savaging and killing plenty of locals who swam, bathed and herded their cattle on the edges of the rivers in the Kavango and Caprivi regions of Namibia. A girl in a bikini, with a large tattoo of a butterfly on the red skin of her back, was sunbathing. An African man with dreadlocks and a runner's build was kneeling on the walkway, pulling out clumps of grass and weed, and another bag that had snagged on the mesh of the cage. A sign warned swimmers that if they pissed in the cage they'd be drinking it later, downstream in Maun. Sonja conceded a smile.

Cheryl-Ann came out onto the deck followed by the men, like a mother duck.

She waited until she had reached Sonja before producing the keys she had collected from reception. "Here you go, Sam, Gerry and Jim. You've each got what they call a treehouse bungalow, on the water."

Sonja said nothing and didn't put her hand out for a key. She had already guessed what was coming.

"Sonja, I'm afraid we didn't book a room for you. The plan was always for the guide to camp in or with the vehicle, to look after it."

"No problem. It shouldn't be too far from the camp site to your bungalows, so you won't have too far to carry your gear."

Rickards made a face behind Cheryl-Ann's back and Sam just rolled his eyes. She cared nothing for the petty point scoring Cheryl-Ann had initiated. In fact, she cared nothing for these spoiled people and their insignificant contribution to the world. "The Land Rover's unlocked. I'm going to check out the camp site."

Sonja headed down the sandy path to the floating swimming cage. The reddened girl was still baking on the wooden deck and the African guy Sonja had seen earlier was sitting on the edge with his feet in the water.

"Morning," he said.

"Howzit?" Sonja said.

"Fine and you?"

"*Lekker*, man." Because of her shortage of clothes Sonja was wearing her bikini under her safari clothes, as underwear. She took off her shirt and slid out of her sandals and shorts and did a shallow dive into the confines of the cage. The water was cool and as soon as she surfaced she felt the current drag her to the downstream end of the enclosure. She turned and started a lazy breaststroke against the river's flow. With a little effort she maintained a stationary position in the center of the floating pool. It was a novel way to get a little exercise, and a good reminder that any approach toward the dam would have to be done in boats with outboard motors. Even though the river was low, the current was still fast, so stealthy kayaks were probably out of the question.

"Looks like you're getting nowhere," the African man said, smiling.

"You don't know how right you are, my friend."

He laughed.

"I saw you pulling rubbish out of the cage before," she said. "Do you work here?"

"No, but it doesn't mean I don't care for the environment. That dam they're building upstream is responsible for too much pollution."

"How so?"

"Plastic bags and other rubbish dumped by the construction workers in the water, oil and diesel from the trucks and bulldozers, unchecked flows of silt during construction. Anywhere else in the world they'd be prosecuted."

"Anywhere else in the world and it wouldn't have been built, for environmental reasons. You sound like you know what you're talking about."

He laughed again, deep and hearty. "Don't let the 'do and the duds fool you, sister," he said, pointing at his dreadlocks and the shiny red baggy board shorts he wore, hanging low down on his arse so his Calvin Klein underwear was showing at the back. "I've got a degree in Environmental Management from the University of Zimbabwe, but the only way I can made a buck is as a guide on an overland tour truck. That dam's going to kill a beautiful thing." The white girl stirred, sat on the edge of the pool and slid in. "The locals won't notice it so much here upriver, but it's going to kill the environment downstream, and hurt the tourism business at the same time. All because of greed."

Sonja nodded. "For water?"

"For money," the guide said. "Some people have big plans for the Caprivi Strip once that dam is finished. It's not just about hydro-electricity and water for Windhoek; there are plans for more mines, including diamonds, and large-scale commercial farming up there." He gestured north, over his shoulder, with a thumb. "Big money."

"That incredible bird, flying just above the water with its bill in the water, is an African skimmer," Sam said to the camera. The boatman had cut the outboard and they were drifting silently, swiftly, down the Okavango.

"It's listed as near-threatened and there are as few as fifteen thousand of these incredible creatures left on earth. It catches small fish by flying with its lower beak—its mandible—just beneath the surface of the water. Amazing."

"Great," Cheryl-Ann said.

"I'm loving this light," Rickards said, panning slowly and pulling back on the focus to take in more of the sky, which was a triple-layer cocktail of deep pink, gold and azure.

Sam looked to Sonja, who was scanning the bank through binoculars. "Why is the species threatened?"

She lowered her binoculars. "Habitat destruction, especially because of dams. Rising waters flood the sand bars and banks where they breed. Also, pesticides and other run-off from intensive farming can kill the little fish that the skimmers feed on. You should put that in your program."

"Jim?" Sam said. The cameraman held up a finger, wanting to catch a few more seconds of vision of the sky.

"Let's not get into politics until we've had a chance to inspect the dam and interview the folks upriver," Cheryl-Ann announced.

Sam was about to argue, but he knew it would be pointless. The more he learned about the hydro-electric power plan for the Okavango, the less he liked the sound of it, but perhaps Cheryl-Ann had a point. There seemed to be a truce between the two women on the boat this evening, but it was still an uneasy one.

Sam had left his treehouse and walked to the campground half an hour before their departure to see if Sonja needed help setting up. Predictably, her small camp site was already established and her gear stowed with military precision. He found her at the pool, where she told him she was enjoying her second swim for the day. She invited him in.

"I can't. I don't want to ruin my hair or makeup."

She laughed out loud and he marveled again at how that simple act could transform her and make him feel so good.

He tried not to stare at her breasts when she climbed out and put her clothes on over her wet swimsuit. "I read that article about you," she said.

He stayed silent and waited for her verdict.

"It's not easy seeing a friend die." She was stating the obvious, but the way she said it made him think it had happened to her, too. "Wouldn't have picked you as a teenage car thief, though."

He'd told Sonja the truth, by the pool, as he looked out over the Okavango, that the car had belonged to David's mum, who had let him use it unsupervised on plenty of occasions before the accident. Denise Rollins was a lush, who let her teenage son take her car so he could drive to the liquor store for her. David had insisted Sam drive that night and had urged him to go faster and faster. David had bought the pot, as well, although Sam had smoked some.

"You didn't tell all this to the judge?" Sonja asked.

"It didn't lessen the fact that I was the driver and my best buddy was dead. I didn't want to make it harder on his mom by dragging their names through the mud."

Rebecca, his former girlfriend, had told him he was a sap for not mounting a stronger defense, when he had told her the same story.

"Good for you," Sonja had said. "Come. The boat guide's waiting for us."

Out on the motorized pontoon Sonja had impressed Sam and the others—even Cheryl-Ann, he suspected—with her ability to spot birds and wildlife, sometimes even before their experienced African guide, Julius. While Sonja and Julius scanned the riverbanks for game, Sam stood in front of the camera.

"Action," Cheryl-Ann said.

Sam cleared his throat and looked into the lens. "The Okavango River rises in the highlands of Angola, to the north of where I am now, where it's known by its local name, the Kabango. From there it passes through this part of Namibia, before entering Botswana. Here it flows as a wide river, fully deserving that title. If you imagine a skillet then where we are is on the handle—in fact it's known as the panhandle here—but as it winds south through Botswana the river runs into ground that's been lifted and rippled by millennia of seismic activity and it starts to split into numerous small rivers and creeks. The Okavango finally peters out in the Kalahari Desert into a myriad of seasonal channels that only flow after the annual rains."

"Elephants," Sonja whispered. "Turn, Julius, quickly, hey. They're coming just now to drink."

"Cut, Sam. I don't see any elephants, Sonja," Cheryl-Ann said.

Julius was swinging the outboard. He pointed with his free hand.

Sam saw the cloud of dust, which was tinged pink by the setting sun's rays. Of the animals themselves there was still no sign.

Another tourist boat saw them turn, and the spreading V of their wake on the shiny brass surface of the water as Julius accelerated. Julius called across the water and the guide on the other craft swung his tiller to follow them. The first of the elephants came into view.

"That big one, in front, with its trunk up, is a female. She's the matriarch, the head of the herd," Sonja said.

Sam saw the elephant sniffing the wind, but if she detected the scent of humans it was not enough to slow her headlong charge for the river, or to stop the pressing crowd of wrinkly gray flesh behind her. Almost lost in the forest of trunklike legs and choking dust was a tiny baby that threaded its way to the matriarch's side. "How old is that little one."

Sonja shifted her binoculars slightly. "Less than a year old. You can tell because he can still fit under his mother's belly. Also, look at the way his little trunk is flopping from side to side."

"I see it," Sam said. "It's like he doesn't know what to do with it."

"Exactly. They have to learn how to use their trunk, and what it's for."

Julius headed for a sandbar island, about twenty meters from the far riverbank, where the elephants had arrived. Their front rank splashed knee-deep into the water.

"Can't you get closer?" Cheryl-Ann asked.

"He knows what he's doing," Sonja muttered.

Julius turned the craft toward the island, revved the motor, and the pontoons' bows shushed up onto the sand. "We can get off the boat, now," Julius said.

"Perfect," said Rickards, who needed no further invitation. "Come on, Gerry. Let's move it. Light's fading."

Sam followed the camera team off the front of the boat and stopped to offer his hand to Cheryl-Ann, who waved him away. She jumped and landed unsteadily in the sand, but regained her balance at the last second. Sonja stepped off and touched the sand with graceful confidence.

"Will they cross the water?" Sam asked.

Sonja shook her head. "See the matriarch sniffing again? She knows we're here. The water is a barrier. They could cross it if they wanted, but see how the rest are drinking now. They're relaxed about us, and they're bloody thirsty."

"The drought?" Sam asked.

Sonja nodded. "Look at the vegetation."

Sam could see trees shredded to matchsticks. The bush on either side of the gently sloping sandy beach that led down to the river had obviously been a favorite feeding spot for the herds that came to drink here. He lifted his own nose to the air and caught the damp, musty smell of the elephants wafting across the narrow channel.

"Ready when you are, Sam, if you want to do a piece to camera," Rickards said.

Cheryl-Ann had been staring at the elephants, as if locked in a trance. It was, Sam thought, a rare lapse in her relentless professionalism, but he liked the fact she had been moved to silence. "Yes," she snapped. "Get in there and give me something that will make me cry."

Sam moved in front of the camera and dropped to a crouch so Rickards could keep filming the herd, which was now framed above his left shoulder. He cleared his throat, then drew a deep breath through his nostrils and exhaled. "This family is close enough for me to smell them. It's a rich, earthy smell, as powerful as the urge that drove this mother and her offspring through the harsh, dry African bush to this temporary sanctuary."

Rickards gave a slight nod of his head and Sam took the cue, and looked back over his shoulder. The herd had parted and Sam could see one elephant, nearly as big as the matriarch, sinking to its knees in the sand. He wasn't sure what was happening. He looked at Sonja, who whispered, "She's dying. Thirst."

Sam nodded. "Who knows how far this herd traveled to reach the Okavango River. What is clear, though, from the scene unfolding behind me, is that for at least one of these mighty animals the journey was too far. That female," he turned again and saw the elephant was now lying on her side, "is dying."

He paused and let the pictures tell the story for a few seconds. The rest of the herd had paused in slaking their thirst and were now standing in a semicircle around their fallen relative. Trunks were sniffing her. A young one, not much older than the matriarch's baby, raised its trunk and let loose a piercing, wailing scream. It lowered its head and started nudging its stricken mother, as if trying to rouse her.

"People ascribe almost human emotions to elephants and it's hard to know where fact stops and legend begins. We do know that elephants will spend time sniffing the bones and carcasses of other dead elephants, as if they are trying to identify the fallen one and, perhaps, grieve for it. You make up your own mind about what's going on behind me."

He paused again and all of them watched the mournfully slow procession as the herd members, one by one, stopped to sniff and lay their trunks gently across the body of the fallen one. The dying elephant's baby was inconsolable, and ran in a circle, trumpeting and shaking its head, refusing to accept the inevitable. The sun was behind the camera crew, bathing Sam's face in soft light. He knew the vision would be extraordinary. Cheryl-Ann was whispering instructions to Rickards, who twitched his head like he was trying to shake off a buzzing mosquito. Gerry watched the scene with his mouth open. Sam moved his eyes to Sonja and when the young elephant cried again she flinched.

Those elephants that had not yet drunk did so, while four others kept vigil over the fallen one. Sam looked back again and could now see the angular protrusion of the cow's hip bones. She raised her trunk, no more than a meter off the ground, and her youngster seized on the tiny movement and moved to his mother's side. He entwined his trunk with his mother's for a few seconds, but when he shifted position and lost his grip the adult's trunk fell to the sand, and didn't move again.

16

"You teared-up, dude," Rickards said from the back seat, looking up from the flip-out LED screen of his camera. "I pulled in tight on that last shot, just after the baby elephant wrapped its trunk about the dead mother. We have tears. I can see you blink."

"Don't get too excited about it, OK?" Sam said, shaking his head.

"Excited? We are talking Emmy-fucking-award-winning stuff here, my man. Tell him I'm right, Cheryl-Ann."

Cheryl-Ann looked up from the printout she was reading. "As much as it pains me to agree with you, James, you may be right. That was some good stuff last night, Sam. And you, too, Jim."

Sonja frowned as she drove and gripped the wheel a little tighter. These Americans treated real life like it was television and vice versa. It didn't matter that they had witnessed a tragedy take place, only how it would look when they beamed it to the homes of a billion people around the world. It didn't matter whether Chapman had tears in his eyes or if he had forced them. They glossed over the problems of global warming and people fucking with the environment by building dams. They didn't have the time or the knowledge or the inclination to mention those elephants were living in a reserve hemmed in by man on all sides, with a finite amount of food and not enough water away from the river. A rich white man's tears were enough to make a story and win an award. That was the depth of their take-home, takeaway experience of Africa.

Sonja told herself she'd been silly to fantasize about the spoiled American after she'd caught him in the shower. She rationalized that her physical attraction to Sam was probably just a reaction to Stirling's dismissal, and told herself it was pointless nurturing some teenage infatuation with a man who lived in a different world to her. In Sonja's world distractions meant danger.

She didn't want to dwell on her own reaction to the elephant's death either. She, too, was sure she had seen Sam blinking back tears and that had set her off. She had turned and walked back to the boat, letting the salt water stream down her cheeks before she was sure she was far enough into the gloom for none of the others to see her wiping her face. She'd scooped a handful of Okavango water and washed away the marks while she waited for them to pack up the camera and trudge back through the sand. First the horse, now this. Was she losing her grip? She forced her mind back to the job. Her real job, not the pretense of nursemaiding these pampered children from a marshmallow-soft society.

They were close now, and her fingers tingled. She loosened her hold on the steering wheel and wriggled them. She glimpsed a flash of fluorescent day-glow green through the curtain of heat haze ahead and geared down.

Cheryl-Ann looked up from the printout, which Sonja had noticed was a joint press release from the Namibian and Angolan governments extolling the virtues of the Okavango Dam. This seemed to be the sum total of the producer's research prior to their visit. "Why are we slowing, Sonja? We've got to be at the dam by ten."

"I know. Roadblock."

Sonja made out the uniforms and the weapons as they coasted up to the red-and-white boom gate. It was a vet control point, designed to stop the flow of meat and dairy products one way as a precaution against foot and mouth disease, fairly common in this part of the continent. What was uncommon, as at the border crossing, were the two soldiers with AK-47s, who stood in the shade of a corrugated-iron hut while the woman in a blue uniform asked them if they had any meat products in the vehicle.

"No, nothing," Cheryl-Ann said across Sonja. "Look, we're in kinda a hurry here, so I'd really appreciate it if we could make this snappy, OK?"

Sonja smiled to herself. If someone ever bothered to write a textbook about how to circumvent African bureaucracy, then Cheryl-Ann's little monologue would have been perfect for the "what not to do" section.

"Switch off the engine and open the back, please," the quarantine officer said to Sonja, who complied and got out of the Land Rover.

Cheryl-Ann stuck her head out her window. "Hey, excuse me! I said we are in a hurry here, miss."

"Open the back, please," the woman repeated. Sonja unlocked and opened the rear door. "I want to see inside the cool-box. What is in all these black cases?"

"Camera gear," Sonja said. She knew there was no point lying.

The woman called out in her own language to the soldiers, who wandered over.

Cheryl-Ann got out of the vehicle. "Look. I asked you nicely if we could speed this up and now you seem to be going out of your way to delay us. I'd like to speak to your superior, miss."

"I am the superior. Open the cooler box."

Sonja hefted a waterproof case sitting on top of the drinks box and set it on the ground. One of the soldiers bent and started fiddling with the clasps on the case.

"Hey!" Jim Rickards opened his door and ran to the back. "Get your fucking hands off that man or I'll—"

The soldier brought his AK up to his waist and yanked back on the cocking handle, chambering a round.

"—or I'll be quite perturbed, my man." Rickards held his palms up and took a step back. "It's just camera gear. We're a TV crew, man. Wildlife World? Heard of it?"

The soldier stared at the cameraman.

Sonja licked her lips. This was going from bad to disaster, very quickly. She had a Glock in her bag and if Cheryl-Ann and Jim provoked the soldiers and the quarantine lady into doing a full search of the vehicle, she would end up in jail before nightfall. Cheryl-Ann would back up the story about her being their security for the trip, but Sonja had nothing in the way of permits or licenses for the weapon. "Cheryl-Ann," she said softly, "don't you have a number for someone you can call at the dam? Some government contact?"

"Right. I was just going to do that."

"All of the cases and bags, out of the car, now," said the other soldier.

"I'm just going to make a call, OK?" Cheryl-Ann said to the quarantine officer.

"Just do it," Sonja hissed, praying they were in a mobile phone coverage area. Sonja opened the lid of the cold-box. "It's hot, hey man?" she said to the soldier still pointing a gun at Rickards. "How about a Coke or a frostie?" The soldier off to one side shook his head. The gunman tightened his grip on his rifle.

Cheryl-Ann had got through to someone. "Where are we?" she asked Sonja.

"About five kilometers south of Bagani-Divundu." Sonja used both names for the tiny village and trading post at the crossroads not far from the dam.

Cheryl-Ann relayed the information then passed the phone to the ranking military man. "It's a man from the dam project. He wants to talk to you."

Sonja waited nervously and exhaled with relief when the soldier handed the phone back to Cheryl-Ann and nodded. "You must wait here. That man will come from the dam and escort you from here."

Sonja didn't need to be told twice. She got into the Land Rover and started the engine while Rickards was still loading his case back into the vehicle. Sonja drove off the edge of the road and parked a safe hundred meters from the roadblock, under a leafless tree. There was precious little shade, but she didn't want the soldiers to have second thoughts and carry out a snap search while they waited for their contact. While they waited, Sam opened the cold-box and handed out soft drinks. Rickards raised one in a mock toast to the soldiers over at the checkpoint. Sonja glared at the Australian. "Don't be an idiot."

"Holy shit," Cheryl-Ann said. "What was that all about? They treated us like we were goddamned criminals or something. I'm going to report those people to their supervisors."

"Welcome to the real Africa and your very first roadblock," Sonja said, not without sympathy. "It may not be the last. The secret to surviving roadblocks is the three P's—be polite, patient but persistent. You don't need to take any crap from police or soldiers or bureaucrats who might try and shake you down for a bribe. You've got to show them that you've got nothing better to do with your time but sit or stand there and talk it out, but as soon as you get angry or abusive you're asking for trouble."

Cheryl-Ann put her hands on her hips. "Excuse me. I was *not* abusive, Sonja."

Sonja was saved by the sight of a white Toyota Land Cruiser *bakkie* with a flashing orange light on the roof of its cab screaming down the road toward them. It pulled up at the roadblock and the African passenger greeted the soldiers and the quarantine officer and spoke with them. All of them, at various times, looked at the Land Rover and nodded at the foreigners. A white man was driving the Toyota and he waved at them. Cheryl-Ann waved back.

When the Land Cruiser turned Sonja saw the logo on the passenger's door—Roberts Engineering Pty Ltd, Windhoek. The vehicle pulled up next to them and the driver got out. He was about six foot tall, and solidly built with a rugby forward's shoulders and muscular thighs that seemed to bulge from his tight blue denim shorts. He wore a two-tone blue and khaki bush shirt, with the same emblem as the truck door embroidered above the heart, and *veldskoen* with no socks. With his red exposed skin, short blond hair and blue eyes he was as Namibian German as could be.

"Howzit?" he said to them collectively. "Miss Daffen?"

"Over here," Cheryl-Ann said, extending her hand. "And it's Ms., but you can call me Cheryl-Ann."

He nodded. "Deiter Roberts. As you are too many and my *bakkie* has only room for me and Hermand, you will please follow us?"

Sonja pushed the Land Rover's accelerator to the firewall to keep up with the Toyota Hilux. Deiter drove like a local—fast. Namibia was a vast, empty country with the lowest population density and some of the best roads on earth—an environment conducive to reckless speeding. However, Sonja kept a steady distance between her and the other vehicle as the corridor along the edge of the Okavango was home to several small villages and plenty of meandering goats and people.

On their left was a turn-off to Bagani airstrip and Sonja slowed to keep the gap between her and the other four-by-four. "Another roadblock ahead. This is the town of Divundu. Don't blink or you'll miss it."

They passed a general store and a shebeen. Half a dozen African men in blue overalls, two with orange hard hats, sat on a bench outside the bar with brown plastic containers of opaque beer in their hand, which they raised as the Land Cruiser drove past. Roberts honked his horn, returning the salute. It looked like the dam was good for business, as there were also two more of the engineering company's trucks parked outside the store.

Sonja geared down as they neared the roadblock. They were just before the intersection of the C48, which they were traveling on, and the B8, the main east-west highway that ran through the Caprivi Strip, which branched off to their right, via a high-level bridge over the Okavango.

Sonja expected more delays. This was a checkpoint like few she had seen. As well as the ubiquitous quarantine ladies in their blue overalls, there were police and soldiers armed with Kalashnikovs. If there were this many guns this far out on the road in full view, Sonja thought, there would be more positions in depth, hidden away but covering the men on point duty.

Her eyes scanned left and right until she found the machine-gun position. It was off to the right seventy meters from the checkpoint and sighted so that it could cover vehicles or people coming from any direction toward the crossroads, including the bridge. She recognized the silhouette of the barrel that protruded above the parapet—a belt-fed 7:62-millimeter Russian-made PKM. The gunner and his loader were in a makeshift bunker of sandbags and corrugated iron, roofed with a sheet of tin topped by a single layer of sandbags. Around the post was a coil of concertinaed razor wire and a seemingly flimsy screen of chicken wire. The mesh, she knew, was protection against RPGs—rocket-propelled grenades. The RPG was designed to take out light-armored vehicles by first penetrating a layer of steel, and then detonating inside, killing the crew. The fence would cause a projectile to detonate before it hit the sandbags, increasing the odds of the men inside the bunker surviving. She could see the number two on the gun raising a pair of binoculars. These men were prepared and alert.

Surprisingly, the boom gate in front of the Land Cruiser was raised before it came to a stop. Roberts thrust his arm from the driver's window and motioned them to follow. Sonja cruised past the checkpoint, taking in the numbers, the guns, uniforms and general attitude of the men and women manning it, without making eye contact with any of them. It was one time she would have welcomed a brief delay, in order to better carry out her recce.

The road had turned from tar to gravel and was now called the D3402, according to her GPS. They had swung west again, the Okavango still somewhere off to their right, and Sonja eased off the accelerator to stay out of the dust cloud stirred up by the Toyota in front. The dry grass to her right was covered in a layer of white grit, a testimony to the amount of traffic on the road. A small *bakkie* with rotating orange warning lights on its cab and a sign saying *abnormal load* emerged from the dust. Sonja moved to the left and rolled up her window as a lorry towing a giant bulldozer on a low-loader trailer trundled past.

Ahead of them, the dust devil chasing Deiter's *bakkie* swung to the right and Sonja indicated to follow them. The cloud slowed after a few hundred meters and, caught by a faint breeze, shrouded the Toyota for a moment. When it cleared, Sonja was close enough to see Roberts had reached a gate set in a chain-link fence topped with electrified strands of wire.

Inside the outer gate there was a boom and a newly erected portacabin, which, like the machine-gun strongpoint, was surrounded by razor wire and mesh. Instead of soldiers, this post was manned by blue-uniformed security guards. Both Roberts and the African man traveling with him, Hermand, were holding out what looked like black nylon identification wallets, with a clear plastic window and a cord that looped around their necks. The security guard, who wore a holstered pistol, passed a clipboard to Roberts while a colleague, armed with a drum-fed automatic shotgun, stood nearby. Another man, with a slung South African–made R5 military assault rifle, stood by the boom, while a fourth looked on from inside the portacabin. All of the guards wore body armor.

Sam leaned forward from the second tier of seats and peered out through the windscreen between Sonja and Cheryl-Ann. "Tight security."

And that was just what they could see. Sonja looked up and down the fence line. She spotted two cameras, and noted portable arc lights at intervals of every fifty meters. Cabling snaked back to a large generator on a trailer behind the portacabin, which must also power the hut's air-conditioning.

Having satisfied the guards, Roberts was allowed through the barrier, and pulled over to the side of the dirt road once inside. He walked back to the boom gate and Sonja rolled down her window as Roberts and one of the guards stepped up to the Land Rover.

"A necessary formality. We are very strict about security here on the construction site. Once you have all signed in I will also have to take you through a full site induction, for your safety."

Sonja and the camera crew got out and, under the instructions of the guard, filed into the hut.

"Why such strict security?" Sam asked Roberts as he stood aside to let Cheryl-Ann and Sonja enter.

"Routine," Roberts shrugged. "We have a lot of valuable equipment and vehicles here. We wouldn't want any to be stolen."

Routine, my arse, Sonja thought. As she filed into the hut behind Cheryl-Ann she noted the gun safe behind the counter, and the flat computer screen on the desk, which was angled enough for her to see it was quartered with constantly changing images from the security cameras. The feed probably went to the construction site's head office, but giving the guards' office access meant they could respond quickly.

Sonja filled in her name and false passport number on a form that the guard behind the counter slipped into a clear plastic wallet with a clip on it and handed back to her. "Please wear this at all times when on site, madam." She nodded. While the others filled in their tags she casually looked around the room. On a whiteboard on the far wall was a shift roster. There were ten names per shift.

She moved to the door and opened it to the oven-hot outdoors. A dust cloud was moving down the fence toward the hut. It was another Land

Cruiser, though this one was the same color blue as the uniforms of the guards in the hut. The fence looked new and the road around it recently graded. The vehicle slowed as it passed the gate and the occupants, in the same livery as those on the gate, waved and continued on. Mobile patrol. That made six guards now. She had to assume there was another vehicle on mobile patrol, while the remaining two men could be taking a break somewhere. The security guards seemed efficient and well armed, but there were not many of them.

With the paperwork completed they filed back out to the Land Rover and got in. The man on the boom checked that they were all wearing their badges, and Sonja motored through to where Deiter Roberts was waiting for them, inside his vehicle with the engine running and the air-conditioning on. He wound down the window, stuck his arm out and motioned for them to follow. Sonja got the distinct impression that this man would much rather be building a dam than babysitting a television crew.

Sonja raced through the gears to keep up with him on the wide but corrugated dirt road that led from the gate through a cordon of dust-covered bush. The gradient increased and Sonja dropped down to second as the vegetation on either side of them began to thin. At the top of the low hill she slowed to take in the view of the dam construction site.

"Wow," Gerry said from the back.

Roberts stopped and got out of his Land Cruiser. "You can get out here," he said through Sonja's window. The film crew got out and stood around him. "This is OK for filming, if you wish."

Rickards took Gerry to the back of the Land Rover and began unloading their gear.

Roberts turned his attention toward his guests. "My job is to explain to you how we are building this dam. I can be interviewed on camera if you wish, though my preference would be not to appear on film. I will not answer questions about why the dam is being built, or anything to do with politics or the environment, other than to outline how we minimize environmental impacts on site, in accordance with our environmental impact assessment."

Sonja got the impression he had rehearsed this monologue.

"There is a man from Windhoek, from the government's Nampower organization—our electricity people—who will talk to you about those things. Also there is a woman from the consortium that developed the plan for the dam who will talk to you about agricultural uses of the water and so forth. Is this clear?"

Sonja noticed that he didn't ask if it was all right.

"Crystal," Cheryl-Ann said. "Though if you don't mind I'll get Jim to film your briefing, so at least we have it all on tape and get it right for the voice-over. We may not use any of your stuff on film, but it's good for us to have it on file."

Roberts frowned, but nodded.

Jim and Gerry mounted the camera on its tripod and plugged in the boom mike and tested their gear while Cheryl-Ann and Sam briefly discussed angles and positioned Roberts so that Rickards could get as much of the construction site in shot while he gave his briefing.

From the top of the hill the Okavango looked like a giant blue-green python that had swallowed a fat *duiker* and was having trouble digesting the buck. The waters had started to back up behind the newly completed dam. Sonja wondered what the destructive force of that water would be once it was unleashed. She forced from her mind images of flimsy African huts and people and cattle being washed away.

Roberts cleared his voice. "The dam on the Okavango River is twelve hundred meters long and four meters high. It has an earth core and is covered in concrete."

Sonja tuned out for the moment. She moved a few paces away from the group, trusting that Roberts was too preoccupied with the camera pointing at him to notice her pulling her small binoculars from the pouch on her belt. She found the far end of the concrete dam, her reference point, and swung slowly to the left. There it was. An eight-wheeled armored vehicle painted camouflage. It was a BTR 60, a Russian-designed armored troop carrier. It could seat sixteen fully equipped soldiers and was armed with a 14.5-millimeter heavy machine-gun in the turret on top and a 7:62-millimeter machine-gun in the hull. The BTR was amphibious, Sonja recalled, making it a good vehicle for use in the defense of the dam site. If trouble flared on the opposite side of the river it could be there soon. She doubted there was just the one vehicle. It faced eastward, out toward the bush beyond the clearing that demarcated the edge of the construction site on the far side of the dam and the border of the Bwabwata National Park. The perimeter on that side of the river was fenced with triple coils of razor wire.

She lowered the binoculars. On this side of the river, below them, were rows of identical portacabins. She saw washing hanging from lines strung between the cabins—overalls mostly—so she assumed this was where the dam construction workers lived. Beside them, however, was an encampment of tan-colored canvas tents. She lifted the binoculars again and saw two soldiers in camouflage uniforms, with AK-47s slung over their shoulders, walking down the well-trodden path between the lines of accommodation. She counted twenty-four tents in all. With, say, four men to a tent, there was enough space to house an infantry company of about a hundred soldiers.

Sonja swept upriver, to the left, to the extent of the construction site. There were the predictable fuel tanks, tin-roofed workshops—open on the sides because of the heat—vehicle parks and a constant procession of dump trucks moving to and from what looked like an onsite concrete plant. Every couple of minutes a cement mixer trundled along the earthen ramp, which had yet to be surfaced, and onto the dam wall. Sonja could see there was still construction going on partway along the wall, and tuned back into Roberts's spiel to hear that work was almost finished on the spillway and the installation of the hydro-electric generator. The noise of trucks and generators and jackhammers rolled up the hill to provide a constant buzzing backdrop to Roberts's monotone delivery of his briefing. Like his introduction, she gathered he had given the speech many times before to other visitors.

Between the army encampment and the construction site proper there was a vehicle park, a large cleared area surfaced with gravel and surrounded by a diamond-mesh fence topped with barbed wire. Inside was a fuel tank mounted on stilts, which in turn sat in a large plastic bath, which she imagined was to catch any leaks. It was a sop to environmental protection, which Sonja considered tokenistic given the dam project was probably going to ruin an entire ecosystem. Parked in the yard were dump trucks, *bakkies* and what looked like a fuel truck. She refocused the binoculars to get a better look and saw a large red warning sign on the side. Interesting, she thought.

Sonja shifted her view again and doubled back over the path she had followed with her binoculars. She had missed something or, rather, she had seen and ignored what looked like a small clump of bushes. Here and there small pockets of natural vegetation had escaped the bulldozer's blade. The odd mature tree still standing had been commandeered by workers on breaks as a place to sit in the shade and eat or drink, but the shrubs Sonja had seen were too small to provide much shade. She focused her binoculars on the one that had caught her attention again. The bush moved, and an African man emerged. He was stripped to his waist and although it was at the extreme range for her pocket binoculars she could tell his trousers were not the blue or bright orange of the overalls worn by the construction workers she had seen so far. They were camouflage.

The man urinated in the open, then climbed back into the copse of bushes. However, now that she knew what she was looking for she saw it was not a stand of thornbush but a prepared position: a foxhole covered with a camouflage net. The man pulled aside the net and for the briefest moment the sun flashed on something. Sonja lowered the glasses again to rest her eyes.

The words of Gideon, the Lozi man she had met outside the Spar supermarket in Maun, came back to her. He'd said the Caprivian force that attacked the dam had been lit up by mortars firing illumination rounds, followed by deadly high explosive. The mortar pit was well sited and when she looked again she saw two other camouflaged positions. Mortars were indirect-fire weapons, which meant they had to fire their bombs high into the air to give them time to arm—they couldn't shoot in a flat trajectory. Therefore, they needed to be as far away as possible from the dam in order to bring fire to bear on them if insurgents breached the perimeter defenses. The pits were at the extreme end of the compound, which made sense.

"So, do you have any questions?" Deiter Roberts asked Sam and Cheryl-Ann. Sonja moved back to the camera crew, as she didn't want the engineer seeing where she was looking.

"Deiter, what about the environmental impact of the construction project on the river downstream. What can you tell us about that?"

Roberts held up a hand. "Like I said, I cannot comment on environmental matters or reduced flows in the Okavango Delta. I mean . . . I cannot comment on issues some people are raising."

He'd made a slip-up and Sonja could see his embarrassment as his already red face colored some more. He'd brought up the thorny question of the effect the dam would have on the supply of water to the delta without even being asked. Sam or Cheryl-Ann would surely exploit this opening.

"No," Cheryl-Ann said, "I think you misunderstood. I wasn't asking about water flows, just about how you were handling run-off from the site and water-quality issues associated with the construction phase."

"Oh!" His relief was obvious. "We are following every environmental regulation and safeguard to ensure all contaminants are contained on site and nothing harmful escapes from the construction site into the river downstream."

Except, Sonja thought, for plastic bags, sewage, rubbish and diesel slicks she'd seen in the river in front of Ngepi Camp.

"That's great, Deiter, just what we need. Thank you," Cheryl-Ann said.

"You will edit out the part where I talked about reduced flows, yes?"

Cheryl-Ann nodded. "Will do. Leave it with us. And you'll get to see a transcript of the interview before it goes to the final edit."

"Good," Roberts said. "That was not as difficult as I imagined it to be."

"You were great," Cheryl-Ann said, touching him on the forearm as he led them toward the vehicles. "Real good natural talent, as we say in the industry. Perhaps we can use a bit more of you in the video?"

He frowned again, but said, "We will see. For now, we must go and see the Nampower man and the lady from the consortium."

Sonja opened the door of the Land Rover and got in and started the engine. She was puzzled. Either she had just witnessed the softest ever television interview of a man involved in the building one of the most environmentally controversial dams in the world, or there was something else in play here.

17

Rickards was, literally, in the child's face. The lens was just a few centimeters from the little boy's nose, close enough to see the flies crawling in and out of his nostrils and eyes.

Sonja turned away from the gratuitous intrusion. The bureaucrat from the Namibian power company had not been at the site office when they returned from their tour of the construction works. He had been delayed by car trouble. Deiter Roberts had phoned the woman from the dam consortium. She was not due to meet with the TV crew for another two hours, but she offered to meet them at a nearby village. The plan had been for her to brief them at the site office first, and for them to end their first day with a trip to the village, but if they reversed the order they could film around the community first and she would meet them there. Cheryl-Ann had been quietly fuming, but to Sonja this was just another day in Africa, where things rarely went according to plan.

Sonja's mobile phone vibrated in her pocket and when she took it out she recognized the number. She let it buzz silently in her hand for a few seconds while she walked away from the camera crew.

She pressed the green button. "What?"

"That's not a very polite way to answer a telephone," Martin Steele said.

"They're filming," she said in a low voice.

"Can they hear us?"

"No, they're busy getting shots of children with distended bellies and mothers carrying plastic containers of water on their heads."

Steele laughed, but Sonja didn't find any of it amusing. "Martin, they may as well be making a bloody propaganda movie for the dam consortium, defending what they're doing up here. It's disgusting."

"I don't know that you or I are in any position to make moral judgments on anyone, my dear, but does it make you hate them even more than before?"

"Yes." He could still put a smile on her face.

"Good. Tell me what you've got."

She looked back at the crew, who were still busy recording misery. "Here, now?"

"I doubt anyone's tapping you up there in the middle of nowhere. Yes, what have you seen so far?"

"Why the rush?"

He paused. "Timing's been brought forward."

"Why?"

"I told them we could put something together in six weeks—and that would give the other element time to train up some new people."

"*Ja* at least." Sonja knew he was talking about the remnants of the CLA, hiding somewhere in Botswana. Gideon had told her there was no shortage of recruits willing to fight for Caprivian independence, but Martin was right: it would take at least six weeks to get men with no military experience ready to go to war.

"Our paymaster spoke to me today. He says a couple of the others are getting cold feet—your ex-boyfriend included. He's pushing to go within two weeks, before they have time to back out of their deal. They've got an update meeting planned for a fortnight's time."

Sonja looked back at the camera crew. Via an interpreter, Rickards was organizing a procession of village women to walk down a path with plastic water containers on their heads. "Shit, Martin. Why don't you just walk away from this one?"

"*You* know why. We're going to be short fifty percent of what was promised for your last job."

She smarted from the implication that the double-cross in Zimbabwe was somehow her fault. "It's too risky."

"We need the money, Sonja. Simple as that. So, what's your assessment?"

She drew a breath then exhaled. "There's a company plus dug in here, with armored support—at least one BTR 60 that I can see, probably a couple more in the bush somewhere if you assume they've allocated a troop. They've also got mortars. Using standard odds you wouldn't get through to the wall with less than a battalion, supported by heavy weapons." One of the basic ratios that all military planners worked on was that an attacking force taking on a prepared enemy position needed a numerical advantage of at least three to one.

"Hmmm. What about a small team, infiltrated onsite covertly?"

Sonja had already thought about that option. "Their civvy security is sharp—better than the local police and military checkpoints further out. No one, not even the bosses, gets onsite without a thorough check of their ID. The perimeter is covered by cameras, vehicle patrols and dog teams. It's mostly for show, I guess, but if the perimeter is breached the army guys inside will be ready for action. You'd have to know someone to get inside here."

Steele paused for a couple of seconds and Sonja, realizing her mistake, knew what he was going to say next.

"Then get to know someone."

"No. I'm not going to do that. Not ever again. No matter how much you pay me."

"I didn't say fuck someone, Sonja. I just said get to *know* someone. Someone senior, in case you need to come back one day soon."

"I thought I was only doing a CTR." She felt a tightness in her chest and then her heart started beating fast, pumping a hot shot of adrenaline all the way out to the tips of her fingers and toes. Steele was playing her, and she knew she should call a halt to this game right now.

"We don't have a battalion, Sonja—not even a battalion minus. You'll see that when you meet them. I'm trying to work a miracle and you're the angel on my shoulder."

She scoffed at his poor attempt at poetry and flattery.

"Whatever," he said. "If you can get back inside you can get a small team in there and do the job. Of course, if you think doing a dam is too big a job for a . . . for you . . ."

The clever, charming bastard was playing every angle and pushing every single button—and he was using a sledgehammer instead of his finger. Klaxons were going off in her brain and she knew, beyond a shadow of a doubt, that she should hang up, walk away from the dam and the Americans and Martin Steele and disappear into Africa.

"It's a ticket out. For you and Emma. Your share will go up, of course, with the added responsibility. If you can handle it."

"Damn right it'll go up. A recce is one thing but what you're talking about is the main game, Martin." She took a deep breath and knew she shouldn't ask the question. "How much."

"A mill."

"Pounds or dollars?"

"Dollars. England no longer rules the world."

"Make it three then."

"One and a half, and that's as high as I can go," he said.

"Bullshit. I know you, Martin. Two or I'm hanging up."

"Sonja, be reasonable, that's—"

"Bye, Martin."

"Wait, wait. OK. Two it is."

"Half now."

"All right. You drive a hard bargain—that'll eat up most of my advance and operating expenses. The money will be in your account tonight."

"Good," she said. She smiled to herself. He liked playing her and she liked him paying her.

"Instead of coming back to Maun the way you came, I want you to head down the Caprivi Strip to Katima Mulilo. Check things out there and cross back into Botswana. Have you heard of a place called Dukwe?"

She thought for a moment. "On the road between Nata and Francis-town?"

"That's the place. I'll see you there in five days' time."

She did the distance calculations in her head. "Where in Dukwe?"

"I'll find you. Oh, and Sonja?"

"Yes."

"Be careful."

He'd never said anything like that to her in the past. "Of what?"

"Don't forget the Zimbabwean CIO is still looking for blood over the supposed assassination attempt. I'm watching my back and you should watch yours. They need a body, and they don't want people around who might tell the truth to the international media."

She was confused. "Are you saying we should come clean and tell the world the assassination attempt was a fake?"

"No, no, no. Christ, Sonja, the last thing I want to do is implicate you—or me—in trying to take down elected leaders, no matter how corrupt they are. Maybe after this current job is over we can leak something. I don't want the CIO to think they can get away with using us like that and the world should know the truth."

"In time."

"Yes," he said, "in time. When you're living the life of a rich, gorgeous single mum retiree."

"Whatever."

"Perhaps I can drop by and see you on your private island off the coast of Mozambique, or your luxury private game lodge in the free-flowing waters of the Okavango Delta?"

She laughed. "Fuck off, Martin."

"Love you too, babe."

The consortium that had partnered with the Namibian government to develop the dam was called GrowPower, one word, with a capital in the middle. Sam was no pedant when it came to the English language but he didn't appreciate people messing with the natural order of letters and cap-

itals, any more than he particularly liked them messing with the environment.

He wasn't thrilled by Microsoft PowerPoint presentations either. He
was an outdoorsman and had never enjoyed being cooped up inside watching images on a wall and listening to someone drone on. All the same, Selma
Tjongarero, GrowPower's Manager, Corporate Communications, was not difficult to look at. He guessed she was aged in her late twenties and she'd arrived
like a visitor from another planet at the village. She was dressed in a well-cut
business suit with a blood red silk blouse that matched her fingernails. She
planted her patent leather high heels carefully in the dust as she eased herself
out of her low-slung BMW ZX4 sports car and pulled her D&G sunglasses
down off her tightly braided hair to shield herself from the midday glare.

Selma had suggested they head straight back to the construction site
office where she could brief them on the consortium and its development
plans for the area. When they arrived at the site they filed into a cabin fur-
nished for meetings. There was a drop-down screen on one wall and a po-
dium sporting a laptop that was connected to a data projector slung from
the ceiling. Selma looked at the projected image of the computer's desktop
and clicked on a PowerPoint file titled "presentation vers 2."

"It's great that you've already seen the hardship under which the rural
people live in this part of Namibia," she said, flicking mercifully quickly
through some slides that showed the scenes the crew had already captured,
including more women with water containers on their heads, and children
with distended bellies. "We can skip these."

Sam glanced over at Sonja, but she was looking out the window of the
air-conditioned cabin, over the construction site. She was interested in neither the presentation, nor him. He already knew she had a dislike of small
talk, but she seemed to have become even more withdrawn.

"GrowPower," Selma said, raising her voice as if to make sure they were
all still awake, "is going to change the lives of rural people in the Caprivi
Strip and northwestern Namibia. The Okavango Dam project will supply
water for irrigation which will open up hundreds of thousands of hectares
of currently barren land for commercial farming." She paused to advance

her slide presentation. The next image showed large swathes of the country turning from brown to green with a single click.

Selma's English was precise with a trace of a German accent. Grow-Power, she had explained at the beginning of the presentation, was a consortium whose shareholders included the Namibian government and its power authority, although the majority partner was a German agricultural company, AG Schwarz. Its president, Klaus Schwarz, Selma said, was currently in Windhoek involved in meetings with the president of the republic and had sent his apologies for not being able to meet the American TV crew in person.

Schwarz did, however, make an electronic appearance, via an MPEG video that Selma clicked on next, and then stood deferentially aside from the screen as her boss picked up the commentary, in heavily accented English.

"Thank you Selma," he smiled, and turned his head awkwardly to the right, and nodded. Selma grinned back adoringly at the little piece of computer-generated trickery. "Ladies and gentlemen, I'm sure Selma has passed on my sincere apologies at not being able to meet you in person during your trip to this beautiful country of Namibia. Beautiful, but barren."

Sam thought from the wooden performance that Schwarz was reading from an autocue, and it seemed like it was the first time he'd read the words.

"Beautiful, but barren. GrowPower is going to change all of that. We are going to turn this dry, underutilized corner of Africa into a fertile, verdant Garden of Eden where the quality of life for everyone living in the region will be improved appreciably. Northern Namibia, including the Caprivi region, will become the new breadbasket of Africa, growing and exporting crops and grain and beef and dairy products throughout the continent."

Sam wondered how many more clichés the guy could fit in before having to draw a breath.

"As well as supplying clean water for drinking and irrigation for agriculture, the new water storage facility will also bring," he coughed to clear his throat, "how you say, power to the people. Demand for electricity is growing throughout Africa, but power generation and distribution infrastructure is struggling to cope with existing requirements. One only has to look at

South Africa to see how disastrous the situation is. The Okavango project will generate enough megawatts to supply the whole of northeastern Namibia well into the future, and to feed excess power back into the national grid.

"Our company, AG Schwarz, has committed in excess of the equivalent of one hundred million US dollars toward this project, to help finance construction of the new water reservoir, and the development of other infrastructure essential for the development of intensive agricultural practices in the region. We expect some three hundred people will be involved during construction, and the same number, at least, in our agricultural precincts."

Sam gave a low whistle. It was a lot of money, and the private sector was in on the project in a much bigger way than he had realized.

"Much has been said and written about the environmental effects of construction of this new reservoir. I would like to assure you all that AG Schwarz has a proud record of environmental compliance at all of our sites around the world. This project is being constructed under the tightest environmental safeguards ever seen in Namibia and will operate under the same tough environmental regulations. The impact on flows downstream has been assessed by independent environmental experts as negligible. The wildlife of the Okavango Delta ecosystem will continue to flourish but, more importantly, the *people* of Namibia will have clean water for their children, food for their bellies and valuable dollars for their economy through a major expansion of the country's agriculture production and export capability.

"Ladies and gentleman, again, my apologies for not being there in person, but I wish you a pleasant and informative stay in Namibia and, if Selma might assist me with one other matter," Schwarz turned stiffly once more to the right, "perhaps you would ask Mr. Chapman if he would be kind enough to autograph one of his DVDs for my ten-year-old daughter, Liesl?"

Selma turned the lights on in the cabin and held up a copy of *Outback Survival*, grinning broadly.

"Fascinating, thank you, Selma," Cheryl-Ann said.

"What?" Rickards's head snapped up and he looked around him, wiping a tendril of drool from the corner of his mouth.

Selma walked around the data projector to Sam. "I'm so sorry you couldn't meet Mr. Schwarz. He's a great guy. Would you be willing to sign the DVD for his daughter?"

"Of course. My pleasure."

"What did you think of the presentation?"

Sam handed the DVD back to her. "Very informative." In fact, Schwarz's use of weasel words such as "water storage reservoir" instead of dam rankled.

"That was great, Selma," Cheryl-Ann said, coming between them.

Sam smarted. He wondered if, in the wake of what had gone on with Tracey, Cheryl-Ann had now appointed herself as his chaperone for the duration of the trip. He would have liked more time to quiz Selma—not because of her beauty, but because of some nagging doubts he had about the dam project. The more he saw and heard about the consortium, the less comfortable he was feeling about making the documentary. Still, he knew there was no way to back out of the contract at this late stage.

"Selma, let's get you miked up so we can film your part of the video now. You've rehearsed your script?"

Sam heard the unspoken "not like your boss" in Cheryl-Ann's tone.

Selma nodded. "I'm a little nervous though. I can speak to an audience, but the camera is quite intimidating."

Cheryl-Ann patted her on the arm. "You'll be fine."

And she was. Sam stood off to one side and watched as Selma delivered her prepared spiel about the benefits of the "water storage facility" and the associated "intensive agricultural precincts" to the good people of Namibia in one perfect take. She was beautiful, black and a woman, exactly the sort of spokesperson the project needed. Watching her glistening, sensual mouth and seeing her bright, animated eyes, and her smile—interspersed at all the right places—made him want to believe the dam was every bit as good as she said it was. The balding, middle-aged white German with slightly crooked teeth hadn't convinced him, but Selma Tjongarero almost did.

Mathias Shivute, the regional head of the Nampower corporation arrived just as Selma was removing her microphone.

He was sweating profusely and had loosened his tie and rolled the sleeves of his white shirt, which was stained with a grease mark. His black suit pants were shiny with wear and the knees scuffed with white dust. He wiped his hand on his belly and introduced himself around the room.

"Sorry I'm late. Two punctures—can you believe it?" he said. "I can be ready in half an hour to begin my presentation."

Sam heard Rickards groan behind the camera. Cheryl-Ann took Mathias aside and politely suggested that as they were running late it might be better if they simply interviewed him for his piece to camera in the corporate documentary. That way, she said, they would gain an understanding of Nampower's involvement in the project and have his comments on the record at the same time. He looked a little put out, but agreed.

While Selma started packing up her things and Cheryl-Ann talked Mathias through his lines, Sonja slipped out the door of the cabin. Sam followed her.

She stood in the shade of the hut, her eyes scanning the construction site in the valley below. She reminded Sam of a predator surveying its savannah hunting ground.

"I wouldn't have thought it possible, but you seem quieter than ever."

She turned and looked at him, not speaking, and he gazed out over the dam.

"You're taking their money to make a propaganda video for them, aren't you?" she said.

He shrugged. "Cheryl-Ann and I are hired by a production house that makes films for Wildlife World. We also make corporate videos for people who pay us."

"And you don't ask questions."

"I've turned down requests from the hunting lobby and the Japanese whalers to make documentaries for them."

"So whales are important but the Okavango Delta isn't?"

"You don't think people are as important as animals? What about all that stuff about electricity and food and water for the local people?"

She shook her head. "The Okavango Delta supports thousands of

people in Botswana who make their living from the safari industry, including, by the way, professional hunting. This project isn't about food and
water, it's about money, and that," she jabbed a thumb toward the door,
"confirmed it. If you can't see that, Sam, then nothing I can say will convince you otherwise."

He was about to follow her toward the Land Rover when Cheryl-Ann
called him to listen to Mathias's interview.

When Sam walked back inside Sonja opened the Land Rover and found her
daypack. She took out her hairbrush, slid the rubber band off her ponytail
and brushed her hair, leaving it hanging loose. She had no makeup, but she
licked her lips and checked her teeth in the rear-view mirror before closing
the door. She undid the third button of her safari shirt and turned up her
collar.

The site office was made up of three cabins, set in a horseshoe arrangement on the ridge overlooking the dam. Cheryl-Ann and the crew were still
in the cabin used for meetings and presentations. Sonja watched Deiter Roberts leave his office, walk to the meeting cabin, disappear inside, then re-
emerge a few seconds later with a laptop under his arm. It was the computer
Selma had used for her presentation.

Sonja waited a couple of minutes after Roberts had returned to his office, then walked over to it. She knocked on the door of the one next to it
and asked to see Deiter. An African woman called through a partition and
Roberts came out to greet her.

"Yes?"

"Hi, Deiter. I think I know all I need to about hydro-electricity and
water storage facilities, so I thought I would see if I could get a coffee."

He looked past her, toward the open door and the next hut where he
had just come from. He was clearly distrustful of the media people, even if
they were here at the company's invitation. The laptop he'd taken from the
conference room was on his desk, next to his PC.

"To tell you the truth," she said, lowering her voice, "I need a break
from my *friends*. Yes, but they're worse than Englishmen."

A smile fractured his face. "Come into my office. The aircon works better so it's cooler in there. Frieda," he said to the African woman at reception, "please, bring us two coffees."

"Yes, sir," the woman said.

"What did you think of the presentation?" Roberts asked her.

Sonja shrugged. "It was pretty interesting. There are obviously a lot of sensitivities about this project, though."

Roberts nodded and motioned for her to take a seat. "Hell, you don't know the half of it. We have to watch every word we say and the Germans in head office check everything ten times. They're forever changing brochures and documents and presentations to make sure every 'i' is dotted and every 't' crossed. The big boss, Schwarz, is fanatical about communications—I only just loaded the version of that presentation half an hour before you arrived. You say the wrong thing to the wrong person on this project and it could cost you your job."

"Very political, hey?"

Roberts rolled his eyes toward the ceiling, then relaxed a little in his chair. "You came up from Botswana, but you're not from there, I think. South African?"

She shook her head. "I was born in Okahandja."

His eyes widened. "So you're a Namibian."

"It said South-West Africa on my birth certificate. My family moved to Botswana after the war. I grew up in the swamps."

"Quite a change from Okahandja. What did your parents do there?"

"In Namibia?"

He nodded.

"My dad was a cattle farmer, but he was called up with the SWATF when the war got busy."

"Me too." Roberts looked out his window over the dam, and she could tell the mere mention of the acronym of the South-West Africa Territorial Force had brought back a cascade of memories. "They put me in an engineering unit after I graduated so I wasn't in a lot of combat, but..."

Sonja picked up the thread. "There was no escaping it, I suppose. Not even us, on the farm. We were attacked by terrorists while my dad was away on call-up. My mom and I were fine, but things changed after that. She wanted to leave the country—she's English—and he wanted revenge. I went to live in England with her for a while and he transferred to *Koevoet*."

Deiter reached into the pocket of his shirt and drew out a packet of cigarettes. He flipped the lid and Sonja could smell the roasted tobacco from the other side of the desk. He raised his eyebrows, but she shook her head.

"Do you mind if I do?"

"It's your office," she said, craving the hit. "Roberts doesn't sound very German."

He lit up and she was momentarily entranced by the orange tip that burned like a tiny sunset. "*Ja.* My mom was from German stock but my father was an Englishman who came here looking for diamonds."

"I'm the reverse," Sonja said. "German Namibian father and an English mother."

There was a knock at the door.

"Thank you, Frieda," Deiter said, as the receptionist laboriously set out the cups, sugar, milk and a plate of biscuits. When she was finished and they were alone again he said: "So, your old man was in *Koevoet*, eh? Hard bastards."

"Too hard." She stirred sugar and milk into her coffee. "My father had to leave the country after independence. We sort of went into hiding in the Okavango Delta. My mom and I came back out and my folks managed a safari camp for a number of years."

He sighed, then blew on his drink. "Terrible, terrible times, Sonja. Wait . . . Sonja?" He snapped his fingers. "Not Sonja Kurtz?"

She nodded. She'd picked his age right, and made sure she mentioned Okahandja and the SWAPO fighters attacking the family farm. She was fairly sure he would recall who she was. It rankled and sometimes in the past when she'd met men of Deiter's age from Namibia she'd given a false surname or deliberately avoided mentioning it as someone always made the connection.

"You're the little girl who killed the terr!"

She shrugged. "I could strip, load and fire an RI from the time I was eleven and I was loading magazines from the age of seven."

"You were the toast of Windhoek, you know?"

Sonja swallowed and smiled at the awkward compliment. She had been twelve at the time.

"You saw more action than I did. I suppose you get sick of people asking what it's like to kill a man?"

"You're very perceptive, Deiter."

He laughed. "So what are you doing with this bunch of American TV people? I was told their guide was going to be a man."

Sonja breathed in the smoke he exhaled as he spoke. "I think I might have one of those, if you don't mind."

He reached back into his pocket and offered the pack to her. She drew it out, slowly, watching his face as she did so. Before he could palm the lighter across the table she placed the filter tip between her lips and leaned forward. He seemed pleased as he lit it, and closed the distance between them.

She inhaled and closed her eyes, leaning her head back, but keeping her elbows on the timber laminate of his desk.

"First one in a while?" he asked.

She smiled as she opened her eyes and caught him raising his eyes from her cleavage. "Mmmm. You've corrupted me, Deiter Roberts."

He coughed, and she wrinkled her nose as she flashed him a smile. She had him.

She sat back in her chair and crossed her legs, cool and aloof now. "*Ja*," she exhaled. "Their guide was injured when he crashed the helicopter they were filming from. I'm a last-minute substitute. I can't say I particularly like them, but it's work, hey?"

He nodded. "And the man, the television star? Chapman?"

She could tell what he was thinking. "I think he's a *moffie*."

"Ah-hah," said Roberts, as though she was confirming his suspicion that any man who worked on television must be gay.

Sonja felt a pang of guilt at perpetuating what she knew was a lie. "From what I've read you were lucky to get your dam finished, what with all the international environmentalists opposed to the project."

Roberts sipped some more of his coffee and took a biscuit. "It's not just the greenies who were against us. These mad bloody Caprivians want to blow us up, as well."

Sonja smiled. "Speaking of blowing things up, are you still blasting here on site? One thing I've learned about these TV people is that they like to film lots of action."

He shook his head. "No, but you might have seen a truck carrying explosives on the road around here, or onsite."

"Yes, I think that's probably what made me think of it." The truck in the vehicle park that looked like a fuel or water container, she suddenly realized, contained explosives.

Roberts leaned forward, resting his elbows on the table. "These Grow-Power people aren't just into farming, you know. They've also bought the exploration rights for this area and they're doing some blasting to look for diamonds. If they find what they're looking for they're going to need a hell of a lot of water for the mines. They park their bloody truck full of Nitro-pril here because we've got good security. Can you imagine what would happen if those damned Caprivians got hold of a truck full of that stuff?"

"Goodness, no," she said, shaking her head. "But you're safe here. I see you have some military back-up. That's a good thing." She looked out the window of the office.

He followed her eyeline to the far side of the river where the BTR 60 was trundling down a dirt road, with a dust cloud in attendance. "Those clowns spend most of their time eating *pap* or snoozing in the shade of their vehicles, but when the bullets started flying last time it was good to have them there."

"One armored car isn't much, though, surely?"

He shook his head. "You misheard me. I said *vehicles*. There are three of them and, yes, you should hear the racket when their guns open fire. Also, we have four mortar tubes covering the site."

Sonja drained her coffee and stubbed out her cigarette. She hated Steele for telling her what to do, but her time with Roberts had already yielded an extra mortar tube and two more armored cars.

Sonja stood and carefully picked a couple of biscuit crumbs off her bush shirt. "I'd better get back to my Americans." Roberts rolled his chair back and she could see the disappointment in his eyes. She had no more need of the man—he had served his purpose.

18

Sonja paused outside the site office to let the heat blast away the imaginary layer of grime that covered her skin and her soul.

She had flirted only a little with Roberts, but she hated Martin for making her feel like a whore, and hated herself for falling for his lines every time. But he knew how to play her emotions as well as he'd once known how to play her body. All she wanted to do right now was blow something up so, in essence, she knew Martin had won her over once again.

The door of the meeting room cabin opened and Cheryl-Ann walked out, chatting to the African bureaucrat who followed her and now looked a lot cooler and relaxed. Jim, Gerry and Sam trailed them, carrying cameras, tripods, sound gear and other paraphernalia. Sonja opened the Land Rover's doors and got in and switched on the engine.

"Get what you wanted?" she asked Sam.

He paused, carrying a tripod and a case, and just looked at her. He'd read the sarcasm in her tone and she looked away. She was still angry, but she knew she shouldn't be taking it out on Chapman. He wasn't the cause of her problems. She turned and walked from him and got back in the driver's seat. Who was she to judge the morals of a television presenter who took money from a legitimate corporation to tell their side of a story? She'd just used the fact that she had killed as a child to get information out of a man who thought he had a chance of sticking his dick inside her. Looking at Sam and remembering how she'd fantasized about him that night in the camp in Botswana made her feel even more ashamed of what she'd just done at Steele's urging.

"We need to stop in at Popa Falls and get some vision there, Sonja," Cheryl-Ann said.

Sonja nodded. She was sick of being a chauffeur, as well.

There was a tap on her window and she saw Deiter Roberts standing there. She rolled down her window and he handed her a card. "It's got my mobile phone number on it. Just call anytime if you're in the area."

"Thanks."

"What was that all about?" Cheryl-Ann said.

None of your fucking business, Sonja thought. "He might have some security work for me." Sonja drove off down the access road, glad for the moment to be out of sight of the dam. She drummed her hands on the hot black steering wheel as she waited for the guard at the perimeter boom gate to sign them out.

"Anybody else thirsty?" Rickards asked from the back seat.

"I am," said Gerry.

"There's the general store at Divundu," Sonja said. "We can get cold drinks there."

When they came to the intersection of the B8 Sonja slowed for the roadblock, but the policeman on duty must have recognized the vehicle, because he motioned with his hand for them to continue. She turned right onto the tar road, then swung immediately to the left to pull into the store and fuel station. The forecourt wasn't paved and white dust swirled around the Land Rover as she drove past a braying donkey. Two mangy dogs watched her and a trio of young boys dressed in rags emerged from the meager shade of the whitewashed store's walls. A shiny black double-cab Toyota *bakkie* with darkly tinted windows was the only other vehicle parked outside the store, occupying the only natural shade in sight, under the bare branches of a stunted tree.

"I am hungry, madam, give me ten dollars," one of the boys said, as he pressed against the driver's side door.

"No." She got out of the vehicle and locked it once her passengers had piled out.

"I will mind this car for you, madam."

"That's my job." Sonja walked over to the fuel station's island, where the female attendant sat, wilting in the heat with her back against a pump. "Afternoon, how are you, sister?"

"I am fine, but it is too hot. How are you?"

"Fine." Sonja looked over at the black pick-up and saw gray smoke coming from its exhaust pipe. "How long has that *bakkie* been there?"

The woman shrugged.

Sonja reached into her breast pocket and pulled out a one hundred Namibian dollar bill.

"For about one hour," the attendant said, reaching up, though still not standing.

Sonja extended her hand, though not all the way. "How many people inside?"

"Ah, four men."

"African?"

She nodded. "But not from here, I think. Zimbabweans. They must be mad. How can they wear jackets in this heat?"

Sonja shrugged, then handed over the money as Cheryl-Ann and the three men emerged from the store. Sonja bleeped the alarm with the remote, thanked the woman and walked back to the Land Rover.

Perhaps, she thought as she headed back toward Popa Falls, she was being paranoid. She glanced in the rear-view mirror again. Nothing. She eased her foot off the accelerator.

Cheryl-Ann looked up from her notebook. "Why are we slowing?"

"The car that just drove past flashed his lights. Could be a speed cop up ahead. You don't want a fine do you?"

Cheryl-Ann lowered her head again. The last car had done no such thing, but Sonja knew Cheryl-Ann was too engrossed in her work to have noticed. Rickards and Gerry were dozing in the second seat and Sam, who was taking a turn at the rear, next to the camera cases, was looking out the side window, mesmerized by the African landscape.

She was sitting on eighty kilometers an hour now. When she checked her rear-view mirror again she saw them.

The black *bakkie* loomed up on them, and she guessed the driver was doing at least a hundred and twenty. The road was clear of oncoming traffic, so there was no reason for the truck not to zoom past her.

It slowed.

Sonja dropped down to fourth and planted her foot. The engine screamed in protest and Cheryl-Ann looked up. "Make up your mind, Sonja."

She checked the mirror again and saw Sam looking backward and forward. "Is that pick-up following us?"

"Wha . . . what?" said Rickards, his head snapping up.

"What's going on, Sonja?" Cheryl-Ann demanded.

"Relax, everyone," Sonja said, fighting to sound calm. "Cheryl-Ann, take the wheel for a second."

"What?"

Sonja slipped back up into fifth, the speedometer needle climbing to one-twenty. The black *bakkie* was three car lengths behind them, matching their speed. "Take the wheel, please, Cheryl-Ann. Just for a moment."

Cheryl-Ann leaned across the center console box and grabbed the steering wheel. She jerked and overcorrected.

"Hey, careful!" Rickards said.

"What are you doing, Sonja?"

She ignored Cheryl-Ann and reached between her legs and under her seat. Her fingers closed around the oily cloth and she slid out the bundle and unwrapped it.

"Oh. My. God."

Cheryl-Ann let go of the wheel as though it was red hot and scrunched against the passenger door as if the pistol was going to go off of its own accord as Sonja transferred one hand back to the steering. She placed the pistol between her legs and wound down her window.

Rickards swiveled in his seat. "Sam, open that black case. Pass me my camera."

"Jim, are you crazy?" Cheryl-Ann asked. "Leave that camera where it is, Sam."

"No," Sonja said. "Let him. Jim, point your camera at them."

"Will someone tell me what's going on?" Gerry moaned.

In the mirror, Sonja could see Sam passing the camera over the seat to Rickards, who wound down his window. "Walkley awards, here we come. Hold on to my belt, Gerry."

Sonja shook her head. Rickards was insane. He was sitting on the sill of the car door, his shirt snapping in the slipstream as Sonja kept her foot pressed hard to the firewall. Awkwardly, he raised his camera to his shoulder and pointed it at the pick-up.

Her ploy worked. She knew the sight of a TV camera would make them reveal themselves and force the driver to act. The Toyota, much faster than the aging Land Rover, moved into the oncoming lane and started gaining on them.

"That's right," Rickards yelled. "Smile for the camera, baby."

Sonja glanced right and saw the black tinted front and rear passenger's windows sliding down. She put her arm out the window so the occupants could clearly see the pistol in her hand.

"Holy fuck!" Rickards turned from the viewfinder. "He's got a gun."

Sonja aimed at the *bakkie*'s front tire and fired twice, but the driver swerved and she missed. She glanced ahead as she heard the *pop, pop, pop* of an AK-47. There was a clang and a jolt as a copper-jacketed bullet punched through the wafer-thin aluminum skin of the Defender.

"Shit! Ow. I'm hit, I'm fucking hit." Gerry slumped down and Rickards flailed in the breeze, grasping for the roof carrier with one hand and holding his camera to his shoulder with the other.

"Jim, get in!" Sonja wrenched the wheel hard to the left and the Land Rover careened off the edge of the road, down the meter-high embankment. The white powdery dust threw up an immediate smokescreen behind them. The Toyota overshot, and though the gunners in the front and rear seats fired back at them, none of their shots found their mark. Ahead of them was a trio of thatched huts. A woman ran screaming from her yard, snatching a bare-bottomed toddler by the arm and lifting the child off the ground as she fled the shooting. The dwellings had stopped the black *bakkie* from leaving the road and the driver was executing a three-point turn further down.

Sonja swung left again and drove straight for a plot of straggly maize. Corn stalks flashed by the windows and were crushed under the bumper bar as the Land Rover bounced over the tilled furrows. Camera cases slid forward onto Sam and the others and Cheryl-Ann kept up a high-pitched, unceasing scream as she gripped the handle on the dashboard with two white-knuckled hands.

Rickards was swearing and yelling insults out the window at their unseen pursuers. Sonja looked back over her shoulder. "Gerry, are you OK? Jim, shut up and check him out. He said he was hit."

Gerry was pale-faced and panting. Sam leaned over from his seat to check. "Here," he said, holding up fingers sticky with blood. "The back of his neck, but it's only a graze and a burn. You'll be OK, Gerry."

The sound man looked far from convinced. Sonja took her foot off the accelerator.

"What now?" Cheryl-Ann said.

"Somebody else drive." Sonja opened her door as the Land Rover slowed to a halt in the maize, its engine still running.

"You can't leave us!"

"Yes, I can, Cheryl-Ann. I know what I'm doing. Are you going to drive? We don't have time to mess about."

"Get out of the way, Jim." Sam had climbed over the back seat and elbowed his way past Rickards, who was standing next to the Land Rover, still holding his camera. "Get back in. I'll drive."

Rickards nodded. "I can hear them coming."

Sonja stepped back as Sam climbed into the driver's seat. "Carry on for about another hundred meters," she said. "You should be close to the river. Turn left when you can see it. Follow the bank as far as you can. Keep driving then cut left again once you're clear of the maize and head back to the road. Go back to the dam and ask for Roberts. He'll take care of you."

"What about you?"

"I'll be fine." She looked at Sam's belt. "Give me your Leatherman."

He fumbled with the pouch and pulled it out. "Why?"

"I want to trade." She held out her pistol to him, but he shook his head. "Uh-uh. No way."

She snatched the pocket tool from his hand and thrust the pistol into his. "You've got Cheryl-Ann and the others to worry about. You know how to use that?"

He looked down at the pistol like it was an alien ray gun. He looked up at her and shrugged. "I guess."

"Good man. It's loaded, but not cocked. Now go!" She banged on the roof of the Defender, then turned and ran into the rows of corn.

"*Benzi!*" Major Kenneth Sibanda screamed in Shona at Sithole, the junior Central Intelligence Organization operative, as the idiot flew past the Land Rover and found himself unable to turn off the road because of the huts.

The smell of cordite filled the air and hot spent casings rolled about Sibanda's shoes in the front of the Hilux. He fired twice more at the disappearing dust cloud as the driver executed a slow, clumsy turn. The noise was deafening in the confines of the *bakkie*.

He turned and looked behind him. "And you, Moyo, you fucking fool, who told you to open fire?"

"The cameraman, Comrade Major. He was filming us."

"I know that, you cretin," Sibanda screamed. "But we are not in Harare now! You cannot go executing journalists because one points a camera at you. If we don't get them I will personally see that you are court-martialed and executed. Understand?"

Moyo nodded and shifted across the back seat of the car so he was on the driver's side as they sped back toward the maize. Sithole, the driver, pulled off the road and the Toyota bucked and bounced on the uneven ground.

Sibanda banged on the dashboard. "Follow their tracks. Faster."

Two vehicle lengths into the stand of straggly crops the Hilux came to a halt, its rear wheels spinning in soil that had been laboriously watered by villagers carrying buckets from the shrinking river.

"Engage four-wheel drive! Didn't anyone ever teach you how to drive properly, you stupid baboon?"

"I have, Comrade Major," Moyo said, wiggling the selector gear and stamping on the accelerator. The engine screamed but the rear wheels kept spinning.

Sibanda leaned the barrel of his AK-47 out of the passenger window. "Get out and push, Moyo. I'll cover you."

The gunman got out, leaving his door open, and peered into the maize.

"Get a move on, man! We have to catch the *murungus*. If they get away we are finished. Move!"

Moyo slung his rifle across his back and moved to the rear of the pick-up. Sibanda looked around and when he saw the big man had his weight against the tailgate he ordered Sithole to accelerate again. Still nothing happened. Sibanda opened his door and leaned out, to check the front wheels. "The wheels are not moving. Did you lock the hubs, Sithole?"

A look of comprehension dawned on the driver's face. "Sorry, Major. I will do it now."

Sibanda shook his head. Every second they wasted was putting the woman further out of their reach. He got out and locked the free-wheeling hub on the passenger's side front wheel, and waved Sithole back to the driver's seat.

"Moyo?"

Sibanda got back in the vehicle, craned his neck and looked out the rear window of the double cab. "Moyo!" he barked again. He couldn't see the man, and presumed he was crouching lower, perhaps with his back to the tailgate now to gain extra purchase.

"Go, go!" he said to Sithole. When the driver floored the accelerator there was a little more forward movement, but the vehicle only managed to crawl a meter before it seemed to bog again. The fool must have spun the rear wheels so much that they had plowed into the soil. "Idiot. I will help Moyo, but if you can't get us out and catch the Land Rover I will shoot you here, in this field, and leave your body for the fucking dogs, Sithole."

"Yes, Comrade Major."

Satisfied with the fear in the driver's eyes, Sibanda got out, slung his rifle and slammed the door.

"Moyo!"

Sibanda trudged through the cloying mud and saw that below the dry crust they had broken through to a thick, gluggy porridge, probably fed by subterranean water. The rear of the Toyota was resting on its springs. "Moyo!"

Sibanda placed a hand on the hot black metal of the truck's side panel for balance as he reached the rear. There was no sign of his other operative. Sibanda felt something sticky under his fingers and when he inspected his hand he saw the redness.

Flies buzzed around her face and feasted on the dead man's blood on her hands.

Sonja blew them away with a quick breath from the side of her mouth. Her heart was pounding and she was breathing fast as she squinted through the AK-47's rear sight. Her heart felt like someone was squeezing it, and her mouth was dry. Sonja heard the man yelling his dead comrade's name and she had a good idea what he would do when he saw the blood.

For the moment, though, she concentrated on the driver's face. He was a target, an enemy combatant. She didn't hate him. He was, she imagined, an underling. She took up the pressure on the trigger and when the green stalks behind her shook under the storm of lead she squeezed the trigger, firing one shot into the driver's temple. The predictable fusillade fired into the bush by the other man had masked the sound of her single aimed shot.

Sonja was on her feet, running at a crouch. She had been no more than ten meters from the car, so there was no way she would miss. The driver must have stamped on the accelerator as he died, because the Toyota's engine blew a cloud of black smoke.

She assumed the man who was spraying indiscriminate fire into the maize was the commander of the detachment. He wasn't driving and hadn't got out to push when they'd become bogged. The man held his finger on the trigger and swung the rifle left and right, covering the direction of the blood and drag trail that led from the vehicle.

But Sonja had circled forward and across the tracks made by the Land Rover as soon as she had killed the first man. She'd wrapped her left hand around the big African man's mouth and drawn the wicked, saw-toothed blade of the Leatherman through his windpipe before he could ut-ter a sound. His blood had soaked her as she dragged him into the corn and unslung his rifle.

The commander emptied his magazine, just as she guessed he would. He trudged back toward the vehicle, which was still blowing smoke.

"Stop revving the engine, you fool!" As he walked he pulled the empty magazine from the rifle, then tossed it into the back seat through the open door. "Sithole?"

"Down!" Sonja yelled, pressing the barrel of the dead man's AK-47 into the soft skin behind the commander's left ear.

He started to turn so she jabbed the rifle harder into his head. "Drop your weapon and get down on your fucking knees."

He complied. She backed off half a step. "Turn your face to me. Slowly." She looked him in the eyes. "Major Kenneth Sibanda, Zimbabwean CIO."

Sibanda nodded. "Miss Sonja Kurtz, mercenary."

"I prefer Ms."

"It appears you have bested me again, *Ms.* Kurtz. You don't die easily."

"You set up the bogus hit on your president."

He said nothing.

"You posed as a member of the opposition and paid my principal, Martin Steele, to organize the hit. I want to hear you say it."

He shook his head.

She pressed the rifle home again. "You're an animal, Sibanda. You sac-rificed and jeopardized the lives of your own men—police, soldiers, the drivers of those limos—to discredit the opposition and protect a man who has bled your country dry."

"You killed them, not me."

Sonja reversed the rifle and smacked the steel butt plate against the side of Sibanda's head, drawing blood. He lurched to one side, but regained his balance, still on his knees.

"Who are you to lecture me on right and wrong, woman?" He spat the last word and she was tempted to hit him again.

"Whose idea was it to set up the assassination? Yours? The president's? I'm curious, what kind of a monster uses his own loyal foot soldiers as bait?"

He laughed, long and loud.

"Shut up. I should just kill you now, but I want your story, on tape, for the world to hear."

He shook his head. "You may as well kill me now. If I told the lies you want, my life would be worthless."

"They're not lies."

"Be that as it may, I am not saying anything to you, woman, on tape or otherwise. And if you do decide to kill me I will look for your daughter in the otherworld. Since she is the spawn of a murderess I might bump into her in hell—and enjoy her."

Sonja shifted the barrel and pulled the trigger.

The bullet tore through the muscle atop Sibanda's left collarbone and the impact sent him sprawling forward so that his forehead clanged against the side of the Toyota. He screamed and rolled in the mud, frantically reaching for the wound with his right hand.

"Don't kill me," he wailed, "or your daughter will die. I promise you."

Sonja dropped to one knee beside him and pushed the hot barrel back behind his ear, pinning him like an insect. "What do you know about my daughter?"

"Everything." His voice was high-pitched, but it chilled her. "Her school. The address of your apartment in London."

She pushed harder. "You're bluffing."

"She goes to fencing practice, in Amersham, on Wednesday evenings."

Sonja licked her lips. They were following her child. Her fist began to squeeze, involuntarily, around the pistol grip of the AK-47, the tension increasing on the trigger.

"If I die my superiors will not let you live. They know the best way to catch a parent is to grab the child."

"You bastard." They were on to her. The CIO had been better organized and better resourced than she'd thought possible. She'd been arrogant, thinking they would have lost her trail after Kasane. Perhaps she'd been safe at Xakanaxa, but they would have had people looking for her in the major towns and airports in Botswana—including Maun. There was a huge population of expatriate Zimbabweans—legal and illegal—living in Botswana and she was foolish to have ignored the possibility of the CIO having a spy network in the country.

Sibanda winced. "We can negotiate. You do me a favor and I will do you a favor. Let us talk, like rational people, please."

"You threaten my child and want me to be rational? You're bluffing. I should kill you now."

"Please . . . you know I know things about Emma . . ."

"If you so much as whisper her name again I will cut your manhood off and leave you to bleed to death."

". . . things about your daughter. My government needs assurances you will not go to the press, as you have threatened to do so. You killed innocent men in Zimbabwe."

"Yes, but it was all part of your plan. You killed them, you bastard."

He ignored her accusations. "In exchange for my life I will organize for you and your daughter to be left in peace . . . as long as you and your employers remain silent. Please . . . I am bleeding to death."

She grabbed his shirt collar and he twitched away, but she wanted to inspect the wound. Blood was flowing freely. It would take time for him to bleed out, but if she did nothing for him and kept him held like this it would happen. He was starting to shake.

"I want money, as well," she said.

"I am offering you the life of your child."

"Yes, and I have your life in my hands. I have people I can call on who might be able to protect my daughter, before your thugs can get to her. But you have no one, Major Sibanda."

He was silent for a few seconds. "One hundred thousand. US dollars."

"Two hundred thousand. British pounds."

"One hundred thousand pounds. That is all I have in my contingency budget. We are a poor country."

She wanted to shoot him for that remark alone. His president, his party and men like Sibanda had grown fat by scavenging Zimbabwe's corpse like a pack of hyenas. As much as she hated dealing with this odious piece of scum she would do anything to protect Emma. "Deal."

Somehow or other she would see that the money got to the families of the men she'd killed in the convoy ambush in Zimbabwe.

"Thank you. My shoulder?"

"Keep still. Move and I'll kill you." She laid the dead man's AK-47 in the grass behind her and pulled Sam's Leatherman from her pocket. It was sticky with the congealed blood of the first man she had killed. She unfolded a blade and cut Sibanda's shirt from his body. She placed her booted foot in the small of his back so she could pull the remnants of it from him.

He yelped and his broad black back was shiny with sweat. Sonja balled the shirt and pressed it down on the wound. "Hold this. Keep pressure on the wound. Do you have a first-aid kit in the *bakkie?*"

Sibanda shook his head. She heard footsteps behind her and looked around.

"Sonja? My God, what happened here?"

"Go back to the Land Rover, Sam. Get the medical kit from my day-pack and—"

Sibanda rolled from under her and smacked his right fist into the side of her face as he rose. Sonja reeled from the blow, landing in the grass. She flailed out with her right hand, dropping the Leatherman as she tried to regain her balance and reach the rifle. Her vision was clouded with shiny silver spots as he kicked her right side.

She fumbled in the dirt for the knife, but Sibanda kicked it aside.

"Hey," Sam called.

"Run," she croaked.

Sibanda kicked her again, then stooped, almost casually, to retrieve the fallen AK-47. "You stupid, gullible white bitch. You think you're so much smarter than us. You and your kind think you can rule Africa with your private armies."

Sonja drew a painful breath to try and stop the dizziness, but the sun was in her eyes as she looked up at him. "My daughter..."

Sibanda smiled. "... will be looking into my eyes when she dies." He raised the butt of the rifle to his shoulder and put his finger through the trigger guard.

19

When Sam saw the African man roll from under Sonja and punch and kick her he raised the gun, pointing straight up in the air, and pulled the trigger as he started running.

Nothing happened.

"Shoot," he said to himself. He looked at it. Think! In movies and computer games they grabbed the top and pulled back. His left hand was slick with sweat and he only managed to pull it back halfway before it slipped and slid forward. He pulled the trigger again and nothing happened.

"Hey!" he called to the man, who was bending to pick up a rifle. If the man heard or saw him, he obviously thought Sam was no threat.

Sam wiped his hand on his T-shirt and yanked back the slide on top of the pistol again. It was much tougher than he expected, but when he pulled it all the way back and let it go this time he heard and felt a satisfying clunk. The man was raising his rifle and pointing it at Sonja.

"Oh, dear God," Sam said. He stopped in the narrow pathway of fallen cornstalks and raised the pistol in a two-handed grip and pulled the trigger.

The noise and the recoil of the pistol made him start. He heard two shots, though he thought he had fired only one. He saw smoke and gases erupt from the barrel of the rifle and the man looked up at him. Sonja was moving on the ground, but he couldn't tell if she had been hit. The man started to swing the barrel of the rifle toward him and Sam fired again.

And again. And again. And again.

When Sam opened his eyes the man was slumped against the black pick-up, a smear of glistening blood following him down the paintwork as he slowly sank to the ground in a seated position. Sam's legs felt like jelly, but he forced himself to walk closer, his right arm up, with the pistol still leveled at the man.

"Sam!" Sonja cried. She was on her knees, a strand of drool linking her mouth to the mud she was trying to free herself from.

The African man was holding his rifle one-handed now. He looked at Sam and weakly tried to raise the weapon.

"Motherfucker." Sam fired thirteen more times, emptying the pistol into the lifeless form.

"No!" Sonja screamed. She got to her feet and stumbled to him. She reached out and grabbed the pistol from him. "Why did you kill him, you idiot?"

Sam stopped and looked from the man he had just killed to the red-faced, screaming woman whose life he thought he had just saved. "Why do you think, Sonja?"

"No, no, no!" She scrunched her free hand into her hair and knelt beside the dead man. She untangled her fingers and placed two on his neck. "Dead. Shit."

"Sonja, sit down. You need to tell me what was going on here. I just killed a man who I thought was going to kill you."

"My daughter. Give me your phone."

"Your daughter?" He pulled his phone from his shirt pocket and she snatched it from him. While she dialed a number he stared at the body and the wide-open eyes of the man he had just killed, watching his blood pool in the mud and dirt around him. Sam started to feel queasy, then dropped to his knees and vomited.

Sonja had the phone pressed to her ear. "Martin, it's Sonja. Shut up and listen. I need you to get Emma collected from boarding school and on tonight's flight from London to Jo'burg."

As she talked she bent down and prised the AK-47 from the dead man's hands. She motioned, with the tip of the barrel, for Sam to follow her while she talked. Sam dry-heaved a couple of times and palmed tears from his eyes. He forced himself to his feet. She was as cold and nasty as a goddamned rattler.

"Business class," she said into the phone. "And book her on the first available flight to Maun tomorrow, then Mack Air to Xakanaxa. Ask for Laurens, the head pilot, and tell him to look out for her. I'll phone Stirling and tell him to find a room for her."

Sam pushed half-broken stalks of corn out of his face as he stumbled in Sonja's footsteps. There was something wet on the toe of his boot and when he bent at the waist to take a closer look he saw it was blood. They were following a trail of it. The caller at the other end of the phone—he gathered it was her security consultant boss, Martin Steele—was asking the obvious question. Why?

Sonja glanced back over her shoulder at Sam, then to her front. She held the AK-47 loose in her left hand, so she obviously wasn't expecting more trouble. She lowered her voice, and Sam had to lengthen his stride to get closer to her so he could eavesdrop.

"Those people we spoke about . . . they caught up with us. No, none of us was hurt and the . . . *visitors* have been dealt with. But one of them threatened Emma, Martin. He told me they would get her if I didn't let him live. He had credible information that told me he wasn't bluffing."

Sam swallowed hard, as he knew the next question and its answer.

"I had to finish him off. Look Martin, I don't care if I have to pay for the flights myself, but I don't have a credit card on me and I need you to get Emma's transport arrangements sorted ASAP. If you don't do this for me then I'm walking, right now. I'll drive to Windhoek and I'll steal the money for a flight to England. If I get there and find my daughter dead then it'll be on your head. Understood?"

She paused for a few seconds. "OK, good. Send Laidlaw and Regan. They're good men and Emma knows them. I'll call her and tell her to pack her bags."

"Sonja . . ."

She held up the phone to silence Sam and pressed some more buttons. "Emma, it's me, listen carefully."

Sam trudged on while Sonja spoke to her daughter. He didn't think it strange that she'd so far neglected to say anything about having a child, as he'd already learned she was not the sort of person to pull out snaps of her family. Sonja's tone with her daughter was brisk and commanding. There was no "missing you" or "I love you," but Sam wasn't surprised.

Sonja ended the call, stopped, and handed the phone back to Sam, without a word of thanks. She dropped to one knee and used the tip of the rifle barrel to brush aside some fallen green stalks. "Help me take this one back to the truck."

Sam saw the lifeless eyes and the gaping chasm of blood, sinew and white muscle that had once been the man's neck and throat. He turned away and retched again. He felt like his body was turning itself inside out.

"Sam, come on. I need your help." She slung the rifle over her back and grabbed the body under the arms. When Sam had the courage to look again he thought the man's head had lolled so far back that it might fall off. He spat bile.

"Man up, for Christ's sake."

Man up? Did this woman think life was a goddamned war movie? Sam swallowed and grabbed the dead man's boots. By the time they reached the Toyota he was cursing and sweating. Together they heaved him into the rear seat of the pick-up, and then placed the body of the man Sam had shot in the front passenger seat. Sam averted his eyes from the interior of the cab, which was painted with the driver's blood, brain and skull fragments.

"Stand back." Sonja raised the AK and fired a single shot into the vehicle's body, just behind the driver's side rear door. Petrol jetted from the neat hole in an arcing stream. Sonja walked to the passenger side, reached into the cab and patted the pockets of the man who had tried to kill her. She took out a lighter and a packet of Newbury cigarettes. One-handed, she placed the open top of the pack to her lips and drew one out. She lit it, inhaled deeply, exhaled through her nose, with the cigarette still in her mouth, and peeled the blood-drenched shirt from the man's shoulder wound. She walked back to the petrol fountain, soaked the rag in fuel, lit it, then tossed it into the pool of fuel.

Sam was speechless. He had the presence of mind to step back as the fireball erupted into the air. Flames engulfed the Toyota and the bodies inside it. Sonja ejected the empty magazine from the pistol, replaced it with a fresh one, and stuffed the gun in the waistband of her shorts.

Sam could smell them burning. He wanted to be sick again, but he was empty inside. He started to cry.

"Come on." Her voice was softer. She held the dead man's cigarette between her blood-stained fingers and closed her eyes as she inhaled deeply.

He stood there, staring, blinking away his tears. The windows popped and the people inside burned like spent Fourth of July fireworks consuming their flimsy wrappers.

Sonja tossed the AK-47 through the front passenger window. It bounced off the melting body in the flaming seat. She stubbed out the cigarette, put the butt in her pocket and placed her hand in Sam's, gripping it lightly. "Come on."

He started to walk and she immediately increased the pace. He glanced back once more at the scene; it was a live cross from hell, except this wasn't television.

Sonja was almost dragging him as he stumbled along. He shook his hand free of hers and stopped. "Who were they?"

She didn't look back at him. "It doesn't matter."

"Like shit it doesn't matter, Sonja! There are three dead men back there. Who were they and why were they trying to kill you?"

Still, she refused to meet his eye. She started walking again and knocked stalks of maize aside as the heat intensified at their backs. "Us, Sam. They were trying to kill us."

"Who were they?"

"CLA. Caprivian Liberation Army. They probably heard about your visit and decided they would kidnap you and the rest of the crew."

"Bullshit, Sonja. A second ago you said they were trying to kill us.

Now you say it was a kidnap attempt. They were shooting at us. And what's all this got to do with your daughter?"

She stopped and turned, and wiped the back of her hand across her brow. It left a red smudge. Sam looked down at his own hands, then wiped them on his shirt. They were sticky with the blood of the man whose throat Sonja had cut. Her clothes were covered in it. She looked like an angel of death. "You don't need to know anything more than those men tried to kill or capture you and you acted in self-defense. With luck you'll be out of the country before the police even find the vehicle."

"*Need to know?* This is not the goddamned army, Sonja. I *need* to know why I just shot and killed a man, and why he was trying to kill you. Frankly, I'm having just the teeniest bit of trouble with taking a human life, although you seem to be handling it all right."

She pulled the dead commander's cigarettes from her pocket and lit a second. She held the pack out to him.

"I don't smoke."

She shrugged and dragged deep. "Booze helps. Maybe see a shrink when you get back to LA. Myself, I find they ask too many questions and don't give enough answers for what you pay."

"How can you joke at a time like this?"

"It's called black humor, and we're going to end up like those *okes* in the *bakkie* if we don't get a move on. Fire's gaining. Let's move."

She set off and he dried his eyes on the blood-encrusted sleeve of his shirt.

Sam had followed Sonja's instructions and, on reaching the Okavango, had driven parallel to its banks for a while before hooking left and back through some sparse cattle grazing areas to the main road. Instead of carrying on to the dam site he had left the others and gone back to look for Sonja. Part of him wished he'd done as she'd first ordered. However, if he had, she would have died and he wouldn't have been able to forgive himself.

The Land Rover was still where he'd left it, parked under a tree. As he followed Sonja toward it he saw blue-gray smoke coming from the tailpipe.

Rickards and Gerry were standing outside in the shade, but it looked like Cheryl-Ann was still inside.

There was a pick-up in the dam construction company's livery nearby, and two men in overalls were chatting to the cameraman and sound man. A white Land Cruiser slowed, indicated and turned off the tar to pull up next to the other four-by-four. The white man who climbed out was Deiter Roberts.

Everyone seemed to asking questions at once.

Roberts addressed Sam: "What's going on here? We got your call for help. Are you guys all right—you're both covered in blood."

"How's Cheryl-Ann?" Sam asked Jim.

"Was that more gunfire we could hear?" Rickards replied.

"Who were those guys?" Gerry chimed in.

Sam saw Sonja ignore the cluster and move to the window of the Land Rover. She tapped on it, waited a couple of seconds, then tapped again. Sam walked over to her as Cheryl-Ann rolled down the window. Her eyes were red and her cheeks streaked with tears. She blew her nose into a tissue. Sonja opened the door, leaned in and wrapped her arms around Cheryl-Ann, holding her face to her chest. Cheryl-Ann recoiled at first, from Sonja's unexpected embrace and her blood-spattered skin and clothing, but then started sobbing again and melted into the other woman's arms.

He was told to "man up" and Cheryl-Ann got a hug, Sam couldn't help thinking cynically. He left the women in peace and Rickards placed a hand on his shoulder.

"Cheryl-Ann's fucked, man. I've never seen someone lose it so quickly and so completely. I had her figured for a hard arse."

Sam looked back at the sobbing wreck who until recently had been ordering them about with such gusto.

Rickards continued. "When you left she told us to leave you and Sonja. I said no, and Gerry said we should wait and she just blew a fuse, man. She started abusing us like you wouldn't believe, then she just kind of made this mooing noise, curled up in a ball and started crying. She was saying she didn't want to die, and shit like that."

Sam knew he'd been very close to losing it in the same way.

Roberts called for everyone's attention. The red-faced engineer seemed to find the displays of emotion particularly annoying. He clapped his hands. "People, listen. I have called the police on my radio and they will be here soon. I also called GrowPower's PR people and Selma Tjongarero spoke to head office. Mr. Schwarz, the head of GrowPower, just called me from Windhoek to say you may use his company's airplane to fly straight to the capital, if you wish. In the circumstances, that might be a very good idea."

Sam thanked him. They were supposed to be going back to Ngepi that evening for some filming on the Okavango, and then catching a charter flight from the airstrip at Bagani to Windhoek the next day.

Sonja brushed Cheryl-Ann's hair from her face and murmured a few more quiet words to her. The American woman had stopped wailing, but she stayed in the Land Rover with her head in her hands.

"You don't want to hang around for the police investigation," Sonja said to Sam. Deiter nodded in agreement. "Also, I think Cheryl-Ann needs to be sedated. The quicker you get her back to civilization, the better."

Sam looked hard at her, wondering where this sensitive, compassionate soul had been hiding when the blood-streaked killer lit a dead man's cigarette and torched his body. She caught his eye then turned quickly to Roberts. "You agree, Deiter?"

The engineer rubbed his jaw. "With the way the police work in this part of Africa you could be stuck here for days. May be better to write a couple of quick statements at the airstrip and leave them with me. I know the chief of police. I also know GrowPower and the government won't want to make too much of this incident. It sounds like a car-jacking attempt to me, Sonja. What do you think?"

She nodded.

"That's not what happened," Sam said.

"Leave it, Sam. Forget about it."

Roberts held up his hands. "Sonja's right, Sam. Whatever this was, you don't want to stick around for the aftermath. Car-jacking is nowhere near as prevalent in Namibia as it is in South Africa, but it is not unheard of. You two should clean yourselves up, get rid of those bloody clothes and get out of here, fast."

Sam held his tongue. He, too, wanted to get away from this place, especially the pall of smoke behind him which reminded him of what he had just done. He couldn't see a way in which the publicity surrounding his shooting of a man in a remote corner of Africa could be turned into a good thing.

"I spoke to the pilot just now," Roberts said, as if delivering the argument's clincher. "The GrowPower aircraft will be ready to leave in thirty minutes. I suggest, for Cheryl-Ann's sake, we get a move on."

Jim and Gerry compared stories as they scribbled statements in Cheryl-Ann's notepad during the drive back to Ngepi camp, where they hurriedly collected their bags. Cheryl-Ann was still too shaken to walk far, so Sonja collected her luggage from her room for her then hurriedly loaded the lot into the Rover. Then they headed straight to the nearby airstrip at Bagani.

"Um, what do we call you in our statements, Sonja?" Gerry asked, as he checked his notes.

"Field guide and security consultant," she said.

"Cool. So our 'field guide and security consultant' fired back at the suspected car-jackers, probably injuring the driver, right?"

"Whatever," Sonja said, watching the road.

Gerry wrote some more and then looked up again. "And then their pick-up went off the road, crashed in the cornfield and caught fire, is that how it went down, Sam?"

"Like the lady said, Gerry."

"Awesome."

Sonja pulled up at a lean-to that was roofed with corrugated iron, which passed for a terminal in this part of the continent, next to a battered old blue Bedford refueling truck, and a pair of white Nissan Patrol four-wheel drives which looked incongruously clean and new. Roberts's Land Cruiser and the other vehicle from the construction site were behind them and stopped next to the Land Rover.

The pilot, dressed in navy shorts and a white short-sleeved shirt that somehow remained crisp and clean in the heat and dust, introduced himself as Dougal Geddes and said he was ready to go as soon as they were.

Sonja had to coax the producer from her cocoon in the Land Rover while the others waited by a twin-engine aircraft which had the green stem and single leaf logo of GrowPower emblazoned on its tail. Sonja supported Cheryl-Ann with an arm around her waist as she walked her across to the airplane, and emerged from inside the aircraft a short time later.

"She's buckled in. Make sure she has some water to drink on the flight and get her to a doctor as soon as you get to Windhoek," she said to Sam.

He nodded. "And what about you?"

"I have to get the Land Rover back to Botswana, remember? The sooner I get going, the better. It's a long drive."

"Right."

She stood with her hands on her hips, not reaching for him or offering her cheek for an air kiss. What was the protocol, he wondered, for farewelling a partner-in-murder in the middle of the African bush?

"Well, goodbye then," Sam said.

She nodded, turned and started walking toward the Land Rover, past the mountain of camera gear and backpacks still to be loaded onto the aircraft. When she reached the vehicle she opened the door, but paused for a moment.

Sam wondered if she was going to look back at him and say something, after all they'd been through. Instead, she climbed up into the driver's seat, started the engine and drove off.

20

Sonja slowed behind a cement mixer as she approached the checkpoint on the B8, near the bridge over the Okavango River.

She'd dragged a good, innocent man into her world of war and killing and now she would never see him again. If she'd been a normal person with a normal life she would have been mad not to reciprocate the attention Sam had showed her. He'd been brave enough to come back for her when he'd thought she was in trouble, and strong enough to kill the man who had a gun pointed at her. Despite their polar opposite backgrounds she'd begun to find him attractive—admirable even—and not just in a sexual way. Why did she always have to push away men who wanted to get close to her? Sonja felt the lump rise in the back of her throat and she sniffed and rolled down the window.

"Good afternoon, madam," the policeman said. "How far are you going today?"

"Livingstone, Zambia," she lied.

"Have a safe journey."

Sonja noted the machine-gun emplacement at the end of the bridge over the Okavango that she had spied the other day. Beneath the cover of the dashboard she selected the camera function on her mobile phone and held it to her ear as she accelerated slowly past the sandbagged bunker. She snapped off a few frames, blindly, as she passed the bored-looking soldiers.

The *O* on the *Okavango River* sign on the bridge had been scratched out. The Lozi-speaking peoples who made up the United Democratic Party and its military arm, the CLA, spelled the river Kavango. It was a reminder of the job ahead of her, now that the immediate threat from the Zimbabweans had been neutralized. Even though she had killed again, not to mention dragging Sam into the bloody mess, she still had a job to do. She thought about the dam and its inevitable impact on this beautiful part of Africa she'd once called home—and she thought about the money, and her daughter. She needed to get herself focused again, and stay in the zone. It was her way of coping.

She breathed a little easier, knowing there was nothing but open road now until she reached the Kwando River, at Kongola, where she would have to pass another checkpoint. She was grateful to the policeman for forcing her to get her emotions in check.

Her phone rang. "Yes."

"Laidlaw and Regan picked Emma up an hour ago," said Steele. She's en route to Heathrow and she'll be on the evening flight. Business class, British Airways, I might add."

"Good. Thank you."

"Are you OK?" he asked.

"Fine."

"Good. Don't forget our next RV."

"I won't."

"I'm worried about you."

"That's very sensitive of you, Martin."

"I'm serious. After this, well . . . after this one is all over and the money's in the bank, I was wondering if you wanted to get away for a while. With me. And Emma, of course."

She said nothing. She couldn't think of the right words. She hated being off guard; losing the initiative.

"Martin, I don't know what to say . . ."

"Think about it. I know I've been a bit of a prick in the past, but we had some good times, didn't we, Sonn?"

He hadn't called her that in a long time.

"Remember that private game reserve near the Kruger National Park?"

She remembered. There was so much beauty, following almost too soon after the horror in Sierra Leone. She could never forget their time at the game lodge. It was sensory overload and even now the memories, the visions, good and bad, flashed across her brain like a high-speed video cut to the deep bass pounding of American rap—the chosen music of their enemy.

After the killing of Danny Byrne in Northern Ireland, Steele and Sonja had been flown to Aldershot military base in England to face a board of inquiry into the deaths of the IRA quartermaster and his bomb-making brother.

Steele sought her out, and while they couldn't socialize on base, he took her to a pub in town where they corroborated their stories about the Byrne brothers pulling guns on the SAS men during an impromptu operation. Sonja was numb over Danny's death and lied to the inquiry about her relationship with him. She felt torn, as though she had betrayed both Danny and her country by sleeping with the enemy in the first place. Martin plied her with booze in the evenings and eventually, inevitably, she ended up in the bed of the only man she could talk to about the nightmares and the pain.

The British press, with the help of some spin-doctoring from Downing Street, hailed the killings as the unfortunate endgame of a well-planned operation by security forces to capture the men responsible for the heinous school bus bombing. There were no tears for the Byrne brothers. Even the republican cause had largely disowned them. Behind the scenes, however, the army was looking for explanations as to how and why Steele and the Det had staged a rogue operation. The end, it seemed, did not always justify the means.

Steele was urged to resign his commission, which he did, after being promoted to major. Sonja was transferred to a signals unit in the north of England. She'd gone from the frontline in the war against the IRA to operating a bank of fax and telex machines in a room with no windows. There was no psychological debrief, as what she had done was classified top secret and no one in her new unit knew anything of her work in Northern Ireland.

Having worked undercover in civilian clothes for so long, Sonja was bored by the mundaneness of barracks life and the pettiness of the NCOs and their inspections. When a female sergeant abused her on the parade ground for having nonexistent mud on her boots, Sonja told the woman to fuck off in front of the other soldiers. The sergeant grabbed her arm when Sonja tried to walk off the parade ground, but Sonja turned and slapped her. She was arrested by the military police, court-martialed and kicked out of the army. She'd lost contact with Martin Steele after her transfer and the last she'd heard of him, from a former SAS man she met one day in a pub in London, was that Steele was working as a mercenary in Africa.

Emma was born nine months after the end of Sonja's disastrous tour in Northern Ireland. Sonja lived with her mother in a flat in London and, with no business or professional qualifications, worked as a waitress in a curry house. It was a difficult time and nothing in her military training had prepared her for raising a child. For a long while she hated the army, and Martin Steele, and what they had done to her. But after the killing she'd seen in Northern Ireland she wouldn't countenance terminating the life growing inside her. She was numb, traumatized by her time in the province, yet she couldn't hate the beautiful child she had brought into the world.

Her work was boring, but it allowed her to give something back to her mother and, in time, as scars started to form over her wounds, she started to think about what she would do with the rest of her life. She knew she needed something outdoorsy and action-oriented, but her dishonorable discharge ruled out enlistment in the police or other security services. An application to join the fire brigade looked promising for a while, but failed. Depression loomed large in her life, but when Emma was three Martin Steele called, out of the blue, and offered her a job in Sierra Leone, working as a signaler.

"Why me?" she'd asked over the phone. "There are a thousand sigs you could choose from."

"Yes," he'd replied, "but there's only one you."

"I'm not going to sleep with you again, Martin."

"It's not part of the job description."

Martin had set up his own private military contracting firm—the new name for mercenary outfits—and had secured a contract to fight the Revolutionary United Front, or RUF, rebels and help train the army of the government of Sierra Leone. The money he was offering was astronomical compared to what she earned as a waitress and the job would return her to the only two things, apart from her daughter, that had ever mattered to her—Africa and military life.

Sierra Leone was chaos incarnate. Freetown, where Sonja was first based, was a besieged, seething mass of people driven to terror and barbarity by years of civil war between the Sierra Leone Army—the SLA—and the RUF. The countryside, mostly subjugated by the RUF under a reign of unimaginable terror, was jungle—as dark-hearted and unforgiving as the rebels they were fighting.

Initially, Sonja spent her days sweltering in a tin-roofed hangar at Freetown airport, manning the communications center, or comcent, a suite of HF and VHF radios. Martin was true to his word and made no sexual advances toward her. However, after a couple of weeks it became clear that he didn't only want her skills as a radio operator. Martin encouraged Sonja to go into Freetown in civilian clothes to visit the bars and clubs on the waterfront and mix with the diplomats, aid workers, journalists, bureaucrats and politicians who partied while the country crumbled. She became a spy, gleaning valuable information about government intentions, potential new contracts and other covert operations going on in and around Sierra Leone. She missed her daughter, but she loved her work.

Not content just to work the cocktail circuit and the comcent, Sonja pestered Martin until he reluctantly agreed to allow her to see more of the country by riding along with a security detail Corporate Solutions had provided to protect an aid convoy heading for Kenema, near the Liberian border.

The convoy was ambushed outside the town of Bo and the driver of the aid truck Sonja was riding in was killed. Sonja climbed down from the lorry and, firing her AK-47 on the run, rushed straight into the jungle, in the direction from which the RUF fire was coming. It seemed to defy logic, but it was the drill she'd been taught in the army to deal with an ambush. Giddy with adrenaline, she'd found herself alone and deep in the jungle, but out of the firing line. She'd hooked back around and snuck up behind an RUF machine-gun crew of two men, who were raking the burning convoy of vehicles. Sonja took up a position behind a tree and shot both men in the back of the head. With their machine-gun out of action, the RUF rebels melted away.

Back at Freetown airport, Martin had given her a tin mug of Scotch and, in the privacy of his tent, held her to him for a full minute, then sent her back out to her radios. She'd won the confidence of the last of the men in the mercenary force who doubted her abilities as a soldier and, over time, they had seen she wasn't there as the commanding officer's camp follower. Martin maintained their professional relationship through the remainder of the tour, but by the end of their three-month contract she knew she would miss him if he disappeared from her life again.

The government of Sierra Leone bowed to pressure from the UN to cease its contracts with private military companies. On the flight out of the country to South Africa Martin said he might have more work for Sonja, perhaps involving what he called "direct action" jobs.

"Killing?" she asked.

"Perhaps. Are you interested?"

"I am," she said.

"Good. We should talk about it. How would you like to come to a private safari camp near the Kruger National Park with me for the next three days?"

She looked at him. "Separate tents, I hope?"

"It's the high season. I've booked the last double. It's a very big tent, though. I could sleep on the sofa. Are you interested?"

He'd been a gentleman and a professional these last three months. There'd been no allusions to their brief affair after the business in Northern Ireland and no suggestion that he wanted her in Sierra Leone for anything other than the tasks he'd assigned her. She was smart enough to know that he was a master manipulator; he was also handsome, a born leader, financially well off and, to the best of her knowledge, single.

When they arrived at their destination she looked around the tent. Unlike the rustic ethnic African theme of Xakanaxa the decor here was British colonial kitsch, but the decorator had stopped just short of the wind-up gramophone, and it was tastefully done. Sonja was aroused with anticipation, but mostly she was nervous.

Martin laid her bags on the night stand. "As you know, I'm not particularly good at small talk."

"Neither am I."

"We're alike, you and me."

She nodded.

"I sensed from the moment I met you in Northern Ireland that you were a doer, not a talker . . ."

Suddenly emboldened by his confidence in her, she placed a finger on his lips and he reached around her. He undid the zipper at the back of her cotton sundress and it was on the floor before they'd finished their first kiss.

"Sonn? Are you still there?" Martin said into the satellite phone.

The tarred black surface of the B8, the main road through the Caprivi Strip, stretched to shimmering infinity in front of her. It was a lonely road, with not much traffic in the scorching heat of early afternoon.

"Yes, I'm still here," she said.

To her left, the north, was the Zambezi River, then war-ravaged Angola and the darker, troubled heart of Africa. To her right were Botswana and the Okavango Delta, the jewel of the Kalahari, whose luster was dying by the day thanks to the twin evils of the dam and the drought. Ahead of her, at the end of this drive, was a date with a man whose business was war and death. Behind her were three more burning bodies. She was alone in Africa, surrounded by despair. Her only child, somewhere in the air, had become a stranger to her. Emma relied on her for nothing more than money now. In a year she would be at university, out on her own. Sonja feared she might never reconnect with her daughter, but at the same time Emma provided her with hope—a belief that she had lived her life in this way for a reason, and not just because she was good at killing. Sonja shivered at the thought of what she had done to pay for Emma's future, and how she had relished every second of some of those deeds.

"I asked," Martin repeated, "are you interested in spending some time together, after this show is all over?"

"I don't think so, Martin. I want to be free after this one."

21

Half a dozen eland took fright at the growl of the approaching Land Rover's diesel, but Sonja had a good look at them as she passed, and they bounded off into the safety of the tree line.

It was an encouraging sign, she thought, seeing the big, muscular antelope, which were considered quite rare in other parts of the continent. The wildlife in the Caprivi Strip had suffered in recent decades from the effects of poaching by hungry locals and refugees from the civil war just across the border in Angola. A wide grassy stretch of cleared land flanked the black top on either side, which meant she could keep her speed up and still have time to brake if an animal strayed out of the trees. The European Union had constructed the B8 and it was in good condition. Unlike when she was a child, one didn't need a four-wheel drive to traverse the Caprivi Strip, but if you deviated off the main road, even a few meters, it was easy to become bogged in the soft sand of the natural floodplain.

The sun was low in her rear-view mirror as she neared Kongola. She was emotionally and physically spent now that the adrenaline from the contact with the Zimbabwean assassins had joined the other horrors of her past, and she didn't want to press on at night in case she fell asleep at the wheel or hit an elephant in the dark. There were plenty of tales of weary travelers running into one of the giant gray ghosts in the night. If the impact didn't kill you, then the angry wounded elephant would make sure you didn't get out of the car alive.

Just before the bridge over the Kwando River she indicated right and turned onto a sandy track. A small metal sign, dented and faded said, simply: *Nambwa km 4x4 only*. The number of kilometers had been scratched out. She'd heard about this place from a South African contractor she'd met in Kabul. The lack of information confirmed what the man had told her, that the camp was something of an off-roader's secret. She couldn't recall how far it was off the main road, and the sign didn't help.

The bush here was thick, and the screen of mopane leaves and trunks glowed golden brown in the failing light. There were mounds of elephant droppings, some old and dry, though one fresh and still covered with tiny flies, and the wrinkled tracks of their big feet—round for the front ones and oval shaped for the rear. There was little risk of her surprising or running into an elephant at the crawling pace she was traveling, but nevertheless she scanned the bush left and right out of habit.

The road climbed and twisted up a low hill and Sonja had to drop to first gear to keep her momentum up the sandy slope. As she neared the crest she saw rusting metal fence poles dripping tendrils of barbed wire on either side of her as she passed through the remains of a gate. The whole area had been occupied by the South African Defense Force during the border war and the fighting in South-West Africa, and as a result the Caprivi Strip was littered with old bases, strong-points, airstrips and bunkers. From the top of what turned out to be a spur she could see the road had brought her close to the Kwando River, and she had a good view over its floodplain. She turned off the engine and got out to stretch her legs.

It was a beautiful spot, but looking around she saw the detritus of war. Concrete foundations showed where military outposts or barracks had stood, and the skeletal remains of a water tower cast a barred shadow over her. The view over the river was as strategic as it was enchanting. Impala and waterbuck grazed on the green grass below and she heard the deep belly laugh of a hippo. A francolin clucked past the front of the Land Rover, bobbing its head in the grass and squawking in alarm when it looked up and saw her. She kicked the sand with the toe of her boot, hoping she might find more evidence of the past conflict. From her knowledge of the border war she thought this might be Fort Doppies. *Doppie* was slang for both an empty beer bottle and an empty brass cartridge case. There was nothing more to see here.

Sonja got back into the Land Rover, started the engine and carried on. As she drove down the other side of the spur she passed through another ruined gate and wondered what it must have been like to be based here, treated to a view of nature's splendor but forced to remain behind the wire like caged animals.

Dusk was falling when she finally saw a dim light flickering on an island in the middle of the Kwando River floodplain. Thanks to the drought the channel separating her from Nambwa Camp was sand rather than water.

An African man in shorts, a T-shirt and bare feet, no doubt alerted by the sound of her vehicle, was ambling down the track to the tiny reception hut when she pulled up. After exchanging greetings he told her what she already knew, "You do not have a booking."

"Correct."

He told Sonja to follow him in her vehicle as he walked back up the track. Driving at the man's slow place Sonja caught glimpses of the other camp sites. She saw now that although she had driven over dry land to reach the island, on its far side the Kwando River was flowing. The sun's dying light turned the channel into a lava flow. A young couple looked up from their *braai*, their faces warmed by the flames of their cooking fire, and waved at her as she passed.

The attendant led her to a site behind a rustic timber ablution block. "You can camp here. We save this place for people who arrive late."

The overflow site didn't have a view of the river, but it was close to the shower, which she needed far more than a view. "Thank you."

Sonja looked up at the sky, which was turning a deep, dark velvet. The first stars were already beginning to twinkle. It was clear. There would be no rain tonight. She climbed onto the roof of the Land Rover and undid the tarpaulin covering the camping gear she had brought for the Americans. She slid out a canvas-covered single mattress, a sleeping bag and a mosquito net. She tied the tarp back in place, laid the mattress and bag on the ground, and then tied the top of the net to the low-hanging branch of a big thorn tree that shaded the site. It was still very warm and there would be no dew tonight.

She rummaged in the back of the Land Rover for the toolbox. In it, she found a can of Spark lubricating spray and a rag. She got back into the vehicle and closed the driver's side door so the interior light went off. She looked out the windows to make sure none of her fellow campers was nearby and, in the dark, began stripping and cleaning her Glock. In the army, you cleaned your weapon each day, before you cleaned yourself.

The lubricating spray moistened her fingers and when she wiped them on the rag she saw the stain was a deep purple. She held her hands up above the dashboard and inspected them in the light coming from the shower block. The blood of the man whose throat she had cut was ingrained in the furrows of her skin, and under her nails. She needed a shower, though she knew she would never be truly clean.

The tear ran off her cheek and landed with a splat on the shiny, lightly oiled working parts of the Glock, but when she flicked the release catch with her thumb the slide shot forward and took the salty drop with it. She wiped her eyes with the back of her grimy hand, put the pistol under her seat and went to wash. Afterward, she sought out the camp caretaker again and paid for her site, given she would be leaving early the next morning.

Despite her exhaustion, or because of it, sleep eluded her for many hours. She lay on her back in her shorts and bikini top, on top of the sleeping bag, gazing at the stars with one arm under her head. Sonja believed she and Emma were safe from the threat of a Zimbabwean hit squad—for now—but that gave her more opportunity to dwell on her next mission, and on the brief conversation she'd had with Martin on the road.

Things had changed between them. After Sierra Leone and their time at the private safari camp, Sonja and Emma moved in with Martin. Sonja worked part-time in the Corporate Solutions office, as an operations-officer-cum-clerk, and while the work was not particularly exciting the hours enabled her to spend more time with Emma and make up for the months she'd lost.

They lasted as a de facto couple for two years. The first was passionate and fun-filled, but after eighteen months Sonja detected changes in Martin. He was working back late, traveling a lot in search of more contracts, and seemed to have less time for sex. He was evasive when she tried to talk to him. One night, when he was supposedly waiting in the office for a conference call from a military contact somewhere in Asia, Sonja called him and the phone rang out. She'd started to worry after her third call went through to the answering machine. She dressed Emma and was about to take her to her mother's and go out looking for him, when he walked in the door, at midnight.

He snapped at her when she berated him for not calling, saying he'd taken the call earlier than expected and gone to a pub.

"Casino, more likely," she said. She'd known, early on in their relationship, that Martin liked to gamble occasionally, but hadn't realized he had a problem until he confessed to losing ten thousand pounds in one night. He'd asked her for money, from the stash she'd saved during her time at Sierra Leone, and she had supported him for two months until the next job came in. He'd claimed to have reformed his ways.

When she stared at him he couldn't meet her eyes. "Yes, it was the casino," he confessed. "But there's more I have to tell you."

The "more" was a twenty-one-year-old croupier. Sonja ran upstairs and grabbed her illegal nine-millimeter Browning and sent him out into the cold, followed by his clothes, which she tossed from the upstairs bedroom window of the house they were renting.

The anger she had felt was softened by the secret relief she had at being back on her own again, with Emma, just the two of them. Better to be alone, she told herself, than to support a gambler who later confessed, over a conciliatory drink and dinner, that he was a serial philanderer with a hopeless attraction to young women. Sonja had reminded him that she was still in her twenties and hardly old. "Is it because of Emma?"

"God, no," he'd said. "And it's got nothing to do with what happened in Ireland. I don't want you to stay mad at me, Sonn. I know it sounds corny, but you really are better off without me. I can't be a good enough man for you."

She'd laughed. "You're right, very corny." She raised her glass of wine and sipped from it while he stared intently into her eyes, ignoring her amusement at his confession.

"You know, I did . . . do love you, Sonn. You're the only person I've ever loved, and I don't want to hurt you anymore."

Somehow, she sensed it was true, although it could have just been more of his masterful manipulation. He'd said he still wanted—needed—her to work for him and, with no other source of income waiting around the corner, Sonja agreed. When the hurt of his betrayal finally wore off she found she still liked him, though not in a romantic or sexual way. True to his word, he stayed a serial seducer of younger women and she had watched half-a-dozen come and go from his life over the years.

Professionally, the job she was about to undertake for Martin, like the assassination attempt on the Zimbabwean president, was in direct contravention to the mission statement Martin had drawn up for Corporate Solutions when he'd formed it prior to their deployment to Sierra Leone.

Corporate Solutions, he'd written in the document he'd shown to her when she and other recruits signed up before leaving for Freetown, *will work only for legitimate governments or reputable private companies. We will not take part in political assassinations* . . . and so on.

A bush rustled nearby. She reached under her pillow and pulled out the Glock. She'd slept under the stars not only because of the heat but also so she could better hear and react to anyone who might want to sneak up on her. She doubted the Zimbabweans had fielded another hit squad, but those in her line of work who weren't cautious were dead.

The next noise was louder. It was a branch breaking, followed by a low grumbling noise. She relaxed. Elephants. Oddly, the presence of the huge beasts was reassuring. If there were men sneaking up on her the elephants would hear them first and let everybody in the camp site know about it. She lay back again, charting the progress of the herd by the sounds of their feeding, and wondering about her future.

Frogs croaked away in the reeds on the banks of the Kwando and a spotlight flashed through the trees as some campers, up late, watched the grazing elephants. The camp site was a piece of paradise where man and animal could coexist in harmony and respect. This part of Africa had once been a bloody battleground and now she was going to help lead the Caprivi Strip into hell once more.

Sonja dozed off and the sound of a vehicle's engine startled her from a dream about being crushed under the falling, burning wreckage of a helicopter.

She reached for her pistol again and lay still, her body as taut as a coiled spring, until she heard the camp manager leading the late arrivals to their camping spot.

Sonja woke again in the pre-dawn cool, but instead of climbing into the sleeping bag she'd been lying on, she got up and rolled and stowed her bedding. She loaded her kit and was on the B8 again, hurtling toward the sun as it showed itself.

There were more signs of human habitation on the eastern side of the Kwando, as she had left the Bwabwata National Park after crossing the river, but this was one of the poorest parts of Namibia. The far-flung northeastern corner could have been a different country to the Germanic orderliness and clockwork-reliable infrastructure of Windhoek, and the prosperous fishing and holiday towns on the Atlantic Coast. If you believed people like Gideon, the CLA and their political representatives in the United Democratic Party, it should have been another country.

Surely these people had the right to choose their own destiny, and to harness their natural resources for their own good? She shook her head. She wasn't even convincing herself. If every African tribe that disputed the lines drawn by colonial mapmakers a century ago decided to take up arms then the continent would never know peace. What she was doing, aiding and abetting this rebellion, was wrong. She pulled her mobile phone out of her pocket and pressed the green button. The last few numbers she had dialed showed up, with Martin's at the top of the list. Her thumb hovered over the call button.

The next major town she would come to was Katima Mulilo, the provincial capital of the Caprivi Strip. She knew that Martin's plan, in outline, was for the main force of the CLA to attack and capture Katima, seizing the police station, government offices and the Namibian Broadcasting Corporation radio and TV studios. At the same time she and a smaller detachment would blow up the dam on the Okavango, at the other end of the strip—though quite how she was going to do this, she still didn't know. The simultaneous attacks at either end of the strip would divide the Namibian Defense Force. The party from the dam would retreat eastward to Kongola, while the main force pushed west to link up with them. They would blow the bridge over the Kwando and the Caprivi Strip east of the river would secede from Namibia.

Martin had told her that CLA agents had done a close target recce on Katima Mulilo but suggested that Sonja take a look at the town as she passed through to provide an up-to-date and independent assessment of police and troop dispositions in the town.

"No," she said aloud to herself.

She would not go through with it. She would call him now and tell him she was out. She would return to Botswana immediately, collect Emma and disappear, perhaps into South Africa. She would pay Martin for her daughter's airfare and say her goodbyes to him. The more she thought about the prospect of starting a war—rather than joining an existing one—the more she realized she couldn't go ahead with this job. It was a liberating moment for her. Her financial situation was secure and Emma's expensive boarding school education would soon be over. Sonja had money put away already for Emma to go to university, and for a sizeable nest egg of her own. She could live reasonably comfortably off the interest and if she sold the flat in London she could buy a mansion somewhere in Africa.

The road had been empty so far this morning, but ahead of her, about two hundred meters distant, a man walked out into the middle of the road. He stood there, on the center line, waving his hand up and down.

"Shit." She put the phone down and changed to third gear. The engine protested, and the Land Rover began to slow. "Idiot."

The morning sun was behind the man, and as she got closer Sonja saw reflective stripes on his sleeve catch the morning light. A few seconds later she made out the silhouette of a peaked cap. Police.

She checked her speedometer, but was sure she hadn't been exceeding the legal limit. It wasn't unknown in Africa for car-jackers to masquerade as policemen, setting up fake roadblocks or just flagging down drivers who might feel disposed to giving a police officer a lift. Sonja reached down between her legs and pulled the Glock from under her seat. She lifted her left leg and slid the pistol under her thigh, out of sight.

The man was still waving his arm up and down, slowly. She complied and now noticed the police markings on the *bakkie* off to the right, under the shade of a tall tree in a demarcated picnic spot. The vehicle's bonnet was open. Sonja relaxed a little—it was one thing to dress up in a fake uniform, but another thing altogether to re-spray your vehicle in police colors. It looked like they had genuinely broken down. She quickly moved her pistol back under the seat. If she had to give this policeman a lift into Katima Mulilo she didn't want him to see her weapon.

She geared down and put her foot on the brake. The policeman moved to her side and smiled widely. "Good morning, madam, how are you?"

"I'm fine. How are you? You have a problem, I see."

"Ah yes, madam, I have a problem. Our *bakkie* it does not want to work and we are in need of assistance."

"I'm sorry, officer. I don't even know how to check the oil and water in my own car," she lied. "Perhaps I can take a message to the police in Katima for you?"

"Maybe you could just get out and have a look at the engine for us?"

Warning bells sounded in her mind. "I don't think that's a good idea. I'm in a hurry, and . . ."

She heard the snicker of a rifle being cocked and looked to her left. A man in a green T-shirt was peering down the barrel of an AK-47, which was pointed at her head. The man in the police uniform reached in and took her keys from the ignition.

"Out, now." All sign of friendliness disappeared as he drew his pistol and pointed it at her.

Sonja could have kicked herself. She'd fought off a team of assassins and now she'd been taken down by some bloody car thieves. The first rule of surviving a car hijack, she knew, was to do as she was told. If these men were just common thieves perhaps they would take the Land Rover and leave her in the middle of nowhere. It would be humiliating, but at least she would live. If they wanted to rape her, then she would make it her mission to kill at least one of them with her bare hands, and die fighting. She thought about Emma, and how much she loved her.

"Out."

Ironic, she thought as she stepped out of the Land Rover, that she might die like this after surviving years at war. "Please, I've got a daughter. She has no father. I will do whatever you want me to."

"Quiet," the man growled. "Search the vehicle. Under the driver's seat, in the console box. She will have a weapon there somewhere. Would you like to tell us where it is?"

She glanced up at him, even though she knew she shouldn't make eye contact. Did he assume any white woman traveling alone through Africa would carry a gun? Perhaps if the plates on the Land Rover were South African—where it seemed everyone carried a gun—but this vehicle was from Botswana, where violent crime was relatively uncommon.

"Under the driver's seat." There was no way she could get to it.

"Here it is," said the man with the AK-47. He stuffed the Glock into his waistband.

The other policeman, who had been standing by the supposedly broken-down *bakkie*, lowered and closed the truck's bonnet then strode over to the Land Rover. He took the keys from the man with the pistol, who still covered Sonja, got into her vehicle, started it and drove off the road into the long grass and trees at the edge of the cleared area.

"Ms. Kurtz," the man with the pistol said.

She kept looking at the ground, surprised that he knew her name, but determined not to show recognition.

"It is all right, Ms. Kurtz. We are not going to harm you, but we had to take certain precautions. We are taking you to meet with Mr. Steele, but we could not allow you to travel all the way to the border and then on to Dukwe. There isn't time."

She looked up at him. "Why not, what's changed?"

He smiled again. "Mr. Steele will explain. We are friends. Please trust us. We are in grave danger from the police and army all the time, so we must take our own precautions. I guarantee you will be safe and I regret any inconvenience to you, but, please, we must leave now."

She nodded.

"I regret, too, that I must take certain precautions from now on. We have been betrayed in the past. I am going to have to cover your eyes. Do you wish to go to the toilet or eat or drink something before we leave?"

"No, I'm fine. Can I have my pistol back?"

"When we arrive at our destination. We will stop for water on the way. We must hurry."

They walked to the police *bakkie* and the man who had confiscated her Glock reached into the cab and pulled out a wide strip of cloth. He held it up and she nodded. She wasn't thrilled about being blindfolded, but at least it wasn't a hood. Before the rag covered her eyes she saw a second police vehicle hidden deeper in the trees. These men were well organized.

"This way, Ms. Kurtz," the first officer said. She felt him take her hand and he gave her instructions for climbing into the back to the secure area at the rear of the *bakkie*. She could tell it was a real police wagon by the odors of disinfectant, urine and vomit. When she sat down she found they had placed a thick foam mattress on the bench seat. Considerate.

She was tired and decided there was no use trying to time how far they were traveling or in which direction. If the men were genuine members of the CLA and had been in touch with Martin, which appeared to be the case, then she had nothing to fear. If this was a setup of some kind, then she would soon be dead. The mattress had been placed length-wise so she found that if she lay back, her head was cushioned from the bumpy ride along the corrugated dirt track. She let the vibrations soothe her to sleep.

•   •   •

"Ms. Kurtz."

Sonja sat bolt upright and tried to stand, banging her head. For a terrible, tense moment she had no idea where she was.

"It's all right. We have stopped. You can get out of the *bakkie* now, Ms. Kurtz."

Recognition flooded her brain and she realized she was safe. "Can I take this bloody thing off, now?"

"Of course. Allow me."

She blinked at the harsh light and, looking up, saw the sun was high in the sky. They must have been driving for hours, but judging by the poor condition of the track they might not have covered too many kilometers. They were at the end of a road, at a collection of mudbrick and thatch huts that appeared empty. She looked around, but knew better than to ask where she was. There was only the one police vehicle in sight—the one she had traveled in.

The man who had pulled her over—she guessed he was the leader—had changed out of his police uniform. He wore a faded and stained blue T-shirt and a pair of torn and tattered shorts. He spoke to the other two in Lozi. One had changed into similarly ragged clothes, while the other was still in his police uniform. The uniformed man nodded, got into the *bakkie* and reversed up the track before executing a laborious three-point turn and driving off.

"Risky," she said, pulling back her hair and refastening her ponytail with its elastic band. "Stealing a police car."

The leader shrugged, then smiled broadly. "Who said we stole it? Come."

She followed him through the eerily quiet settlement.

"This was once a thriving community—my home, in fact, but it has ceased to exist."

"Why?"

He talked without looking back at her, his eyes scanning left and right as they walked past the stripped, rusted hulk of a VW Golf. "AIDS, poverty, the Namibian Defense Force . . ."

She'd heard of ghost villages in parts of Africa—communities that had ceased to exist because of the impact of HIV-AIDS. Typically, the menfolk contracted the disease, often by sleeping with prostitutes, then passed it on to their wives. If both spouses and other members of the extended family died off, their children might end up in an AIDS orphanage. Even if a mother survived, without her family's breadwinner she would probably be forced to move from the village and seek work in the nearest town or city.

The man continued, "In our case, it was much more than a disease. After the last attack on the dam the police and army came to many villages, looking for CLA supporters. Many of our people fled across the border, into Botswana. Some brought tales of rape and beatings by the policemen and soldiers." He stopped, and so did Sonja. He looked around him. "All I want is to come back here one day, to live. Let us keep moving—there is no time for sentimentality."

Sonja smelled stagnant water and, once they passed through the remnants of the village, the man led her into a wall of pampas grass, taller than she was. They were on a very narrow pathway and she saw the deep four-toed indentations of hippo tracks. The black earth beneath her hiking boots slowly became softer, until the ooze was ankle deep.

"Normally this area should be flooded, with the water right up near the village," he said. "The water here used to be free-flowing and sweet to drink, but now . . . It is the drought and global warming. Just one more problem for us."

Sonja glanced back and saw the other man with them had an AK-47, as well as her Glock, and her pack on his back. Every few paces the man stopped and turned, checking the track behind them and listening.

Weaver birds chattered as they brushed through the reeds, making the birds' intricately woven nests dance and sway like Chinese lanterns on flimsy poles. Somewhere ahead she heard a hippo grunting. She was glad it was another scorching hot day, so the sensitive-skinned creatures would be unlikely to be out of the water grazing. If they ran into an angry hippopotamus out of water then even the AK might not be enough to save them.

The leader paused and held up his hand. The tail-end Charlie stopped and covered their rear. Sonja stayed put as the man lowered his profile and crept forward. Sonja could see the glitter of sun on water through the reeds. He waited for a few moments then waved her on.

Sonja squelched forward, the mud and water over the tops of her boots now. The leader was bent over and hauling on something. She joined him and saw he was dragging a long *mekoro* from its hiding place in the pampas. The *mekoro*, a dugout canoe usually carved from the trunk of the sausage tree, was the traditional means of transport throughout the swamps of the Okavango Delta and neighboring wetlands that spilled over into the Caprivi.

The leader held the *mekoro* steady for her, and nodded for her to get in. "I will sit in the front, then you. My colleague will be the poler."

She thought colleague an unusual word for a fellow warrior. She stepped into the narrow canoe and, gripping the sides, sat down. "Before this, what did you do?"

He placed Sonja's pack further back in the *mekoro*, so that Sonja could use it as a backrest, then waded to the front of the long, narrow boat, which was barely wide enough to accommodate his quite ample backside. He checked the safety catch on the AK and climbed in, in front of Sonja. "I was the village schoolteacher."

"And now?" she probed.

"And now, I am taking you where you need to go."

She felt the canoe tip and grabbed the sides to steady herself as the second man pushed the *mekoro* out into the muddy water and nimbly jumped aboard. He stabbed a narrow wooden pole, its length nearly twice his height, into the bank and the vessel slid quickly and easily into the channel.

Reeds and pampas taller than the poler shielded them from view as the *mekoro* glided silently down the waterway, which seemed no more than two or three meters across at its widest.

"Too shallow for hippos to spend the day here, in case you are wondering," the leader grinned back at her.

"And crocodiles?"

He kept his gaze ahead now, adjusting the assault rifle on his lap and wrapping his right hand around the pistol grip. "Ah, plenty."

Sonja had traveled by *mekoro* many times in her youth, but she never tired of it. To her, it was the only way to travel through the swamps. It was as close, literally, to nature and the delta as a human could be. "How long will we be on the water?"

"Two, maybe three hours, depending on the strength of the man behind you." The poler chuckled.

Sonja unzipped her daypack and pulled out her bush hat. One thing she remembered about traveling on the waters around Xakanaxa was how easy it was to get sunburned out on the water. Next, she unlaced her right boot, slid off her sock and rinsed it by trailing it in the water, which was just a few centimeters below the top of the canoe's sidewall. She squeezed the water out of her sock and wriggled her toes, letting her feet dry.

The leader looked back, disturbed by her slight movements, and looked down at her pale foot and smiled. "One boot at a time, eh? Like a good soldier."

"My father taught me that." The memory came from her subconscious. It was a pleasant one of them going for long walks on the cattle farm at Okahandja, tracking kudu and impala and other wild game that also lived on the property. Sometimes he would shoot for the pot, and on other occasions they would go just to watch the graceful antelope. He'd told her, when she wanted to stop and massage her aching and blistered feet after wearing some new boots, to take off one at a time, and replace and lace the one boot before taking off the other—in case she had to suddenly run from danger.

"But Papa," she'd said to him, "you always told me not to run from lions or leopards."

"People, my girl. In case of bad people."

It was her first, but not her last lesson in the art of war and bushcraft from her father. As much as she despised him now, some of what he'd taught her had saved her life.

The leader returned his gaze to the front.

By two in the afternoon she could tell from the sun's position that they were more or less heading south, which figured. She pictured the map of the Caprivi Strip in her mind. South of the highway, the B8, on this eastern side of Caprivi, was a series of wetlands not unlike the country in the Okavango Delta. On the Namibian side of the border were Mamili and Madumu national parks and this seasonally flooding environment continued across the border into the Linyanti swamps of Botswana. It was a good place to hide a rebel army—remote, inaccessible and easy to get lost in if you weren't a local.

Many refugees from the Caprivi region had settled in Dukwe, which was where she had been supposed to meet Martin, but that was a long way south of the border, well into the dry heartland of Botswana. She wondered if the Botswana government had deliberately chosen a spot so far from the border in order to avoid the refugees fomenting trouble too close to their former homeland.

Pop, pop, pop.

Sonja swiveled to look up at the poler. "My pistol. Give it to me!"

The leader looked back over his shoulder. "Relax. It is all right. We are near."

"That was an AK-47," she said, suddenly feeling naked and trapped in the boat without her sidearm.

"Very good," replied the leader.

A faster burst of gunfire erupted somewhere up ahead.

"And that?" asked the leader.

Sonja cocked her head and waited for the next burst. "Seven point six two millimeter, again. A PKM, this time, I think."

"Close," the teacher corrected her. "Good guess. But it's actually one of the new MAG 58s that have just arrived. We are conducting weapons training today. I prefer the RPD myself—it's lighter and easier to move with."

Sonja agreed. "The drum magazine is simpler to change during an assault."

The leader laughed, deep and loud, obviously relaxing a little as they neared their destination and no longer having to worry about making too much noise. "I can see we are going to have much to talk about. Perhaps we can learn a few things from you. I understand you have been in many battles."

"A few. And you?"

He stayed looking ahead, but she could see his shoulders sag ever so slightly. "Only two," he said softly. "The raid on the Katima Mulilo police station more than ten years ago, and the attack on the dam. Both went badly."

She wanted to say something encouraging, but she had already decided that she wanted no more of this operation. Once she had briefed Martin on her recce she was still determined to turn her back on Corporate Solutions and take no part in bringing war to a country at peace, no matter what injustices these separatist rebels may or may not have endured.

The machine-gun continued to fire in desultory bursts of three to five rounds at a time. Above and in between the cacophony was the even louder voice of a man screaming in a local language, which sounded like Lozi.

"Is ammunition a problem for you?"

The leader shook his head. "No, we have plenty of ammunition and weapons, though by now you may have heard that we could use more men. Why do you ask?"

"Those are machine-guns that are firing. Those men need to be told to use them like machine-guns. They need to get used to firing twenty-round bursts. It's an area weapon, not a popgun."

The leader turned and looked at her, and she read a look of surprise on his face. He'd obviously just been making conversation when he'd mentioned that a woman might be able to teach them something about war.

"But surely it is better to conserve—"

The voice was screaming now and it had lapsed into heavily accented English. "Cease fire. Listen to me, you stupid bastards . . . I won't tell you again. THIS IS A MACHINE-GUN. FIRE IT LIKE A *FOKKING* MACHINE-GUN, NOT LIKE A *BLADDY* POPGUN!"

After a brief pause the gun started firing again and it kept going until the whole belt of seventy, eighty, maybe a hundred rounds was finished. Sonja heard the metallic clunk as the empty breech block locked itself in the open position.

The leader was saying something to her but she wasn't listening. She was gripping each side of the *mekoro* tightly. Her head was spinning and her blood was pumping so hard and fast its noise was deafening her.

She told herself she had to be wrong. It couldn't be him.

22

The poler pushed them toward a chink in the curtain of papyrus and when Sonja looked up she saw a man in uniform waiting for them.

"Good afternoon, madam."

"Gideon!" It had taken her a couple of seconds to recognize him. His head was shaved and he was wearing a smartly pressed short-sleeve camouflage shirt and trousers. He braced up into a position of attention, then shuffled carefully down the muddy bank to catch the bow of the *mekoro* as it slid between the long stems of grass. "How are you?"

"I am fine, madam, and you? Are you well?"

"Yes, I am well." The leader stepped out and Sonja politely waved off Gideon's hand and stepped off the canoe. It was good to stretch her legs again. Gideon did look fine. As she shook his hand, three times in the African manner, she saw the whites of his eyes were clear and his breath no longer smelled like a Sunday-morning shebeen. Gideon exchanged a few words with the leader, who bowed to Sonja and told her again he was sorry for her inconvenience, and that he must rejoin his men. The poler pulled her Glock from his shorts and handed it to her.

"Come, madam," Gideon said. "I am to take you to the general, our commander. He is with our senior instructor and operations officer, who also wants to meet you."

She felt her legs weaken, as though they might give out from under her, and mentally cursed herself for her weakness.

It couldn't be.

Gideon made small talk as he led her on a well-trodden path that became firmer and drier with every step. They were on a sandy island and ahead of her was a cluster of mature sausage trees and mahoganies. She heard an authoritative deep voice speaking loudly in Lozi.

The reeds gave way to long grass as they approached the shade of the trees. Sonja saw thatched roofs and as the grass became progressively shorter she saw the dwellings were actually open-sided *lapas*, or shelters. They were long and narrow and beneath the thatch were chairs and tables, like an open-air bush schoolroom.

Gideon motioned for her to wait, with a gentle hand on her arm. Sitting cross-legged in the clearing, facing them, were a dozen young men in camouflage fatigues. Her arrival had been noted and the men couldn't help glancing at the white woman who had emerged from the long grass. Addressing the trainees was an older African man, also in uniform, with a cap of tight gray curls and a black swagger stick tucked under one arm. His deep voice was rising to a crescendo, as if he was fighting to keep their attention. Eyes dutifully flicked back to the general.

Beside the pontificating commander was another old man, but this one was white. There was much less hair on top than she remembered, and what there was now hung long and lank and gray almost to his shoulders, which seemed a little rounded with age. The legs were bandy, but the calves muscled. His exposed skin was nut brown, except for the top of his head, which was red and mottled with dark sunspots. He wore a faded T-shirt in the camouflage pattern of the old South African Defense Force, denim shorts and rafter sandals.

She could tell by the way his head was moving slowly from side to side that he was watching the eyes of the young recruits. He would have noticed their distraction.

When the general finished his address he turned to the white man, who turned sharply to his right and saluted the African general. The commander reciprocated and turned and walked away.

"Course," the white man said.

There were no more doubts, and hearing his voice up close merely confirmed her worst fear. She wanted to turn and run away.

"COURSE! On your *bladdy* feet, you useless pack of bastards!" The recruits scrambled to stand and snapped to attention. "Course, dis-missed."

He turned away from the troops, who milled around in the clearing chatting to each other, and walked toward her.

He smiled and she took in his face as he approached her. He wore rimless glasses now and his beard was long and white, except for the yellow tobacco stains around his mouth, which matched the color of his teeth as his mouth contorted into a wide grin framed by deep wrinkles. He spread his arms wide as he closed the distance between them.

"Hello, my girl. It's been a long time."

She turned away from him and again she felt the urge to flee from his touch.

"Sonja, wait, let's—"

She changed her mind and turned back to face him. Putting every ounce of her weight into the swing, she slammed her fist into the left side of his jaw.

He staggered, reaching out with his right hand to steady himself, but recovered from the blow and straightened himself up again. He worked his jaw from side to side and placed his fingers gently against the left side of his face.

The soldiers behind him stopped their chatter and a couple had the temerity to laugh.

"SHUT UP YOU BASTARDS." He didn't look back at them, but his words were enough to silence and disperse the troops. He stared at her.

"Hello, *Papa*." She turned on her foot and walked away from him, toward a brown canvas army tent into which the general had just disappeared.

"Sonja?"

She ignored him.

·   ·   ·

She opened the flap of the tent and a soldier seated at a fold-out table with a tactical radio set on it stood up. "Hey!" He reached for a pistol in a holster on his belt.

"Relax, Mishak. We are expecting this woman," said the older man.

"I take it you're in charge here," she said to the man without preamble.

"I am. Leave us, Mishak." The young soldier looked at Sonja, fastened the flap on his holster, and walked out. "And if you have come to serve in the Caprivi Liberation Army, Ms. Kurtz, in whatever capacity, you will please address us as 'sir.'"

When he'd said "we" were expecting her she had thought the general was referring to his entire force. She could see now he favored the royal "we." Not a good first impression. "I haven't come to serve anyone or anything. I was on my way to meet my employer, Martin Steele, when your men kidnapped me."

"Kidnapped?" He sat down behind another folding desk and motioned for her to take a seat in a canvas-covered director's chair.

She shook her head. "I don't intend on staying long. Where is Steele?"

"*Major* Steele is on his way here now. Respect for rank is important, Ms. Kurtz. We did not give orders to kidnap you, Ms. Kurtz, we gave orders to *protect* you."

"From what?"

"You were involved in a gunfight with three men who were trying to kill you near Divundu. After that, you were tailed all the way along the Caprivi Strip by two men in a Nissan Patrol."

That was news to her. The road had been pretty empty and she was sure she would have spotted a tail. "How do you know all this?"

"The Caprivi is our homeland, Ms. Kurtz. We have eyes and ears everywhere. Nothing happens there that we do not know about."

Sonja wondered how, then, "our" troops were able to walk into an ambush at the dam construction site that left scores of the general's soldiers dead, wounded or captured, but she resisted the urge to inject the barb.

"We were told," he continued, "that you were a professional, Ms. Kurtz, whom we could learn from. Personally, I doubt our men could gain much from the experiences of . . . of one so young, but Major Steele was very persuasive. I wonder now, however, if you will bring us trouble."

She didn't need to take this tinpot Idi Amin's abuse, though she was concerned if she was being followed. "Who was tailing me?"

"That," he reached into the pocket of his starched fatigue shirt for a packet of cigarettes, "we shall know soon, Ms. Kurtz."

She heard footsteps behind her and turned. Her father was standing at the entrance to the command tent. He stepped across the threshold and saluted. The general sat upright, with his clenched fists on his tabletop. "Enter, Major Kurtz."

"Thank you, sir."

Sonja rolled her eyes at this parody of military discipline.

"Begging the general's pardon, sir . . ."

"Ah, you wish to spend time with your daughter. I understand, Major. Please do so, and appraise us of her intentions at your convenience."

Sonja turned and brushed past her father, not bothering to indulge the general's Napoleon complex any further.

"Sonja . . . wait."

She strode across the clearing, looking for the man who had brought her here, or Gideon . . . anyone who could get her out of this place of madness. She felt his cool, rough skin on her arm and she rounded on him, dropping her hand to the butt of the Glock sticking out of her shorts.

He stood there, mouth open. He blinked. "You would raise a gun to your father?"

"To stop you hitting me, or any other woman again. Yes."

He looked at the ground. "It's what I wanted to talk to you about. For so long. I've changed, Sonja."

She turned again and started walking away.

Walking toward her, gingerly stepping around the line of MAG 58 machine-guns that rested on their bipods on the ground, was an African woman with an elaborately braided hairdo piled on the top of her head. In her arms she carried a toddler, a little boy whose skin was several shades lighter than hers. The woman looked at Sonja as she came alongside her.

"Don't you at least want to say hello to your half-brother?"

Sonja stopped in her tracks and looked back. The woman with the child had moved to her father's side and Hans Kurtz put his arm around her.

Sonja was speechless.

Her father took the little colored boy from his mother's arms and kissed him. "Hello my boy." He set the child down. "This is your big sister, Sonja. Say hello to her, Frederick."

She opened her mouth to speak, but the words wouldn't come. It was as if she'd been struck dumb. There was so much to be said, but she'd been happy a second ago to leave it unsaid and walk away from him forever.

The woman walked toward her and extended her hand. "Hello, Sonja. My name is Miriam. Your father has told me much about you."

Sonja looked down at the woman's hand, but didn't take it. She could never tell with African women, but she thought this one, this *Miriam* was no older than she—perhaps even a few years younger. Miriam lowered her arm and clasped her hands in front of her. "I understand . . ." she began.

"You understand nothing." Sonja glared at her father, ignoring the woman, and thought of the lost years when he had drunk his way out of her life. She thought of the wasted time she had spent living with him, when her mother, who knew better, stayed in the UK. She remembered the biting sting of his palm across her face and how she'd vowed no man would ever touch her like that again.

Something brushed her leg and she looked down. It was the child. He had moved, unseen, between Sonja and his mother. He reached up and patted her on the thigh, where the sticky plaster dressing covered the wound that was almost healed.

"Ouch," the little boy said.

She stared down at his upturned coffee-colored face.

"Your father told me of the bad things he did to you, and your mother, Sonja," Miriam said quietly, as Sonja looked into the wide green eyes of the little boy. "He told me about his drinking, and the violence toward you. He no longer drinks alcohol."

She tore her eyes from the child and looked at the withered man with the bushy white beard. He had the sense not to say anything, but simply nodded.

"And he has never raised a hand to me."

"No," Sonja rounded back on the mother. "Only me and my mom."

"And I have seen him, heard him, pray for forgiveness for those acts many times."

She couldn't recall her father ever setting a foot inside a church, except for funerals. Also, as she looked at him, trying to see through his eyes, she heard the countless, repetitive, objectionable words he'd had for black people. *Kaffir, coon, wood-head, munt, nigger* . . . and so many more. The racist jokes; the way he'd make fun of his farm workers without them realizing it; the things he'd said he would do, when he thought she was out of earshot, to the terrorists who had raided the farm in his absence.

And he'd done it. They were not idle threats.

She'd met a white Namibian, an ex-*Koevoet* man, working as a contractor in Iraq. He'd told her he'd served with her father and had been full of praise for the old drunkard. "You know, hey, that we caught those terrs that raided your farm and tried to kill you and your mom?" the man had asked her.

She didn't know. She heard his words now, spoken with admiration. "It was about a year later, after your dad had transferred to us in *Koevoet*. Our bushman trackers led us to a SWAPO camp. We slotted four of them and took one alive. Your dad decides to *interrogate* him, in the field, if you know what I mean." She could only guess. "So your pa finds out where this gang has been operating and whatnot, and it turns out this terr was on the raid on your farm. This young *oke*, he was full of spite. A real nasty piece of work. When your pa asks him what kind of men are sent to kill defenseless women and children, he points out that you, when you were a little girl, winged one of his comrades. He said you were hardly defenseless. Your old man, he actually smiled at that and we had a bit of a chuckle, us and this terr. Then the *oke* turns nasty again and says, 'But white man, we were not only sent there to kill them, we were told to rape them first.' Your father beat him to death. It took a long time."

Miriam placed a hand on her arm, gently, breaking into her thoughts. "Your father also told me what he did in the war, and he prays for forgiveness for those many acts, as well."

"Hello," said the little boy at her feet. He seemed miffed at being left out of the conversation.

Sonja put a hand on his springy hair. It was soft. She ran her fingers through it. "Hello." He smiled up at her. She removed her hand.

So what? He had found God and fallen for a black woman, but he had abused and hurt her and her mother and driven them out of his life, and away from Africa. What right did he have to expect he could now come back into her life and think that all would be forgiven?

"Steele told me you have a daughter," her father said.

She snapped her head around. "That's none of your business."

He shrugged. "No, but I would like it to be. How is your mother?"

It was easy now, to see clearly again. "Dead. But what would you care?"

"Sonja, please . . . don't talk like that. I'm sorry about your—"

"Don't you fucking tell me how to talk. I don't care if you've changed your life. You pissed our life away up against a wall. I wish you well, second time around," she added, not bothering to hide her sarcasm, "even though Mom and I never got a second chance."

Sonja strode away from them, even though she had no idea where she was going. She saw the *mekoro* she had arrived on and headed for that. Something else the old man had just said popped back into her mind. *"Steele told me you have a daughter."* How long, she wondered, had Martin Steele known her father was tied up with this band of rebels? The manipulative bastard was always looking for ways to control her life. He knew she would have refused to have anything to do with the CLA if she'd found out her father was serving with them. She imagined his gloating. He'd think that now there would be some tearful reconciliation with the old killer who had found God and become a born-again lover of black people. Well, the Kumbaya Rainbow Nation bullshit wasn't going to work with her.

Hans followed her. "I tried to contact your mother plenty of times. She never returned a single letter."

"Was that before or after you found your new girlfriend?" she asked without looking back.

"Come, Frederick," Miriam said softly. She took the confused little boy's hand and led him away. Sonja had hoped for a rise from her. She wondered where and how his father had met her. Had he ended up drinking in African shebeens?

"Shame," the ex-*Koevoet* man had told her in Baghdad, "an old army buddy of mine who works as a professional hunter in Bots these days told me he'd seen your dad begging on the streets of Maun a few years back. It's terrible when a white man has to do that, hey?"

It was terrible when anyone had to do it—black or white—but the news hadn't softened her feelings for Hans then, any more than his alleged transformation did now.

Sonja had the manners to wait until Miriam was out of earshot before she broke the silence. "When did you decide the only good black wasn't a dead one?"

He shook his head and brought his hands together, fingers interlocked, like he was about to start praying. Instead, he began wringing his hands. "We . . . I, Sonja, was responsible for so much evil during the war. I had to live with that—still do—but I should have sought help sooner. I kept you and your mom in the war, living it in my mind and my dreams every day, every night. I thought the booze would make it go away, but it made things worse, as you know."

She nodded. But her mother wasn't stupid. She knew it was the ghosts from the war days that were tormenting him and driving him to the bottle. She'd pleaded with her husband to go to AA, or a doctor, or a psychiatrist, but he'd brushed her concerns aside like an empty bottle.

"After you and your mom left, and I lost the job at Xakanaxa, I tried to pull myself together. I wanted to come after you, but when the dreams came the bottle was always there. I had a couple more jobs, as a guide, and then in Maun, at a taxidermy place, but I crashed the company Land Cruiser when I was drunk. No one would employ me. They stopped serving me booze at the Sports Bar, same at Trackers. I got into fights and they banned me. I ended up drinking in the shebeens."

It was cold comfort to Sonja to see how she'd guessed his downfall. "Is that where you met Miriam?"

His eyes flared; it was eerie, like looking into her own eyes. "Say what you like about me," he hissed, "but she is a good woman from a good, up-standing family. If you must know, her father was a Methodist pastor. He took me in, when he found me lying, bashed, in the gutter in Maun outside a bar one Sunday morning on his way to Church. Through the booze and my pain I can recall seeing at least three lots of whites drive past me that morning. I swore abuse at them as they drove past me, and I swore at Miriam's father when he stopped for me. I told him to keep his mother-fucking shit-eating filthy kaffir hands off me as he was loading me into his car and asking me if I needed food. That man . . . that man . . ."

Sonja looked away when she saw the tears welling in his eyes and the way he wiped them away angrily with the back of his hand. He took another step toward her and she took one back.

"He locked me in a garage—more a cage—behind his home in Maun, and he kept me there until I dried out. Miriam brought me food and she washed me and cleaned me while the demons tried to kill me in that *bladdy* room. You don't ever want to go through that hell, Sonja, believe me. They're Lozi, from the Caprivi, and we talked, a lot, about the past, and what had happened to our tribes."

"Tribes?"

He nodded. "It's all about tribalism, Sonja. He, the pastor, helped me see that. It wasn't about black versus white. He helped me understand that in one way we could never understand or explain why it is that one tribe treats another so badly. He said the Lozi had been screwed by the Ovambo the same way the Afrikaners and the Germans in South-West had been screwed by the British in the old days. Anyway, he told me about the politics of the Caprivi Strip and how the CLA and the UDP had done a deal with SWAPO and Sam Nujoma that guaranteed that the people of the Caprivi would be able to vote for self-rule after independence."

He was talking animatedly, like a born-again Christian who feels the need to convert every lapsed believer he encounters. "I saw it then, Sonja.

We—the white settlers in Namibia," she had never heard him refer to the country as anything other than South-West Africa in the past, "had our turn at power and we abused it and we blew it. We had ourselves to blame for the war, because of the way the South Africans imposed their apartheid regime on us, and we lost and we got screwed. But the Lozi—the people of the Caprivi—they had nothing before the struggle; they got nothing out of the struggle; and now they continue to get screwed to this day."

"I've heard it all before." She did not want to get into any kind of a debate with him. She just wanted to be gone from this place.

"Miriam's father was a man of peace, opposed to military action to take back the Caprivi Strip, but she was secretly in contact with the CLA. She knew of my background and she told me that God had sent me to her people to train the CLA for war."

"Do you know how lame that sounds? What are you now, 'God's instrument?' His shield, His sword?"

He waved his hand across his face. "I didn't say I believed it, but I knew there was only one thing I was ever any good at in my life, Sonja. I was *kak* at farming—we were nearly broke before we moved off; I was useless as a lodge manager and safari guide—I drank the profits and mostly I hated the clients. The only time I was ever good at anything was in the military, and in *Koevoet*."

"I'm leaving."

She started to turn and she felt his hand on her arm. She shrugged it off but didn't look back at him.

"You know what I'm saying, don't you, Sonja?"

She shook her head, not wanting to meet his eyes.

"Look at me."

She refused.

"Steele told me about your time in the British Army, in Northern Ireland, then Sierra Leone, Indonesia, Iraq . . . Afghanistan."

"No."

"Yes. You know the irony of this whole *bladdy* life I made for us? If I hadn't wasted so many years at the bottom of a whiskey bottle I probably would have ended up working with you, alongside you, in all those places."

"No."

"Yes. Look at me when I'm talking to you, girl."

She turned and glared at him. "You gave up the right to tell me what to do the day you hit me in the face. I came back for you. I knew you were having problems because of the war and I left my mother in England to come back to help you and you repaid me by calling me a 'fucking bitch' and punching me. Go back to your freedom fighter wife, your cause and your child. And don't you fucking dare try to say you have something in common with me."

He ran a tongue over his lips. "No, Sonja," he said quietly. "I don't have anything in common with you, other than the fact that I passed on to you the ability to shoot well and kill well. To tell you the truth, I'm glad that I was too drunk and too stupid at the time to find work as a mercenary, because it would have been *wrong.*"

She leaned back from him, as if trying to readjust her focal length to get a clearer picture of his face. "Wrong?"

"Yes, wrong. I know you don't care what I say to you, and you're a hundred percent correct that I forfeited my right to give you parental advice a long time ago, but just let me say two things to you before you leave this place. First, I love you, Sonja . . ."

"Stop." She held up a hand. "I don't care."

He grabbed her wrist, though not painfully. "I love you, Sonja, and have since the day you were born. The second thing I want to tell you is to give up this life. It doesn't matter what else you do or even if you're no good at anything else in your life, but you cannot take money from a man like Martin Steele to fight other people's wars."

She laughed at the absurdity of this man lecturing her on morals.

He let go of her and held up his hands to still her. "You are being paid to wage war on a democratically elected government in a peaceful African nation, and to destroy a vital piece of infrastructure that will provide water and electricity for hundreds of thousands of people who need both. What you are doing is criminal and it is wrong, Sonja."

"I . . ." She searched for the words but again he was stealing them from her, and she hated him for it. She was not a child. "What do you think you're doing, then?"

"I am helping a people—my people, as it now happens—to reclaim custody of a piece of land that has been in their care for generations. The Lozi have nothing in common with the Ovambo or the rest of the peoples of Namibia. They were a proud, independent nation, Linyanti, before the whites even came to this part of Africa. Ethnically, linguistically, culturally, they are and deserve to be a nation of their own once again."

"Pah!"

"Don't scoff. These people took me in when my own had abandoned me. I am one of them now." He grabbed her arm again. "This is my chance to make things right, Sonja. You do not belong here and, quite frankly, now that we have the guns and the air support that the money from the lodge owners in the delta are paying for, we do not need any more white mercenaries here to tell us what to do and how to fight."

His eyes were burning with the searing, white-hot intensity and destructiveness of a zealot, or a madman.

No, she told herself as he stood there, still holding her, letting his words sink in. Not mad, just a believer. She knew which was worse—she'd seen the charred remains of the work of believers on the streets of Baghdad.

"You're fighting for money, Sonja, and it's not a good enough reason to kill for or to risk your life for, or to risk your child's happiness over. Go to her, Sonja. Leave this place now. Steele and the people who work for him are like hyenas, scavenging and growing fat on death."

God, she was so confused all of a sudden. She had been on her way to the *mekoro*, to get her things and paddle herself away from this swamp. The man she had despised for so many years had just compared her to a hyena. She shook her head and almost smiled at his analogy. As well as being scavengers, hyenas were also ruthlessly efficient hunters and killers, and the females ruled the clan.

"Sonja," he said, looking deep into her eyes, "this isn't an exercise in reverse psychology. I'm not telling you to go, and that your work is wrong because I want to goad you into staying and proving a point. I know you;

you're like your mother. You're stubborn and if someone tells you not to do something it just makes you want to do it even more."

Damn him, she thought.

"There's something else." He lowered his voice. "The general likes Steele and he likes the idea of professional, paid soldiers training his men and going into battle with them. It's part of the reason why I'm here. However, the general is mad."

Sonja snorted.

He moved closer to her. "I'm not mad, despite what you might think. But listen, we don't need any more mercenaries here. The head of the Okavango Delta Defense Committee, Bernard Trench, has been bankrolling us for months, but I don't need Steele to tell me how to win in Caprivi."

"Well, it looks like you're saddled with him anyway. Trench might be supporting your plan for regime change, but what he and his kind really want is for the dam to be destroyed."

Hans nodded. "I know. Apparently Steele is providing a team of specialists to blow the dam. We've been tasked to arrange covert transport to the dam site for them. The rest of us will . . . well, we have other targets in mind."

She respected the fact that he wasn't telling her what those targets were, for security reasons. However, she knew from Steele's concept of operations that he had presented to the safari lodge owners that the CLA would try and take Katima Mulilo, and probably the military and civilian airstrip at M'pacha, an old South African military airbase near the provincial capital.

"That *team* would be me," Sonja said.

"What do you mean?"

"I'm the 'team of specialists.'"

"*Jissus*," Hans said, running his bony hand through his thinning hair. "How much are you getting paid?"

She smiled at his tone, then became serious again. She didn't like the way the conversation had turned into precisely that—a conversation. They'd had their confrontation and now they were talking like a couple of professional soldiers about the pros and the cons of the plans they had either made or had forced upon them by their superiors. This was wrong, she told herself. They were not army buddies and, as far as she was concerned, they were no longer father and daughter. "I'm getting paid enough to ensure my daughter and I can see out the rest of our lives in peace and anonymity."

He took off his glasses and rubbed his eyes. "Money won't buy you peace, Sonja, any more than it will buy you love or happiness. Go now and make a new life for yourself and your child."

He made it easy to stay angry at him. "Don't tell me what to do. You forfeited that right, remember?"

He nodded, then put his glasses back on. "But don't kid yourself that what Steele is doing is right because it's supposedly about striking a blow for the environment. Money's the only thing that matters to that man. Myself, I think we should capture the dam intact and hold it, along with the rest of the Caprivi Strip. If we can hold the Caprivi for long enough to start negotiating with the Namibian government we can use the dam and the hydroelectric plant as bargaining chips."

"But Steele's contract is based on the dam being destroyed. He's only using your *liberation* movement to provide the manpower to make this operation a success."

Hans pulled out the last cigarette and inspected it. It was broken. He looked disappointed. "Using us as a diversion, more like it. He's hoping that when we attack Katima Mulilo and the NDF is in chaos, trying to reinforce its garrison there, his 'specialist team' will be able to infiltrate the dam's perimeter and blow it up. That's the price we have to pay for the arms, ammo and air support he's providing." He screwed up the cigarette and threw it away. "You should leave, Sonja. This is the CLA's last roll of the dice and it's going to be bloody. I don't want this granddaughter I've never met to be left without a mom. People are going to get killed."

She was still mad at him, and his show of concern for her welfare. She saw that the color of his shaking fingers matched the beard around his mouth and imagined nicotine was the only drug left for him. Sonja pulled the cigarettes from her shorts and offered him the pack.

His eyes brightened. "Newbury, from Zimbabwe?" He took one and lit it, pausing to greedily inhale, then spat some flecks of tobacco from his tongue. "These things will kill you."

"You should tell that to the guy I took them off."

The smell of it made her want one and she was angry at herself for starting again. She pulled one from the pack with her lips and he raised his lighter. She had to lean close to him. Damn him, she thought. She nodded as she took her first drag.

"I heard you had some trouble at Divundu," he exhaled. "The general said that according to police radio chatter there were three Zimbabweans *braaied* in a Hilux not far from the dam. Did you kill them?"

She saw the purple grime under her fingernails as she brought the cigarette to her lips. Lady Macbeth had it right. "Yes."

"How many men have you killed over the years, Sonja?"

It was the question everyone wanted to ask, but very few people dared. "More than most people; not as many as you. You taught me well."

He'd finished his cigarette already and he pinched off the end and put the butt in his pocket, in the way that old soldiers do, not wanting to leave anything behind for the enemy to track them by. Her left hand went to her pocket and she felt the three *stompies* in there. Curse him for coming back into her life; for never leaving it.

"Yes, I did, and may God forgive me."

23

Sam's back and arm muscles were burning and he was light-headed. He couldn't lie back in the canoe; every time he tried, the guy using the pole or paddle or whatever behind him would kick him viciously between the shoulder blades. The more he sweated into the hessian hood over his head, the more humid and cloying the limited air available to him became. He felt like he was choking on his own breath.

He'd been wearing a tank top and shorts when they'd dragged him and Jim at gunpoint from the rented Nissan Patrol they had taken from Bagani airstrip, and he could almost hear the exposed skin on his legs, arms and shoulders crackling under the sun's heat as he roasted. Jesus, he could have been sipping a chilled beer by the pool in the Windhoek Country Club by now, instead of wondering how soon it would be before he died.

No. If they had wanted to kill him and Rickards they would have done it by now. He shifted his butt a little. That ached as well. The man behind him gave him a kick for good measure and said, "Still."

His wrists were bound together behind him with plastic cable ties, and though he could still wiggle his fingers they felt cold against each other now. His shoulder muscles cried at being pulled back at such an unnatural angle and every now and then streaks of pain shot up the insides of his thighs.

Rickards's idea not to catch the flight to Windhoek with Cheryl-Ann and Gerry, but to go looking for Sonja instead, had been crazy. Oddly, though, Sam hadn't needed much convincing.

"I'm a freelancer, Samuel," Rickards had told him as they stood by the open door of the GrowPower private aircraft. "I go where the news is. And that chick," he jabbed his thumb toward the dust cloud Sonja left in her wake, "is news with a big N."

"What about Cheryl-Ann?" Sam said.

"Step away from the camera bags, dude," Rickards said to the pilot, who was plainly getting impatient to leave Bagani. "Cheryl-Ann's fucked, mate. She's busted her last ball. I've seen it happen before. Sometimes it's the toughest, cockiest journos who cry for mummy and make small potty in their pants when the bullets start flying. I'm a news cameraman. I've seen stuff that would make a mortician puke, and I *know* there's trouble brewing here in paradise. Also, now that your producer's on her way to the laughing academy, that's the end of your documentary. It's OK for you—you've still got a contract with Wildlife World—but my gig just ended and I probably won't see a cent."

A mange-ridden donkey nosed inside a discarded plastic shopping bag full of rubbish that had been deposited by the last occupant of one of the Nissan rental trucks. Sam rubbed his jaw. "I don't know."

Rickards walked over to the vehicles and Sam followed, reluctantly. Jim checked the windscreen of the nearest Nissan, which was parked near the tin-roofed structure that served as the airstrip's terminal and office. The cars had presumably been dropped at the airstrip by GrowPower employees or contractors and the vehicles were awaiting collection by the car rental company whose name and number were on a sticker on the windscreen. It wasn't a big-name firm, which made it more likely, he reckoned, that they would do a deal over the phone if Sam gave them his Wildlife World expense account credit card details. "Are you with me, compadre? Think of the exposure, Sam. With your words and my beautiful pictures we might be able to come up with something that'll take you off cable and onto the networks. You could be rich and famous, Sam."

"I'm not interested in fame or money."

"Yeah, right. Spoken like a true TV celebrity. Once more with feeling, dude. Listen to me, Sam. If not for fame or cash, then do it for the only real reason that counts in this godforsaken world of ours, my man."

"What's that?"

"You want to have sex with Sonja."

"I do not."

His case mounted, Rickards stood there in the dust, leaning against the Nissan, in silence.

"Give me the number," Sam had said.

The company had agreed to let Sam take the car, but only after he'd explained who he was. The consultant from the rental firm was a big fan of Sam and Wildlife World, but her boss insisted on an astronomical deposit and a promise they would drive straight to Katima Mulilo and the company's nearest branch office to fill out the paperwork, before revealing that the quantity surveyors who usually hired the vehicle had hidden the keys in the tail pipe.

Sonja had a good hour's lead on them and Sam and Jim had no idea how far she would drive before stopping, or where she would stay. Come to think of it, Sam had no idea what he would say to her when he did catch her. He guessed her reply would be short and to the point—probably no more than two words and one would be a cuss.

So why had he done it? Maybe Jim was right about him wanting to sleep with her. He wasn't so sure that Sonja was involved in some mercenary plot to foment war in the region, but Rickards was.

"Corporate Solutions, man," he said as Sam floored the accelerator and raced through the gears. "They're mercenaries. I bet all that shit that guy Steele laid on about her coming along to protect us was just a cover. Were you watching her at the dam?"

Sam admitted he hadn't been. Well, no more than usual.

"She was scoping the place out, big time. When we were checking in she was practically counting the cameras and the guards. She was casing the place."

"Professional curiosity?" Sam ventured.

"Whatever. And let's not forget the three African gentlemen in the shiny black ute who tried to whack us. Or have they slipped your mind already?"

Sam knew he would see the face of the man he had killed for the rest of his life.

"Nope, she's up to something, my friend. And she owes it to us to tell us what it is, seeing as she very bloody nearly got us killed."

At the first roadblock, at the junction of the B8, the policeman on duty told Sam that the white woman in the Land Rover had driven through about an hour before them, and headed east, toward Katima Mulilo.

Sam and Jim pressed on, winding the Nissan up to a hundred and forty. At the veterinary control point at Kongola, just across the bridge over the Kwando River, they again had the chance to ask after Sonja. It was already dark.

"No, there has been no woman in a Land Rover through here," the woman at the checkpoint had answered.

"You're sure? How long have you been on duty?"

"All day. I am sure. And now I am going off duty."

"Say, we passed some signs to a couple of camp sites a little way back," Sam said to the woman. "What can you tell us about them?"

The woman shrugged. "The one at Bum Hill is suitable for two-by-four vehicles, but Nambwa is for four-by-four only."

Sam turned the vehicle around and headed back over the bridge. "What do you think?" he asked Rickards.

"I'm thinking Lara Croft is more a four-by-four kinda girl," Jim said.

Sam nodded.

The route had challenged his sand-driving abilities but they'd made it, after taking a wrong turn and almost ending up in a swamp. Retracing their tracks they saw the small metal sign they had missed. When they arrived after ten in the evening the sleepy camp-site attendant said he hadn't seen a single woman in a Land Rover enter the campground.

"How long have you been on duty?" Sam asked the man.

"Only two hours."

Sam looked at Jim. "She could have arrived earlier. I'm going to look for her."

"Good luck," Jim said. "I'm knackered. I'm going to sleep in the truck."

Sam had stumbled about the camping ground for a while, checking each of the demarcated sites along the river front and although he saw a Land Rover it had South African plates and was part of a trio of expedition vehicles. He started to move away from the water in search of other camp sites, but the sound of tree branches snapping halted him in his tracks. Sam jumped when he felt a hand on his shoulder.

"Sir," the African man who had been at reception said, "you should go to bed. There are elephant in those bushes. It is not safe for you to be walking around." Reluctantly, Sam agreed.

He was awake with the sun but when he got up and walked around the rest of the camping ground there was no sign of Sonja or her Land Rover.

A different man was now on duty in the reception hut. "Ah, but the lady in the Land Rover she has already left, earlier this morning."

Sam wanted to scream in frustration. "Why didn't the other guy tell me she was here?" he seethed.

"This lady, she did not have a booking, so I put her in the overflow camp site. My brother did not know about her."

Sam and Jim packed in a hurry. The drive out through the deep sand drifts didn't seem nearly as long or as challenging as Sam gunned the Patrol's big engine and raced to catch up with Sonja.

When the uniformed policeman strode out into the middle of the road and started flagging him down, Sam was sure he'd been busted for speeding. The fine would have been richly deserved as he'd been pushing the vehicle to its limits.

"Our luck might be in," Rickards had said, pointing to the police pickup on the side of the road with its bonnet open. "Looks like these guys might just be broken down and looking for a lift."

Sam rocked forward then backward as he felt the nose of the dugout grind to a halt in mud or sand.

"Up!" the man behind him ordered.

It was easier said than done. Sam couldn't use his tied hands to grasp the sides of the canoe, and when he brought his knees up and tried to boost himself up he found his legs had gone to sleep from staying in the one position too long.

"Up!" He felt a hand grab the back of his shorts and haul him roughly to his feet. His leg muscles prickled with pins and needles and he lurched forward, bumping into Rickards's back. The Australian swore.

"Sorry," Sam said.

"How fucked do you think we are?" the Australian whispered.

"It's not good." Sam straightened up and put one foot tentatively in front of the other. "But I figure if they wanted to kill us they would have done it by now."

"Silence!"

Sam cried out in pain as something blunt and unforgiving punched him in the small of the back. At the same time another hand grabbed the shoulder strap of his tank top and dragged him.

"Lift your feet," the voice said to him. Sam followed the orders and noted the accent of the new voice was different. It sounded European, maybe Dutch. He hadn't spent any time in South Africa other than transiting through the airport on his way to Botswana, but he thought the voice might have been that of an Afrikaner. The accent was similar to Sonja's, but harsher. Sam stepped into a mush of water and mud but his next footfall was on dry land.

"Stop there," the man said. "Hold your hands steady." Sam felt the cold steel of the flat edge of a knife's blade rest against the inside of his wrist and he flinched. "I said steady, unless you want me to cut you."

He heard a snap and then felt the blood pulsing back into his hands and fingers. The relief turned quickly to pain.

"Rub your hands together. Massage your wrists. *Jissus* man, if you'd put these *bladdy* things on tighter this *oke*'s hands would have dropped off," the man said, presumably to one of the men who had kidnapped them. "Strip them."

Sam swallowed as he felt hands lifting his top over his head. Any hope he'd had that the man with the Afrikaans accent might have been kinder on them was fast disappearing, along with his shorts.

"Oh fuck, no," he heard Rickards whine. "Please don't rape me!"

"Shut up!"

Sam heard a chuckle and some words exchanged in an African dialect. The men laughed some more and Sam reddened under the hood he was wearing. He felt vulnerable and very afraid. This, he figured, was what they wanted.

"On your knees. Now!" the Afrikaner voice barked.

Sam lowered himself and placed his hands in front of his pubic area.

"Arms up! Reach for the heavens. You won't protect yourself that way. If you lower your arms you will get a beating, understood?"

"You're making a . . ."

The blow between his shoulder blades pitched him forward and he grazed his palms in the sand trying to break his fall. Rough hands pulled him back up onto his knees again. He heard breathing close to the hood. "You don't speak unless you're answering one of my questions. Name?"

"Sam Chapman. I'm a presenter for—"

A hand slapped the back of his head. "Arms up! All I asked you was your name."

"You?"

"Jim Rickards . . . sir."

Sam heard a thump and a squeal of pain as Jim received the same treatment.

"Play smart with me, Aussie boy, and I'll cut your fucking balls off. Understand?"

"Um . . . yes."

Sam heard footsteps behind him and again sensed the man close to his face. "I see from your passport that you are a Mr. Samuel Charles Chapman, citizen of the United States of America. Now, Mr. Chapman, I want you to tell me who you are working for."

"I'm a television presenter for the Wildlife World documentary channel. I'm in Africa making a film about the Okavango Delta and—"

Sam doubled over and felt only pain when he tried to draw a breath. He fell to his side and clutched his chest.

"Up!"

Hands dragged him up. He was gasping but couldn't get any air in his lungs. He thought he might pass out.

"Hands up!"

A hand grabbed his hair through the hood, forcing the coarse fabric against his mouth as he managed a ragged breath.

"No bullshit, American. I don't want your fucking cover story—who do you work for?"

"I told you, I work for Wildlife World it's a—"

"Shut up, you fucking liar." Sam heard the slick sliding of metal on metal then felt something press against his temple hard enough to ingrain the weave of the hessian on his skin. "Feel that? It's a Browning nine-millimeter pistol. But don't worry, I'm not going to shoot you with it."

Sam was too scared to utter another word. He felt the pressure removed from the side of his head.

"I'm going to shoot your Australian friend here. Mr. . . . James Edward Rickards."

"Don't shoot," Sam heard Jim wail. "He's telling the truth, you fucking psychopath. This dude's a TV talking head and I'm—"

The gunshot shook Sam's whole body. "JIM! Nooo!"

All Sam could hear was a muffled, gurgling sound. He felt the gun pressed against his head again. He could feel the heat of the barrel through the hood. "He's wounded, Samuel, but not dead . . . yet. Want me to put another bullet in him and finish him off, or are you going to tell me the truth? Who are you working for and why were you following the woman?"

"I TOLD YOU, I'M SAM CHAPMAN AND I WORK FOR—"

"Papa? What the fuck are you doing, you bloody idiot . . ."

The pistol was moved and Sam tried to shrug away from the fingers he felt at his throat.

"Sam, it's me, Sonja. Relax. It's OK, Sam."

He was almost hyperventilating but her words stilled him. He felt the fingers again. Soft, delicate, as she unpicked the knot at his throat. He smelled her through the bag. Not perfumed, but a raw, woman's smell. He coughed. "Son . . . Sonja?"

"*Ja*, hush for a moment while I get this off."

He risked the wrath of the other man and dropped his hands to his groin again.

"Get this man's clothes. Now! And the other one's, you fucking maniacs," she said.

Sam blinked as the hood came away from his head. He saw Sonja, though her face and ponytail were a black silhouette against the sun streaming through leaves above. He coughed and spat fibers that he'd sucked into his mouth and throat over the past hours. He looked to his side and saw a black man in camouflage uniform struggling to remove the hood from a thrashing, swearing Rickards.

Sam stood and snatched the shorts from the man who held them out to him, then stepped into them. As he pulled his singlet top over his head he twisted around and saw an old man with a Santa Claus beard holding a black pistol at his side. He felt Sonja's hand on his arm.

"Jesus, Sonja, do you know these madmen?" he asked.

"Hands off, motherfucker," Rickards said as he wrenched his hood the rest of the way off and hopped from one leg to the other as he tried to pull on his pants.

"That one," Sonja pointed to the man with the beard, "is my father."

The man looked at Sam and shrugged.

Sam and Jim sat on a log in front of a camp fire. Scattered around the clearing were more tents hiding beneath trees and nets. Every now and then an armed African man in uniform wandered past and gave them a suspicious glance.

Sonja lifted a blackened kettle off the embers and poured boiling water into three tin cups. She took a pewter hipflask from the pocket of her shorts and poured a shot of something into each cup.

"Make mine a double, GI Jane," Rickards said.

Sam saw that, despite the bravado and wisecracks, Jim's face was still very pale. Sonja handed them each a steaming mug.

Sam smelled coffee and brandy. He sipped it, closed his eyes and let the double-barreled heat work its way through his tortured body. He opened his eyes and looked at Sonja. "That man is your *father*?"

She nodded. "It's complicated."

"Seems pretty straightforward to me," Rickards said, coughing as his first mouthful hit home. "Crazy little fucker tried to kill me because he thought Sam was some kind of spy."

Sonja smiled. "If he wanted to kill you, you wouldn't be sitting here now. He was just trying to scare you."

"Well it worked. I thought he'd shot you, Jim," Sam said. "I didn't know what to say."

"One of the other dudes put his hand over my mouth just as Kris Kringle shot his wad into the ground by my foot, is what happened. Your dad is one sick fuck, Sonja."

She rocked her head slightly from side to side, as if weighing up the observation, but didn't say anything. Sam wondered whether Jim had hit the nail on the head.

"He was trying to protect me. They were watching you from the time you left Bagani airfield. You shouldn't have followed me."

"Who are *they*, Sonja?" Sam took another slug of medicine.

"I'm not at liberty to tell you that."

Rickards stood up and tossed the dregs of his coffee in the fire. A small blue flame danced in the coals. "Enough with the 'need-to-know' bullshit, Sonja. You owe us an explanation."

She crossed her legs and looked up at him. "Really, Jim? How do you work that out?"

He ran a hand through his greasy black hair. "How do *you* feel about telling me to hang out the window of the Land Rover to film those clowns following us in the black Toyota? Did I draw their fire OK for you?"

She frowned and Sam could see Rickards had scored about half a point.

"I thought if they saw you filming they'd be too scared to do anything and would back off."

Sam shook his head. "Now I'm really confused. Who the hell are '*they*'?"

"None of your business, Sam."

It was his turn to lose it with her now. "I *killed* one of those men, Sonja. I think that kinda makes it my business."

Rickards was pacing back and forward. "OK, so Miss Plausible Deniability here isn't going to tell us anything, Sam. Let's do a little deducing. What's the only armed rebel group that's been active in this part of the world in the last few years?"

Sam searched his memory for the acronym. "The CLA, right?"

Rickards nodded. "Caprivi Liberation Army. I actually came up here years ago, in the nineties, when the CLA tried to take over the police station at Katima Mulilo. I got squat—the war was over before it began—but I remember a rumor going around had it that the CLA was being trained by bitter and twisted whites from the old South-West Africa looking to get a little payback against the Namibian government."

"How about it, Sonja?" Sam asked. "We getting warm?" She ignored him.

"And so Sonja's dear old dad," Jim went on, "is one of those old soldiers looking to refight the war against the SWAPO terrorists who now run his former home."

Sonja said nothing.

"Lion got your tongue, Xena?"

She glared at Rickards, but didn't rise to the bait. Sam thought he might have to put a restraining hand on the Australian soon if he didn't calm down—not that he could blame the guy. He had, after all, just nearly been shot.

"So you," Jim pointed between Sonja's eyes, his fingers cocked like a pistol, "work for Corporate Solutions. Cheryl-Ann swallows the line that you're a bodyguard, but no one wants to listen to Jim Rickards when he points out that CS is a mercenary outfit that specializes in wreaking havoc on the African continent."

Sonja turned to Sam, still blanking Rickards. "Why did you follow me, Sam? Why not just go off to Windhoek?"

Sam looked up at Jim, who returned the glance and drew a breath. He answered for Sam, his voice calmer and lower now that the fear-induced adrenaline was subsiding. "I'm looking for the story, Sonja, but Sam here was genuinely worried about you after those goons tried to kill us."

She looked at the camp fire.

"What's CS doing up here, Sonja?" Jim pressed. "Are you training the CLA? Running guns?"

"If you expect an answer to that then you should know it'll be followed by a bullet."

"You going to deliver it, or are you going to leave that up to psycho-daddy?"

She shook her head. "No, I'm not going to hurt you. I was trying to leave this place when you two showed up." She leaned forward in her chair and motioned with a hand for Jim to resume his seat on the log, which he did. "I don't think my father will harm you now that he knows who you really are, but I can't be sure about everyone else here."

"Are you leaving?" Sam asked.

She sucked her lower lip between her teeth and chewed for a second. "I wanted to, but I can't see them letting you go right now."

"Right now?" Jim whispered. "What's going on here?"

She shook her head.

"The dam?" Sam asked.

"Don't ask any more questions," Sonja said. "They already think you know too much. You're a liability to them."

"There we go with 'them' again," Rickards said. "Who are they? Who's pulling the strings on the puppets with the guns here?"

The three of them sat in silence, thinking about their next move.

"I can try and get you out of here. Quietly. Tonight," Sonja said.

Rickards surprised Sam by shaking his head. "No way. I want in."

"You want *what*?" Sonja beat Sam to the question.

Jim stood again. He seemed to feel better asserting himself when he was on his feet. "This could be the African story of the decade. Sam—let me ask you a question. Before you came to Africa and that guy Martin Steele told you and Cheryl-Ann about the so-called security situation in the Caprivi Strip, had you ever heard of the Caprivi Liberation Army or the Free Caprivi movement?"

Sam shook his head.

Jim snapped his head around to stare at Sonja. "See?"

She shook her head. "I don't follow."

"PR. These dudes have been fighting a silent political and military battle to regain sovereignty over their ancestral homelands, against an unfeeling and allegedly cruel government dominated by a different tribe. Right?"

"Pretty much," she agreed.

"And no one has ever heard of them. The CLA needs some good public relations and *you*, young lady, are going to arrange with your dear old dad for *me* to be embedded with whatever hit squad these rebels are putting together."

Her laugh burst like a grenade. "You're insane."

Rickards nodded enthusiastically. "Agreed. It's part of the job description for a TV cameraman. But think about it. Unless your dad is going to kill us—which somehow I doubt—we're going to leave here and sex symbol Sam is going to sell his story for a mint to *OK* or *New Idea* or *Entertainment Tonight* or whatever, about how he was captured and psychologically tortured by this loony rebel commander. Right Sam?"

He shrugged. "I'm sure there will be questions about what happened and I'll answer them as objectively as I can."

"Bullshit. Stop being so polite, Sam. I mean, I know you've got a crush on Sonja and all . . ."

"Jim," he hissed.

Sonja turned to him and Sam looked away into the fire.

"Whatever." Rickards started pacing again. "Well, speaking for myself, I am going to get in front of every print, cable and free-to-air journalist in southern Africa when we get out of here and tell them my tale of woe. Win, lose or draw, your pop and his rebel army are going to come off looking as bad as Marlon Brando in *Apocalypse Now*. Wasn't he a Kurtz as well?"

Sonja ignored the levity. "I can see where you're going, Jim, but my father—not to mention the general commanding the CLA—won't agree to taking a civilian cameraman with them on any operation. Not that I'm saying there is an operation."

"Sonja. Listen to me . . . from what I know the Namibian government has done a far better job convincing the world that Africa needs this dam to give electricity and water to the teeming masses. Correct?"

She nodded.

"It's going to be the same once your war starts in the Caprivi Strip. The Namibians are going to brand these guys as terrorists and criminals. They're going to lock the strip down and not let any foreign media in. The CLA will have lost the information war before it even begins. I want to be the one who shows the world the other side, the truth—the first pictures of the freedom fighters of the CLA in action, taking back their homeland from a heavy-handed oppressor. And Sam here can tell their story."

"I can?"

Jim kept looking at him, waiting for an answer. "Think of it, Sam. The ultimate reality program—*Coyote Sam Goes to War*. You don't look convinced." Rickards paced to the edge of the fire pit and back. He raised his right hand as if seeing letters in thin air in front of him. "I can see the headline . . . 'CHAPMAN TELLS—MY TIME WITH THE ECO WARRIORS WHO BLEW UP A DAM TO SAVE PARADISE.'"

Corny, Sam thought, but he could see there was something in this for the CLA rebels. As Rickards had said, other armed forces—both insurgents and government-led around the world—used the media to help fight their wars. He looked at Sonja, trying to read her face. He was coming around to Rickards's point of view and he wondered how much of that was due to him searching for a way to spend a little more time with the woman next to him.

"Sonja," Sam said, "do you think the CLA has a legitimate grievance against the government?"

She shrugged. "Maybe."

"Yet you're willing to risk your life to help them fight a war and blow up that dam on a 'maybe.'"

"Wait a minute." She raised her hands. "No one said anything about a dam or a war. Besides, I just told you, I'm not even staying here. I'm leaving. I was kidnapped off the road—just like you two."

"I don't believe that," Sam said. "Jim was watching you at the dam and now that I think about it, I thought your behavior was a little odd as well. You *used* us as a cover to get on to the construction site and you work for a mercenary outfit. What do you think about the dam?"

She chewed her lower lip again and sat with her elbows on her knees, staring into the fire once more. "I don't have to tell you anything."

"You're right. You don't. But tell me, in case I get dragged into this thing any deeper, in your heart of hearts do you believe that dam should be destroyed?"

She looked across at him. "I don't know if I believe in the CLA's cause or if they have the right to take on an elected government in an armed strug-gle, but I do know that from what I saw in the delta—the lack of water in places that should still have had some, even in a drought—that the dam has to be destroyed or the world will lose a piece of its heart and its soul."

Rickards shifted from foot to foot. "I want to be there when that fucker blows. The world will call the CLA environmental heroes—green commandos."

She turned to Sam. "Do you want to be part of this?"

Sam stared at her and knew it was madness to go along with what Rickards had suggested. His answer would depend on hers. "Do you?"

She closed her eyes and nodded.

24

"I think it's a brilliant idea," Martin Steele said.

Sonja stood in the Caprivian general's command tent and watched the men carrying on like bull elephants locking tusks, trying to assert their dominance. Steele's comment, siding with Rickards, who had just put his proposal to the general and her father, surprised her. But then Martin was always full of surprises. It was partly what had attracted her to him in the early days—his ability to think outside the box.

"We are not convinced," the general said. "Our Major Kurtz is right— the television man and his camera operator will get in the way, and if they are killed in action we will be blamed for their deaths."

Sonja looked at her father and saw the slight nod of agreement and self-satisfaction. He was a different man to the one she'd seen teaching the recruits how to fire the machine-guns. She knew the drink would have taken a toll on him in the years she'd been away, but she'd been surprised at his long greasy hair, his stained beard, his knock-knees and his tatty shorts and T-shirt.

The man who glanced back, however, looked every inch the seasoned warrior. He, or his new African wife, had taken to his hair with clippers and reduced it to a steel-gray fuzz that flanked the tanned skin of his balding pate. His beard, too, had been trimmed to a neat, short silvery goatee. She knew his father, her grandfather, had served as a German army panzer commander in Russia during the Second World War and emigrated to South-West Africa in 1946, and though the man had died before her birth, her grandmother had shown her crinkled black-and-white pictures of her grandfather in uniform. She saw that same cold, ruthless face again now. He winked at her.

He wore a camouflage fatigue shirt and trousers in the same pattern as the CLA recruits and a tan canvas South African Army assault vest with pouches on the chest bulging with curved magazines for the AK-47 that was slung over his right shoulder. Sonja guessed he had been, or would soon be, test-firing his rifle, psyching himself up for the coming battle. Sonja looked back at Martin Steele, who was wearing his old British Army disruptive pattern camouflage uniform, which he always wore on operations. Sonja knew both men had dressed for a private war. She gave her head an almost imperceptible shake at the theater of it all.

Her father was the training officer for the CLA but she guessed—and the general had just confirmed it—that he also acted as a military adviser to the commander. Hans always claimed Sonja had inherited her stubborn streak from her mother, but in fact her parents were as intransigent as each other. By all accounts her father had been an excellent leader of men in the field in his day, as well as a ruthlessly efficient killer, and she was sure he resented the presence of Steele in the CLA camp. He may have even seen the mercenary as a threat to his position in the chain of command. Also, as an Afrikaans-speaking German from the old South-West Africa, he was, she knew, no fan of Englishmen.

"General," Martin said, "when we take Katima Mulilo and we blow the dam, the rest of the world will turn its attention to the Caprivi. Without pictures—video—of our actions, which will mostly occur at night, your victory will gain a few seconds of air time at best or a news crawler at the foot of a CNN bulletin. With some high-quality images of your success and an interview with yourself, the world will know not only who you are and what you have done, but why you have done it."

The general pursed his lips and nodded, contemplating both sides of the argument. Sonja hadn't missed Martin's careful use of pronouns. "*Our* actions," as though he would be in the thick of the fighting—which she doubted; and "*your* victory"—a deliberate sop to the bombastic little man's ego.

"We understand, Major Steele, but Major Kurtz has a valid point about the unpredictability of the media. What guarantee," he asked everyone in the command tent, "do we have that we will not be portrayed as criminals or terrorists?"

"General . . . sir," Jim Rickards said, "as an accredited news cameraman I give you my word that Sam and I will report fairly and objectively on what we see. I can't tell you what the world will think of whatever it is that you have planned, but I can tell you that without the words and images we want to take to the world they will have made up their minds by the end of the first Namibian government press briefing. The world can either see you explaining that you're blowing up the Okavango Dam to save the environment, or they can see pictures of little babies dying because their mothers can't get enough clean water to drink or electricity to lead a decent—"

"What?" Sonja's father exploded. "Why is this *bladdy* TV man talking about an attack on the dam?" He stared accusingly at Steele. "What have you told these people?"

"Nothing," Steele fired back. "But they're not stupid. They know the strategic and political importance of the dam, and so too does the Namibian government. That's why they've got the dam protected by mortars and armored cars. The Namibians know we want it—you *tried* once before, after all."

Sonja saw the red fill her father's face and his hands ball into fists. For a moment she thought he might grab his AK and shoot Martin. Kurtz gritted his teeth, biting back the anger, and exhaled, slowly. There was no hiding his attempt to control his rage. He fixed Steele with his green eyes. "Yes, we tried, and we failed, thanks to a traitor."

The general tapped his swagger stick lightly on his desk. He, alone, was seated. "Please, gentlemen. We are all on the same side here. Major Kurtz, you know we dealt with four traitors who supplied details of our attack plans to the NDF."

Kurtz squared his shoulders. "We don't need you, Steele."

"No, but you do need the grenades, RPGs, mortars, other heavy weapons, uniforms and helicopters I've brought with me. This offensive wouldn't be happening without me and my backers from the Okavango Delta Defense Committee."

Sonja wondered if her father would explode, or if he had truly learned to control his temper. She saw the rage bubbling beneath the tight skin of his hard-set face. Her father and Martin faced each other off, but they were at a stalemate.

The general slapped his cane hard on the desk this time. "Enough! We are not amused."

Out of the corner of her eye Sonja saw Jim Rickards quickly raise his hand to his mouth and fake a cough to cover his laugh. Sonja turned away until she could force the smirk from her face.

"We have made our decisions." The general cleared his throat. "Major Kurtz will lead the attack on Katima Mulilo and the M'pacha airport and air base. Major Steele will coordinate air support, as previously agreed, and assume command for the covert team that will target the Okavango Dam."

Sonja's eyes flitted from man to man and she saw that both Steele and Kurtz seemed placated.

"Mr. Rickards and Mr. Chapman will be traveling with neither assault force," the general said. Rickards began to speak, but the general silenced him by lifting and pointing his swagger stick first at the cameraman and then at Martin. "Major Steele will assume responsibility for our television crew. Mr. Rickards and Mr. Chapman will be flown to Katima Mulilo when and if Major Kurtz deems the situation safe enough for a helicopter to land. You will film our valiant troops moving through the town and taking control of the police station, government offices and the NBC broadcasting studios."

"What about the dam?" Rickards interrupted.

The general looked annoyed, and flicked his head as if trying to shoo away a wasp. "Without revealing the details of Major Steele's plans, an exfiltration helicopter will be in the near vicinity of the dam when the wall is breached. Filming will be possible from the air."

"Awesome. Thank you, your generalship," Rickards said.

"You now know too much for us to let you leave this place until our offensive begins," the general continued. "You will consider yourselves as our honored guests. You are free to move about the training area, but you will be escorted at all times; and if you try to leave you will be shot."

The general had obviously given some thought to the public relations opportunities the attacks provided—right down to camera angles. Everything was in place and they had all agreed upon their parts in this operation. Steele hadn't briefed her, but Sonja assumed that as he hadn't arrived with an army of Corporate Solutions mercenaries—in fact, he had come alone— then she was going to be the one to blow up the dam. Sonja looked around the tent, from man to man.

They were fucking mad. All of them.

"Hello my girl."

"Mum? Where *are* you? What's all this about?" Emma said into the phone.

"I'm not too far from where you are. I'll explain everything when I see you. Are you all right?"

"'Spose. Uncle Martin was great. At least he treats me like an adult. He met me at the airport at Maun and flew in the light plane with me to Kaka—whatever this place is called."

"Xakanaxa. It's where I grew up."

"Whatever. Anyway, Uncle Martin organized me this luxury safari tent. You should *see* this place. Oh, right . . . you lived here. Was it like this in the old days?"

"I'm sure *Uncle* Martin organized everything just fine. I can't wait to see you again."

"Are you working with him? Is he with you now? And why was I virtually abducted from school? Not that I'm complaining."

She didn't want to start answering any more questions over the phone, no matter how secure it might be. "Did you meet Stirling?"

"Who? Oh, you mean the manager guy?"

"Yes. What do you think of him?"

"He's treating me like I've got fucking herpes or something. Can't stand to be around me. He's been quite rude, actually. I told Martin, and—"

"OK, OK. You can tell me all about it soon."

"Is Uncle Martin all right?"

"What do you mean?"

"I mean, I know you don't tell me half of what you get up to when you're away working, doing your bodyguarding or whatever, but I assume it's dangerous—like, if people need protecting or whatever. And if Uncle Martin's there, I just want to know if he's safe."

It might have been nice if she had spared a thought for her mother's safety as well. "Whatever."

Sam stood outside Sonja's tent and heard her on the phone. He wanted to talk to someone, and to get away from Jim Rickards and his incessant enthusiasm for five minutes.

Rickards had convinced their guard, a man who looked to be in his late teens, to pretend to be patrolling through some bushes while Jim filmed him to get some B-roll to go with his report.

"I'm just going to see Ms. Kurtz," Sam had said to their guard, and pointed to Sonja's tent. The man had smiled and waved, obviously enjoying his new role as a television star.

"Good luck, soldier," Rickards had said, before returning his eye to the viewfinder. "Take one for the team."

Sam waited until he heard Sonja finish her phone call. Knocking didn't seem to be the right thing to do on canvas, so he cleared his throat.

"Who's there?" Sonja appeared at the entrance to her large canvas safari tent and gave him a small smile. "Hi."

"Hi. I guess you're busy . . ."

She shrugged. "Not really. I was going to wash my hair as soon as I'd finished cleaning my AK."

"Oh, right, well I'll come back . . ."

She laughed. "Just kidding. Don't take everything so seriously, Sam. It's not like you're going off to war."

It was his turn to smile now. He thought again how much her face changed when she was happy. Was she happy now? Was it possible, he wondered, to be relaxed and contented the night before going into battle?

"I was wondering if you'd like to . . . actually, what I mean is I'd really like to talk to someone and . . ."

"Other than Jim?"

"You got it."

She laughed again. "I was just talking about you, actually."

"Really? I thought no one was supposed to know we're here."

"You're right. It was my daughter. I've just had her taken out of school and flown halfway around the world to be with me. I mentioned you were here in Botswana and it turns out she's a fan of your programs. It's possibly the longest conversation I've had with her in months—it lasted all of three minutes and most of it was about you. She wants an autograph."

He smiled. "I'd like to meet her some day. Anyway, what I really wanted to ask is whether you have any tips for . . . well, to be quite honest, for surviving."

She looked at him and he could tell she saw the fear in his heart. "Well, the first thing I'd suggest is you stay as far away from Jim as possible."

"That's going to be a little hard, since he's my cameraman. Do you want to come outside . . . maybe get some fresh air?"

She poked her head out of the tent a little further and saw Rickards directing the young soldier. "Pretend you're fighting. Guns up!" they heard the Australian say.

She shook her head. "Come in here, if you like. I don't want to get shot by Rickards."

She moved a stack of magazines about guns and four-by-fours off one of the two military stretchers in the tent and motioned for him to sit down.

"I don't trust him, Sam, and neither should you. I'm not saying he's dishonest, but I've seen a thousand guys like him. He's a glory hound. He's not afraid to die to get the best possible shot and he's going to take you down with him if you're not careful."

"Aw, c'mon Sonja. He's mostly talk. You heard him say he'd covered plenty of wars in the past."

She shook her head again. "I heard him and read between the words. He's shown up late, after the massacres and the shooting were all over. He's never been in a real firefight, apart from what happened at Divundu, and his first battle is probably going to be his last. He can't wait to get in among the bullets."

Sam thought about it and realized he probably had the same opinion of Rickards. The cameraman had been foolish to go off after Sonja, and Sam was a fool to have followed him, even though he'd done it for different reasons.

"Did you come here for me?" she asked him.

He looked at the pile of magazines on the floor of the tent. "You read this stuff?"

"*Ja*, my subscription to *Cosmo* ran out last month."

He laughed.

"Well?" she asked.

"I was worried about you . . . after those men tried to kill you—tried to kill us."

"You killed a man, Sam. You and I both know the smartest thing for you to do would have been to get on the first plane home to the States."

He picked up a copy of *Magnum* magazine, which seemed to be about handguns, and flicked the pages, though he wasn't at all interested in the merits of the .357 versus the .44. "Why do you do what you do, Sonja?"

She leaned back on her stretcher, placing her palms behind her on the canvas. "Because I hate typing and I was a lousy waitress. Why do you make TV shows instead of camping out on the prairies researching coyotes?"

He shrugged. "This way I can get messages about conservation and endangered species out to a much wider audience than if I was just doing my research. And the money is good, too."

She gave a small smile and nodded. "I'd be lying if I said it was just for the money."

"Don't you ever want to stop?"

"Don't you? We both whore ourselves, you and me, but we both secretly enjoy it. Are you *judging* me, Sam?"

"No. No, no, not at all. It's just that . . ."

"What? You don't think a *woman* can be a mercenary? You don't think a woman can kill for a living?"

"No. It's just that I don't want to think of you maybe not being around any more the day after tomorrow."

She was ready with another retort, another salvo of the same old ammunition she'd had to use every time some damned man tried to tell her she had no place being where she was. His words, however, were like hearing your firing pin click on an empty chamber. It was chilling—terrifying. You were supposed to count your bullets and never be caught off guard. She didn't know what to say. She liked him . . . really liked him, and she didn't want him to come into her world and get hurt.

Sam stood, stooping a little in the confines of the tent, and took the space that divided the two stretchers to sit down beside her. The springs squeaked and the canvas creaked. Sam picked up the AK-47, gingerly, in case the thing accidentally went off.

She opened her mouth, but no sound came out as she watched him move the rifle to the other cot. "You should go."

"Deal." The stretcher sagged beside her and he felt her roll, slightly, involuntarily, closer to him. "But only if you come with me."

She looked at the nylon mosquito mesh of the tent flap, as if worried someone might come barging in any second. Or was she, Sam wondered, looking for an escape route? Maybe a little of both. He moved an arm around her and placed his hand down on hers, on the canvas, behind her. She didn't move her hand.

He could smell her now. No perfumes or body lotions, just the cheap soap and damp hair from an outdoor shower. She was a wild thing—a predator as at home in this hostile environment of men, animals and guns as a lioness, and just as dangerous. He didn't want to tame her—he'd die trying—but he wanted to be with her. She reminded him of what he could have been. Honest.

She moistened her dry lips with the tip of her tongue. No gloss. No need. "I want to go, Sam, but I can't." Her voice was hoarse.

He leaned closer. "You don't have to do this for money. If you're in trouble I've got plenty..."

She widened her eyes and shifted away a little, maintaining the distance.

Shit, he thought. "That came out wrong. It's just that... it's not worth..."

She reached up and smiled as he recoiled. He thought she might be about to slap him, but instead she placed the tip of her right index finger on his lips. "Hush," she whispered, "I know what you mean, and I'm touched, but I take hand-outs from no man." She licked her lips again; left them parted ever so slightly.

"Sonja?" said a voice from outside.

She unzipped the tent and exhaled noisily. She ran a hand through her damp hair and hoped her cheeks weren't as flushed as they felt, or that her scent wasn't as strong as she imagined. She felt the trickle and the warmth, and the ache.

"Oh, hello," Martin said when Sam followed her out of the tent.

Martin wasn't crass enough to say he hoped he hadn't interrupted anything, but his raised eyebrow did the job anyway. "Do you have a minute?"

"Of course," she said to him. "Sam, perhaps we could finish our chat later?"

He nodded, turned on his heel and walked over to where Rickards was filming a line of CLA rebels queued outside the open-sided mess tent.

"Let's walk."

She fell into step beside him.

"Chatting? Is that what they call it these days?"

"It was nothing, Martin, and none of your business anyway."

He nodded. He carried an AK-47, and she wondered if it was to compensate for the fact her father had been armed during the briefing. "I thought I'd better brief you on the dam job."

"It might be a good idea," she said, "since I've never blown up a dam before. It had better be a good plan or I'm walking away."

They moved out of earshot of the camp, down a narrow path between stands of reeds and papyrus, toward where the boats had landed. She forced the image of Sam's handsome face from her mind. The temptation to make a run for it with him had been almost overpowering, despite what she'd said. What was he suggesting, she wondered, with the crack about money? He didn't seem the sort who would have a kept woman on tap. Was he talking something more? He knew about Emma, and that, in her experience, was normally enough to kill a first date. "I take it there's no one else from CS about to show up?"

"No. It's just you and me. Bigger share of the loot that way. I've already had your share wired to your account."

"Thanks, but do you expect me to carry ten tons of explosives in a backpack as I climb over the razor wire around the construction site and sneak past the Namibian Army, or will you be coming along to help me carry it?"

"Very funny. I'll take questions after the briefing."

She stayed silent. It was the army way.

"There's a mobile HIV-AIDS testing clinic that visits the dam construction site once a month. It's a converted truck with an air-conditioned cab on the back. There are two people on board—a registered nurse and a driver who is qualified as an ambulance paramedic. Because of other stops it makes on the way, the truck normally arrives at the dam at last light— sometimes after dark. The clinic's only been going to the dam for the past three months—it's a relatively new initiative and a bit of PR window-dressing funded by the German partner in the dam project, Grow-something or other."

"GrowPower," she corrected him. "Their PR person's pretty sharp."

He frowned at the interruption, but nodded. "Whatever. I don't know anything about her or them. Doesn't matter. The point is that it hasn't been the same two people driving the van onto the site more than once, so the gate guards, while accustomed to the visits, don't know who will be driving it. As long as their credentials are in order they'll be let through. The next visit is due tomorrow night. The van is going to arrive at the front gate, at

1900 hours local time, but it's not going to be the same nurse and driver who set off from the last stop. It's going to be you and the CLA's RSM-type, Gideon. You'll intercept them at a bogus checkpoint on the B8."

"If you're planning on killing the nurse and the driver, then this briefing ends now."

"I said no interruptions." He swatted a mosquito on the back of his neck. It was getting dark. The path led them beside the river and its surface rippled with molten gold leaves. Frogs began warming up for the evening chorus. "They'll be pulled over by CLA dressed as police—they're good at that, as you found out—tied up and left in a hut in the bush somewhere. They'll be set free after the show's all over, unharmed if they don't try anything stupid."

"But—"

He raised a hand. "Before you interrupt me again, let me explain. The nurses are provided by a German-backed AIDS charity. They're travelers—white girls who squeeze in a month of do-gooding and then go back to backpacking and shagging anything that moves. The drivers are rotated, as well, so Gideon won't raise any suspicions."

"How do you know all this?" Sonja stopped on the path, hands on hips.

He sighed, as if resigning himself to the fact he couldn't stop her interruptions. "Trench, the chairman of the Okavango defense committee, told me about it. He's got a safari lodge in Namibia and the mobile clinic visits his place as well as the dam."

"What about the site manager, Deiter Roberts? He knows me. You made sure of that by telling me to make eyes at him."

Martin shook his head and they resumed walking. "Herr Roberts's nice home in Windhoek is going to catch fire in the next few hours and the fire brigade is going to get a call a short time later. I predict our Deiter will be on the road or the first flight out of Divundu some time tomorrow."

She studied his face—the small smile, the thin cruel lips. She knew he could be a thorough bastard when he put his mind to it, and he was in his element tonight. "Who's taking care of the arson?"

He shrugged. "Some freelancers in Windhoek. Don't worry about it—they're cheap. They won't be cutting too much from our pie."

"You've been busy these past couple of days. So once inside the construction compound—presumably with an AIDS testing van full of explosives—how do I blow the dam?" Sonja asked.

"Have you seen that old war movie, *The Dambusters*?"

"You're going to drop the van from an airplane and it'll bounce down the river, right?"

"Very funny. The reason those bombs skipped along the water was so they could clear torpedo nets the Germans had erected, and then come to rest against the dam wall, where they would slowly sink to the bottom of the lake and then detonate at precisely the right depth. The force of the water in the lake, behind the bomb, enhanced its effectiveness and the power of the shock wave. So you, in the same way, need to get your bomb to the bottom of the dam wall, under water."

"How? And in any case, I doubt I'd be able to cram enough explosives into an AIDS testing van, no matter how big it is, to blow up a dam."

"You're right. In fact, you'll only be smuggling in about eight kilograms of high explosives in the van."

"Eight?"

He held up a hand. "Let me explain. Was there an explosives truck in the vehicle compound at the dam construction site?"

"Ahh." She nodded. "Roberts told me GrowPower's into blowing holes in the ground, as well as planting crops."

Steele smiled. "The AIDS van, according to Trench's sources, is usually parked overnight in the yard with the other valuable construction vehicles. There's a twenty-four-hour security presence and the nurse and her driver usually sleep in a demountable building allocated for overnight site visitors. At precisely 0300 hours Gideon's going to engage in a bit of arson himself. One of the demountables housing construction workers is going to catch fire. The buildings, you'll recall, are near the vehicle park. While you organize the security guard who watches the park to help fight the fire, Gideon is going to be allowed into the vehicle park to fetch the AIDS van, which doubles as an ambulance. Once he's brought the ambulance to you he's then going to slip back into the unlocked compound and get to work on that truck full of explosives."

"Get to work on it?"

"I've had two high-explosive charges rigged up, in sequence, for the job. Gideon will fasten these to the underside of the truck. The first charge is what's called a kicker, and the second, which is the larger of the two, is the initiator which will blow a hole through the steel tank containing the Nitropril and detonate it."

She gave a short shake of her head. "But how do we get the truck full of explosives in place?"

"I was coming to that," he said. "Get in your ambulance and tell whoever will listen that you've got a burn victim or two in the back and you need to take them to the clinic in Divundu. Gideon, hero that he is, will have started the explosives truck by now. He'll tell the security man that he's moving the truck away from the fire in case it catches light, which is nonsense, of course, but no one's going to argue with him. Gideon's the sort of person people listen to in a crisis and if they don't, he'll dispose of them, quietly. Gideon will drive into the inky night, but instead of heading for the administrative compound he'll drive on to the dam wall and you'll follow him."

Sonja nodded. Despite her earlier misgivings she was impressed by the simplicity and audacity of the plan. Some things were being left to chance, but that was inevitable in what was essentially a two-person operation. It might just work. "And halfway along the dam wall Gideon takes a left, jumps out, and lets the truck roll over the edge into the water."

"Precisely." Steele grinned. "The truck will sink or roll down the rear face of the dam wall, underwater. There's a barometric detonator on the high-explosive charges which will go off at the right depth to do maximum damage. The first charge, the kicker, will actually roll the lorry onto its side, so that the maximum surface area of the container carrying the Nitropril will come into contact with the wall. The initiating charge will go off a couple of seconds later, blow a hole in the tank, and detonate all that lovely bulk explosive inside."

They stopped again, pausing naturally as the sun disappeared beneath the bottom of the layer of dust haze. At another time, in different circumstances, it would have been romantic. "Bang goes the wall—hopefully," Sonja said.

"It won't happen right away. The blast should weaken the dam wall, but it will actually be the force of the water that breaks through the damaged section."

She gazed out over the darkening river and thought about the havoc they were planning on wreaking in one of the most beautiful parts of the world. Was Sam right? Was it worth it? Still, part of her felt the tingle of excitement, as real and as hot as the touchpaper Sam had lit in a different part of her body. The plan was simple, daring and mad. The best kind. "How do I get out?"

"Picture the scene. It's going to be chaos. You'll have picked up Gideon in the ambulance and you'll be off the dam wall before the barometric detonator sets off the explosives. Shortly afterward, the dam will be no more and most of the army garrison will be on the opposite side to you. You'll just slip away."

She laughed. "*Slip away?* Just like that? *Pfft . . .* gone, like a will o' the wisp." She clicked her fingers.

"I'll be in the air, in one of the choppers, circling nearby just across the Botswana border, with our trusty TV crew on board, and a ready reaction force of six of the CLA's finest. You and Gideon will both carry search-and-rescue beacons, a GPS and handheld radios. Ditch the AIDS van, find a quiet spot in the perimeter fence, cut your way out and head into the bush. Find a safe-ish LZ and talk us in."

She stared at him, hands on her hips. "Sounds like you've skimped on the planning of our escape. Don't you think we'll make it that far?"

"You don't think you can manage it?" he countered.

She bit her lip and thought about it for a few moments. "I could do it blindfolded, and you know it."

25

Sonja wanted to find Sam, but first she had to go and see her father.

The CLA had apparently been using this camp for some time, because many of the men had built traditional huts of mudbrick with reed thatch for themselves and their families a short walk from the military tented camp, at the far end of the island in the swamp. Her father wasn't the only member of the force who had a wife and children with him, though his son—her half-brother—was the only one of mixed race. She saw the boy toddling along with a stick in his hand, trying to keep up with two older boys, of seven or eight, playing at soldiers. The others ducked in and out of the bushes around the cleared compound between the huts.

"Bang, bang," her father's son called.

"Where's your dad, hey Frederick?" She dropped to one knee and gently took the stick from his hand. "You don't need this at your age, my boy."

The child started wailing. Sonja knew, from her own experience, what that sound would do.

"Frederick?" Miriam emerged from a hut wiping her hands on a tea towel. Sonja was a little surprised if this was where her father was living. She would have expected him to have a more substantial house than the rest of the men. In truth, she thought he would have had a white man's house. "Oh, Sonja! Hello."

Sonja bobbed her head in greeting and looked down at the little boy, then up at his attractive mother. "My father . . . is he here?"

"Come, Frederick, your dinner is ready. No, he has gone out with the men, into the swamps. Some last-minute training and rehearsals, he said. He works them day and night, so much that even the young ones look like they will die sometimes, but your father, he has the strength of a man a third his age."

She made a quick calculation—he would be sixty now. "Well, it was nothing important anyway. I'll see you, Miriam."

"No. Wait, Sonja. Let me get Frederick settled and we can talk. It's good that you came to see your father."

"You don't know what it was I was going to say to him."

Miriam scooped the little boy up into her arms and headed back toward the hut. She said, without looking back: "The anger is going from you. I think you came to find out who he has become."

Sonja bit her lip. What did this bloody woman know? "I don't care who he's become. You didn't know him as he was."

"No. When I found him he was a dead man. Still breathing, but dead."

"He never hit you."

Miriam set the child down at the entrance to the hut. "No. But he told me, soon after he was sober, what he was capable of when he was drunk. He told me what he remembered of the day he lost you, and how it broke his heart so badly that he thought he would bleed to death on the inside. He loved you," Miriam said. "He still does."

Sonja felt out of place here. She was not one to turn the other cheek or forgive and forget. In her world the meek didn't inherit the earth—they had their villages burned and their husbands killed. But when she glanced around she saw green T-shirts and camouflage uniforms drying on a washing line. Perhaps she was wrong about Miriam. What kind of a woman took herself and her small child into the swamps to join a rebel army; sent her man off to work with his gun and his ammunition in the knowledge that he was probably training to die to make a political point? Maybe Miriam was stronger than she gave her credit for.

"He drove my mother away," Sonja said. "He drove me away, even when I decided to stay with him."

Miriam knelt by a blackened pot just outside the door and spooned a mound of white maize meal onto a battered enamel plate. Next she scooped a rich, thick sheba sauce of beans, meat and gravy from an aluminum saucepan.

With Frederick seated and clumsily feeding himself by taking a handful of maize meal and dipping it into the sheba, Miriam straightened and looked at her. "He was sorry, but he knew it was too late. He started his life again and I just hope—I pray—that he lives long enough to see Frederick grow to manhood, in a country of his own."

She looked down at the little boy, contentedly stuffing his mouth. She remembered Emma at the same age. "Why, Miriam? Why do you love him? You're different ages, different colors, from different worlds. What do you see in him?"

Miriam wiped her hands again. "I saw a man imprisoned by his demons and tormented by his past sins. Then I saw that man—that prisoner—set free when he found the Lord and gave away alcohol. You have never met this man, until the last two days. You don't know him at all. Your mother must have known him, a long time ago, before the war changed him. She must have loved the man that I love now."

"Yet he's going back to war," Sonja said. "That might destroy him again."

"Perhaps his body, but not his soul. His soul is saved, and if he dies it will live on here, with Frederick and me, hopefully in a free land."

"How can you be so bloody accepting?"

"How can you believe your father ever stopped loving you?"

Confused and lonely. That was how she felt; and it angered her.

She took some solace in the small routines of her work. She removed the magazine from her Glock and laid it down on the stretcher beside her. The gas lantern hissed beside her, but the glowing mantle raised the temperature and it was still stinking hot outside, even though night had fallen.

She could strip and assemble her weapon blindfolded, so she turned off the gas. She racked the pistol, slid out the locking pin and eased the slide off. Next she removed the spring and the barrel. She found solace in the simple, practiced movements of her hands, and the solid weight and engineered lines of the components.

She was never one to vacillate. She never dithered or agonized over the choices she made. In a battle it was better to make a decision and stick to it, even if it proved to be the wrong one. You could always change a plan midway through, but if you never left the start line you never reached the finish. She hated not knowing how she felt, or what she should do next.

Sonja had been surrounded by men in disproportionate numbers all her adult life, yet she had nearly always been alone, romantically. Except for the brief periods in her life when she had let Martin Steele into her world—times as disastrous as they were passionate and fun—and a few one-night stands, she had been alone. But never lonely. All she wanted now was to be wrapped in someone's arms and be told that everything was going to be all right.

Stupid. She didn't know why she felt so emotional all of a sudden. It wasn't time for her period. Perhaps, she thought, it was seeing little Frederick that had reminded her of her guilt at missing so much of Emma's childhood. It took too little, at the best of times, for her to convince herself she'd been a crap mother.

She placed the working parts of the pistol down on the canvas and assembled the brass cleaning rod, screwing the pieces together and attaching the bristly brush at the end. She pushed the rod down the barrel and drew it back and forth, cleaning the inside. She pulled the rod clear and wrapped a small square of flannelette around the brush, then squirted some OX 18 gun oil on the material. Sonja heard a footfall on dry leaves outside her darkened tent. Working quickly, she reassembled the pistol, slapped the magazine back into the butt and cocked the weapon.

"Don't shoot!" Sam stood at the opening of her tent.

She lowered the pistol. "Sorry, force of habit."

"I just wanted to say goodnight," he said.

"Where's your chaperone?"

Sam looked back over his shoulder, "With Jim, and a couple of ladies of the night, getting drunk on something called palm wine."

Sonja winced. "That stuff will kill him before he gets near his first war."

"The CLA guys think he's on their side."

She motioned to a fold-out camp chair that had been leaning against the back wall of the tent. She didn't want to do the thing with the stretchers again; she knew she wouldn't be able to trust herself if he sat close to her again.

"Thanks," he said, sitting in the chair. "I interviewed a couple of them. They've got some sad and scary stories about the way they've suffered at the hands of the Namibian authorities."

"Be careful, Sam. Africa can be a sad and scary place. Different tribes screw each other all the time on this continent, and the Namibian government happens to be one of the better-run and most honest."

He leaned forward, his elbows on his knees. "Yet you're going to war against them."

"It's the dam I don't agree with."

He nodded. "Yeah, there was something about that German guy from GrowPower on the video that gave me the creeps. That whole 'good afternoon ladies and gentlemen . . .' was kind of like 'welcome to my web.'"

She thought about the presentation and what Klaus Schwarz from GrowPower had said. A chill ran from her heart to her fingertips. "The Botswana government doesn't want that dam to go ahead any more than the landholders in the Okavango do. They won't go to war over water and wildlife, though."

"Is the environment a good enough reason to go to war?" Sam asked.

"It's better than religion—that's what most wars are fought over these days."

He smiled. "That's true, I suppose. Hey, about before . . ."

"Yes?" She pressed the magazine release button and it slid out into her left hand. She set the bullet-filled magazine down and racked the pistol, catching the ejected round in midair. She pointed the pistol at the ground and pulled the trigger.

Sam flinched as the firing pin struck nothing. "If it seemed, when I was sitting next to you, that I was coming on to you, or . . ."

"Or?"

His face colored a little. "I just . . . I just wanted to let you know that . . ."

She leaned across and put the unloaded pistol on the other cot, then reached for his hand.

He rose and moved to her, sitting down on the stretcher beside her, where he'd been before Steele had interrupted them. She moved to him and their kiss was like the first electric storm of the rainy season. Longed for, wished for, but terrifying when it came. He encircled her in his arms as their mouths melded.

"Ow." She reached under her bottom and slid her Leatherman out of the way. Sam laughed and it set her off. When he reached for her again the springs supporting the cot screeched loudly. "We'll wake the camp."

He stood and took her hands, lifting her to her feet. They kissed like that, standing. She tugged at his T-shirt and he backed off half a pace and whisked it over his head. He reached for her tank top, but she placed a palm on his chest and pushed him gently but firmly back into the camp chair. When he reached out to her she grabbed his wrists and placed his hands on his knees. Her look told him to sit still.

She stood in front of him and slowly pulled the green singlet over her head. She turned her back to him and undid the button at the top of the shorts—the ones he'd bought for her. Sonja felt a rush of pure sexuality flow from her core, as if the force of it was taking over her body, directing her movements. She unzipped halfway and lowered her shorts just a couple of inches, so that they hung low on her hips. She looked back over her shoulder and saw the wonder, the longing in his hungry eyes. She gave him a little smile and reached behind her for the clasp of the black bikini top she'd worn as a bra. One shoulder strap at a time, she removed it, but kept her back to him.

"Sonja . . ." he whispered.

"Shush." She took a pace backward, then turned and placed one hand on his shoulder. Her other arm covered her bare breasts, hiding them from him. His knees were wide apart and the sight of the bulge in his shorts made her lick her lips in anticipation. She lowered herself onto one of his legs and he snapped his hand out of the way—perhaps worried the show might stop if he touched her. Sonja slid herself slowly down the length of his muscled thigh, the movement grinding the fabric of her pants against her. She closed her eyes as she leaned over him. She kissed him again, then stood.

Sonja started to move her hips, slowly, rhythmically and then changed her stance so that her khaki shorts started sliding down her legs. She arched her back as they fell to the floor of the tent and looked down over the mounds of her breasts to see him leaning closer to her, his mouth now close enough for her to feel his breath on her belly.

She hooked her thumbs in the elastic of the waistband of her briefs and slowly started to lower, once more stopping after just a few inches. If he didn't make a move soon, then she would . . .

Sam stood and embraced her, then lifted her off her toes, his hands cupping her arse. She wrapped her legs around him as his tongue invaded her; claimed her. He turned around and she wondered if he would fuck her, like that, standing. It looked good in the movies, and men loved the idea, but she knew the reality was often different to the Hollywood fantasy. Instead, he lowered her. He was strong and she realized the hours he'd spent in the gym didn't only make him look good on television. Effortlessly, he placed her down on the chair where he'd just been sitting. His hands were in her pants now, tugging, and almost ripping them off her. He dropped to his knees and placed his hands on her legs, parting them. He lifted her legs so they were over his shoulders and he opened her with his fingers. She slid down a little, offering herself to him.

She knew how wet she was, but the length and certainty of his finger sliding into her took the breath from her. She groaned as his lips formed a perfectly sealed "O" around her clitoris and he drew her into his mouth.

He kept her there, not from lack of experience or knowledge, but almost as a payment for the teasing she'd subjected him to. She felt the crescendo growing, slowly at first, then the sensations rushed up, threatening to overwhelm her. "More, Sam . . . please."

At that point he removed his tongue and fingers and went back to kissing her puffy flesh, running his lips over her screaming, sensitive nerve ends. She grabbed his head in her hands and tried to pull him closer. When he plunged his tongue into her she thought she might slide off the chair into him.

He stood and reached into his pocket, fishing out the foil-wrapped packet. She grabbed for his shorts, pulling them down with the same force and speed he'd used on her. His cock sprang free, hard and purpled with anticipation.

"Let me," she said, reaching for the condom. She took it, ripped it open with her teeth and rolled the latex over him, fingers sliding down his shaft. She looked up and loved the way he shivered and half closed his eyes.

"Stand," he ordered, once more in control.

Her legs felt like rubber and he had to hold on to her hands to steady her as he took her place in the chair and she lowered herself onto him. She wanted to hang on, to draw it, to tease him as he had her, but the games were over between them now. She wanted him, like she'd never wanted anyone so much before in her life. Not even Stirling.

His kiss muffled her cries and she felt herself begin to clench, hard, before she had lowered herself all the way down, all the way home.

Sonja reached up over him and underneath her daypack, which he was using as a pillow. She pulled the Glock out and his eyes widened theatrically.

"I won't tell anyone, you know. You don't have to kill me."

"Hah, hah." She lay half on and half off him, their bodies slick with sweat. It was hot in the tent, he thought, and hotter still inside her. She slid the magazine into the butt of the pistol.

"Come back to the States with me," he said surprising himself almost as much as he surprised her, judging by the look on her face.

"I won't hold you to that."

"I'm serious." And he realized he was. He wanted this beautiful woman to grow old enough to forget how to handle the tool in her hands.

She shifted herself and relaxed on him again and reversed the pistol, offering it to him butt-first. "Take this, Sam."

He shook his head. "I don't want to go there again."

"Things can go wrong. Things will go wrong. You're going to need this."

He looked into her eyes. "You said I should leave. We can leave."

"*You* should leave."

"Usually it's the guy telling the girl to leave before the gunfight."

"I'm a new-fashioned girl and I know what I'm doing."

"And I don't? Is that it?"

"Yes. Rickards is crazy, but you aren't. I can get you out. Now. Take the gun. I'll talk to my father—Lord knows he owes me one—and I'll make sure they don't come after you. Besides, this madness will be over before you find your way to a telephone."

He shook his head. "No. I'm staying with this. You're right, it is madness, but it also seems somehow right."

"Don't kid yourself, Sam. What we—my father and I—are doing is wrong. He's fighting for a lost cause and I'm here for the money. He's the idiot and I'm the whore—neither of us is right, but we do what we have to do. You have to go and make documentaries."

He was getting annoyed now. "No. Jim's right. Someone needs to be here to report on your father and his men—to explain their cause to the world. Also, someone needs to show that dam being breached, and explain it was done for the right reasons."

"Don't fall for Jim's bullshit, Sam. Journalism isn't about right and wrong and balanced reporting. It's about a three-second clip of a big explosion or some guys firing their guns and running past the camera. We'll be a blip on the hourly satellite news channels until some celebrity gets caught fucking someone else. Oh, sorry . . ."

"What?" He suddenly realized she was talking about him. He waved her apology away. He realized now how pointless and frivolous his time in the public eye—his life—had been so far. Who cared about who his ex-girlfriend was sleeping with? He was among people fighting for their freedom, and the future of one of the world's remaining natural treasures. He knew Sonja was trying to sound more detached than she really was. "Will you follow me, to the States, if I leave now?"

She laid her head on his chest so she wouldn't have to look him in the eyes. She placed the gun on the bed beside his head. "I will."

"And you'll bring your daughter?"

"I will. But she's a pain in the arse."

He laughed.

"You'll leave?" she asked.

"I'll think about it."

She sighed and he felt her body relax against his, so that even more of her was touching him. He wished they could stay like this forever, and that at least one of them would do as they'd just promised.

26

There were too many loose ends. Too much unfinished business. Too many ifs.

Sonja punched in the number and waited for the call to be relayed by satellite.

"Xakanaxa Camp, good day. How can I help?"

"Tracey, it's Sonja Kurtz."

"Oh. Right."

"I need to speak to my daughter. Please fetch her."

There was no pretense of civility between them and Tracey put the phone down on the desk with a thunk. Sonja heard muffled voices—one of which she recognized as Stirling's. Then a high-pitched whine from Tracey, summoning a staff member to fetch Emma.

"Sonja? Is that you?"

Stirling's voice was hushed, as if he didn't want Tracey to overhear him. Perhaps she'd gone out of the office. "Yes."

"I don't have much time. I didn't have your number, but I told Emma to tell me the moment you called. I hoped you would."

"What is it, Stirling?"

For a moment she feared he was going to apologize, to tell her it had all been a mistake—him and Tracey—and that he wanted her to come and live with him at Xakanaxa. She would feel no remorse about telling him no. It wasn't that she wanted to get back at him, just that things had changed overnight.

"Sonja, please don't hate me, but I couldn't go through with it."

"Go through with *what*, Stirling?" He was making no sense.

"That plan. The dam. I don't know how much I should say over the phone, but . . . oh, to hell with it. I called the Namibian government, Sonja—their ministry of defense. I told them there was an imminent plan to blow up the dam. I wanted to warn you. Please, Sonja, wherever you are, don't let Steele drag you into this. This has to end, now. Tell him, if you like, that the Namibians know what the CLA is planning. I don't care whether you save him, but just save yourself. And please don't tell him it was me who told the Namibians."

To think, she had wanted to spend the rest of her life with him. He hadn't stood up to the other safari operators, or to Steele, and now he had ratted them out. He was scared Steele would kill him.

"Have you told anyone else what you've done?" she asked.

"No. No one. Who would I tell?"

"Good. Keep it that way."

"Sonja," he said, "I don't believe the dam should ever have been built and I hate to think what effect it will have on the delta, but innocent people will get killed in this war they're trying to start. It's not worth it, Sonja . . . it's just not worth it."

"Where's my daughter?"

"Um . . . hang on."

He put the phone down and she heard Tracey's voice in the background, then Emma saying "Coming . . ." A couple of seconds later she picked it up. "Mum?"

"How are you?"

"Annoyed, is how I am. Uncle Martin has disappeared and you're off somewhere you couldn't tell me about. Mum, look I'm not stupid enough to think that all you do is bodyguarding, but this is weirding me out. When am I going to get out of here?"

"Soon."

"I'm not an idiot and I'm not a child. I deserve to know what's going on, and there isn't any Internet access here."

"What do you need the Internet for? Go on a game drive, or get one of the guides to take you out on a boat."

"I don't fancy African men. But thanks for the idea . . ."

Sonja held the phone away from her ear and breathed. In. Out. "Emma, don't taunt me. Just listen to me. All right?"

"All right."

"I should be with you in a couple of days' time. If I'm not at Xakanaxa or you haven't heard from me by Saturday, I want you to get Stirling to put you on a plane to Maun. Change your return flights and get to Johannesburg and then back to London as quick as you can. All right?"

"No. Not bloody all right. What's going on, Mum? What's all this 'if you haven't heard from me' crap? Where are you and what are you doing?"

"I'm fine. There's nothing to worry about."

"Well I am bloody worried. Where's Martin? Are you up to something with him?"

"Emma, I just wanted to tell you . . ."

"What?"

"I love you, Emma."

"Whatever."

Her father gave his orders and Sonja marveled, again, at the transformation from the wreck he had been.

"The first helicopter sortie, with two birds, will lift the recce platoon, with me leading it, to M'pacha airstrip, here." He used a long straight stick to point to the black ribbon on the ground to his right. "We catch the air force detachment asleep and we deal with the sentries as quickly as possible. Our intelligence tells us there is a Hind gunship there, two Mi-6 troop carrying helos and three fixed-wing light aircraft. One and two sections destroy the aircraft with explosive charges and three and four sweep through the barracks. Understood?"

The officers and noncommissioned officers of the Caprivi Liberation Army—about thirty in total—sat and stood two deep in a semicircle around him and the mud map and models he had placed on the ground. They all nodded.

"By this time Alpha and Bravo companies will already be in position, south of Katima Mulilo, here." He scribed a line along one side of the collection of wooden offcuts that represented the largest settlement in the Caprivi Strip. Several of the blocks had pieces of paper stuck to them, reminding the audience what they represented. "Key targets, in order, are the police station, government offices and the NBC broadcasting studios." He tapped each of the blocks in turn. The men in the audience nodded. "Charlie Company will move up in reserve and take and hold the Zambezi Shopping Center."

There were a few muttered jibes among the ranks as those in the lead companies ribbed their comrades who had the comparatively easier task of seizing the Pick n' Pay supermarket and, no doubt, the nearby bottle store in the new low-rise shopping mall.

"Enough," Hans said. There was silence. "We don't know how long we'll have to hold the town against counterattacks. The shopping center will be our headquarters and our commissary for the duration of any siege. The core precinct we need to defend will stretch to here," he used his pointer again, "down the street to the broadcasting offices. We don't need to hold the police station, but we do need to neutralize it, and empty its armory so it's of no use to the enemy."

Sonja nodded to herself. The police station and government offices were on the road out of town that led to the Ngoma border crossing with Botswana, on the Zambezi River, about a kilometer from the main commercial strip of the town. She looked over at Steele and saw he was making notes.

"Delta Company," her father continued, "will lay an ambush on the B8, covering the main road on the Kongola side of Katima Mulilo. If the enemy sends a reaction force by road, it can only come from that direction. Questions?"

Steele looked up from his notebook. "It's a good plan, Hans, for taking and holding the town, but what about breaking out, if things go according to plan—pushing down the strip toward Kongola and even Divundu?"

Kurtz's mouth creased in annoyance.

"Well, *Martin*, if we hadn't been forced by circumstances outside our control to launch this mission earlier than planned, we would have had time to recruit and train enough troops to take over more of the Caprivi. I know what the rush is all about—your rich safari operators are worried the hydro-electricity plant is going to be completed ahead of schedule and the Namibian government will be showing journalists around the world all these poor African people getting access to cheap electricity and pumps to irrigate their bone-dry fields. Your backers can't bear to think anyone might benefit from the dam, and you're blackmailing us into launching now because we need the heavy weapons and ammo those fat cats are paying for. As it is—and I don't need to remind you—our infantry companies are companies in name only. They're little more than platoon-plus groupings. I've got enough men to take and hold Katima, and put M'pacha out of operation, but that's about it."

Her father looked away from Steele and swept his men with his green eyes. "Remember, men, this war is as much about politics as it is guns and bullets. Every day we hold Katima Mulilo is another day that strengthens the legitimacy of our claim on our homeland. If we can fight off the inevitable counterattacks then the Namibians will have to negotiate with our political leaders. We are buying them a seat at the government's table, and we need to buy them time, as well. The world, too, will be watching us, thanks to our *friends* here." He pointed at Rickards and Sam with his stick. "I do not need to tell you all that the majority of the people in Katima Mulilo are your people—your family in some cases—so every care must be taken to avoid civilian casualties. Rest assured, gentleman, that if one of your men does mistreat, wound or kill a local, then our representatives of the media will see it and film it. Likewise, Mr. Rickards and Mr. Chapman are not to be harmed or mistreated in any way."

Sonja was mad at Sam for staying, and terribly afraid for his safety, but she had failed to convince him to run. She didn't think he was being brave or noble—just stupid.

She'd gone to him, the day after they'd made love, and sat with him in private by the banks of the river. She'd told him that she had enjoyed the night before but that she did not love him. She told him she did not want to live in the United States or take her daughter there, and that she would not be the kept woman of a TV star. She wanted, she said, to continue working as a military contractor rather than living the life of a courtesan.

He'd remained silent, tossed a rock into the water, got up and walked away from her. She'd hugged her knees and swallowed back her tears. She was angry her lies had failed to convince him.

"Men," her father said, his voice rising as he drew her back to the present, "in this world divided by hatred and fear and ignorance and intolerance, you are about to fight for the two things that are, above all, sacred to any warrior, and the only things truly worth fighting for. You leave here to fight for freedom and for your homeland. May your God and your families, past, present and future be with you all and keep you safe. Caprivi!"

"CAPRIVI!"

Most of the CLA soldiers left straight after her father's morning briefing. They had a long way to travel, out of the Linyanti swamps by *mekoro* to the border with Namibia. There they would lie up for the afternoon before sneaking across when it became dark. From there they would move to their assault positions.

Hans was talking to a young man with lieutenant's pips on the epaulettes of his camouflage shirt. He was laden with a pack, water bottles and an AK-47. Her father clapped the man on the arm and sent him on his way. She wondered if he was going to his death.

"Hello," she said.

Hans nodded. "Hello."

She looked him in the eye. "We need to talk."

"Yes, we do."

"I spoke to Miriam. She told me what happened to you."

He nodded and pulled a cigarette packet from his pocket and offered it to her. She took one and he lit it for her, then one for himself. "So many bad things you've inherited from me."

She tried a small smile. "And some not so bad ones. I'm a good shot."

"Sometimes I wish I'd died in the war against SWAPO."

"No," she said, exhaling. "You can't say that. You got us to safety, to Botswana, and it was an OK place for me to finish growing up, in peace."

"It didn't work," he sighed. "You still went off in search of a war. Because of me."

"I probably would have gone even if things hadn't ended the way they did between us. I wished you dead for a long time."

He nodded and drew on his cigarette.

"But I've been to some of the places where you went," Sonja said. "I know about the nightmares, and if I hadn't been pregnant with Emma I might have tried to drink my problems away, like you did."

"Tell me about your daughter. About Emma."

She nodded. "She's a handful. She doesn't like me, most of the time. She hates that I'm away so much. I remember missing you, during the war years, when you were away."

"Sit," he said. They moved to a log and sat beside each other. "I gave up the right to give you advice years ago, but you know what I'm going to say to you, about her, don't you?"

Sonja nodded. "Go to her. Give up this life. I know you think I'm wrong doing what I do, but I'm working for her—for Emma—for her future."

"It won't be much of a future if she hasn't got a mom, Sonja. Anyway, it's not you being a mercenary that I'm worried about right now. We have bigger problems."

It might have been the nerves, but the cigarette was tasting vile. She ground it out and put the butt in her pocket. When she looked up she saw her father smiling at the action. "We do have bigger problems. We need to talk about this plan."

"Agreed," he said, pinching off the end of his cigarette and doing the same. "But first I need to know something."

She looked at him. "What?"

"Will you please be my daughter again?"

Sonja shrugged. "I can't say I love you, if that's what you want, or even that I forgive you. Not yet. But I never stopped being your daughter. And I think I understand, a little, of what you went through, though it excuses nothing."

He placed his hand on her knee, and she didn't recoil from his sandpapery touch. She swallowed hard, then placed her hand on his.

"That will do me for now, Sonja."

"The plan," she said, "to take Caprivi. It's not going to work. Stirling's already tipped off the Namibian government that there's going to be an attack on the dam."

He grinned at her and his eyes glittered. "I knew someone would talk. This is the worst-kept secret in Africa."

"We've got a lot to talk through," Sonja said, "but first, tell me what you know about this supposed roving missionary, Sydney Chipchase."

His look changed. "I can tell you everything about that murderous bastard."

27

The bush raced past her dangling feet, seemingly close enough for the toes of her boots to brush the tops of the trees. She watched the long, dry yellow grass flatten in waves as the helicopter's downwash passed over it. The air blowing in through the open door cooled her face and chilled the sweat that lingered under her black long-sleeve T-shirt and matching jeans.

Beside her in the Bell 412 were Gideon, in the green overalls of an ambulance paramedic, and two other CLA soldiers dressed as Namibian policemen.

The afternoon sun burned red as it was engulfed by the layer of dust that hung above the horizon. She saw the Okavango ahead, the river the color of blood.

"Two minutes." The pilot's voice crackled in the headphones she wore. She held up two fingers to Gideon and his comrades and they all nodded and flashed the V sign back to her in acknowledgment, grinning to hide their nerves.

Sonja checked the GPS on her wrist and confirmed they were approaching the landing zone. She yanked back the cocking handle of her AK-47 and the others copied her. She looked at Gideon and winked. He smiled. She grabbed the carrying handle of her pack as she felt the nose of the helicopter rise and the machine's airspeed drop as the pilot flared her.

She pulled off her headset and dropped it on the nylon troop seat beside her, then swung her legs out into the slipstream.

"Go! Go! Go!" The pilot yelled over the scream of the jet engine. Sonja's feet were already on the right skid. She dragged the pack off the floor and stepped off. She took three paces and dropped to her belly, facing out into the long grass down the barrel of her assault rifle, which rested on her rucksack. She scanned the bush at the fringes of the LZ and felt the tingle and jolt of the adrenaline pumping her heart faster. Behind her she heard the change in engine pitch as the helicopter started to climb, then felt the loose twigs, grass and small rocks sandblast her back through the thin fabric of the T-shirt.

Silence.

She looked behind her and Gideon gave her the thumbs-up. She stood and grunted as she hefted the pack onto her back. Gideon had wanted to carry the explosive charges, but Sonja wouldn't hear of it. She strode off the clearing into the bush, setting a brisk pace as the men fell in behind her.

The soft sounds of the bush replaced the alien clatter of the helicopter as Africa's night creatures slowly came to life. Sonja checked the red-lit face of her GPS and made a small correction to their route. She waved Gideon forward. Sonja would navigate and Gideon would take over as the lead scout, watching for people and animals. Sonja pointed ahead, slightly to their left, and Gideon nodded and moved off.

A Scops owl gave a high-pitched *brrr, brrr*, as it called to a nearby mate, and Sonja found the sound went a small way toward comforting her nerves. She wasn't scared, but all her senses were on edge as she waited for the adrenaline rush of the landing to slowly subside. They were in the Bwabwata National Park, two kilometers south of the main tarred B8, and four east of the military and police checkpoints on the bridge and crossroads at Divundu. According to their maps and the Caprivian soldiers' local knowledge there were no villages in the area, but there was still the remote but dangerous chance they might come across poachers. Of greater worry was the presence of wild animals, particularly lion and leopard, which were more active at night, or elephant and buffalo, which she knew could be even more dangerous if surprised by humans.

Gideon held up a hand and Sonja stopped and mirrored the field signal so the men behind her would see it. One of them stumbled and nearly fell against her. She looked back in annoyance. They were not as well trained or bush-savvy as Gideon, it seemed. Gideon caught her eye and cupped a hand to his left ear. She heard the rustling in the bush and raised her AK to her shoulder, staring down the barrel into the darkness. Her thumb rested on the safety catch.

It—or he—was making a hell of a racket. Her right index finger slid inside the rifle's trigger guard. It wouldn't be an elephant, she told herself, as despite their size the giant beasts moved on their thickly padded feet with uncanny silence. Buffalo? she wondered. Or a man?

She drew in her breath as the snapping of twigs and brushing of leaves grew louder. Perhaps it was more than one man.

Gideon looked back and grinned broadly. Sonja craned her head and saw the two porcupines. They waddled like a pair of short fat brides with spiky trains trailing behind them. With their rear-most spines extended each animal was over a meter long. Stealth was no defense for the porcupine and their spines scraped along whatever lay on either side of their path.

Sonja exhaled and turned and smiled at the men behind her, who had been wide-eyed with fear just a few moments earlier when Gideon had called the halt. Gideon led off.

Her back was damp with sweat and her shoulders ached, but Sonja forced herself to remain alert, and watched every footfall to ensure she didn't make as much noise as a porcupine. Gideon called another halt when they heard a vehicle engine. It sounded like a large lorry, she thought, and her GPS told her they were less than a kilometer from the road. She stopped and whispered to the men behind her to take off their packs and to sit. Sonja and Gideon also shrugged off their loads and, after warning the other two to keep watch for their return, she and the veteran guerilla moved off at a faster, but still cautious pace toward the road. The cool night air chilled her wet back, and it was a relief to be rid of the weight. She felt light on her feet and her heart started beating faster again as the bush thinned in front of her.

She checked the GPS and motioned for Gideon to turn a few degrees to the east. "It should be just ahead . . . a hundred meters," she whispered.

"There," Gideon said a couple of minutes later. Sonja had to look hard to see the Namibian Police Force *bakkie* parked under the overhanging branches of a large tree and covered in a camouflage net laced with fake plastic leaves. A little further on, past the hidden vehicle, she saw the ribbon of tar road on the far side of thirty meters of cleared ground where the long grass had been scythed.

Sonja and Gideon lay down and watched and listened, to make sure they were alone.

"I will go back, for your pack. You stay here," Gideon said after a few minutes of silence.

Gideon returned with the other two and set the explosives down. Sonja pulled a satellite phone handset from her pocket. She dialed Martin Steele's number.

"Yes" was all he said.

"Tiger," she said. "White." Tiger was the code word to let Steele and the Caprivian commander know that Sonja and her team were in position. The color white told Steele that she was safe and not under duress.

"Acknowledged. ETA is three; I say again, ETA is three."

"Acknowledged," she replied, then ended the call. She clicked her fingers to attract Gideon's attention, as he had been looking down the road. "The mobile clinic ambulance will be here in one and a half hours."

Gideon nodded. Under the code she had worked out with Martin he would double the estimated time of arrival of the vehicle. The CLA had a watcher posted in Kongola and his job was to call headquarters as soon as the mobile clinic passed through the police and veterinary checkpoint on the Kwando River.

Half an hour later, Sonja stood and did some quick stretches. "Get up," she said to the men dressed as police officers. One was dozing so she nudged him with the toe of her boot. As he woke he involuntarily lifted the barrel of his AK-47. Sonja snatched the flash suppressor and pushed it down. "Take your finger off that fucking trigger. Do you want to get us all killed?"

Defiance glittered in the man's eyes at being spoken to in such a way by a woman, but he lowered his gaze when he saw Gideon, standing beside her, shaking his head like an angry bull elephant. Sonja extended a hand to the man and he took it, allowing her to pull him to his feet.

"Get the net off the *bakkie* and move into position," she said.

"It's early," the sleeping man said, checking his watch.

"Do as she says," Gideon commanded.

The other fake policeman raised a hand. "Quiet." He pointed. "Vehicle coming." They all turned to the east and saw the approaching headlights.

Hans Kurtz kissed his wife and son goodbye, and wished he'd been able to do the same to his only daughter when she'd left on the same helicopter he was about to board.

There had been a reconciliation of sorts, but probably not enough to absolve him of all his past sins. It was as good as it could be, he told himself, though he would have liked to have hugged her one more time. He remembered her as a baby; the clean, soapy smell of her before she started to grow up and the war changed everything. He remembered Sonja's mother's face when he was allowed in to see her in hospital, cradling Sonja in her arms. "Look what we made, Hans," she had said.

Look what I made, he thought, as he gave the thumbs-up to the helicopter pilot and ordered his men to board.

"I love you," Miriam yelled over the whine of the jet turbine.

He nodded, shouldered his pack and turned. He took two steps and looked back at her. "I love you, too. Both of you."

Miriam held his son in one hand but she moved the other to her face so he wouldn't see the tears. He was fairly sure he wouldn't see them again. He jogged to the open door of the Bell 412, threw his pack in and sat on the floor, with his feet on the skid. The pilot looked over his shoulder to check if they were all on board, and Hans gave the man another thumbs-up. The helicopter lifted off.

Martin Steele was with the general and they both craned their heads to watch the helicopter's departure. See you both in the next life, Kurtz thought. It would be even hotter there than the bloody Caprivi Strip.

"Caprivi!" he shouted and raised and clenched the fist that wasn't gripping his AK-47.

"CAPRIVI!" his young lions roared back at him, and he could hear them loud and clear and ominous as a big cat's call in the night.

Hans Kurtz was not a man given to deep philosophical thinking—he left that to his wife. He was a farmer who became a soldier who became a drunk, who became a Christian, who became a soldier again. In his dreams and his promises to Miriam he went full circle and ended his life as a farmer once more, teaching his little son how to work the land.

As a father and a Christian he knew in his heart of hearts that if he truly wanted to atone for the way he had treated his first wife and child then he should do everything he could to gain their forgiveness, and then spend the rest of his life loving and caring for his new family. In the meantime, he would be going to war again.

The Ovambo had won their war and created their new country in their own image: Namibia. The whites who had stayed had not fared badly. Namibia was peaceful and, by African standards, prosperous, and while whites could no longer count on guaranteed access to easy government jobs with life tenure, they were generally treated equally and with respect. How, Hans wondered, could the new government treat its old enemies so right and its former allies, the Caprivians, so wrong?

He shuffled backward on his bottom into the cargo area of the helicopter and a couple of his warriors dragged packs and machine-guns and an RPG 7 out of his way so he could get up on one knee. He pointed at the headset hanging on a hook between the pilot and copilot and one of his NCOs handed it to him.

He pushed the transmit switch on the small box on the cord and said, "Howzit?"

The South African copilot looked over his shoulder. "*Ja*, all fine, bru. We're in Namibian airspace. Going low, under the radar. Should be over M'pacha in," he checked his watch and the glowing instruments in front of him, "twenty minutes."

"Sorry, man, but there's a change of plan. Turn west and I'll give you a new coordinate to head to."

"What?" The pilot shot a glance back at Kurtz, but quickly returned his eyes to the ground rushing close beneath the aircraft's nose. "No one briefed us about any change of plans."

"Trust me. I know what I'm doing. Turn to—"

"I'm calling headquarters for confirmation," the copilot said.

Hans thumbed back the hammer on the nine-millimeter pistol he had already quietly drawn from the holster slung low on his right leg and pressed it into the copilot's temple. "Not a good idea, *bru*. Now, get out of your seat."

The policeman yawned and prodded the fire in the cut-down oil drum with a stick. The music from the veterinary control officer's radio coming from inside the checkpoint building was tinny and blurred with static. Either her batteries were nearly flat or she hadn't tuned the station in properly.

"Can't you do something about that tuning, sister?" he called to her.

"What?"

He shook his head. She was a fine-looking woman, but so far she had resisted all of his charm and his best lines. She had a nice round arse and big tits that were still sitting nice and high on her chest. He would try asking her again if she would come to the bar with him on Friday night. She'd said no once, but she might just be playing hard to get.

He took a sip of warm Coke. Later, after his senior officer had done his customary "random" check on him at ten o'clock, just before going to bed, he would break out the beer. The empties would be gone before the sun rose. Perhaps the veterinary control lady would join him in a drink or two tonight. It was warm still, and hopefully it would get hot with her later on. He rubbed his face to stave off the tiredness that was already starting to grip him, even at this early hour. Too much beer last night, he thought, and not enough sleep in the heat of the day. Who could sleep in such weather?

The noise banished the fatigue. It was a siren. He stood and moved the red-and-white-striped boom. The wail was getting louder and he could see the lights flashing on top of the oncoming vehicle.

"What is it?" the veterinary control lady said, poking her head out of the building. She had turned down her radio.

He walked to her and leaned inside, retrieving his AK-47 from where

he had left it leaning against the inside wall. It was too heavy to keep hanging over his shoulder—especially at night and in between "random" inspections. "Police. He is in a hurry."

"Are all you policemen in a rush to get somewhere?"

He ignored her joke, but filed away her flirtatiousness for future reference. He stepped into the middle of the road, pulled out his torch, and
turned it on. He waved the light slowly up and down so the man behind the
wheel would see him. The vehicle slowed as it came up on him. He could see
clearly now, as it approached, that the *bakkie* had police markings as well as
the lights.

The *bakkie* stopped and the driver turned off the siren, but kept the
lights flashing.

"Evening comrade," the driver called.

"Evening. Where are we rushing to?"

"Here, comrade! There has been a road accident, not far from here. I
was just passing. I have two men in the back, one seriously injured. One has
just had a cardiac arrest and I revived him. I was trying to make it to Katima,
but I don't think the man will make it. I radioed and MARS are sending a
helicopter."

"Serious?" It couldn't be good if the Medical Air Rescue Service had
been called.

"He is a tourist. From Germany. I have told the helicopter to land
here."

"All right. I will wake my supervisor, if your siren hasn't done so already."

"Wait, comrade. Please. I think I hear him calling from the back.
Come help me."

The policeman looked over his shoulder. The woman was standing
there in the doorway, her shapely figure silhouetted by the dim light from
the hut. His supervisor could wait if there was a tourist in trouble. "All
right."

The uniformed man moved to the back of the *bakkie* and opened the
door. The officer from the checkpoint peered into the darkened area usually

used to hold arrested suspects. As usual he caught the twin odors of urine and disinfectant. However, there was no injured German tourist inside— just two men dressed as policemen, but pointing AK-47s at him from the gloom. He felt the hard tip of a pistol in his ribs.

"Quiet, comrade. Just take it easy and you will live to see a new dawn in a new land."

28

"How are you going to blow up the dam?" Sydney Chipchase glanced into the rear-view mirror of his Land Cruiser as the security guard at the entrance to the Okavango Dam construction site lowered the striped boom gate behind them.

Although security at the site was tight, Sonja had correctly assumed that Chipchase, as a regular visitor to the dam construction site, would not be made to traipse into the office to log in and be issued a pass, as she and the TV crew had. Instead, the guard had brought a clipboard to the boom gate for Sydney to register his name and time of entry.

"Keep quiet, Sydney, and keep driving. Slowly," Sonja said, keeping the barrel of the pistol pressed into the back of his neck, from her hiding place in the back of Chipchase's Land Cruiser.

From her father, Sonja had learned that Chipchase timed his regular trips to the dam construction site to coincide with the visits of the mobile HIV-AIDS testing van. Chipchase traveled the same route as the German nurse and her driver, though he usually preceded them. The idea was, Hans had told her, that the missionary was available to tend to the construction workers' spiritual needs while the clinic cared for their corporeal issues. "Gives him a good cover for his goddamned spying," her father had added.

Sonja's first change to the plan was to hijack Chipchase's vehicle rather than the mobile clinic.

"You can put that away," Chipchase said, looking back at the pistol.

"I don't think so, Sydney."

"Sure and I can't let you blow up the dam, Sonja."

His Ulster accent reminded her too much of her past. It grated. She was in charge of this operation now. "Pull over up there, behind the manager's office, in the dark."

He did as she told him, then turned off the engine. She checked her watch and opened her door, keeping the Glock pointed at the Irishman. "I need a tire lever, or a long-bladed screw driver."

He nodded and got out and walked to the rear of the four-by-four. He opened the door and reached in.

"I'm watching you."

"Don't worry. I know your record."

He slid out a black plastic toolbox and opened it. Sonja moved a pace closer to him and looked over his shoulder. It was a perfect place to conceal a weapon, but all she could see were tools. He drew out a screwdriver, slowly, and handed it to her. "Come with me," she said.

She motioned for him to move ahead of her and when they got to the door of the demountable building that housed Deiter Roberts's office she gave the tool back to him. "Open it."

Chipchase looked at her for a second, then at the barrel of the pistol. He slid the flat tip of the screwdriver into the gap between the door and the jamb and pushed against it. The door splintered with a loud crack and swung open. Sonja checked over her shoulder to make sure no prowling security guard had been startled by the noise. "Get inside."

It was hot inside the prefabricated building without the air-conditioning on and she began to perspire immediately. "Down the corridor, on the right." Deiter's office was even stuffier. "Sit down," she said when they entered the office, "behind the desk."

Chipchase walked around Roberts's desk, pushed back the office chair on its castors and took a seat. The laptop computer that had been used in the GrowPower presentation was sitting on the desk, next to Roberts's PC. Sonja had noticed it as soon as they'd entered the office and was pleased she didn't have to search for it.

"What now?" Chipchase asked.

"Turn on the laptop." Chipchase opened it and pushed the power button. The screen came to life and bathed his face in an eerie glow. She sat down opposite Chipchase and pointed her Glock at the mouse.

"What am I looking for?" He peered at the screen and clicked a couple of times.

"Look on the desktop for a couple of PowerPoint presentations."

He leaned closer and blinked a couple of times. "OK. There's something called 'presentation,' then 'presentation vers 2.'"

Good, she thought. She remembered how Deiter Roberts had spoken about GrowPower's fixation with amending documents and presentations, making sure everything was just right. She recalled, too, that the version of the presentation Selma had shown the TV crew was called "vers 2." Roberts had spoken about loading an updated presentation on the laptop just before they had all arrived at the dam site.

"Open the first version—the one called 'presentation'—and play it."

He jiggled the mouse a bit, freeing dust from the ball, then clicked. Sonja leaned in slightly and saw Klaus Schwarz's face appear on the screen.

The video started and Schwarz's voice sounded loud in the quiet, dark room. *"Thank you, Selma,"* he said, then turned stiffly to look at where his PR lady would have been standing during the presentation. *"Ms. Daffen, Mr. Chapman, gentlemen, I'm sure Selma has passed on my sincere apologies at not being able to meet you in person during your trip to this beautiful country . . ."*

"Stop it there."

Chipchase clicked and ended the video.

"Play the other one—version two."

Chipchase exhaled and wiped his damp brow, then selected the second video and clicked on play.

"Thank you, Selma," Schwarz said again, in the same emotionless voice. *"Ladies and gentlemen, I'm sure Selma has passed on my sincere apologies at not being able to meet you in person . . ."*

Chipchase clicked stop and looked across at her.

"You saw the difference?"

He nodded. "What do we do now?"

"It's been a setup all along. What we do now is stop him doing what he's trying to do."

Chipchase shook his head. "I can't let you go through with this, Sonja. It's not enough to take to a court, either. You can't prove what they're up to on the basis of a throwaway line in a presentation."

She raised the pistol. "I don't want to kill you, Sydney, but I will if you try to stop me."

He stared back at her. "I need more proof."

She checked her watch again. "Come with me. I'll show you."

Sonja moved quickly, but silently, through the remnant bush that screened the administrative compound from the perimeter fence and gate of the construction site. She held up a hand as the lights of the checkpoint came into view.

"What now?" Sydney whispered as he lowered himself into the dry grass next to her.

"We wait." She looked at the luminous face of her watch again. "Any time now."

It seemed like an age, but it was just eleven minutes before they heard the whine of an approaching engine. They were about two hundred meters from the checkpoint, but the night was clear and with the lights around the gate there was no need for binoculars. They could easily make out the faces of the African driver and the white female passenger when the mobile AIDS testing clinic pulled up.

"Look at the guard on the gate," Sonja said quietly. "He's got an AK-47 at the ready. You've been here plenty of times. Have you ever seen him armed with anything more than a pistol?"

"No, but the Namibian government and GrowPower know an attack of some sort is imminent. It's not surprising security has been beefed up. The NDF detachment is on high alert as well."

The driver and the passenger opened their doors and got out. The guard raised his rifle, glanced quickly over his shoulder then back at the pair. "Get down! On the ground!"

The man and woman looked at each other through the open doors of the truck. The woman said something in German, but her voice was drowned out by more yells. Two men emerged from the shadows behind the security checkpoint office, while two others stood up from the long grass at the side of the access road.

"Down! Down!" the men yelled at the pair.

"What is going on here?" the woman tried in English as she lowered herself to her knees.

One of the men who had emerged from the grass ran up behind the nurse and pushed her in the back. She reached out with her hands and yelped as she grazed them on the tar of the road. The man put his foot on the small of her back as a second kneeled beside her, laid his AK-47 out of reach and began to frisk her.

"Get your hands off me!"

"Leave her!" the African driver yelled, but he was silenced by the crack of a rifle butt to the side of his head. He, too, was searched roughly once he was face down on the ground.

"Clear," the guards yelled across to each other.

"Get them on their feet," said one of the guards who had stepped back.

The woman screamed as she was pulled to her feet by her long hair. Sonja winced at the spectacle and wished there was something she could do. However, she was sure the couple would be fine once the guards searched the back of the ambulance and found nothing.

"What is the meaning of this? I demand to see Herr Roberts and—"

The woman's protests were silenced by a backhanded slap in the face by the guard who seemed to be in charge. He pointed his rifle at her chest. Another man kept his weapon trained on the driver, who was now on his feet, holding a hand to the side of his head.

"Move!" the man in charge said in a loud clear voice. He pushed the German nurse in front of him with the barrel of his rifle and they moved toward where Sonja and Chipchase were lying.

Sonja gripped her pistol tighter, but the head man and another guarding the ambulance driver stopped about twenty meters from them and looked back at the empty ambulance. The other two gunmen stopped as well. They lowered themselves to one knee and raised their rifles to their shoulders.

"The vehicle," their leader said. "Fire!"

"Jesus Christ Almighty," Chipchase whispered.

Bullets thudded into the radiator and pinged off the engine block, ricocheting into the night. The ambulance's windscreen disintegrated in a shower of shattered glass. One of the gunmen paused to reload then moved slightly to one side. He took aim at the petrol filler cap on the side of the truck and pulled the trigger. The fuel ignited with a *whoomf*. The leader of the security gang kicked the woman in the back of her right knee, causing her to crumple to the ground. "Get down," he ordered her. The driver was also down, his captor forcing his face into the dirt.

The gunmen lay down as well. A second later the vehicle exploded.

Sonja and Chipchase lowered their faces into the grass as bits of metal and shards of glass whizzed over their heads. When she looked up Sonja saw the mobile clinic was nothing more than a fiercely blazing skeleton.

"UP!" The driver and the foreign nurse were dragged to their feet once more and marched back toward the wreck.

"Please, please, please," the woman wailed. "There has been some kind of mistake. Please, tell us what is going on."

"We have to do something," Sonja hissed. "I didn't think it would go down like this."

"Quiet," Chipchase whispered. "It's five against one, Sonja. You'd be cut down before you got close."

She shook her head and raised herself slowly to her knees. She knew she had little chance of hitting the men with her pistol now they were walking away from her. She would have to move closer. They seemed mesmerized by the inferno in front of them and one of them was whooping with animalistic joy at the destruction he'd wrought.

"Run!" the man covering the woman barked.

She looked back at him and Sonja could see her face was streaked with tears and dirt. *"Nein, nein . . . bitte."*

Sonja stood.

"Come back," Sydney hissed.

Sonja's heart was thumping. No, she thought. This can't happen.

The leader pushed the woman in the small of her back with the barrel of his rifle and she took a few tentative steps in the direction he wanted her to go—ninety degrees from the side of the vehicle in which she'd been sitting. The man guarding the driver was doing the same thing, but motioning for the African man to move in the opposite direction.

"No!" the driver said. "Sabine . . ."

The woman looked around, past the flames and saw the security guard pull the trigger on his AK-47. The ambulance driver pitched forward, arms out, and hit the ground.

"No!"

The woman screamed again, turned and started sprinting.

The man laughed.

Sonja felt Sydney's hand on her shoulder and she stopped. She knew it was pointless going any further. The leader of the security detachment raised his rifle to his shoulder, took aim at the fleeing German girl, and fired.

Sam and Jim sat on a log outside the general's command tent at the rebels' hideout across the border in the Linyanti swamps. Sam slapped the back of his neck. The mosquito that had been distracting him for the past ten minutes was a distraction from the thoughts that filled his head and churned his insides. He was almost sad when he inspected his fingers and saw the blood.

"Waiting's a bitch, isn't it?" Rickards said.

Sam admired the Australian's cool and wondered how much of his nonchalance was an act. Sam checked his gear again. In his daypack was a liter water bottle, two wound dressings a rebel medic had given him, spare batteries for Jim's camera, and four tins of what was optimistically billed as Texan beef. The pistol Sonja had given him was stuffed in the rear of the waistband of his jeans. When he leaned forward the unforgiving steel dug into him. On no level was he comfortable about carrying the weapon he had used to kill a man. He squeezed his eyes tight to try and force away the image of the blood spurting from the man's mouth as he died.

"Headache?"

Sam shook his head.

"Take a swig of this." Rickards reached into his own bag and pulled out a water bottle filled with a cloudy liquid.

"What is it?" Sam wrinkled his nose as he sniffed the acidic vapors that escaped when he unscrewed the cap.

"Palm wine. One of the Caprivian soldiers gave it to me. Dutch Courage. Don't drink too much of it or you won't be able to see where you're going—ever again." Rickards laughed.

Sam took a swig and coughed out half of the bitter fluid. The rest felt like it had exfoliated several layers of skin from the inside of his throat. "Holy shit." Sam heard footsteps behind him. Martin Steele, in his neatly pressed camouflage uniform, emerged from the command tent, drew a thick cigar from the pocket of his fatigue shirt and tapped it from its aluminum container.

"Any news?" Sam asked.

Steele shook his head and held a match to the cigar. He puffed a few times until the tip glowed orange. He took the cigar from his mouth and exhaled into the night sky. "Too early."

A ringtone chirped and Steele reached into the side pocket of his cargo trousers and pulled out a satellite phone. He moved three paces away and answered the call. "I understand. Good work." He ended the call.

"Who was that?" Sam asked.

"Sonja. She is inside the construction site perimeter and they're on their way to plant the explosives. You two should get your shit together and be ready to move at short notice. Understood?"

Sam nodded, and so did Jim. He sensed Steele's warning order had put an end to Rickards's bravado and wisecracks. Perhaps the cameraman really was as nervous as Sam.

The flap of the general's command tent twitched and a wide-eyed Caprivian soldier appeared. "Mr. Steele! Come quick, please. It's Major Kurtz, on the radio."

Sam and Jim got up and followed Steele, pausing at the tent opening as he moved to a wooden trestle table that was bowed under the weight of four different military radio sets. A signalman with headphones on looked up at the new arrivals and turned a switch activating a speaker.

The overweight Caprivian general slapped his swagger stick on the sliver of clear tabletop, making the young soldier manning the radios jump. "How could this happen?" the commander barked.

"*... Fish Eagle, this is Eland ... I say again ...*" Sam recognized Sonja's father's voice, though it was distorted by static and intermittent popping sounds. "*... say again ... we have been ambushed. Forces at airfield are far more than expected ... armored vehicles ... mortars. The helicopter can't get to us ... ground fire is too heavy. I've ordered it to return to your location. Suggest you recall main force ... over.*"

The general opened his mouth to speak, closed it, then opened it again, but no sound came out. He stared blankly at Steele. Sam felt like someone had trickled cold water down his back.

"I agree with Hans, sir," Steele said to the general, who slowly nodded in acknowledgment, but still couldn't speak. "Where exactly did the main force cross the border?"

The general looked dumbly at the large-scale topographic map pinned to a board behind his desk, then back at Steele. Sam knew that the two parts of the operation—blowing the Okavango Dam, and taking the strategic town of Katima Mulilo and nearby M'pacha airbase—had been planned in isolation from each other, because of security concerns.

"Tell me ... sir. I suggest we move the ready reaction force to the border immediately to cover the withdrawal of the main body of troops. We'll use the helicopter and keep it on station on the Botswana side to provide air cover with machine-guns, in case your men are pursued, and to act as a case-vac. Do you concur, sir?"

The general blinked several times and coughed to clear his throat. "Yes ... yes, Major," he croaked. The commander moved to the map and pointed to a spot on the border between Botswana and Namibia. "Here."

"Grid reference?" Steele looked from the general to the two soldiers manning the radios.

"Give it to the major," the general said to the elder of the two men. The signaler took out a notebook, wrote down the coordinates and handed them to Steele.

Steele took the piece of paper and put it in his pocket. He snatched up a radio handset. "With your permission, sir?"

The general nodded, struck dumb once again.

"Eland this is Fish Eagle, over," Steele said into the handset. He paused, then repeated the call.

"*Eland, go. Is that who I think it is?*" Kurtz replied.

Steele keyed the microphone. "It is. I can try and get through to you, with the ready reaction force. Can you break contact and RV with us away from the target, over?"

"*Negative,*" Kurtz said, his message punctuated with the popping of more gunshots. "*It'd be suicide for you to try. Did you copy my last?*"

Steele looked around the tent at the silent, apprehensive men. "Roger, Eland. Main force is being recalled and we'll cover their exfiltration. Any last message, over?"

There was a pause as everyone waited for the reply. "*Tell . . . tell my wife, my son and my daughter I love them. Eland, out.*"

"A brave man," Steele said.

"There's nothing you can do for him?" the general said.

Steele shook his head. "No, sir. However, we can save the bulk of your forces and Major Kurtz and his men won't have died in vain. The Namibians won't be able to keep the attack on M'pacha a secret. It'll be all over the world's news tomorrow."

"Not without any pictures, mate," Rickards said.

Steele looked at him.

"He's right," said Sam. "We still need to get some vision of the Caprivian troops in action—even if it is a tactical withdrawal, or whatever you call it."

Steele rubbed his jaw. "I'm not sure."

Sam didn't think Steele was the kind of man to voice indecision, so he jumped back in. "There'll still be the explosion of the dam. We have to get that on video, and pick up Sonja and Gideon."

"All right," Steele conceded. "But my first priority is covering the evacuation of the rest of Kurtz's men from Namibia. Sonja isn't due to blow the dam for another two hours—close to dawn. I'll get the reaction force in place then come back with a helicopter and pick you up. You can get the shots at the dam and then we'll go back on station at the border. By that time you should see Caprivian troops crossing as the sun comes up. Will that satisfy you?"

Sam ignored the sneer in Steele's voice and looked at Rickards, who nodded.

Steele looked at the commander, who still seemed in a state of bewilderment. "General?"

"Yes . . . yes, of course, Major Steele. Carry on."

Sam and Jim moved away from the opening of the tent, back out toward the empty clearing. "This waiting is killing me," Sam said. "What are we going to do for another two hours?"

Rickards grinned. "I know what I'm going to do, Sammy boy. A bit of stress relief."

Sam shook his head. "You're mad."

"No, just perpetually horny."

"Promise? Promise?"

Jim raised his voice as much as he dared, hoping the prostitute wasn't too drunk to wake. One of the Caprivian soldiers he'd been filming the day before had invited him back to his tent for a drink after Jim had finished shooting video footage of the soldier and his machine-gun for the camera. After splitting a dozen beers and half a bottle of palm wine with him the African had told his new best friend that he needed to go find a woman.

"Where?" Jim had asked.

"There are always girls who follow soldiers. They camp on the island near us. The general doesn't approve and Major Kurtz is worried about diseases, but . . ."

"Nothing ever changes," Jim had observed. He'd meandered after the soldier along a pathway through the reeds that flanked the river and through a patch of ankle-deep water and glutinous black mud that he guessed divided one low-lying island in the swamps from another, until they had come across a pretty girl with tightly braided hair wearing a faded floral sundress. In a sweeping glance he saw he'd come to the right place. She had high, firm breasts with nipples challenging the thin cotton; smooth, firm thighs below the frayed hem; and a wide, beaming smile. It had been weeks since he'd had a woman.

"She's nice," he'd said to the soldier.

"Promise?" The soldier had looked askance. "Her arse is too small. Take her. I'm looking for Goodness."

"Promise," he whispered now, at the hanging blanket that served as a door to the reed and thatch hut where he was fairly sure she lived.

The blanket twitched. She stood there, dressed in a nightie that reached the dirt floor. She blinked twice, still half asleep. "James?"

"I have to go soon . . . to the battle. I don't have much time."

She smiled, though her eyes were heavy with sleep. "Come in, big man. Sit, sit, sit."

He looked around. There was no chair, just a crude palliasse, a mattress made of coarse hessian stuffed with straw, and an upturned plastic beer crate that served as a small table. He didn't care. He laid his camera down on the box and undid the webbing belt with the pouches that held his spare batteries and tapes. He knelt down on the mattress and looked up at her.

He was nervous—not because of being with the woman, but because of the fight to come that didn't seem to be going as planned. He hoped he'd be able to perform, but when she raised her nightie up over her head and revealed herself to him again the doubts disappeared. While her face was covered, as she fumbled slightly to pull the gown off, he smiled to himself and leaned over the beer crate. He pushed the "record" button on the camera's hand grip. The wide angle lens was fitted.

She came closer to him. "Put on a light," he said.

"Why?"

"I want to remember every inch of you . . . just in case."

"Don't say such bad things, James. You will be fine. You must come back to Promise."

"I promise."

She giggled as she picked up a paraffin lantern from the dirt floor, raised the glass mantle and lit the wick with a match.

"That's better," he said as she adjusted the flame so that the lantern filled the hut with warm, soft yellow light. "Now I can see you better." Forever, he thought lasciviously.

"What you want, James?"

"Get down, like before."

She smiled and winked at him, looking back over her shoulder as she positioned herself on all fours on the thin mattress. He unlaced and kicked off his hiking boots then unzipped his jeans and began running his hand up and down his growing erection. When he was hard he took a condom from his pocket and shrugged off his pants.

"You are in a hurry?"

"Just to get started, baby." Promise faced forward again and Rickards looked across at the lens and winked as he rolled on the latex sheath, then knelt behind her.

Promise pushed back against him and Rickards grabbed her hips and drove hard enough into her to make her raise her head and gasp. Promise kept her gaze fixed on the wall of the hut and Jim glanced at the camera, smiled, and then lifted his right hand from her bottom to give a quick salute to the audience that would one day watch this masterpiece of his. He returned to the business at hand. He was going to come soon, but what the hell, he thought, he could always go again. There was plenty of time.

"Get ready, baby." Rickards closed his eyes.

Promise shuddered and he felt her head and shoulders drop to the floor. He opened his eyes and saw her breasts were on the mattress. "Nearly there!" It felt like she was trying to pull herself off his cock so he dug his fingers into the flesh of her hips to hold her.

"Don't stop now, baby," he breathed. There was no point holding back now. "Aaaaaah . . . yessss!" His hands were slippery with perspiration and as he came he lost his grip on her and she fell forward onto the mattress. He panted hard. "Promise? Promise, are you OK?" It looked like she'd passed out. "Woo baby! Who's the man?"

He threw back his head and started laughing, but when he looked down at her again he saw the blood spreading on the hessian of the mattress cover. It welled from the side of her head.

"Holy shit!" Rickards jumped up, his semierect penis flopping about. He turned and saw the man, and the pistol with the unmistakable extra length of the silencer screwed to the end. He'd shot Promise and Jim had been too engrossed in his own climax to notice. Rickards smelled the cigar smoke that had followed the man into the confines of the hut. "You?"

Martin Steele's mouth curled into a half-smile. He looked pointedly from Rickards's startled eyes to his limp penis. "Don't worry, Jim, I'm sure she didn't feel a thing."

Steele leveled the pistol and fired twice.

Sam checked his watch. It was less than twenty minutes until the helicopter was due to collect them, and there was no sign of Jim.

Six heavily armed men sat or stood in the tree line at the end of the grassy clearing where the helicopter had been taking off and landing. Sam knew they were the ready reaction force, which would be dropped at the secret border crossing to cover the withdrawal of the rebel troops who should have been attacking Katima Mulilo. One of them was a tall, fit-looking lieutenant named Edison. Sam had learned the man was the son of a chief, and it was clear by his bearing and the way the other soldiers deferred to him that he was born to rule.

Sam hoped Sonja's father had somehow survived the ambush, but he knew the chances were remote. Even if he did, Hans Kurtz had even further to go than the main force of his men in order to get back to safety in Botswana. The Caprivian soldiers smoked and talked in low voices. Edison was moving from man to man, checking their weapons and equipment. He made each soldier jump up and down a few times on the spot, in order to check if their gear rattled and made too much noise. There was none of the exuberance he'd witnessed when the others had set off. These men had been defeated without firing a shot, and they had no doubt lost comrades in the fighting at M'pacha. One of the men sat on the ground with a belt of machine-gun bullets draped across his lap. He seemed to be checking them, perhaps for dirt or mud, but the way he fingered the copper and brass made Sam think of someone fondling worry beads. The man looked up and Sam saw the fear in his eyes.

"Don't leave without me," Sam said to Edison. He tapped his watch. "Five minutes, OK?" The lieutenant nodded.

Sam strode back through the deserted camp, past the commander's tent and the smoking remains of the camp fire, which had been doused with water. It was quiet, except for croaking frogs, the squeak of a night bird somewhere nearby and the occasional grunt of a far-off hippo.

Sam trod the sandy path to the huts on the fringe of the camp. He knew what Rickards was up to—the Australian had been crude enough to tell him. He had no idea which hut the woman would be in, but only one of them showed a light. A dog gave a low growl from somewhere. He heard a small cough, perhaps from a child. Sam looked around and moved closer to the hut. He heard the hiss of a gas lantern. Insects clouded around the chink of light that bordered a blanket that was hanging over the entranceway.

"Jim," he called softly. "Jim, it's time to go, man. You in there?"

Sam licked his lips. The last thing he wanted to do was walk in on them while they were in the act. He paused by the door and listened, but there was no sound. Maybe they had fallen asleep.

"Jim?"

Sam grabbed the edge of the tattered blanket and pulled it to one side. "Holy shit!"

He moved in and dropped to one knee beside the two bodies. Jim lay on his back, with a dot of red blood on his forehead and his eyes wide open. There was another bullet hole in his chest, near his heart, and blood all over the coarse mattress. The African woman was face down and both of them were naked. "Oh, Jesus, no."

Sam reached over to the upturned beer crate that served as a beside table and grabbed the metal swinging handle of the gas lantern. He placed it on the earth floor next to Jim's face as he reached out and touched Jim's neck. There was no pulse, but there was the faintest trace of warmth on his fingertips. He checked the woman and saw there was nothing he could do for either of them. He started to retch, but swallowed hard. Why hadn't he heard gunfire? He took a deep breath to steady himself and moved back to Rickards. He slipped a hand under the Australian's head. There was no blood on the back though; no exit wound. It was a tiny hole in Jim's forehead. He wondered who could have been responsible. Perhaps, he thought, it was a jealous husband?

Sam looked around the room and saw the red light on the video camera that was pointing at him and the two bodies. He shook his head, then stood and went to it. He picked the camera up and pressed the "record/pause" button on the hand grip. He knew a thing or two about cameras and located the "play," "fast forward" and "rewind" buttons on the side of the Canon. He pressed "rewind," waited a few seconds, then hit "play." In the small flip-out LED screen he saw Jim and the prostitute having sex. At one point the woman slid forward onto the mattress. Jim stood and looked at the camera, shock plain on his face. Sam was too slow to press "stop" before he saw the sickening vision of the Australian's death. As he replayed the scene, Sam saw Jim raise a hand. His lips were moving, then he crumpled to the ground. Sam felt nauseous and light-headed. He put the camera down. He needed to hear what Jim had said.

Beside the camera was Jim's black nylon backpack. Sam unzipped it and rummaged around until he found a set of headphones. He located the audio jack on the side of the camera and plugged them in. When he hit "play" and "rewind" again he heard the high-pitched squeal of voices. He went back past the scene of Jim's death and caught a few seconds of the two people having sex. Sam drew a deep breath to steady himself as he watched the woman fall limp on the mattress.

"*Don't stop now, baby . . .*" Sam heard Jim grasp.

After screaming out his orgasm, Jim seemed to grasp what had happened.

"Holy shit!" Sam saw Jim jump to his feet on the tiny screen, then turn and say: *"You?"*

Sam heard an English-accented voice, delivering a final insult before a silenced pistol coughed twice. Sam couldn't see the man who had uttered the words, but he recognized immediately who it was. "Steele," he said out loud.

"Very clever, Sam." Sam turned to look at the doorway. "Silly of me not to check the camera."

29

Chipchase was panting by the time they made it back to the construction site's administrative compound. Twice they'd had to lie low in the bush as a Namibian Defense Force Land Rover and a BTR 60 armored car had raced past on their way to the gate. Sonja kept the pistol pressed to his ribs to make sure he didn't try and alert the soldiers.

"I can't believe Steele would have had you killed," Chipchase said between ragged breaths. "What's going on between you two?"

"I wish I knew," Sonja said. An innocent man and woman had been gunned down because the security guards at the gate had mistaken them for Sonja and Gideon. "I didn't think he was going to kill them. I thought the idea would have been to arrest them—us."

"So Steele's working for GrowPower—for Schwarz—not the Caprivians."

Sonja knelt in the moon shadow of the site office, catching her own breath while the Irishman wiped his brow with the back of his sleeve. "Yes. There was something about Schwarz's recorded message in the presentation that didn't sound right and I couldn't quite put my finger on it until I spoke to my father."

Chipchase nodded. "Steele told Schwarz that you were going to the dam site on a secret reconnaissance mission, using the American film crew as cover."

"Yes." It was Schwarz's reference to *ladies* and gentlemen in his recorded message to them during Selma's briefing that had been the clue she had subconsciously picked up. "Schwarz knew I was going to the dam, but no one else on site—not even Roberts, the construction foreman—was expecting me. Schwarz changed his message to include me, as well as Cheryl-Ann in his opening remarks. He was a victim of his own obsession with getting his presentations correct. He knew there would be two women in the audience at the briefing, but no one else did. Even the smartest criminals make mistakes."

"Well he'll be in big trouble now—from both the Namibian and the German governments for ordering the killing of innocent civilians. He's overstepped the mark this time."

"I'm not so sure," Sonja said.

"What do you mean?"

"If it'd been Gideon and me in that ambulance then Schwarz and the Namibian government would have had the world's media there tomorrow. They would have been able to show the bodies of a mercenary and a Caprivian rebel. My guess now is the wreckage of that mobile clinic and those two bodies are going to disappear very quickly."

"You could testify, and—" Chipchase said.

Her look silenced him. "Who do you work for, Sydney? The Namibian government?"

"I told you. I'm a missionary."

"Bullshit. I thought for a while that maybe you worked for GrowPower, but you wouldn't have let me witness the killing of the nurse and the driver if you were secretly in cahoots with Steele. You didn't know about any of it, did you?"

He stared at her, but she knew she was right.

"I give you my word, Schwarz and GrowPower—and Steele—will pay for the murder of that young woman."

Sonja started nodding. "Not the black African driver? The German government doesn't care about him, does it?"

Chipchase was silent again, but she'd worked it out. "If you didn't work for the Namibians, which was unlikely in any case, and you weren't employed by GrowPower, then who else has an interest in everything that goes on in Namibia? The Germans, of course. I understand now. I'm sure you had an arrangement with Schwarz and the Namibians, though. What did you do, Sydney . . . have little meetings every now and then?"

His eyes betrayed him as he looked away from her.

"It was you who infiltrated the CLA, wasn't it? You were the freelance white mercenary who helped them with their training and then sold them out. Your information allowed the NDF to almost wipe the rebels out, didn't it, Sydney? I bet you set up some innocent Caprivians to take the rap as spies. Their blood's on your hands . . . you're no better than Steele and Schwarz."

"Don't lump me in the same category as Steele," Chipchase said. "Namibia has friends in Europe and it's in Europe's interest for this part of Africa, at least, to be at peace. This region also needs the water and electricity the dam will bring. GrowPower might be rotten, but that doesn't change the fact that this dam will save lives. We knew you and Steele were active in the area from information MI6 supplied us. No one knew about the Zimbabwe job, but I was ordered to keep tabs on Corporate Solutions. I figured, rightly, that Steele was going to hawk himself—and you—to the CLA. What I didn't know was that he was double-crossing them and working for Schwarz."

Sonja stood and looked down at Chipchase, who stayed lying in the grass. "Get up, you're coming with me. I've got work to do and you're my insurance policy if we get stopped."

"I'm not going anywhere, Sonja, and I'm not going to be a party to the destruction of this dam."

"Fine," she said. "Then I'll have to kill you."

"Strip," Martin Steele said to Sam.

Sam stood in the hut with the two dead bodies and the man who had killed them. The nine millimeter Sonja had given him was in the small of his back, in the waistband of his pants, but if he reached for it Steele would shoot him dead. He guessed Steele wanted him naked so it would look like he'd been killed in some sort of ménage à trois with Rickards and the prostitute—perhaps by a jealous boyfriend. "You're going to a lot of trouble."

Steele drew on his cigar, while keeping the pistol pointed at Sam. "You're an American TV star. The rest of the world won't give a fuck about what happened to the Caprivi Liberation Army, but this place will probably be swarming with the bloody FBI forty-eight hours after you're gone."

"Why should I make killing me any easier for you?"

Steele shifted the aim of the pistol and fired. The report was a silent cough, and Sam flinched. His left arm felt like someone had grabbed the skin near his biceps with a pair of pliers and yanked it back. Other than the immediate sharp sensation there was no pain, but there was blood. He lifted his right hand to the wound and blood pulsed through his fingers. He started at it.

"Because if you don't, I'll kill you very, very slowly. The next shot will be in your balls. The twenty-two is a small round, but it's still very deadly. The quickest way for me to kill you is a head shot, but there's nothing to say a jealous lover wouldn't have taken his time with you. Now take your kit off."

Sam started to sweat and feel unsteady. He licked his lips and glanced down at the wound again, but then looked away. The sight of the blood, as much as the wound, was making him woozy. "I . . . I feel . . ." He staggered and went down on one knee. Steele shifted his position. "I'm still watching you."

Sam nodded and moved his hands to his belt buckle. His right was slippery and sticky with blood, so it wasn't easy. He reached out for support, toward the makeshift bedside table.

"Steady. Hands where I can see them."

Sam swayed and nodded. Steele took a step back.

Sam grabbed the lantern, ignoring the burning sting of the glass mantle, and hurled it straight at Steele. The light shattered on the arm that Steele raised instinctively to protect himself. Steele, however, was an SAS officer, trained in close-quarter battle, and his other reflex action was to fire two snap shots at his target.

Rolling away, Sam felt one of the small-caliber bullets snatch at his billowing bush shirt. He wasn't nearly as weak or shock-affected as he had made out. He swung his legs in a wide arc, feet together, and kicked through the flimsy grass and reed wall of the hut. Behind him there was darkness and Steele's cursing. He rolled once more then got to his feet, blindly crashing through jungle outside the back of the hut. His eyes were still partially blinded by the sudden change from the light to dark, but Steele would be suffering the same disability. Sam got to his feet and drew the pistol from his trousers. He pivoted at the waist and fired three shots back in Steele's direction. He doubted he would hit anything, but the thunderous crash of the unsilenced weapon would alert the Caprivian troops waiting at the helipad.

Sam sensed more shots flitting through the bush like angry bees beside him as he ran, as fast as he could, back toward the camp. Behind him he heard a whoosh of displaced air. He slowed and risked a glance back over his shoulder and saw the night sky flare orange and a volcano of sparks and glowing embers shoot up from the hut in which Jim and the woman had been killed.

Not watching where he was going, Sam ran headlong into a barrel-chested African soldier toting an AK-47. Sam stumbled and the man wrapped an arm around him. It was the lieutenant in charge of the ready reaction force, Edison.

"He has a gun!" Edison said.

Sam found himself pushed to the ground and facing a semicircle of armed warriors, all pointing automatic weapons at him. He tossed Sonja's pistol in the dirt and held his hands up, then placed them on his head. "Steele . . . Major Steele is trying to kill me. He killed my cameraman—"

"Silence!"

Sam turned and saw Steele standing in the pathway, the silenced pistol raised and pointing at him.

"Step away," Steele said to the rebel soldiers. "This man is to be summarily executed. *He* killed the fellow he was with, and one of your women, from the village. I want a firing party of five men. Now!"

Edison shook his head. "We need orders from Major Kurtz."

"Major Kurtz is dead," Steele said. "He and his men were killed in an ambush at M'pacha. You men need to get saddled up and ready to go as soon as we've killed this saboteur. We have to protect the withdrawal of the main force back across the border."

"An ambush you set up, Steele." Sam turned back to the lieutenant. "This man is working against you, not for you."

Steele laughed. "Preposterous. I'm the only person who knows what's going on here. With a bit of luck we can snatch something out of today's defeat. This man is a bloody *journalist*, he's never been on your side."

"I have seen this man on television, on DSTV," Edison said. Both Sam and Steele stared at him.

"You have?" Sam said, taking the words out of Steele's mouth.

Edison nodded. "On *Outback Survival*. I trust this man."

"Oh, for fuck's sake," Steele said. He took a step closer to Sam and pointed the pistol at the side of his head. "I don't have time for this."

Edison cocked his AK-47 and shifted its barrel slightly so that it covered Steele as well as Sam.

"Go get the commander . . . please," Sam said to one of the men arrayed behind their officer.

Steele licked his top lip. "Don't waste your time. This man killed the general and the two signalers in the command tent. He's a spy and he needs to be executed immediately."

"What?" Edison looked down at Sam, who was still kneeling.

Sam suddenly comprehended the enormity of Steele's deceit.

"I just stopped by the headquarters tent," Steele continued. "All three of them are dead. We need to kill this man now and get going as soon as possible. There may be other enemy agents in the area. Listen . . ."

Sam lifted his face to the night sky along with several of the other men. The far-off drone of the helicopter's engine was soft, but growing stronger.

"Wait," Sam said to Edison. "Check the bodies in the command tent and look at the bullet entry wounds—and exit wounds if there are any. Compare them to the pistol I had," he moved a hand and pointed at Sonja's weapon down on the ground, "and that silenced popgun Major Steele is holding. Ask yourselves who the assassin is."

"Right," Steele said, marching forward. "This has gone far enough." Defying the men who faced him he grabbed Sam by the epaulette of his bush shirt and hauled him up.

Edison moved as well and grabbed Steele's wrist in a huge hand. The two men stared each other down. "Julius."

"Sir?" one of the other men answered the lieutenant, who still held Steele's arm.

"Go check on the general and his men. Come back and tell me if they were killed by a two-two or a nine-mil. You have one minute."

"Yes, sir!"

Edison looked back at his subordinate and motioned his dismissal with a nod of his head.

Steele shook off Edison's hand while he was momentarily distracted, pointed the silenced pistol at his chest and pulled the trigger. Only one shot came out, but it took the big man in the chest and he staggered back, collecting one of his other troopers as he fell. Steele looked around him, threw the empty pistol at Sam and ran.

Sam picked up the wounded officer's AK-47, pointed it at the fleeing Englishman and pulled the trigger. The AK reared high and to the right as thirty rounds tore into the grass and reeds around Steele. Other rifles joined the cacophony, which reached a crescendo as the helicopter raced low overhead, toward the landing zone. Those men not firing knelt beside their tall leader, who was gasping for air. Blood was spreading across Edison's camouflage shirt.

"Get him to the helicopter," Sam said to the leaderless troops. "Hurry."

"What about Major Steele?" one of the others asked as four men grabbed the wounded man's arms and legs.

Sam shook his head. "I don't know. We leave him. He's a dangerous animal and he'll be worse now he's cornered. What he said was right—there might even be other people converging on this place while we stand around here. Let's go!"

It seemed wrong to leave Jim's body, and Steele running around the bush alive, but Sam's fear was growing rather than dissipating with the disappearance of the rogue mercenary. If Steele had killed the Caprivian general and Jim, planned to kill Sam, and set up the ambush of Hans Kurtz at M'pacha, what had he planned for Sonja?

They ran toward the noise and buffeting downwash of the helicopter, which was settling into the long waving grass of the LZ. Sam clasped the hand of Edison, who had saved his life, as they all moved, bent at the waist, to the helo. "Hang on!" he roared over the turbine's nose as the man's comrades slid him into the cargo hold of the machine. A man already inside grabbed the wounded officer under his armpits and dragged him the rest of the way aboard. When Sam looked up he was shocked to see the short, wiry figure of Hans Kurtz, his face streaked with black camouflage paint.

"Get in," Kurtz waved to him.

Sam and the other men needed no urging and they climbed aboard. It was a tight squeeze, and they had to be careful where they put their feet around the casualty. Kurtz maneuvered himself so he was sitting next to Sam.

"I thought you were dead," Sam yelled over the engine noise as the pilot increased power prior to take off.

Kurtz grinned. "Not yet, but the night is still young." He slapped Sam on the thigh and then pitched forward.

The pilot turned his head and screamed: "Incoming fire!" He lifted the helicopter off the ground and it seemed to Sam they were rising at a rate of inches per hour. For the second time in the last fifteen minutes he snatched up a wounded man's rifle and pulled the trigger. Nothing happened. A Caprivian soldier sandwiched between Sam and another man snatched the AK from him—his own machine-gun was resting on its bipod half under the wounded officer—yanked on the cocking handle and then fired out into the night. Tracer streaked away from the helicopter like trailing green ribbons. The fuselage behind them rattled with the noise of pebbles thrown on a tin roof as the pilot yelled at no one, willing his machine higher, faster and further away from the ground fire.

Hans slumped back in the nylon webbing troop seat.

"Are you all right?" Sam's voice was almost lost in the exchange of gunfire.

Kurtz felt his side and showed Sam fingers sticky with blood. It reminded Sam of his own wound and again he felt the queasiness. "I'll be fine. They need to see to him first," Kurtz said, pointing down at the officer. The medic was cutting away Edison's shirt. His black skin was slick with blood, but his eyes were open and he was breathing, albeit in ragged gasps.

The medic looked up from his patient and caught Kurtz's eye. In his right hand he held a curved AK-47 magazine with a bullet hole through it. "This took most of the force of the bullet, and the projectile glanced off his rib cage. The young chief, he will live." Edison forced a painful smile.

Kurtz gave a thumbs-up as Sam tugged on his sleeve to get his attention. "What about Steele?"

Kurtz winced and looked out the open cargo door. "We'll get him, Sam. We'll get him."

The medic worked on Hans during the rest of the flight, removing his fatigue shirt and cleaning the wound in his side as best as he could, then wrapping it in a dressing and a tight bandage around his torso.

"We never went to M'pacha..." Kurtz winced as the medic fastened the bandage.

"Where then?" Sam asked.

"It was a feint, designed to fool Steele. Sonja and I were both pretty sure he was working for the Namibians, and for those crazy Germans who are building the dam, but we couldn't be a hundred percent sure."

"And the general?"

Kurtz tried to scoff, but the small action caused him pain, so he grimaced instead. "That fool was bamboozled by Steele into thinking the best way to regain the Caprivi Strip was to seize the capital. I argued against it—there was no way we had enough troops to take and hold both Katima and the airfield at M'pacha. Besides, I knew from my spies in the field that the Namibians were amassing an unusually large ground force at M'pacha. It was the ambush that Steele had kindly arranged for us."

"So where are your men, if not at Katima?"

Kurtz grinned. "They are where we're going right now, at Kongola, halfway down the Caprivi Strip between Katima Mulilo and the dam. We're not going to take Caprivi—we're going to split it. Kongola's on the Kwando River, which divides the strip in two. It was easier to take than Katima and it'll be a damn sight easier to hold than a town—it's no more than a few buildings and a bridge. We're going to stop east-west traffic in this part of southern Africa. The Namibians and the rest of the world will have to take notice of us now."

Kurtz explained, in between painful breaths, that the main force of his men had crossed the border as planned, but instead of making for Katima Mulilo they had secretly rendezvoused with a fleet of civilian trucks and buses which had sped down the near-empty highway to Kongola. Instead of flying to certain death at M'pacha airfield, Kurtz and the rest of his small assault group had flown straight to Kongola and met up with Gideon, who had split up from Sonja and overpowered the small police detachment at the bridge over the Kongola River. "We've taken Kongola and split the Caprivi Strip in two without firing a shot—except for here," he said.

"What about Sonja?" Sam asked.

The helicopter was starting its descent and Sam could see headlights flicking on and off on the road below. Kurtz looked at him. "Like me, she was calling in fake reports to Steele and to the general, but we had worked out our own code, between us, to fool the rest of them. The last I heard of her she was at the dam and safe. Beyond that . . . I don't know."

Sam felt anger slowly spreading from his heart to his head and his fingertips, dispelling the fear. "Goddamn it! Don't you care about your daughter? You said Gideon went to Kongola—does that mean she's going to blow the dam all by herself?"

Kurtz shrugged as the pilot flared back the nose of the helicopter and the skids settled on the black tar of the main highway. "If anyone can blow a dam up by herself, it's my daughter. She's very stubborn once she puts her mind to something." Kurtz clapped him on the shoulder, then eased himself painfully down out of the helicopter. He winked at Sam. "You'll learn that in the years to come. Goodbye, Sam."

Sam blinked, not fully able to comprehend all that the old man was saying to him. He watched as the soldiers on board helped Edison from the helicopter. The young officer was fully conscious now and although he limped he politely waved away his men. "Hans! Sir!" Sam called.

Kurtz was easing on a new fatigue shirt that one of his men had waiting for him, to cover the bright red and white of the bandages. Kurtz walked slowly back to the helicopter. The pilot looked over his shoulder and twirled his finger in the air, signaling to Sam and the two armed men who had stayed on board with him as a security detachment that it was time to take off. Sam held up a hand. "Sir?"

"What?" Kurtz said, buttoning his shirt.

"I think I love your daughter, sir."

He nodded. "Don't tell me, tell her. Go!"

30

Sonja and Chipchase got in the Land Cruiser and then ducked out of sight behind the dashboard as a spotlight swept over them. The blinding beam bounced back off the driver's side wing mirror and filled the cab with a flash like lightning.

The light was followed by the grumbling clatter of a big diesel engine and, as the noise passed, Sonja peeked up over the steering wheel and saw the disappearing bulk of a slow-patrolling BTR 60 armored car. "They're nervous."

"So am I," Chipchase said. "What do we do now?"

"Wait a little longer, until things settle down."

"Have you got a pick-up arranged? Is that it? Who's double-crossing who tonight, Sonja? If you knew Steele planned on killing the AIDS nurse and her driver then you're as guilty as he is, for letting it happen."

She gave a snort. "I told you, I thought they were just going to be arrested. Don't lecture me on morality—you sent nearly a hundred Caprivians to their certain death when they tried to stop this dam while it was still under construction."

Chipchase hissed through gritted teeth. "That's a lie. I didn't mean for that many to die."

She kept the gun on him. "*That many?* What does that mean? You set them up for a fall, but didn't expect them to make it into the killing ground?"

"I can't say."

"Bloody hell. Give up the spook routine and give me a straight answer."

He looked out the windscreen. The armored car was nearly out of ear-shot, but from the hill where the site office was perched they could see it trundling cautiously along the dam wall, its light sweeping left and right. He said nothing.

"You still haven't told me. Who do you work for? MI6? The Germans? South Africans? CIA?"

He shook his head. "All of those governments have one thing in common—the desire for peace, democracy, stability and development in Africa. Namibia and Botswana were the closest things to showpieces for all those and now you and Steele and co have started a war here."

"Schwarz and Steele wanted to ensure *stability* by drawing my father and his men, and me, to our deaths. Is that the kind of peaceful development you and your masters are protecting?"

"No." Chipchase banged a fist on the dashboard of the Land Cruiser. "Damn it, Sonja, no one wants to see Schwarz and Steele get away with murder, but Africa needs this dam and the electricity, irrigation and development it'll bring. The Caprivians would have led this part of the continent back into civil war, one way or another."

"So they had to be killed." She felt her anger rise and knew she should contain it. Maybe he was trying to goad her into a rage so he could make a move on her. She forced the calmness into her mouth. "What about solar power and boreholes? There's water and power if a government cares enough about its people to provide it. This dam's a quick fix for big business, and you know it. I'm not going to let Schwarz and his cronies win. Get out of the car."

Chipchase opened his door and climbed out. Sonja kept the pistol trained on him as she did the same. "Turn around."

"Can't look me in the eyes, eh? Are you going to kill me now?"

She probably should, she thought. Chipchase, who used his cover as a missionary to get where he wanted in order to lead his flock to the slaughter, was as bad as Steele—or her, for that matter. If she somehow managed to get out of the Caprivi Strip alive he would be able to identify her to whoever was paying him. She held her hand out and pressed the barrel of the pistol into the soft skin at the base of Chipchase's skull. Her finger curled around the trigger. He didn't flinch or say a word.

"You don't care about dying, do you?"

He shrugged. "My job was to infiltrate the CLA posing as a mercenary trainer and gather intelligence on their numbers, bases and weapons. It became very clear they were being funded by wealthy outsiders—a group of safari lodge owners in the Okavango Delta, the same people who are paying you and Steele to blow up the dam."

"You lived with them, Sydney," she said, shaking her head. "You befriended them—my father included—and you sold them out. You're no better than Steele, no matter who you're working for."

He clenched his fists. "I reported what I learned, that a raid on the dam was imminent. I disappeared to maintain my cover. I thought the Namibians would tip off the Botswana authorities and the rebel training camp would be busted by the local police. Instead, I think Steele and Schwarz found out about the plan and encouraged the Namibians to stay quiet and suck the Caprivians into an ambush. It was a dirty business."

Sonja wondered if Chipchase was telling the truth. She didn't have time to find out and it didn't really matter to her. Chipchase had sold out the Caprivians because he thought it was the right thing to do to maintain stability in the region. Steele had sold the same people out for money, from Schwarz. Martin was also double-dipping, continuing to play both sides and taking money from Trench. Martin had decided to use this operation to get rid of her, as well. It was all clear to her now. Steele had set her up to fail in Zimbabwe and had assumed she would be killed by the CIO man, Sibanda. When she had survived he had conspired with his other employer, Schwarz, to allow Sonja to be drawn in with the CLA, who would have been walking into an ambush at the dam if Martin had had his way.

All that had been missing was the "why," but she knew now it was all about the money. Her money. Martin, the compulsive gambler, was probably not only broke, but also owed money to people. It must have been a lot, she imagined, for him to go to such extreme lengths. He had made a big song and dance about saying he had already paid her share of the down payment for the Zimbabwean job into her account, just as he had with the up-front payment from Trench and the other landholders. He was adding to her nest egg, which he wanted for himself.

She turned her attention back to her hostage. At least Sydney was working to his own code of honor. Too bad she couldn't buy him, as the job would be harder by herself, but he clearly wasn't for sale. She raised the pistol and brought the butt of it hard down on the back of his head. The Irishman crumpled to the ground, and when she checked his eyes she saw he was unconscious.

Sonja opened the rear door of the Land Cruiser and climbed in. On the floor, under a blanket, was her pack containing the two-stage high-explosive charge. She unzipped the bag and when she was satisfied the explosives were ready she pulled the satellite phone from the pouch on her combat vest and dialed her father's number.

"*Vis arend,*" he answered. "Are you . . . are you all right?"

She'd only intended to say one word in reply to his use of the Afrikaans for fish eagle, which told her he was at Kongola and that the rebels held the bridge crossing, but his wheezy question worried her. "*Bateleur,*" she said, giving him the code that told him she was safe and in position inside the compound, and ready to set the charge. "I'm fine, but how are you? Are you hurt?"

He coughed. "Nothing, nothing . . . just a scratch. Your *Engelsman,* you were right about him. He's been killing people back at the camp."

"How is . . ." She stopped herself from saying Sam's name, just in case someone in the region was monitoring satellite calls. "How is the American? Please tell me he's safe."

"*Ja,* he is, and on his way to your location. His *boet* wasn't so lucky. They'll be with you soon. You don't have to go through with this plan now. You realize that? Don't do it for that . . . that bastard."

"No," she said firmly. She wasn't doing it for Steele. "I'm doing it because it's the right thing to do, for the delta and for your people."

"*Ag,* follow your head. You'll do the right thing. *My* people are a bunch of superstitious natives, but I love them. They say the water belongs to them, but they also need electricity. That's Africa for you, hey? I don't know how I ended up here."

"You could leave them to it," she said.

She heard another ragged cough on the end of the line and her level of concern for him went up a couple of notches. "No, I'm like you. I'm too stubborn to walk away from a fight."

Sonja swallowed hard and felt her eyes start to sting. This was crazy. She needed to stop talking and get to work. "I . . ."

"I love you," he said.

She paused for a moment. "Me too, Papa. See you soon."

"God and Mikhail Kalashnikov willing."

Sonja hung up the phone. It seemed their lives had always been ruled by the gun and the bullet. She hoped the future would be better for Emma, but she didn't have time to spare to call her now.

Sonja got into the driver's seat of the Land Cruiser and turned the key. The engine started first time. She put it into gear and drove out of the administrative compound, down the hill toward the workers' huts and the vehicle park where the truck full of Nitropril waited. Sonja drove slowly, so as not to arouse undue attention. She knew that the military garrison would be awake and on full alert.

Sydney Chipchase sat up and groaned. The egg at the base of his skull hurt like hell when he touched it, so he stopped touching it. He felt dizzy as he got to his knees, but forced himself to stand.

He couldn't have been out for long. He had to stop her. Sydney looked around him and was surprised to see his black plastic toolbox sitting in the dust. It was still open from when he'd found the screwdriver for her. He rummaged through the tools inside and grabbed the handle attached to a tray near the bottom of the box. He pulled it up, accessing a hidden compartment at the bottom, which held a Browning nine-millimeter pistol. "Not as clever as you think, are you, Sonja." He picked up the weapon and worked the slide.

Pain stabbed him in the back of the head with each pace as he ran down the hill. He had a good view of the whole construction camp and military tent lines. Sydney stopped and raised a hand to his eyes when an explosion erupted below him, in one of the demountable buildings where the workers lived. He blinked and saw an orange-black ball of burning petrol twisting and rolling into the air. The building was on fire and men ran from it, screaming.

"Diversion," he muttered to himself. He started jogging again. She was a long way from the dam wall, so she had to be after something down there, near the workmen's quarters. He could hear panicked yells and confused orders being relayed as soldiers and hardhats tried to work out what was going on. He shifted his gaze to the vehicle park and saw his Land Cruiser parked inside the gate. "Bloody hell."

The noise of the big diesel engine starting and being revved carried across the beaten earth of the building site. A horn blasted and Sydney saw the antlike security guard scuttle out of the way as the truck rolled out of the gates of the compound. Even though it was dark Sydney recognized the vehicle. It looked like a water tanker, but the large red diamond on its side, visible even from this distance thanks to the flames from the burning building, told him it wasn't carrying anything so innocuous as water.

The truck slowed as it came to a T-junction. The road to its right, the one Sydney was running down, led up to the administrative compound and the gate. To the left was the gravel road and earthen embankment that became the dam wall. Sydney stopped, planted his feet apart, drew a deep breath and raised the pistol in his right hand. His left hand was wrapped around the right to steady his aim and absorb the recoil. He was an expert shot, but this was close to maximum effective range for the pistol, and a night shot to boot. He fired twice.

Sydney heard a grating whine as Sonja missed a gear. He knew he'd hit the vehicle somewhere. He wasn't a demolitions man so he didn't know if a bullet would detonate the bulk explosives on board. If she went up with her home-made bomb, then so be it. He started running again while she fought the gearbox, and despite slipping on the loose gravel and nearly falling, he was able to close the gap between them a little. He paused again as she began to accelerate and he emptied four more bullets at the lorry, which was trundling along the access road to the dam. He'd been aiming for the tires and scored a lucky hit at extreme pistol range. One of the pair on the right rear was already blown. It slapped and clattered around the steel rim, but the remaining tire held the vehicle's weight for the time being. Sonja was still moving, and although the blow-out had slowed her a little she was still able to drive far faster than he could run.

"Hands up! Stop!"

Sydney turned around and saw two uniformed Namibian Defense Force soldiers trotting down the road, their AK-47s held at the high port.

"Drop the gun!"

Sydney did as he was told. "You have to stop that truck. It's full of explosives and the driver's going to blow up the dam."

"What?" The soldiers had him covered, their rifle barrels rising and falling as they panted. "You're the missionary, aren't you?"

Sydney nodded. "The vehicle that was destroyed at the gate just now by the security guards—it had a bomb on board, right?"

The soldiers looked at each other, wondering if they should confirm what they had been told.

"Well," Sydney continued, "their information was wrong. There were no explosives in that ambulance—they're all in that vehicle heading to the dam. You have to stop it!"

The men looked at each other again, confusion and indecision paralyzing them. One raised his rifle to his shoulder, though held his fire.

"There's a patrol on the other side of the dam, on foot like us," the other soldier said. "I'll get them to set up a roadblock at the end of the dam wall."

"For Christ's sake, man, don't be daft. That vehicle's not going to make it to the other side. The bomb's going to be detonated halfway. You have to stop it now!"

"I'm going to aim for the tires," said the man with the raised rifle. He fired a shot, adjusted, then pulled the trigger again. The tanker was several hundred meters away, but traveling broadside to them. A hand appeared from the driver's window and all three men ducked instinctively at the sight of the pistol and the popping of return fire.

One of the soldiers ducked. The other squeezed off a burst of automatic fire at the disappearing lorry.

"You'll never stop it from here now." Sydney scanned the far side of the dam. "Where are the armored cars . . . the BTR 60s?"

One of the soldiers took a walkie-talkie from his belt and radioed through a hasty summary of what was going on.

"Yes, sir," the soldier said in reply to a question Sydney couldn't hear. "We're trying to stop it, sir, but it's almost out of range." He looked at Sydney, who mouthed the words "armored car" to him. "Sir, can you order the BTR 60 on the far side of the river to engage the explosives truck?"

The soldier put the radio back in the pouch on his belt.

"Well?" Sydney said.

"The BTR's on patrol at the far end of the camp." He pointed upriver to where the troops' bivouacs were. "My platoon commander said it won't be able to beat the Land Cruiser back to the dam and the bush is too thick for it to fire on your truck from where it is."

"Shit. We're sunk," Sydney said.

The soldier smiled. "No. We are floating!"

Sonja fought the steering wheel continually to keep the truck more or less straight on the road. The second of her two right rear tires was gone and the truck sagged and groaned as the bare rims scraped and sliced twin furrows into the dirt surface. As long as she was still moving she would be OK.

The gunfire behind her had faded to a desultory *pop-pop* now and then and she knew she was out of effective range of whoever was shooting at her. She was only a few hundred meters short of the dam and the wall stretched away in front of her like a puckered white scar on the dark skin of the land.

Sonja blinked and held her left hand up as bright white light filled the cab of the truck. She swerved and then wrenched the steering wheel to the right to stop herself slewing off the road. Her vision was dazzled and she screwed her eyes tight for a couple of seconds as she felt the beam find her once again.

Pah-chunk, pah-chunk, pah-chunk, pah-chunk . . .

She opened her eyes to the deep, rapid-fire sound and a green comet of tracer raced toward her from the left and then flashed past her windscreen. Another chased it.

"Shit!"

Her brain tried to work out what was happening. The gunfire seemed to be erupting from the black nothingness of the Okavango River. The road surface was suddenly smoother underneath her three remaining sets of wheels as she finally hit the surfaced top of the dam wall, leaving the dirt access road behind.

Pah-chunk, pah-chunk, pah-chunk, pah-chunk . . .

The lorry rocked on its springs as the first three of the rounds found their mark and punched holes through the rear of the cab, not far behind her back. Sonja swerved, though she was side-on to the weapon, so the evasive maneuver achieved little. The gunner was leading her, firing slightly ahead now so that his projectiles would intersect with the cab as she moved forward. She didn't know if a stray shot through the tank would ignite the store of granular explosives. It seemed the gunner was trying to kill her rather than set off a huge bomb on top of the dam. The safety wall on the water side of the dam wasn't finished yet and small cement blocks, each no more than a meter high, were laid like the crenulations on a medieval castle in order to stop drivers going over the edge. Two of them were blasted away as she neared them.

Sonja had already identified the BTR 60's main armament as part of her reconnaissance for Steele. She hadn't expected at the time she'd first spotted the armored car that it would one day be firing at her—or that her boss and former lover would betray her so comprehensively. A hit by just one of the 14.5-millimeter heavy machine-gun rounds would tear her apart. The gun was designed to shoot down an aircraft, so it would shred her in a puff of red mist.

The searchlight mounted on the top of the armored car was shining on her again and the beam bobbed up and down. Likewise, the next salvo of fat slugs from the armored car's gun zinged overhead. "It's on the water," she said out loud as her brain assembled the pieces of the puzzle. The commander of the BTR 60 must have taken his amphibious vehicle into the water upstream to draw a bead on her as quickly as possible. Smart and gutsy. The gunner fired again.

The truck shuddered again as a round tore through the engine bay and she ducked behind the dashboard as the bonnet popped open and slammed against the windscreen before falling away. The next bullet entered the cab via the passenger side window and exited near the front door pillar above her right arm. If she hadn't ducked it would have torn her head and torso from her body. Sonja screamed as two more rounds shredded her seat back and the passenger side upholstery. A storm of foam stuffing swirled around her.

The steering wheel bucked hard in her hand and she felt the left front side sag. Metal screeched on tarmac as she realized the tire had disintegrated. Sparks flew from the steel rim. She was driving on only two points of rubber now and the truck was just about uncontrollable.

Sonja was a third of the way across the dam now. She looked to her left and spotted the BTR 60 when the night sky was lit up with an incandescent bloom. A flare slowly floated to earth under its parachute and picked out the armored car's silver wake across the otherwise dark waters of the man-made lake. Mortars, she thought, firing illumination. High explosive would follow soon and if one of those hit the truck she would be vaporized.

The gunner on the armored car kept the beat on his machine-gun, blasting chunks of concrete and more barriers from the wall. Masonry bounced off the holed panels of the truck, and smoke and dust filled the cab through the gap where the windscreen had been. Far off, she detected the feint *crump, crump, crump* of more mortar rounds leaving their tubes. Something fell off the vehicle with a loud clunk.

Steam sprayed from the truck's radiator and was blown back into the cab, stinging Sonja's face and arms. The truck was disintegrating around her. A geyser of water erupted ahead and to the left of her as a ranging high-explosive mortar round detonated. The next mortar round exploded on the dam wall fifty meters ahead of her. The crews would know their bombs weren't strong enough to damage the dam wall, but a direct hit from one would be the end of her and the mobile IED. The Namibian commanders had obviously decided it would be safe to destroy her and the truck. If the Nitropril went off on the dam wall the force of the explosives would be directed up and out into the atmosphere. There might be a crater on top of the dam wall, but the structure would survive.

Sonja's father had helped her swap the barometric device on the high-explosive charges for a radio-controlled command-detonated device, quickly fashioned by a Caprivian rebel who had once made a living in Katima Mulilo repairing mobile phones. Her plan was to drive the truck into the river and swim clear, then detonate the charges once she had swum to land on the far side of the river. She couldn't be sure the explosives would detonate at exactly the right spot, but nor did she want to become a martyr. She loved the Okavango Delta, but not enough to die for it. Using her right hand she reached around for her seat belt, brought the strap across her body and clicked it home. A mortar bomb exploded in front of her and she swung the steering wheel to the left. Shrapnel peppered the dying lorry as Sonja launched the vehicle off the dam wall.

Sam saw the green tracer arcing through the blackness, then raised a hand to his eyes as night turned momentarily to day.

"Illumination round," Sam heard the pilot say into his headphones. "Someone's deep in the *kak* down there."

Hans Kurtz had outlined Sonja's plan to him, which involved her quietly rolling the hijacked truck full of explosives into the waters of the lake forming behind the dam wall.

"It's like bloody Baghdad down there," the pilot said as he banked the helicopter to get a better view.

Sam saw two explosions, one in the water and one on the dam wall as a mortar bomb landed in front of a swerving truck. Sparks were trailing from the vehicle which looked like it was running on bare metal rims rather than tires.

"Holy shit! It's going off the edge."

Sam watched as the lorry turned to the left and hurtled off the dam wall, nosediving into the water.

Sonja braced herself with her hands on the steering wheel but the force of the truck hitting water and the seat belt cutting into her chest took the breath from her lungs. She sucked and wheezed, trying to drag in some air as she fumbled for the belt release button. Water was rushing in through the shattered windscreen and the film-coated remnants of glass crumbled like paper and wrapped around her. She brushed the glass blanket away from her and managed a ragged, painful breath as she freed herself from her seat.

With water rushing over her lap Sonja climbed out through the hole where the windscreen had been. She could see the silver moon, but it was eclipsed for a second by something flying by. The helicopter, she realized. Perhaps she might make it out alive after all. The gun on top of the BTR 60 commenced firing again. Splashes in the water around her and the ping of lead on steel told her she had no reason to be optimistic. Sonja took a deep breath and duck dived. As she swam away from the truck underwater she heard more heavy rounds slamming into the ruined cab.

Above her Sonja could hear the zip of bullets entering the water where she had last been. Her whole body shook and then felt like someone had squeezed her in a giant fist as a mortar bomb exploded somewhere nearby. She forced herself to keep swimming, even as the first signs of dizziness flashed a warning in her brain. She knew she had to get as far away as possible from the sunken vehicle and then get out of the water before she detonated the explosives. If she did it while she was still in the water there was no way she would survive. If the shockwave didn't kill her she'd be drowned as the water rushed through the breach—assuming the bomb worked.

When she couldn't take any more she forced herself to do a few more strokes and angled up toward the surface of the water. When she broke free she drew in huge rasping breaths of air, ignoring the residual pain from the seat belt. She looked around to get her bearings. The mortar had stopped firing high explosives, but another flare burst high above her. She heard the

churn of the amphibious armored car's engine and saw it, just as the searchlight mounted on top of the BTR 60 found her. Its gun opened up an instant later and bullets smacked into the water around her. She drew a final
breath and dived deep.

It would head toward her, she thought, and the crew would expect her
to swim toward the shore or the dam wall.

"Go lower! Get down there," Sam shouted into the microphone attached to
his headset.

The pilot shook his head. "No way. You see those glowing green blobs?
That's tracer and I'm not flying into it. My orders were to stand off and wait
for a signal from whoever's left alive down there. Every other bloody order I
got has been changed tonight, but this is one I'm sticking to."

"Goddamn it," Sam said, and banged his fist down on the top of the
pilot's seat. He felt helpless, watching the floating armored vehicle rake
the water with machine-gun fire. So far the troops on the ground and the water
hadn't noticed the helicopter, which was flying without its navigation lights
turned on. "Look! There, in the water. That searchlight just found someone."

"Still no dice," the pilot said as he banked away from the river to circle
out over the bush of the Bwabwata National Park. "Even if you did spot
someone down there in the water we'd be blown out of the sky—or they'd
be killed—before we even got close enough to lower a cable."

"Take me down," Sam said.

"No way."

"The soldiers down there won't open fire on you. You're a civilian helicopter. They'll think you're a medivac."

"Wanna bet?"

"Christ, that's Kurtz's daughter, Sonja, down there. Do you want to be
the one to tell him you let her die?"

The pilot glanced back and Sam could see the concern on his face. He
guessed the man felt bad about leaving someone stranded down there, no
matter how tough his talk about following orders.

"Come in behind the armored car," Sam said. "Low and fast. Drop me off in the water and you'll be gone before they even draw a bead on you. You'll take their attention off the woman."

"You're fucking crazy, man."

"Sonja might be injured. If we do nothing they'll find her and kill her. Just do it."

"This is madness," the pilot muttered to himself. "Get ready. One pass and I'm not coming back until it's all clear. Take a radio with you."

Sam took off his headset and moved to the jump seat where the two armed Caprivian rebels were staring apprehensively out each side of the open cargo doors. "Give me your radio!"

The senior of the two men unclipped the walkie-talkie from his belt and Sam stuffed it down the front of his shirt.

"Take these," the other man said. He pulled two hand grenades from pouches on his combat vest and handed them to Sam, who stuffed them in the pockets of his jeans, where they were held tight against his thighs.

The pilot looked back and caught Sam's attention. "Ready?"

Sam nodded and gave a thumbs-up. The helicopter banked sharply upriver of the dam and headed back toward the wall. The pilot pushed the nose down until the skids were almost touching the water's surface. Sam thought momentarily of the bird, the African skimmer, how it flew with effortless ease with its lower beak slicing the waters of the Okavango. If any part of the helicopter connected with the river they would all cartwheel to their death. Sam could see the dam wall ahead and the angular bulk of the amphibious armored car. The searchlight mounted on top of the vehicle stabbed the dark in search of Sonja. Another illumination round exploded high in the sky. The gunner was sitting on the sill of his hatch, perhaps to get a better view. The noise of the helicopter's approaching engine made him turn.

"Ready . . ."

Sam stood with his feet on the left skid of the helicopter and one hand gripping the door pillar. He felt the nose lift slightly as the pilot bled off a fraction of his forward speed.

"Go!"

As Sam jumped he tried to bring his arms up in front of his torso and face to protect himself, but he was so close to the water he hit before he could bring his body into a streamlined position. He bounced hard, like he'd done a couple of times when falling off waterskis, but this was more painful. He was vaguely aware of the helicopter disappearing low over the dam wall as he went under water. When he bobbed back up again, gasping for air, he saw the armored car's turret was already swinging toward him, along with the searchlight's beam.

Sonja had swum toward, not away from the BTR 60. She heard the throb of its engine getting stronger then looked up to see its dark bulk churning toward her. It slowed, then stopped and she struck toward it. She broke the surface between two of its eight massive rubber tires, hidden from view. She breathed heavily.

"Don't shoot, don't shoot! American civilian, don't shoot!"

Sam? She couldn't see him, and couldn't believe what she was hearing, but there was no doubt the voice was his. The bloody fool, she thought. The mad, idiotic, gorgeous bloody fool.

"Pass me my AK-47," she heard a man say from up on top of the armored vehicle.

Sonja reached up and wrapped her hands around the top of the tire and heaved herself up.

Bang. Bang.

"Hey, don't shoot!"

Sonja groped for a handhold on the smooth cold steel skin of the BTR 60. The bloody man was opening fire on Sam—shooting first and asking questions later in case it was a trick. Smart guy, she thought.

"He's got a grenade!" she heard the crewman yell.

She heard the squeak of rubber boots above her and as she found a climbing rung and pulled herself up on top of the vehicle she saw the green metal orb land and bounce along the roof right toward her. The crewman was too preoccupied climbing back into his turret to notice her. Sonja reached out and batted the grenade away and it rolled off the angled side of the Russian armored car and into the river with a plop. She crawled across the top of the machine, using the machine-gun turret to conceal her from the sight of the panicked crewman and from the blast that she knew would come any second from the grenade.

The hatch slammed shut, but there was no explosion. Sonja looked around and saw Sam's head break the surface of the water. "Sam!" she hissed. He raised a hand and waved at her.

A burst of machine-gun fire raked the BTR 60, with half a dozen bullets zinging and ricocheting off the steel around her. Sonja ran along the water-slicked armor and slid down the sloping rear as the driver engaged gear and the car started to move. "Sam, hurry!"

He swam toward the rear of the vehicle as another long burst of fire landed in the water around him and pinged off the car. "Machine-gun on the dam wall," Sonja said. She clung to a climbing rung at the back of the car, half in and half out of the water, and reached out her hand. Sam struck out toward her, then reached for her.

"Got you," she said. "You crazy bastard. What are you doing here?"

"Coming to rescue you."

Sonja almost laughed at the absurdity of the remark, but the machine-gun was joined by the *pop-pop* of rifles and more bullets started zeroing in on them.

"Why are they firing at their own guys?" Sam asked, ducking his head half into the water as a bullet whizzed low over them.

"They know they can't hurt the guys inside the armored car, so they're trying to pick us off. The guys inside don't want to stick their heads out so my guess is they're going to just head toward shore. If we let go the soldiers on land will just pick us off."

The BTR 60 turned for the riverbank and chugged slowly through the water.

"And if we keep hanging on to this thing?"

"They'll shoot us when we get to shore," Sonja said.

"Got any ideas?" Sam said.

"Only the one." Sonja undid the flap of a pouch on her combat vest while still hanging on to her rung with the other. Sam held on to another metal bracket. He pulled out a radio transmitter. "In case this doesn't work, Sam, for the record, I think I love you."

He blinked water from his eyes. "Did I hear you right?"

"I hope so. Now hold on."

Sonja pressed a button in the middle of the transmitter and the sequential high-explosive charges detonated. A bubble and geyser of water erupted from the surface of the lake, at the base of the dam wall, and a split second later an even bigger fountain shot into the night air. The shockwave created an instant rippling tsunami that fanned out from the site of the underwater explosion.

The BTR 60 bucked in the water as a wave washed over the vehicle's bow and threatened to capsize it. Crewmen inside were yelling at each other as water gushed in through open hatches, but the car righted itself and didn't take in enough to sink. Sonja and Sam clung to the metal handholds on the back. Like the panicked crew, they didn't want to go under.

The gunfire from dry land had stopped. "The dam wall's still there, Sonja. It didn't work." The waves had passed them and the water was calming.

"Hold on," Sonja said. "Just wait."

He shook his head. The BTR's engine was vibrating beneath them and they were headed toward the shore again. "It didn't work," he said, freeing one hand and wiping his face, then twisting his finger in one of his ears.

Sonja took his hand and placed it back on the bracket he'd been clinging to. "Hold on! Wait . . . listen . . . it's going!"

Another shake partially restored his hearing and he picked up the rumbling: soft at first and then slowly growing louder and stronger like an oncoming train. The water started to swirl on either side of them and the armored car and he felt the stress on his arms increase as the BTR started moving faster through the water.

"Hold ON!"

The explosion deep beneath the surface had fractured the dam and the pressure of the accumulated water was doing the rest. The base of the dam wall was cracking and the water, at first a few isolated jets shooting out under intense pressure, was now ripping its way through the barrier, dislodging concrete, earth and rocks, which were shooting out from the face of the dam like jagged cannonballs.

Sonja was grinning wildly as they hung on for their lives. The BTR 60's engine screamed as the driver floored his accelerator and tried to turn out of the riptide that was sucking them toward the dam wall.

The dam wall gave way and water rushed through the narrow gap. A swirling undertow dragged the armored car toward the breach, faster than its screaming engine could resist. Sam felt like his arms were being ripped from their sockets and both he and Sonja yelled at the top of their lungs with pain and adrenaline and fear and wild exultation. The amphibious vehicle rode high on the wave that coursed through the breach but the stomach-lurching dip as they went over the gap forced their bodies to slap back down hard against the unforgiving angular steel edges of the armor. One of Sonja's hands was torn free but Sam reached out and grabbed it so that the pair of them hung there, one hand each on the vehicle and one on each other. They dragged themselves back to their respective handholds and waited for the ride to slow.

Down the Okavango they went, past farmland and mud huts on one side and the bush of the national park on the other. Hippos honked and snorted from the riverbanks where they had been grazing and lights came on along the shore in their wake. Sam watched as the river burst its banks, the mini tsunami inundating the land on either side of their path. Boats and *mekoros* slipped their moorings and were drawn into the flood, racing behind and beside the Russian armored car as it careened on, its engine powerless to change direction. Someone inside was screaming. Sam couldn't blame the crew for being terrified—he was as well.

As their movement gradually slowed Sam and Sonja were able to pull themselves up onto the back of the armored car. They sat on the engine cover at the rear, panting and coughing water they'd both inadvertently swallowed. "Do you have another grenade?"

"One," Sam said, "but I don't want to kill these guys. They were just doing their job."

She took the hand grenade from him. "I don't think there's much risk of that. Shush . . . listen."

There was noise coming from inside the gunner's turret and the rasp of steel on steel was followed by a squeak as the hatch slowly began to open. As the gunner's head came into view Sonja grabbed the lip of the hatch and reefed it back. Sam grabbed the lapels of the soldier's fatigue shirt and hoisted him up. With the hatch fully open, Sonja wrapped an arm under his chin and rabbit punched him in the throat, killing off his alarm cry. The man tried to rise up as they pinned him on his back on the top of the ar-mored car, but Sam punched him hard enough in the chin to snap the man's head back against the steel. Sonja pointed to the side and she and Sam hefted the dazed gunner overboard. He landed with a splash, but immediately be-gan flailing his arms and swimming, albeit poorly, toward shore.

"Hey!" cried a voice from inside. "What's happening, comrade?"

"This, *comrade!*" Sonja pulled the pin and dropped the grenade down the hatch.

The other two crewmen started screaming and scrabbling and the front two semicircular hatches, above the driver and commander's seats, popped open. Sonja was waiting, with pistol drawn, as the two men emerged, scrambling over each other in their rush to get out.

"Move! Out of the way!" she said.

Sonja rode the rocking of the floating car easily, legs apart, her pistol hand raised. She inspected the men's uniforms. "Relax, Lieutenant, Corporal. I'm pretty sure that grenade was a dud. Now, if you'd be so kind as to leave us."

The men looked at each other, as if wondering if they could overpower the woman. They glanced rearwards and saw Sam standing there, also hold-ing the pistol Sonja had given him. Sonja took aim and fired a round just to the left of the officer's arm. The two men dived overboard.

"Ever driven anything like this?" Sonja asked.

Sam smiled and shook his head.

"Climb into the driver's seat, big boy. I'm taking you for the ride of your life."

"What do you call our little surf just then?"

"Oh," she grinned, "you ain't seen nothing, yet. Now we're going to war."

31

Every time he pulled the trigger the recoil of the AK-47 sent a fresh shot of pain through his body. He was fairly sure he was dying.

Two army trucks were stopped at crazy angles across the road to Divundu in front of him. One was still engulfed in fire, with its burning tires sending oily black pyres into the clear blue morning sky; the other was a charred, smoking skeleton. There were two bodies lying in the dirt at the edge of the highway and already half a dozen vultures were circling in a thermal high above them.

The last of the assault force of infantrymen from the Namibian Defense Force were retreating. Hans wasn't sorry that he'd missed the man he'd just fired at. There had already been enough killing. It wasn't their aim to destroy the NDF—just buy themselves some time.

He looked at the sky and his watch, then surveyed their position for the hundredth time since the sun had come up. Behind him was the long bridge over the Kwando River, with the police and customs barrier post on the other side, closer to Katima Mulilo. His troops had formed semicircular perimeters on either side of the bridge and he had men dug in on both banks of the virtually dry Kwando, upstream and downstream of the bridge. Hans's men had blocked the bridge by driving an old Volkswagen Golf hatchback and a Toyota *bakkie* owned by the local veterinary staff at the checkpoint onto the structure and shooting out the tires. Tactically, the river crossing wasn't a bad position to hold. He had good fields of fire in all directions and his perimeter was tight enough for his force of a hundred and thirty men to defend against ground attack.

They were very vulnerable, he knew, to air and artillery bombardment, so every second man was digging into the soft sandy soil as if his life depended on it. Until more of the NDF arrived every third man was foraging for timber, corrugated iron and any other bits of natural or man-made material they could find to reinforce their fighting pits.

Hans knew, as did all of his men, that if the Namibian government did not want to negotiate with the CLA and their political wing, the UDP, then they would all die here. His men were confined to a small space, hence their vulnerability to artillery shells and aerial bombardment. But if the government wanted to kill them that way then they would most likely lose the bridge as well, which they'd hesitate to do.

Strategically, Hans had cut a main arterial highway and put an end for the time being to tourist and commercial traffic between Namibia, eastern Botswana and Zambia. His men had already turned back several startled foreigners in rented four-by-fours and a party of rebels had driven in a commandeered Land Rover down to the luxury lodge and campground at Nambwa Island, about fourteen kilometers south of the bridge, and overseen an evacuation of the worried holidaymakers staying there.

It was no longer business as usual in the Caprivi Strip and if the government wasn't prepared to bomb or shell them out of existence, then they would have to negotiate. Hans was confident his men were well trained, armed and dug in enough to repel conventional infantry attacks for many days to come.

Edison, the young lieutenant and chief's son, had not been seriously wounded by Steele's bullet and was walking the line, stopping to talk to his men and offering words of encouragement. He was a good man, and would make a fine leader of his people one day, Hans thought, unlike his pompous oaf of an uncle who had taken control of the CLA after his wiser brother had died.

"How are they holding up, Edison?" Hans asked, then coughed.

"The men are fine, sir. But I think you should rest a little while."

"Don't bloody tell me what to do." The pain was making him irritable and he cursed his bad luck. He knew the boy was only worried for him. "I'm fine, Edison. Go check on the mortar crew." Edison nodded and walked off.

Logistically they weren't completely cut off, but nor were they assured of support. A network of Caprivian women, children and older men were standing by to ferry more food and ammunition out of Botswana along the Kwando, though the Botswana Defense Force would get organized soon enough and put a halt to any more illegal cross-border movement. Hans figured they had four to six days to wait at the crossroads. By that time they would either all be dead, or a truce would have been negotiated. Hans had told his men they might need to hold on until the United Nations could be forced to intercede, though based on past form that never happened quickly.

"Radio message from OP Alpha, sir," a young Caprivian soldier with a radio on his back said. "They want to talk to you."

"Thank you, Jonas." Hans smiled at the nineteen-year-old boy. Like the others he was excited and still buoyed by the minor victories of taking the bridge and destroying the two trucks, which had been achieved with well-aimed rifle and machine-gun fire. Hans had antitank weapons, but he was saving them for any armored cars that might come their way, or for use against helicopters that tried to land on the road on the approaches to his position. He had small observation posts set up covering the main road about two kilometers out in either direction.

OP Alpha, covering the road to Divundu, reported that the stragglers from the first attack on the bridge were passing them by, heading back up the road. Kurtz acknowledged.

"Wait one," the man in the concealed observation post said, instead of signing off.

Kurtz licked his chapped lips as he waited for the trooper to report.

"I hear a vehicle, over."

Kurtz snapped his fingers to get Gideon's attention, who had been walking among the troops in Edison's wake, checking their ammunition. "Gideon, get one of the RPG teams ready to move."

"Yes, sir."

"Armored car. One BTR 60, coming around the bend." The young soldier in the OP was unable to keep the excitement out of his voice. "Coming your way, over."

"Roger. Keep it under observation, over," Kurtz said to the man on the radio, then passed the handset back to the signaler. To Gideon he said, "Send a five-man fire squad to cover the RPG—the best you've got. I don't want that BTR 60 getting close enough to do us damage. Catch him on the other side of the hill."

"I'll go, sir," Gideon said.

"No. I need you here."

"With respect, sir, I'm the best we've got. I can't send these young men out without someone who has been in battle."

The teams were already assembling and Kurtz stared hard at Gideon. He clapped him on the arm. "All right, you old lion. Go show these young cubs how it's done."

Gideon grinned and gave his orders. Three of the men in the fire team carried AK-47s and the fourth hefted an RPD light machine-gun. Together with the two-man team armed with the RPG-7 rocket-propelled grenade launcher and spare projectiles, they set off up the hill on the Divundu side of the bridge. Halfway to the crest Gideon led them off the road and they melted into the long dry grass and parched bush on the right-hand side.

Edison had been checking the far side of the perimeter and arrived at a jog as Gideon was disappearing. "Sir," he said, unable to contain his annoyance, "why was I not sent with those men?"

Hans raised a hand to his bloodied side. "Because they might not come back, Edison. If we lose Gideon, we lose our most experienced noncommissioned officer. If we lose you, Caprivi loses its future."

"I would rather die than send another man to face the enemy in my place."

Hans nodded. "Believe me, Edison, we will all face our enemy today."

•   •   •

Gideon understood and respected Major Kurtz's wish to keep NDF casualties to a minimum. He just didn't agree with it.

He wanted to kill some of the men who had been responsible for the repression of his people and the theft of his homeland. He crawled from man to man, checking their positions, weapons and ammunition.

"No firing until I give the order, or until I fire first, understood?"

A young volunteer nodded. Gideon could see the mix of fear and excitement in the boy's eyes. "Aim for the center mass. Here." Gideon tapped the base of his own sternum and the lad nodded.

"You," he said, stopping next to the man who had the RPG-7 already balanced on his shoulder, as he knelt behind a stout tree trunk. "You know to lead the BTR 60—to fire just ahead of it if it is moving fast, yes?"

"Yes, sir," the man said.

"You have fired the RPG-7 before?"

"Once—several months ago."

Ammunition was scarce, Gideon knew—or at least it had been until the recent influx of money and equipment that had come from the rich white safari operators in the Okavango Delta. "You will get a lot more practice in the coming days."

The man grinned.

Gideon cocked his head. "They are coming." He saw them now. The BTR 60 was leading, driving slowly, followed by a Unimog truck with its tarpaulin removed. In the back were fifteen soldiers sitting on bench seats, and all the infantrymen were facing outward with rifles and machine-guns at the ready. "The truck will stop and the infantry will dismount as soon as the RPG fires. Their job is to provide protection for the armored car—to sweep through the bush and kill us," he said loud enough for them all to hear. "But we will do the killing first."

"For Caprivi!" one of the men said, too loud, but it was too late to chastise him.

"Fire!" Gideon yelled.

The rebels' RPD machine-gunner opened up, firing low at first. By watching the puffs of dirt kicked up by his 7:62-millimeter rounds he was able to adjust his aim and walk his bullets up and into the truck. One man tumbled out of the back of the vehicle while it was still moving.

"Fire the RPG!" Gideon looked at the anti-armor crew and saw the gunner had the RPG-7 off his shoulder and was frantically pulling the missile out of the tube. "What happened?"

"M . . . misfire, sir," the man stammered under pressure.

"Hurry up. Reload! Keep firing, the rest of you. Aim for the truck—for the infantry."

The Unimog had pulled over and the soldiers on board were leaping out. A medic had rushed to the fallen soldier, but the rest were very much alive and had shaken themselves out into an extended line and were running toward the rebel position, trying to get off the grassy killing ground as quickly as possible, and into the fringe of bush and trees.

Gideon raised his AK-47 to his shoulder and fired once. A Namibian soldier fell in the grass. He watched the BTR 60 turn to the left so that it was facing them. The turret rotated and the big 14.5-millimeter anti-aircraft gun pointed toward them. The sound when it opened up was almost deafening. Leaves, bark and shredded twigs rained down on them as the gun fired high. "What's happening with the RPG?"

"Loaded."

"Well fire the fucking thing!"

"Firing now."

There was the pop of AK-47s and the chatter of the machine-guns but no whoosh and roar of a departing rocket-propelled grenade. Gideon looked at the team. The gunner and loader were tugging the second round out of the launcher. "Another misfire. Sorry, sir."

"Fall back, fall back," Gideon commanded them. Two out of two misfires was very bad odds indeed. "Reload while we're moving. Go!"

Black smoke belched from the BTR 60's exhaust and the armored car started advancing up the rise toward them, firing on the move.

Gideon felt the punch of displaced air pass him by and when he looked to his left he saw one of the members of his squad had fallen. The heavy-caliber machine-gun rounds had taken almost all of his head off and blood fountained from the gory mess that remained. The young trooper Gideon had spoken with just before the shooting started stopped to look at what remained of his comrade. Gideon grabbed him by the straps of his chest webbing and yanked him away from the gruesome sight. "Get moving, I said!"

The boy staggered and Gideon had to hold tight to stop him falling. The trooper looked at his left hand and saw his index finger was missing. "Move!" Gideon yelled at him. Gideon turned and emptied the magazine of his AK-47 at the pursuing troops. One-handed he tore open the waterproof packet of a field dressing with his teeth and passed the bulky cotton pad and bandage to the boy. "Tie that around the wound."

"R . . . reloaded, sir. Ready to k . . . kill this time," the RPG gunner called from behind him.

"Keep going, the rest of you," Gideon ordered the team as he knelt beside the RPG man and changed magazines. "Steady," Gideon said, resting a hand on the man's shoulder. "Aim well."

The BTR 60 charged on toward them, flattening grass and saplings in its path. The heavy gun in the turret tracked the fleeing men and Gideon heard another scream of pain amidst the unceasing clatter.

"Firing now," the man said.

Gideon fired two bursts from his AK-47 at the NDF infantrymen who were running to keep up with the armored car they were supposed to be protecting.

There was no sound beside him. Nothing.

"Run!" Gideon stood and fired off the remainder of his magazine. He and the RPG gunner sprinted after the rest of the patrol, who were silhouetted against the crest of the hill. On the other side was the bridge and the rebel position, but for these few seconds they were all perfect targets. Heavy machine-gun fire swept the ridge and two more men fell.

One man was killed instantly when a bullet sliced through his heart, but the other had lost his right leg below the knee. He lay writhing and screaming in the dust. "Help me," Gideon said to the RPG man. Between them they dragged the wounded man upright and held him between them.

The man bellowed in pain, however, as the RPG gunner fell. Gideon staggered and dropped to one knee. The RPG man was dead, having taken an AK-47 round in the back of the head. Bullets large and small hissed around him as he grabbed the one-legged soldier by his webbing straps and heaved him up and over his shoulder in a fireman's carry. Gideon bent and snatched up his own rifle from the grass and staggered over the brow of the hill. One of the others from the squad in front of him paused and turned. "Keep running . . . I'm fine," Gideon assured the man.

"Covering fire!" Hans lifted his AK-47 and started aiming at the Namibian troops who were coming over the hill. The enemy was trying to kill his men and Hans felt no remorse now when he saw another NDF soldier fall. Heavy machine-gun rounds started plowing the dirt in front of his position. Hans lowered his rifle and pulled a pair of small Zeiss binoculars from the pocket of his shirt.

He scanned the crest and saw the turret of an armored car. The commander of the vehicle had cleverly stopped just below the top of the hill and had his gunner train his gun down to its maximum angle of depression. The vehicle was all but impervious to direct anti-armor fire. In any case, it was out of range of his RPGs from here. He guessed the RPG crew he had sent with Gideon had missed the vehicle with every round.

Around him other men were pouring a noisy but largely ineffectual stream of lead at the Namibian troops, whose advance had lost momentum once they saw the fortified bridge. The enemy infantry had lain down in the grass on either side of the partially concealed BTR 60. "Mortars . . . two rounds, high explosive, at that armored car; fire!"

Hans kept his binoculars trained on the armored car. It was firing its main gun in short bursts now. He guessed the gunner and commander were conserving their ammunition. By his recollection the car only carried about five hundred rounds and they wouldn't last long. A movement in the distant grass made him lower his field glasses. He saw another of his men, moving slowly, bent and burdened and lagging behind the other men. He focused again. "Gideon!"

Hans looked over his shoulder. "What's going on back there? I said two rounds, high explosive!"

A bare-chested soldier who had been passing bombs to the mortar crew came running over to him and said, "There is a problem with the bombs. They are not going off, sir."

"Shit."

He looked back at Gideon's men who were retreating. The fastest runners were almost at the perimeter of the bridge position. "Get those men over here, now!"

Gideon was still staggering after them and Hans could see now it was another man he was carrying, on his back. He was about to send two men out to help his friend when he saw the first green glowing fireball of tracer land at Gideon's feet. Another followed and he could hear shouting carrying down the hill from the Namibian position.

"Sir . . ." a sweat-drenched soldier panted as he stopped next to Kurtz. "You wanted to see us."

"What happened?"

"The RPGs, sir . . . they would not work. They all misfired. The sergeant major, he told us to run, sir."

He thought about the misfiring rocket-propelled grenades and the mortar rounds that had just failed to launch. They were all from the new batch of ammunition delivered courtesy of their new financial backers. "Steele."

Kurtz, like every other man at the outpost, watched Gideon, who staggered through the grass along the verge of the wide tar of the B8 highway. He made use of the downhill slope and was keeping up a steady pace. His mouth was open wide, sucking in air as he ran.

"Come on, come on!" some of the men urged. Others whistled.

Pah-chunk, pah-chunk.

The BTR 60 fired two more ranging shots and they bracketed Gideon and his wounded charge perfectly; one landed just behind him and the other just in front.

"Bastards," Kurtz said. They were taking their time.

"Mortar . . . fire smoke!" Kurtz yelled. "The rest of you . . . anyone with a smoke grenade, throw it now!" He hoped that the smoke would at least obscure the gunner's aim.

"Misfire, sir!" a man called from the pit where their sole mortar was dug in.

Edison arrived at Kurtz's side. "The mortar rounds—they're all duds. We have been betrayed."

Hans nodded. Martin Steele had played a final double-cross. With no RPG anti-armor weapons and no functioning mortar bombs to deliver their own indirect fire, their available time at the bridge had just shrunk from days to hours.

Yellow and red smoke grenades popped and fizzed into colorful, billowing clouds beyond the perimeter, but Gideon was still further away than the strongest man could throw, so he was left exposed to the gunner's mercy.

"Come on!" Hans yelled. "Nearly there!" The effort of calling out to his friend seemed to rupture something else inside him and he doubled in pain, but shook off the offer of a helping hand from Edison. "I'm fine."

The men around him were all cheering and yelling now and the firing had stopped from the NDF soldiers on the hill. The range was perhaps too far for them, but not so the gunner behind the heavy machine-gun on the armored car.

Pah-chunk, pah-chunk, pah-chunk.

The explosions of dirt followed Gideon and were close enough to spatter against the man bleeding to death on his back. Kurtz allowed himself to hope. "Throw another smoke grenade!"

Kurtz signaled to a medic. "Get ready to treat that man as soon as he's safe. Remember to put on two sets of rubber gloves, hey." The soldier nodded. Even in the heat of battle Kurtz had to remind his men to guard against the ever-present specter of HIV-AIDS. There was no doubt that a significant proportion of the fighters, perhaps even the medic, were carrying the disease.

The smoke canister was thrown and it popped and sputtered into colorful life. Gideon was no more than a hundred meters from them now. The sergeant major dropped his rifle and he readjusted his grip on the wounded soldier and seemed to prepare himself for a final sprint. He lifted his muscled legs and the fall of his boots sounded like clapping as he found a surer footing on the tarmac highway. The men in the rebel camp were silent now. The fresh plume of orange smoke started to take form and rise around Gideon's knees.

Edison put down his weapon and vaulted over the barricade of sandbags. He started running toward Gideon. Hans tried to protest, but the words were killed by the pain in his side.

Pah-chunk, pah-chunk, pah-chunk.

The grenade had done its job and Gideon and the man on his back were obscured. Edison disappeared into the billowing orange curtain. Not a man dared breathe, until the light breeze carried the smoke north toward Angola.

Edison reappeared first. He stood, oblivious to the bullets that continued to fall around him, and raised two clenched fists to the sky. He threw back his head and bellowed with the mix of rage, remorse and fear as the smoke cleared, revealing Gideon, and the man he carried, lying dead on the road.

32

A Caprivian agent living in Divundu, whose job was to deliver frozen meat and vegetables to the construction camp and garrison at the Okavango Dam, called Hans on his satellite phone to tell him the wall had been destroyed and the lands downriver were in flood. When the helicopter hadn't returned to Kongola with his daughter and the American on board, Hans had feared the operation had failed and they were both dead.

The news raised a half-hearted cheer from the garrison, but the death of Gideon and the others, and the realization that so much of their ammunition was dud, had sapped their morale. What little appetite the men had for fighting was further dulled by the rest of the news from Divundu—the army garrison there was on its way to Kongola to seek revenge for the breaching of the dam. When the observation post along the road radioed to confirm that a convoy of army trucks was approaching, Kurtz ordered his sentries to pack up and return to the bridge as quickly and quietly as they could, before they were ringed by NDF forces.

Edison had contained his grief and was moving up and down the line again, trying to reinvigorate the demoralized rebel soldiers.

Kurtz's phone rang again. *"Ja,"* he said, unable to hide the tiredness and pain.

"It is Webster, Major, in Katima Mulilo."

"What news?" Kurtz asked his agent in the provincial capital.

"The people, Major. They are on the streets."

Webster, unaffected by the deaths at Kongola, was ebullient in his description of people thronging the streets outside the government offices, and of convoys of cars blocking the B8, honking their horns in protest against the government and in celebration of the news about the dam. According to Webster the unofficial flag of Caprivi-Itenge—two black elephants with their trunks entwined, on a background of horizontal bands of black, white, green and blue—was flying in the streets and being waved from car windows. The police were in the streets, but so far neither side had resorted to violence.

As soon as he finished the phone call his signaler passed him the radio headphones and handset again. The OP was making a final report, as it withdrew, that the BTR 60 armored car, which had disappeared from sight at the top of the hill after Gideon's death, was being refueled and rearmed, and that close on a hundred troops were debussing from the army trucks which had stopped on the far side of the hill.

The sun was high overhead and Hans Kurtz took a moment to sit in the shade of a water tower beside the customs post. His signaler had vanished, but returned a few minutes later with a lukewarm mug of coffee. "*Dankie*," Kurtz said. He took a sip, then, suddenly weary, rested his elbows on his knees and his head in his palms.

"Daddy!"

He looked up. It was his son, running toward him, followed by Miriam, dressed in jeans and a green bush shirt. The boy threw himself into his arms, but Kurtz was able to mask the pain and smile for him. "What are you doing here?" he asked his wife.

"We came with the other women and children, in the boats and the *mekoros*."

"You were told to stay on the other side of the border and be ready to help with evacuation of the wounded."

"You look pale, are you hurt, Hans? Move, baby, let Mommy take a look at Daddy."

Kurtz shook his head and held the boy closer. "No. You shouldn't have come, Miriam. It's not safe to bring the boy here."

"The *boy* will be a man one day and he deserves to be with his father in his own land, not across the border in a foreign country. Besides, haven't you heard, Hans? It's happening. It's really happening—it was on the BBC this morning. People are rising up all along the Caprivi Strip. They're coming out of their homes in Katima and Divundu, onto the streets and waving our flag. People have had enough."

Hans looked up at the hill and at the stain on the road where Gideon and his comrade had fallen. "The NDF hasn't had enough yet, Miriam. They'll be coming for us soon. You shouldn't have put our son at risk."

She stared at him. "What do you want me to do?"

"Go back to the river. Wait downstream. I will come if it gets too serious."

She gave a snort. "You'll never leave. I know you. But I will take our son into the bush for a little while longer. Come to me, my boy."

His son looked up into his eyes and Hans ruffled his hair. "Go with your mom. I'll be with you soon."

The boy turned and slowly walked back to Miriam. What she saw made her raise her hand to her mouth, but it took little Frederick a couple of seconds before he noticed the stain and the wetness on his white T-shirt. "What is it?" he wailed, patting his father's blood with his fingers.

"Come to me, now, my boy," Miriam said. "Hans . . . I'll get help."

"The medics are busy with others. I'll wait my turn, and . . ." He raised a hand to stop his own words and hers. "Listen." They both heard the *crump, crump, crump.* "Mortars! Take cover! Run, Miriam, into the bush. Hurry!"

The barrage was almost dead on target. The first two bombs fell just outside the perimeter, and the third landed right in the midst of the rebel stronghold. A man screamed and smoke and falling dirt were swept through the rebel camp on a hot wind. Miriam was crouched in the lee of the customs shack, but Hans took her by the hand and forced her to start running. "Downriver, as fast as you can. Go!"

"Sir!" a soldier called. "Look! Infantry on the move, and that armored car is back."

Hans could see the men swarming over the crest of the hill, the squat angular bulk of the BTR 60 cruising slowly along behind them. The armored vehicle had a row of smoke launchers fitted to it and these fired, sending out canisters ahead of it, which provided an instant smokescreen to cover the advance. The 14.5-millimeter gun started firing.

"Infantry in the open . . . eight hundred meters . . . Machine-guns, fire!" Hans called. Their own limited arsenal of automatic weapons opened fire, at long range.

Explosions were going off around him now as the mortars found their mark, landing on either side of the Kongola Bridge. Hans called another squad of men from the east bank to reinforce the west, where the attack would hit. He had to trust his man in Katima that there had been no reports of a military force leaving the capital or M'pacha—yet. He imagined the Namibian government would keep a strong presence around the largest town in the Caprivi Strip for the time being.

The BTR 60 emerged from its smoke barrage and started firing at the rebel positions on the western side of the bridge. Men screamed and fell as the virtually unstoppable slugs tore through sandbags and flesh with impunity. The armored car climbed out of the grass and onto the main road, where it settled into a sedately menacing pace, firing in long bursts as it advanced, but never getting too far ahead of its screen of infantry, who trotted along on either side of it, gaining courage and confidence from the vehicle's presence.

An RPD machine-gun fired furiously at the BTR 60, but the 7:62-millimeter bullets bounced harmlessly off the vehicle's sloping armored front and sides.

Kurtz cursed himself for not testing some of the RPG rounds before leaving Botswana, but knew he could not have risked firing the mortars around their hideaway. The dud ammunition had forced them to improvise. "Molotovs!" he yelled.

Two men rose from the grass on the downriver side of the road and touched cigarette lighters to petrol-soaked rags stuffed in glass vodka and gin bottles filled with petrol. One of them was shot immediately by a Namibian infantryman and when the rebel staggered his Molotov cocktail slipped and broke at his feet. He was engulfed in flames and lurched around in circles, setting fire to the grass around him as he died an agonizing, screaming death. The other man raced toward the BTR 60, evading the bullets that kicked up the dirt and whizzed around him. He tossed his flaming bottle at the armored car, but missed any hatches or openings. His improvised bomb smashed on the steel side of the vehicle, but the fire didn't catch. The man was gunned down as he tried to run back to cover.

The gunner in the car took aim at the customs post where Hans had been sheltering. As he crawled from the shack the 14.5-millimeter bullets tore it apart, showering him with wood, tin, masonry and shredded paperwork.

"Sir!" his signaler called from the other side of the road at the end of the bridge. "Here comes another one!"

Hans raised his head above a sandbag parapet and saw that another BTR 60 had just come over the hill, on the main road, and was speeding down to join the first.

"What do we do, sir?" the signaler asked.

Kurtz pressed his hand against the wound and when he pulled it away his hand was wet with blood. "We fight, and we die." He rested his AK-47 on the top of the sandbags and started firing. The soldier with the radio did the same. The BTR 60 kept coming, though, and it kept up its merciless raking of the rebel positions. The line started to crumble.

"Fall back, fall back," Kurtz yelled. "To this side of the bridge!"

His men needed little urging and those on the far side of the river began running toward him. Two died on the bridge and the others were chased by rifle and heavy machine-gun fire all the way. Kurtz looked back over his shoulder and saw the armored car moving onto the bridge. He and his men had packed explosives around the piers supporting the bridge, but Hans had a terrible feeling nothing would happen when he gave the command to blow it.

Hans fired carefully aimed shots at the infantrymen advancing beside and behind the BTR 60. "Blow the bridge!"

He looked at the sergeant who was the closest they had to a demolitions expert. He had rigged the explosive switch for Sonja's truck bomb and that had obviously worked. The man pressed the electronic detonator switch and nothing happened. He looked at Kurtz. "Dud, sir. Like the RPGs and the mortar bombs."

Kurtz swore. The BTR opened fire on them and the men ducked low behind their hastily erected parapets. "It's all over, sir, isn't it?" the demolitions sergeant said.

"Gather the women and children, Sergeant, and make a run for it. Any man who wishes to leave can do so. Go into the bush and make for the Botswana border."

The sergeant looked around him. Fifteen or twenty men had gravitated toward the command position. "No, sir, we're staying . . . if you are."

"I'm wounded," Kurtz said. "I'll give you covering fire. Go now, while you can. Save yourselves and your families. Go back to Botswana."

"No, sir. Our home is here and we would rather die on Caprivian soil than rot in another country."

The BTR fired another salvo and a man fell, his head split apart like a melon. "So be it. Let's show them how real soldiers fight, eh?"

Kurtz stepped back up to the firing line and took aim at the armored car's vision slits. It was no more than a hundred and fifty meters away. Men were shooting on either side of him and he saw the madness in their eyes and heard it in their voices.

"Medic!" a man yelled further down the line.

Kurtz turned and saw Miriam rushing behind him. He caught her by the arm. "What are you doing here, woman? I told you to go."

She shrugged off his grip. "I've sent Frederick into the bush with one of the other women. I couldn't leave. My place is here. There are not enough people who know first aid." She ran off, toward a fallen rebel.

The BTR 60 was on the far side of the immobilized car and *bakkie* that blocked the bridge's passage. The driver slowed to drive around it. Kurtz had planned for this choke point to provide a perfect location for his RPG crews to open up on Namibian vehicles, but the anti-armor weapons were useless.

The end is here, Kurtz thought to himself.

"Faster!" Sonja said.

"I've got my foot flat to the floor," Sam said.

They'd left the river well downstream of the breached dam, but by using dead reckoning and a network of old tracks carved out by the South African

Defense Force when it had been based in the wilds of the land now known as the Bwabwata National Park, Sonja had navigated the BTR 60 north to the B8. Once on the main road they raced toward Kongola.

Just ten minutes earlier they had caught up with the truck convoy of troops from the dam site who were heading for the rebel stronghold at Kongola. Sonja, who was sitting in the gunner's turret, had closed her hatch and told Sam to just keep driving. Soldiers on the roadside waved at them and gave close-fisted salutes as they trundled past.

When Sonja risked opening the hatch again she saw mortar bombs landing on the CLA's fortified position on the far side of the bridge over the Kwando River at Kongola. Ahead of her, dismounted infantry were advancing on either side of another BTR 60, identical to theirs. As Sam motored down the hill she saw the other armored car approaching the bridge, all the while firing into the Caprivian troops and the barricades they had constructed around the crossing.

"They're murdering them," Sam yelled over the engine noise.

"I know. We've got to stop them."

The BTR 60 in front of them was spinning its huge wheels as it pushed against one of the two vehicles blocking the bridge. The small Volkswagen hatchback was slowly being slid out of the path of the armored car. At the same time, every burst of fire from its main gun destroyed another section of fortified wall or killed or wounded another two or three of the defenders. Despite the hopeless odds, the rebels were returning fire. Sonja heard rounds zinging off their vehicle as some of the Caprivians shifted their fire. She pulled her hatch closed.

"Drive right up his arse, Sam."

He looked back over his shoulder and grinned at her. "Is it wrong for me to be enjoying this?" They slowed and weaved around the burned-out trucks.

"Welcome to my world."

Sam floored the accelerator and the car charged onto the bridge.

Through the vision slits in the turret Sonja could see NDF riflemen in camouflage uniforms pouring onto the bridge as well. The arrival of the second armored vehicle had given the Namibians another shot of courage and they all wanted to be part of the kill now that victory seemed certain. The soldiers showed no indication that the second BTR 60 wasn't expected.

"Get me close, Sam."

"You got it." The other BTR 60 had almost created a gap in the two-vehicle blockade big enough for it to get between the car and the pick-up. Sam pulled up just fifty meters behind it.

"Firing now!"

Sonja thumbed the firing button on the heavy machine-gun and the turret filled with smoke and the clatter of ejected brass casings as the slugs from the gun struck the other vehicle at almost point-blank range. Most of Sonja's bullets bounced off the target's armor, ricocheting off at wild angles. Soldiers on the ground halted their advance and took cover wherever they could, confused by the sudden burst of what looked like friendly fire.

Sonja aimed at the base of the other turret, where it met the main hull of the car, in the belief that this would be one of the weakest points. She also wanted to distract the other gunner, even if she couldn't kill him.

The driver of the other armored vehicle was trying to put some distance between him and Sam and, with a nerve-grating screech of buckling metal, the BTR 60 finally squeezed through the gap between the truck and the car. "He's got his wheels turned toward the side of the bridge," Sam yelled over the din of firing.

"So?" Sonja screamed back, focusing her concentration on aiming the big, unfamiliar weapon.

"I'm going to ram him. I'll try and push him off the bridge."

"Go for it!"

The opposing gunner was now well and truly aware of the danger behind him and he was rotating his turret. Sonja conserved her ammunition and waited for the next round of the dual. She figured the slit where the 14.5 millimeter protruded from the turret would be another natural weak point. No doubt, though, her adversary was thinking the same thing. It would be decided by who was quickest on the trigger and the best shot.

Sam pumped the accelerator a few times, revving the big engine, then let the armored car surge forward. "Hang on!"

Sonja braced herself in the turret but still banged her head on the gun sight as the pointed hull of their vehicle slammed into the vertically sloping rear of the other car. The impact of the collision pushed the other vehicle three meters, and into the steel crash barrier at the side of the bridge.

Sonja recovered her wits and pumped another long burst of fire into the enemy gun turret as Sam backed up and revved the engine again. She could hear the other driver gunning his own engine and grinding his gears. "Go, Sam!"

Sam stood on the gas pedal again and rammed into his target once more. The sharp bow of the other vehicle broke through the barrier and was now overhanging the bridge, but the gunner had succeeded in swinging his turret almost all the way around.

"Keep pushing, Sam!" Sonja yelled, waiting for her chance.

Sam gunned the engine and smoke started to pour from all eight of the big rubber tires as they spun and squealed on the road surface. Inch by inch they were pushing their opponents to the edge.

"Come on, come on," Sonja willed the other gunner.

They were so close now, nose to tail with the other vehicle, that the tips of the barrels of the two heavy machine-guns would be little more than a couple of meters apart when they met on the same traverse. Almost there, she thought. "Fuck it," she said, and pushed the firing button.

Nothing happened.

"Sonja?"

"Blockage!" she yelled, cursing the Russian technology and ammunition as she opened the feed cover, cleared it, closed it again and furiously yanked back on the gun's cocking lever.

"Get down out of the turret!"

"No, Sam, I'm nearly there!"

She looked up out of her viewing slit at the mouth of the other gun's barrel, which was now pointing straight at her face. She reached for the firing button, but knew she was probably too late. "Aaargh!"

"What is it?"

Sam's question was answered by the intense heat of a fireball that rolled over their vehicle, sending stinging, acrid smoke and fumes through their narrow vision slits. Sam ducked as the storm brewed around them. He rammed the gear lever into reverse and backed away.

Sonja popped open the hatch of her turret and peeked out. The top of the other BTR 60 was engulfed in fire, and men screamed from inside it. Even as the flames burned there were other men—Caprivian rebels— swarming out from behind their shattered barricades and surrounding the burning vehicle.

The driver's hatch opened and a man climbed out. Immediately he was engulfed by flames. A rebel soldier silenced his screams with a single shot. One other man got out without being burned and was taken prisoner, but the third crew member cried for a little while longer. Opening the hatches had allowed the fire to spread to the inside of the car so it was impossible to get in to rescue the trapped man. Rebels put their hands on the hot steel and tried to push the stricken armored car over the edge.

Sam revved his engine again and moved forward, scattering the troops. He nudged into the rear and accelerated. Without the driver inside working the breaks the vehicle rolled easily off the bridge. As it fell and flipped on its top side in the sandy bed below, the ammunition inside started exploding. A few seconds later the fuel tank caught fire and erupted.

A bullet flew past Sonja's ear. She turned and saw the NDF infantry, who a few minutes earlier had been full of enthusiasm for the fight, had now clustered at the far end of the bridge, lying in the roadway and on grass verges, and taking other cover where they could find it.

"Come on!" she yelled at the rebels who were gathering and cheering around them. "Finish the job!"

She and Sam closed their hatches again and Sam reversed and made a three-point turn. With the gun's breech cleared Sonja started firing again. Sam moved the BTR forward at walking pace but had to increase his speed to keep up with the charging, firing Caprivians who swept down the bridge on either side of him and Sonja.

The Namibian soldiers had no stomach for the fight and ran back up the hill in the direction from which they'd come, back toward Divundu.

Sonja stopped when she came to the remains of the rebel stronghold and opened the hatch again, grateful for the fresh air. She stood on top of the armored car and reached out a hand to help Sam climb up out of the driver's compartment. He hugged her and she wrapped her arms around him.

He held her away from him and looked at her. "We did it!"

She nodded and looked into his eyes. He kissed her and they hugged again and she never wanted to let him go. Her heart was pounding madly and, for once, she didn't think it had anything to do with battle.

"Sonja?" she heard a weak voice call.

Sonja looked down and there was her father, walking down the bridge toward them. She looked at Sam.

"Go to him, Sonja."

She climbed down, smiling wide. She was so happy to see he was alive. The fight wasn't over, but they had blown the dam and fought off a determined counterattack. The NDF would be wary about making another, and worried about losing more men. If the rebellion gained popular support they might still be able to negotiate peace and a deal for an independent Caprivi without more bloodshed.

"Papa . . ."

He reached out his arms to her, but just as she was about to reach him he staggered and dropped to one knee.

"Dad . . . you're hurt." She felt the lump swell in her throat and the tears prick her eyes. She knew he'd sounded in pain on the satellite phone. She saw the blood on the side of his shirt, and on his hands. "Medic! Help me . . . medic!"

Miriam came running from the far end of the bridge. Her little boy was in the arms of another woman, but he wriggled and struggled until she let him go and went toddling after his mother. In defiance of Hans's orders to evacuate, his wife and son had clearly been hiding close to the Caprivian defensive position.

Hans slipped to the roadway and Sonja knelt beside him, cradling his head in her arms. "Papa, please don't die, not now . . . not now that . . ."

"That we've found each other?" He coughed.

"Not now that you owe me a case of beer for saving your life."

He tried to laugh, but the pain was too much. Blood welled at his lips.

"Not now, Papa. Hang on. You'll be fine."

He forced a smile. "Reassure the patient, hey? One of the first rules of first aid. Did you learn that in the army, like me?"

She wiped the perspiration from his forehead. "I learned it from you, Dad. You taught me first aid. On the farm, remember?"

He blinked twice. "Yes, my girl. I remember. Reassure me some more."

"I love you, Dad, and I missed you for so long. You can't leave now."

He coughed again, and more blood came with it. "If God wills it, I must go."

Miriam came to the other side of him and dropped to her knees. She took his hand in hers and a few moments later their son arrived and clung to his mother.

"We're homeless, you and I, Sonja . . ." His skin was terribly pale and his breathing shallow. He winced in pain. "The country we were born in has a new name and neither of us can go back to Botswana now."

"You've helped make a home for all these people, Papa . . . for Miriam and Frederick."

He shook his head, and the effort seemed to drain almost the last of his strength. "No, Sonja. Countries . . . flags, they don't matter. Here is our home, in each other's arms. Go to your daughter. Don't leave it as long as we did. Find your home and be . . . be happy."

Sonja took her father's free hand and, together with Miriam and Frederick, sat with Hans until he died.

33

"She's gone, Sonja. I thought you knew," Stirling Smith said when she asked to speak to her daughter.

"I don't know what you're talking about. Gone where? With who?"

"With your *friend* Martin Steele, of course. To Johannesburg and then Mauritius, I gather."

"Jesus Christ."

"Sonja? What happened at the dam . . . was that you?"

"When did Steele leave?"

"It was wrong, Sonja, blowing it up."

"For God's sake, Stirling, shut up about the bloody dam. Steele . . . when did he leave; what else did he say?"

There was a pause on the end of the line. "He only left a few hours ago, on a Mack Air charter to Maun—same plane he arrived at Xakanaxa on. He'll be on the Air Bots flight later today. He stayed long enough to meet with that bloody Bernard Trench and collect the rest of his money—your money."

Sonja tried calling Emma's mobile phone, but it went straight to voicemail. "Emma, if you get this, my love, please, please, please get away from Martin as soon as you can and go to the nearest police station. He's dangerous. I'm coming for you. Call me." Sonja left her number, for the third time. She ended the call and dialed another number on her satellite phone.

"Yes," said the weary-sounding male voice.

"It's Sonja."

"You've got a bloody nerve," Sydney Chipchase said. "I've got half the bloody Namibian Police Force here with me now and they only just let me out of custody. They thought I was in on it, even though I tried my hardest to stop you."

She heard voices around him in the background. "Can you talk now?"

"Hang on." After a few moments he said, "What do you want?"

"Steele."

"You and everyone in this country—and Germany. News has just broken about the death of the nurse and her driver. He's going to be a marked man. I wouldn't want to be him when GSG-9 catches up with him."

"I want him first."

"Why should I help you, Sonja? You nearly got me killed and I'm in big trouble with the people who pay my bills."

"He's got my daughter with him."

She could tell Chipchase was weighing the pros and cons. She had guessed he was working for German intelligence and his reference to GSG-9—Germany's equivalent of the SAS—had confirmed her suspicions. If he could facilitate the elimination of Steele without his employers having to launch a major international operation, he might yet gain some kudos and make up for failing to save the dam. Sonja added, "You can track him using my girl's passport, Emma Jane Kurtz. Steele will be on a false one, but he won't have had time to get her one. He's said he's heading for Mauritius, but I'm sure that's a false trail. I doubt he'll risk leaving Africa, though."

"Leave it with me," Chipchase said.

"Call me back as soon as you have a destination." She ended the call.

Sonja was dirty, smelly and ached all over from the battering she'd received in the river and from being thrown around inside the armored car. All she cared about, though, was getting her daughter back. She looked at Sam. "You need to get across the border and get the hell out of Africa."

He shook his head.

• • •

He took her shopping in Johannesburg Airport. He bought her clothes, perfume, cigarettes, some expensive vodka and two swimsuits—a bikini and a one-piece. He even bought her shoes—high heels—which seemed quite a pervy thing for an old bloke to do, but she liked it. She liked him.

Emma drained the last of her white wine and watched him walking toward the bar again, threading his way among the other travelers and their bags. He was well old—old enough to be her father—but there was something about him, many things in fact, that she found incredibly masculine and sexy. Being with him was like surfacing after too long under water. It felt so good to breathe again after the crushing drudgery of boarding school.

She was excited, but she was also nervous in an edgy, thrilling, tingly sort of way. She analyzed her feelings and decided freedom was better than any drug her mother might think she'd tried. Emma had known Martin Steele—*Uncle* Martin—all her life, but it was only in the last year or so that she'd discovered just how much she loved him, and how much he loved her. It wasn't an uncle-niece sort of love. Not by a long shot.

Emma hated boarding school—something her mother never seemed to grasp—and Martin's emails from exotic places around the world had helped take her away from the gloom of English winters, the bitchiness of the other girls and the dour faces of the teachers. When he'd suggested they chat on MSN the frequency of their contact increased, as did its intensity.

He treated her like an adult, which she liked, and she felt she could ask him anything. Somehow—she couldn't quite remember the precise moment—their chat had turned to the topic of sex. She'd asked him if he had a girlfriend and he'd said no. He'd asked her if she had a boyfriend, to which she'd replied, "not really." He'd made some remark about reading a survey that said the vast majority of girls over the age of sixteen in the UK were sexually active, so she was probably getting more sex than he was. He'd warned her to be careful and had launched into a bit of a parental safe-sex talk. She'd been a bit shocked, but she'd also been very keen to let him know that she was still a virgin. She'd had rows with her mum about boys and sex—once because she wanted to bring a boy she'd met on summer holidays home for an overnight stay, because he lived in the country. Her cow of a mother had told her she couldn't have a boy over, no matter what she did when she wasn't around. She'd told her mum that she hadn't had sex with the boy—or anyone else—but she could tell her mother didn't believe her. She'd told all this to Martin and he'd been very sympathetic.

After that, she'd noticed that Martin had become much more formal with her in his emails and messaging, and she felt like she'd said something to upset him.

He walked back to the table with a glass of white wine in each hand and when he smiled at her she felt her heart melt and flow to her fingertips and toes, and everywhere in between. She'd resurrected the topic of love, romance and, yes, even sex, in their online chats, and she'd let him know that although she hadn't actually done it, that didn't mean she didn't think about it a lot.

It had been like having an adult best friend and she had found herself unburdening all sorts of things on him. He was interested in what she liked—in boys—and what made her excited and what didn't. She'd had two semi-serious boyfriends between the ages of fifteen and sixteen and while there had been some kissing and touching during the holidays, things had never progressed any further. With one of the boys she indulged in some cybersex. She hadn't found masturbating while he wrote in broken text-speak particularly arousing, but she sometimes found herself feeling very turned on while chatting with Martin. When they moved, slowly, inevitably to indulging in sex play online, she'd found his words were like poetry, or the book of literary erotica one of her friends had lent her. It didn't seem wrong or dirty or inappropriate and he'd been at pains to stress that there was no way in the world he wanted to have actual sex with a girl under the age of eighteen, even though the legal age of consent was sixteen.

All the same, when she'd arrived in Botswana it had been very, very odd seeing him in the flesh. It was the first time they'd seen each other in person since their chat had become so explicit and she'd blushed like crazy when he'd given her a chaste peck on the cheek. That first night in Xakanaxa Camp she'd wondered if he would come sneaking into her tent. In fact, she fantasized about it. But he paid her no attention. Although he was old he was even more handsome than she remembered, and she realized she was now looking at him through a woman's eyes, not a girl's.

Once more she was left wondering if she'd said or done something wrong, to make him lose interest in her.

"Cheers, beautiful," he said, and they clinked glasses. "Not long until the flight."

She loved that he thought she was beautiful. "You'll get me drunk." She sipped the wine. It was her fourth glass. She could hold it as well as any girl at school, but she felt light-headed around him. He put a hand on hers, on the small round table in the bar, and she thought she might catch alight from the heat of him.

She glanced around the crowded bar and caught the eye of a businessman in a suit who was looking up from his laptop. Emma wondered what the man was thinking. Did he think they were father and daughter, or did he pigeonhole them as a dirty old man and his younger mistress. She leaned over and kissed Martin on the cheek and smiled to herself as the businessman looked away.

"What was that for?"

She shrugged and drank a big gulp of wine. "For the dress, for the other clothes, the shoes . . . everything. I feel free at last, Martin, to be who I want to be. I'm still worried about Mum, though. I wish we could call her."

"Well, as I told you before, she's out of mobile range where she is at the moment, doing a security job for me, but I'll call her, or she'll probably call me when she has a signal again. Leave her to me, Emma."

"Yes, you can have her, but won't she be mad at you, when you tell her about . . . about us?"

He shook his head. "It doesn't really matter, my love, because in four short months you'll be eighteen—officially an adult—and you can do whatever it is you please."

Emma felt lost without her mobile phone. She'd searched her tent, the dining area and everywhere else she could think of before they left Xakanaxa. Like every girl she knew, her phone was like another body part—inseparable and essential to her day-to-day existence. She couldn't imagine where or how she lost it, and Stirling had assured her none of his staff would have stolen it. It was annoying, but Martin had promised to buy her an iPhone, as soon as they got to where they were going.

He'd been such a gentleman—in real life, that was—unlike some boys she'd met who only wanted to get into her pants. On the second night at Xakanaxa, while her mother had been away in Namibia bodyguarding, Martin had arranged for the two of them to have a private dinner on the balcony of his tent. He'd told her, then, across the candlelight and with the sounds of the African night as a soundtrack, that he loved her and that he wanted to take care of her when she finished school later that year. She'd been stunned, but part of her had been relieved because she'd played this scene out more than once alone in her bed at school. She told him that she wasn't going back to school, that from now on she would only go where he was going. They'd been brave words and she'd had second thoughts in the last couple of days, but the excitement of traveling somewhere new and exotic had galvanized her.

A woman's voice came over the Tannoy advising them that this was the first and final boarding call for the Kenya Airways flight to Nairobi. He smiled at her and she knew then and there that she wanted him. Forever.

Sonja turned on her phone while she and Sam were queuing in the center aisle of the Boeing, waiting to get out and into the terminal at Johannesburg Airport. The message alert beeped so she dialed the number to retrieve it.

"It's me," she heard Sydney Chipchase say. "Mombasa. They left Jo'burg for Nairobi last night, just after midnight. They would have been on a connecting flight earlier this morning. Probably there by the time you get this. Steele's traveling under the name of Craig Joseph Regan. Call me."

She did, and when he answered he said: "You got my message?"

"Yes."

"Are you going there?"

"Of course. Next available flight. I'll need hardware."

"Someone will meet you at Moi Airport. We only know his destination, not where he'll be staying. Good luck . . . you're going to need it."

Sonja followed Sam out of the airliner and ended the call. She knew where Steele was going, and that he was going to need a shitload more luck than her when she caught up with him.

34

Compared to the sparkling newness of Johannesburg Airport, which Martin had told Emma had been upgraded for the FIFA World Cup, Nairobi's Jomo Kenyatta Airport was old, dowdy, crowded and hot. They cleared customs and had to walk across the road to the domestic terminal. Amazingly, it was older, dowdier, more crowded and hotter than the main terminal.

It was a relief to get on board the smaller jet to Mombasa, and even more so once the pilot finally switched on the air-conditioning. Emma's eagerness to get to their destination, however, was dampened by a rising, nervy feeling inside her that she was going to have to confront the moment of truth very soon. She didn't really believe Martin—or she—could wait four months to have sex.

After their dinner at his tent he had kissed her, on the mouth. She could still feel and taste his lips. She'd started to open her mouth to him, as she'd done to other boys, but he had broken the kiss then, rather than taking her hint, leaving her feeling frustrated and insecure.

He put his hand on hers on the armrest as they started to descend. He'd made no move on her, or even touched her other than the odd brush, during the five-and-a-half-hour night flight from Johannesburg to Nairobi. She was tired and had a bit of a headache from the wine she'd drunk at the terminal and the small bottle she'd polished off on the flight.

"Nearly there," he whispered to her.

She smelled his aftershave and it made her spine tingle. The boys she'd known were barely shaving. One wore cologne, but she'd thought it revolting.

When she walked down the stairs the heat rising from the tarmac at Daniel Arap Moi Airport engulfed her like a duvet. She found it hard to breathe, but Martin took her arm gently and steered her toward the white terminal building with its series of high-pitched, steeply gabelled roofs. They collected their bags and Martin negotiated a price with a taxi driver who loaded their stuff, including the several shopping bags she'd collected, into the boot.

Kenya was very different to Botswana, and the little she'd seen of South Africa. Right up against the airport's perimeter fence there were people living in shanties made of tin and cardboard. The air was heavy with moisture, unlike the dusty dryness of the Okavango Delta, and the tarmac roads looked like they'd been hosed that morning. The vegetation was lush and green and threatening to overrun the ramshackle houses.

The city of Mombasa, Martin explained as they drove, was on an island, and they soon crossed a bridge and entered the chaotic, exhaust-choked center of town. There seemed to be no order to the traffic which moved from three, to five, to six lanes and back again at any one time as minibus taxis, cars and scooters honked at each other for no particular reason.

Many of the men wore long flowing white robes and some of the women were covered from head to toe in black. She was used to seeing Islamic people in England but, funnily enough, she hadn't expected it in Africa. There seemed to be as many Arabic people as black Africans. They passed fruit markets and a Libya Oil service station. The air, when she wound down the window of the taxi, was a mix of flowers, spices, smoke, engine fumes and raw sewage. It sickened and excited her at the same time. Martin's thigh was against hers, through the sheer fabric of the new sundress she'd changed into in the cramped toilet on the airplane. She'd fantasized, while standing there in her bra and knickers, about him tapping on the door, coming in and taking her, standing up. She rested a hand on his thigh and he smiled. She could do this. It was going to be OK.

"This is the main road," Martin said, breaking into her thoughts.

Arching over the road was a giant pair of grubby cream-painted elephant tusks. As they drove under them she could see they were made of pieces of tin plate, riveted together. "What's that all about?"

"That's a monument to Uhuru, which is what the Kenyans call their independence from Britain."

She liked that—independence. She was nearly eighteen and it was time for her to start living her life the way she wanted. She would finish her studies and enroll in university when it suited her, not her absentee mother, who had long ago forfeited the right to exert any control over her. "Tell me again about this house where we're staying. It belonged to your gran?"

"My great-aunt, actually. I spent several summer holidays here in Mombasa when I was a boy, at boarding school. I loved it here—it was a great escape from England. She died a spinster and left it to me."

"Cool."

The cab took them over another bridge and she started seeing signs for Nyali, and Nyali Beach, which she knew was where Martin's house was. She took a deep breath. Things were coming to a head. The houses here were more western than the crowded, jumbled bazaar of the city. They looked old, and while some were run-down, others were freshly whitewashed and enclosed behind fences festooned with bougainvillea. Emma liked it. It all seemed so romantic and reminded her of old movies she'd seen.

Martin told the driver to stop in front of a black steel sliding gate set in a white-painted concrete wall that was topped with razor wire and a three-strand electrified fence. Martin pressed a button on the intercom and a few seconds later the gate rolled open. To her surprise, Emma saw two African men in green uniforms. Both had rifles slung over their shoulders. Martin had told her that crime wasn't a particularly serious problem in this neighborhood so she didn't know whether to be alarmed or reassured by the presence of the security guards. He spoke to the men for a few seconds in what she guessed was Swahili.

She got out of the car, glad to be free of the sticky vinyl seat, and walked through the gate. "Oh, Martin, it's wicked!" She walked on a sparkling path of crushed coral flanked by manicured lawns and palm trees. Exotic flowers and creepers framed a sprawling single-story white house with a red terra-cotta roof. The house seemed split into two halves and through the middle was a wide open space with cane furniture and huge puffy pillows. She could see the pristine sand of the beach and turquoise of the Indian Ocean beyond and she wanted to run to it. An African man in a starched white robe, said: "*Jambo,*" and smiled brightly at her.

"Um ... *Jambo.*"

Emma's new heels clicked on the polished tiled floor of the lounging area and she walked to the edge. The sand was no more than fifty meters away, on the other side of another strip of lawn, though another electric fence prevented intruders straying into the house. She heard his footsteps behind her and felt his hand on her shoulder. "It's beautiful."

"Not as beautiful as you, Emma."

She looked past him and saw the servant and security guards had disappeared from sight. She tilted back her head and closed her eyes as he kissed her. Just like the last time, she opened her mouth to him, but this time he didn't stop. She felt his tongue and she liked it. He pulled her closer and she felt his erection swelling against her belly. It excited her and scared her at the same time.

Still holding her, Steele smiled, then lowered his lips to her ear. "Do you remember the things we chatted about online?" he whispered.

"Um ... yes."

"Good," he said. "Would you like to go for a swim now?"

She laughed. "Yes." He was teasing her and it was maddening, but if he wanted to play games, then she could give as good she got.

He loosened his hold on her and seemed to study her face. It sent a shiver down her back. "You look so much like your mother when she was younger." He reached out and brushed a strand of auburn hair from her forehead. "So beautiful."

She felt the redness rising up her throat and into her cheeks. "Maybe I should go and change?"

"Of course. Your room is down the hallway, second on the right."

Emma walked quickly down the hallway and when she opened the second door she saw her backpack and shopping bags were laid out on top of a low, intricately carved blanket box at the foot of a queen-sized bed topped with a duvet in a starched white cotton cover. She closed the door, leaned her back against it and exhaled loudly. She was so turned on she thought she might melt.

Sam asked for a Coke from the attendant on the flight from Nairobi to Mombasa. He was too nervous to eat, and Sonja hadn't ordered anything either. She stared out the window at the African landscape far below.

She'd started to open up to him, on the flight from South Africa to Kenya, though she'd retreated into her thoughts again. Sonja's theory, about Steele, was that he needed her money. "I've been a complete bloody idiot," she had told him. "I changed my will before I left England and made Martin Emma's legal guardian until she turns twenty-one. I didn't trust my own daughter to spend my money wisely, if anything happened to me, and Martin has control over her and my bank accounts. I misjudged Emma, and by not crediting her with the brains and maturity to look after herself I've made her resent me even more than she did and set her up as a target for Steele. The bastard was trying to kill me, Sam, in Zimbabwe and at the dam—all for bloody money. He's a gambler. He's probably lying low in Mombasa waiting to see if I'm still alive before he pays off whoever it is he owes this time."

Sonja had told Sam of her time in the British Army, and her service in Northern Ireland. She'd stopped the story when she told of the death of a young IRA man, Danny Byrne, whom she had befriended as a means of trapping the terrorist's brother. Steele had been involved in the raid in which both Byrne boys had been killed. She'd started the story in response to his question about how she had met Steele. It seemed odd that she even spoke about what he guessed was a sensitive military operation, but he sensed it had something pivotal to do with her past relationship with Steele.

"You never finished telling me about your time in Northern Ireland," Sam said now. She lifted her forehead away from the window and looked at him. "You said you and Steele were part of an operation where two IRA men were killed, but that you both had to leave the army soon after. Why was that? In the US Army you would have been given medals."

She shook her head. "Northern Ireland would have been too complicated for the US Army, Sam. For any army. I used Danny Byrne to set up his brother, Patrick, who was responsible for blowing up the school bus. I was convinced Danny wouldn't have given his brother the explosives to make the bomb if he'd known the target. In fact, Danny wanted to roll over, become what we used to call a 'super grass' and give up everyone he knew. He was sick of the war, and sick of the killing. He agreed to invite Patrick to his cottage and let me know when it would be, on the condition that his brother be taken alive, and that I would be there."

"As insurance?" Sam said.

"No. I don't think so." Sonja looked back out the window again for a few seconds, remembering. She turned back and looked Sam in the eyes. "I think he loved me, Sam. And, maybe, I think I loved him too. We'd become very close. I slept with him. Martin had encouraged me to win him over—to do whatever I felt was necessary—but when Martin found out what I'd done I think he was furious. He never said as much, and tried to play the cold hard professional, but the way he looked at me made me feel like a whore, and I suppose he was right to think that. Part of me wanted to run away with Danny—he was going to be offered relocation and witness protection—yet the other half of me wanted to make things right with Martin. I was so young, and so confused."

He felt for her. She had barely been out of her teens at the time. Sam had been at university, though still recovering from the shock of life in juvenile jail. Poor Sonja. He thought he'd had a rough start to adulthood, but it was nothing compared to what she'd had to deal with.

"How the hell," she continued, "did I trust this man with my daughter's future and my life? I wonder how much he owes the loansharks. Why didn't he just con someone or knock over a bank like a proper criminal? I don't know, Sam, maybe he hates me for ending his promising military career all those years ago."

She blinked a few times, and he wondered if she was fighting back tears. He knew, instinctively, she needed to get all this out of her system. She would no doubt disagree, but he knew it helped to talk sometimes. "What went wrong in Northern Ireland . . . you were about to tell me?"

Sonja nodded and took a deep breath, then exhaled. "The night of the raid, Danny and I were in his room and his brother was in the next. Patrick thought we were in bed together, but we were both fully clothed, just waiting for Martin and Sergeant Jones to arrive. I'd thought there would have been a bigger assault force, but Martin had said he wanted to keep it within the unit. It didn't seem right to me, but he was the officer, and very experienced.

"When the raid happened, Danny and I were wide awake and ready. The front door burst open, with no warning, and a stun grenade went off. The noise was terrible and we clung to each other, waiting. I knew Patrick had a gun somewhere, but the surprise worked. We heard Martin and Jones run into the house and kick open the door of Patrick's bedroom. He was swearing, but then I clearly heard Patrick say, 'Jesus, don't shoot . . . Please . . . I'm unarmed.' Then I heard the shooting."

Sonja paused and swallowed hard.

"You don't have to tell me if you don't want to," Sam said.

She shook her head. "Danny said to me that Steele had double-crossed him and executed his brother. He had a gun I didn't know about, hidden in his wardrobe, and he grabbed it. I told him to put it down, that everything would be all right. He told me to shut up and called me a lying bitch. I was speechless, Sam. I wasn't part of any betrayal, but he wouldn't listen to me. He opened the bedroom door and started shooting. He hit Jones and killed him. I knew he was going for Steele next. I had a pistol, and I drew it. I shot Danny in the back, Sam. I killed him."

"You were doing your job," Sam said.

"No!" She lowered her voice as the attendant walked past. "No, Sam. No one was doing their job that day. Steele had come to execute both men. It was an unauthorized operation. I should never have agreed to any of it. When we got back to England Steele concocted a story about how we had

acted on the spur of the moment, after discovering Danny and Patrick together in a pub. He hadn't reported any of our earlier activities. He was a
glory hound who wanted to claim sole responsibility for killing the man
who had blown up all those children. I was a pawn in his game. He used me,
manipulated me into sleeping with Danny, then couldn't stand it once I did
what he wanted. He seduced me when we got back to England and made me
lie to cover for him. It's only now that this is finally becoming clear to me,
Sam. At the time, I was happy that Patrick Byrne was gunned down in cold
blood . . . I wanted to believe that the ends justified the means, and that
Steele was right. The army saw through him, though, and they made him
resign his commission because they knew he was a maverick, and they
wanted to cover things up. I went along with the lies for too long."

"What year was that, again?" Sam asked.

"Nineteen ninety-two."

Sam did the arithmetic. It was pretty simple. "That must have been the
year Emma was conceived."

Sonja nodded. "I started to show after the investigation into the Byrne
brothers' death was wrapped up. There were rumors about me circulating
through the intelligence community. Steele and I were both forced out of
the army and we ended up together, after we both served as contractors in
Sierra Leone. He made a point of saying it didn't matter who Emma's father
was; I was happy not to know, and physically Martin and Danny were pretty
alike, so it was never obvious. A little over a year ago, though, Martin came
to see me and told me he wanted to know, for sure. He said he was re-writing
his will and had been thinking about Emma a lot. He'd grown close to her
over the years and he wanted it out in the open once and for all, and if she
was his, he would write her into his will. I guess I wanted to know, as well."

"What did you tell Emma?" Sam asked.

"Nothing. When she was young I'd told her that her father had died in
a car crash shortly after we'd started going out, and that my one regret was
that we'd never had a picture of the two of us taken together. I bought a
paternity testing kit online—all you need is to get a cheek swab and then
send it to a lab. I didn't know how I'd get the sample from Emma without

telling her what was going on, but I got lucky. Emma had braces at the time and would sometimes develop mouth ulcers. She asked me to take a look at one and I made up a story about needing to use an applicator this time to put on the numbing liquid she usually used. I switched swabs after taking a sample, and sent it off, with Martin's swab."

Sam grimaced, but said nothing. How could he stand in judgment— his life had been equally messy.

"Anyway," Sonja continued. "The test came back negative. Danny Byrne was Emma's father. Martin said he still wanted to be close to Emma and me, but I could tell at that moment that things changed again between us. I wonder if finding out, for sure, made him hate me . . . made him . . ."

"Want to kill you?"

She shrugged. "It looks like it. That, and the money. But I'm more worried that it gave him some kind of green light to do something worse, Sam. Emma's always liked him, but she's a sensible girl. She wouldn't have gone off with him if she knew I was coming to get her. I think something terrible is about to happen, Sam."

He suddenly shared her fear.

35

They swam and sunbathed on the beach during the afternoon and one of Martin's servants brought them gin and tonics. She felt so sophisticated.

Martin didn't kiss her again, although she wanted him to. At one point, as he lay beside her, he lifted himself on one elbow and leaned over and brushed a strand of wet hair from her eyes. He smiled down at her and she grinned back at him. "I don't want to rush things, Emma. You're a mature young woman, but..."

"But you want to wait until I'm eighteen. I know. But Martin, I am old enough to make up my own mind, you know, and I'm past the age of consent."

He nodded, but didn't rise to her bait. "We need to get back to the house and get changed. I've got a surprise for you."

"Naughty."

"Not that."

"What is it?"

"It won't be a surprise if I tell you."

She showered and changed back into the dress he'd bought her. This was so unlike school it wasn't funny. She stared at herself in the mirror, dabbing some extra foundation on an annoying spot that had chosen this moment, of all moments, to appear. She wondered what he saw in her, but she knew, then, that she was happy that he was interested in her, and that she had agreed to come away with him. Her mother would be furious, of course, but Martin was right. She was a woman. She slipped on her new sandals, took a breath and opened the bedroom door.

Martin was in the open living area wearing white linen trousers and a matching shirt, with the top three buttons open, but he was barefoot.

"You won't need shoes where we're going." Beside him was a large pic-nic hamper, which he picked up. "Come on." He held his hand out to her and she took it.

They walked out of the house and back onto the beach. It was late af-ternoon, nearly five, and the breeze had picked up. Two people were out kitesurfing, scudding across the ocean's surface. One lofted high up into the air, did a loop, and then came back down and stayed upright.

Ahead of them, where the water lapped the sand, was an inflatable rub-ber boat. Martin led her to it and placed the hamper on board, then held out his hand to help her get in. A true gentleman. "Is this your idea of a roman-tic boat trip?"

He laughed. "This is just the entrée. The main course is out there. See her? It's the dhow, out there in the deeper water."

Emma shielded her eyes and saw the ancient-looking wooden boat. She'd seen others sailing slowly past during the afternoon, with their exotic triangular sails and dark-skinned crews.

Emma sat in the back of the boat as Martin rolled up his trousers and pushed them out into the water. He got in and she shifted awkwardly to the middle as he edged past her and started the outboard. Soon they were speed-ing across the choppy water. Emma's hair streamed in the breeze and she couldn't stop grinning. She watched the kitesurfers zoom past them. This, she thought, was living.

There was a man on board the dhow, who waved as Martin approached. When they pulled alongside she recognized him as one of the security men from the house. He forced a smile, but didn't look particularly happy. Emma hoped he wasn't going to be hanging around during dinner. Emma wanted to tell Martin that she found it a bit weird having servants waiting on her, but she also didn't want to offend him. Martin and the man exchanged some words and the guard reached out a hand to help her on board. "I'm fine, thanks," she said, grasping the gunwale and hauling herself up. She didn't want him touching her.

"Well done," said Martin. "We'll make a sailor of you yet."

When Martin was on board the African man climbed over the edge and into the rubber boat. He started the engine and headed back to shore.

"Are we alone?" Emma asked.

"Yes. Is that all right?"

She nodded.

"Right," Martin said, "I'll get dinner on." There was a low table in the middle of the deck, laid with glasses, plates and cutlery set on a white table-cloth. Instead of seats there were large cushions. Toward the rear of the deck was a box of sand surrounded by walls of corrugated tin. A charcoal fire glowed in the center and an old-fashioned black teapot sat on a metal stand. Beyond the brazier was another nest of pillows.

There was a pop, which made Emma start, as the cork sailed out of a bottle of champagne. Martin poured two glasses and began laying out dinner from the picnic basket: cold chicken, salad and a plate of peeled cooked prawns.

Martin stood beside her and held up his glass. "What shall we drink to?"

She shrugged, feeling suddenly self-conscious. "The future?"

"An oldie but a goodie." He clinked his glass against hers. "My turn, next. To you, the most beautiful woman I've ever laid eyes on."

The African driver in the loud shirt had been waiting for them at the air-port and once they were inside the black Korean four-by-four he passed a padded envelope to Sonja, who was sitting in the front passenger seat. She undid the staples and slid out the nine-millimeter Sig Sauer, two magazines full of bullets and a screw-on silencer.

Sonja loaded the pistol and racked it. "What should I do with it when I'm done?"

The driver honked and swerved to miss a man on a motorcycle with a pillion passenger in a burqa. "There is plenty of water around here."

"Maybe we should go to the police," Sam said from the back seat.

"Too complicated," Sonja said.

Sam rolled his eyes. He was in love with a mercenary, and he knew there was no turning back now. Sonja told the driver the address, at Nyali Beach, and the man nodded. Sam was too nervous to pay much attention to the crowds in downtown Mombasa.

"The house is around the next corner," said the driver. He slowed the vehicle along a treed street lined with security walls. "Maybe I should leave you here?"

"Yes," Sonja said.

"Thank you," Sam said as the driver pulled over. Sonja was already out of the car and striding down the street. Sam had to jog to catch up with her. She was in hunting mode, he reckoned; totally focused. "What do you want me to do?"

"Stay here, or get a cab back to Mombasa. Find a nice hotel for us to stay in."

"Very funny," he said. "I'm not a handbag, Sonja. I'm here to help."

She stopped and looked at him. "I don't think you're a handbag, Sam. However, this is a job that's best done by one person."

"No way. I'm not leaving you. Just tell me what you want me to do."

Sonja thought for a few seconds. "OK. If Martin's got security, which I'm sure he has, they may have been briefed to watch out for me. He won't know yet whether I'm dead or alive, but the dam blast has been all over the news, so he'll be worried. I doubt he'd be expecting you to tag along, so you're going to be my diversion." She outlined her plan to him and he nodded. It was simple, and crazy.

Sonja melted into the lengthening shadows, down a laneway roofed with overgrowing bougainvillea. The alley ran between two grand old colonial homes and looked like it led to the beach. It was getting close to dusk.

Sam walked up to the steel security gate and pressed the button on the intercom.

"*Jambo*," said a tinny voice through the tiny speaker.

"Er, *Jambo*," Sam said. "I'd like to speak to Mr. Steele, please. I'm a friend from the United States."

"*The* bwana *he is not at home now*," said the voice.

Phew, Sam thought. If Steele was in, his plan was to disappear. Sonja had insisted on it. She would be waiting at the end of the alleyway, and if Steele was in, Sam would hurry to her and they would reassess the situation. If he wasn't in, then Sam was to distract the guards for as long as possible.

Sam pressed the button again. "I need you to take a message, then. Please come to the gate."

"*What is your name?*" the voice asked.

"It's Bates. Jim Bates," Sam said. Jim Bates, apparently, was a CIA agent based in Africa. Sonja had told Sam that she and Martin had met Bates a couple of times over the years, in Iraq and Afghanistan. If the guard wanted to check with Martin by phone, then Steele would be surprised, but hopefully not too concerned to hear the American had tracked him down.

"*You can come back tomorrow*," said the voice.

"No," Sam said. "Mr. Steele will want to see me and if he finds out you delayed the message I have from reaching him then you'll be in for an ass-kicking, my friend."

"*A what?*"

"You will be in big trouble. Come to the gate and I'll give you the message. That's all I want." Sam checked his watch. The five minutes was up. There was no further conversation and he stood there, nervously tapping his foot. He heard a rumbling and grating and the gate began to slide open. It stopped when it was wide enough for a man to walk through.

An African man in a green shirt and trousers filled the gap. "What is the message?"

Sam held his nerve. The man was as tall as he was, and solidly built. He noticed the bulge under his overhanging shirt and presumed it was a pistol. "I need a piece of paper and pen."

The man shook his head. "Tell me."

"No, it's private. Go and get me a piece of paper and a pen. Please."

The guard sighed and turned. Sam started to follow the man as he walked across the gravel, but the guard stopped and put up his hand to stop him. His other hand hovered in front of his waist. "You cannot come in here, without Mr. Steele's permission. Please, you must wait at the gate."

Sam raised his hands. "That's cool. Don't want to upset anyone. Say, you couldn't get me a glass of water, too, could you? It's awful hot out here."

"I am not a waiter. Stay at the gate, and I will—"

The sound of something crashing to the ground inside made the guard turn back toward the house and reach for the gun at his belt. Sam lowered his head and shoulder charged him, knocking him to the ground. The man fell, sprawling in the sharp white gravel, but rolled onto his side with frightening speed and got himself on top of Sam. He raised a fist and slammed it into the side of Sam's face. He grabbed Sam's throat in one huge hand while the other reached again for the pistol in its holster. "Who are you?"

"I'm Jim Bates, CIA station chief here in Mombasa, and if you kill me, you're going to bring a world of hurt down on your ass."

The man laughed as he slid his gun out, then suddenly pitched forward as Sam heard a thud like someone hitting a punching bag with a baseball bat. Sam wriggled out from underneath his attacker and saw Sonja standing over him with a security guard's wooden truncheon in one hand and her pistol in the other.

"Here," Sonja said, reaching out a hand. Sam took it and she lifted him to his feet, almost effortlessly. Sam stared down at the unconscious man. Neither Sam nor the guard had seen or heard her approach. "House is empty, except for one more of these." Sonja produced a curly telephone cord that she had presumably ripped from a handset inside the house, and knelt by the motionless guard. She used the phone's cord to tie his hands behind him. "No sign of Emma?"

Sonja shook her head. "The other guard told me Steele took her out to his boat."

Sam followed Sonja inside. Looking out over the lawn he saw that the gate leading to the beach was open. He wondered if she had shot the lock off. She'd evidently entered unnoticed, as the second security man lay on the tiled floor, which was spattered with blood. He had a rag stuffed in his mouth, and his face was beaded with perspiration. Sonja had tied a tourniquet around his leg, below the knee and above the bullet wound in his calf. The man's eyes widened and he shrunk away from her. "He needed some persuading," she said.

Sam made a mental note to try very hard never to do anything to upset his new girlfriend. "Is he going to be all right?"

"Yes he is, but at this moment, Sam, I don't particularly care." She walked through the open-plan living area and Sam followed her. Across the beach they saw a rubber boat speeding toward shore. It beached and a man got out and dragged the craft up the sand. "Quick! Get out of sight, Sam!"

"What?" Sam was too slow to react and just as he saw the man Sonja had pointed at, the man saw him. He started pushing the boat back into the water.

"Shit," Sonja said. She ran across the sand, with Sam in her wake. This part of Nyali Beach was quiet as twilight approached. The man splashed into the sea, jumped aboard the inflatable boat and yanked on the starter cord. The engine roared to life at first pull. "Stop, or I'll shoot!"

The man must have recognized Sonja. He lowered himself between the bulbous sides of the boat and gunned the outboard. Sonja spread her feet, lifted her pistol hand and wrapped her left around her right. She fired a double tap, and then another two shots. The man dropped out of sight completely and the boat began circling back toward shore in a wide turn. The inflatable slowed and, as Sonja waded out into the water, it started to sink. "Bloody hell. I must have holed both watertight compartments."

Sam stood at the edge of the Indian Ocean. He realized the man must be dead, part of his body somehow pressing on the outboard tiller to make the boat turn. "Let's call the police, Sonja. You can get Steele for abduction, if nothing else."

She turned and glared at him, the pistol hanging loose in her right hand. "There's no time, Sam. Martin could be up to anything out there. I'm not wasting time waiting for the police to arrive." She kicked off her shoes, stuffed the pistol in her shorts and started jogging up the beach, toward a young man who was folding a beach umbrella, under which a sandwich board said *Kitesurfing lessons.*

Emma felt light-headed and guessed it was a combination of sun, fresh air and alcohol. The sun was setting and the water looked as though someone had covered it in a floating blanket of gold foil, like the chocolate-money wrappings she remembered from childhood Christmases.

"How was dinner?" Martin asked.

"Lovely."

"We've got strawberries for dessert, but would you like to stretch out for a bit first?"

"Mmmm. That would be nice," she said without thinking it through. He stood and held out his hand, and she let him lift her to her feet and lead her to the pile of cushions behind the warmly glowing brazier. He eased himself down and she joined him.

They lay side by side, propped up on their elbows, looking at each other. He took her hand in his. "I'm worried about your mother," he said.

She looked down at their intertwined fingers. "I told you she'll have a cow. But we can deal with it."

"No, there's something else. Did you see the news video on the flight from Johannesburg to Nairobi, about the dam in Namibia being blown up?"

Emma nodded. A feeling of dread started to enshroud her heart and lungs, making it suddenly hard for her to draw a full breath. "Was Mum up there? Is that why we haven't heard from her?"

He looked into her eyes. "Has your mother ever told you what she does—what we do—for a living? What she really does?"

"She says she's a bodyguard, but I know she does more than that for you."

Martin he set his drink down on the wooden deck and rolled back to face her. He took her hand in both of his now. "Your mother and I work as private military contractors, what some people call mercenaries. She was . . . is very passionate about the environment, and the Okavango Delta, where she grew up, and where we were both staying."

"I know all that. She used to talk about it sometimes, but I thought it was a bit of a dustbowl. What are you saying? Oh my God, what? Are you saying she . . ."

Martin nodded, silencing her. "Yes, Emma, your mother blew up that dam. She was paid to do it—we both were—but she took on the job because she wanted to save one of Africa's true paradises. I didn't want to tell you until I was certain . . . but if she was OK, I would have heard from her by now. She was very brave, Emma."

Emma snatched her hand back. "What are you saying, *was*? Is she dead? Did she die blowing it up?" It was too much to take on board. She had her problems with her mother but she couldn't imagine her not being there, even if "there" was halfway around the world. "No."

"I should have heard from her by now. She was supposed to call me yesterday and then the plan was that she would fly to Mombasa and meet us. I'm worried, Emma. I think something terrible has happened to her."

"No!" Tears sprang to her eyes and the lack of breath made her choke. She started crying and Martin put his arm around her. She felt rotten, thinking back on all the horrible things she'd said to her mother recently. She pressed her face against Martin's chest and sobbed and sobbed.

"She might be OK, Emma, but I needed to tell you my fears. I have to be honest with you. I want you to know that whatever has happened I will look after you. I will care for you forever."

His words sounded muffled and she couldn't concentrate on what he was saying. She felt his finger under her chin and she raised her face, although her whole body was racked by convulsive sobs. He kissed her wet cheek and she blinked her eyes. He was looking at her funny now, as if he was thinking something deep and dark. Emma sniffled and tried to draw a deep breath to still her shaking. He leaned closer to her again and kissed her on the lips. She felt his tongue.

"No!"

"Emma . . ."

This was all suddenly so wrong. Emma realized he had deliberately held off telling her about her mother's death so he could continue seducing her, and now she was supposed to fall, simpering, into his comforting arms. The bastard. "No!" She put her hands on his chest and pushed him away. "Get off me! This isn't right."

"Emma, it's OK. I know how you feel. Let me hold you close. You're going to be all right. We're going to be—"

She wriggled away from him, drowning in the mass of pillows. "We're not going to be anything." He reached out and grabbed her wrist. It hurt. "Fucking let go of me!" She lashed out with her other hand and punched him in the chest, but he didn't release or ease his grip. "Let go!"

Martin got to his knees and managed to grab her other hand. "Listen to me," there was no gentleness in his tone now, "your mother's dead, Emma. You have to face facts. She made me your guardian in her will."

"She what? Let go of me. I'm going to scream."

He smiled. "Scream away. We're too far out for anyone to hear. Get it out of your system. Listen, I know you're hurting right now, but I *am* going to take care of you and we *are* going to be fine together. Remember the things we chatted about online, Emma . . . Remember the things we talked about doing, the things you've fantasized about. It can all be real, now, Emma, now—"

"Now that my mother's dead? You sick fucking old pervert. Did you kill her? Did you kill her so you could have me?"

"Of course I didn't. Calm down, Emma."

She took a breath and narrowed her eyes, seeing him as he really was, for the first time. She was too smart to believe in coincidences—her mother dying just as Martin had taken her into his life in real time. She saw the hours on the Internet for what they were—what teachers had warned the girls at her school about so many times—she had been groomed by a man who wanted not only her body, but her money. How could she have been so gullible, so stupid? She forced herself to think this through, to think what her mother might do in this kind of situation.

"OK." She took another breath. "I'm OK, now. I'm fine. Just don't rush me, all right? This is a lot to take in." She forced her body to relax back into the pillows and when he let go of her wrists she lashed out at him, raking her fingers across his cheek, drawing blood.

Steele yelled in pain and Emma rolled from under him. She leaped to her feet and started running, barefoot, along the deck. She had reached the brazier when she felt his hand grab the hem of her dress. She felt the pressure against her skin, then heard the fabric tearing. She reached down and grabbed the blackened teapot from its stand. The handle burned her palm, but she ignored it. Emma flung it back past her body and yelped as a jet of boiling water shot across her bare thigh.

The scream that came from Martin, however, was far worse: an animal cry of pure pain as the lid popped off the kettle and a wave of boiling water drenched his chest and arms. He dropped back into the cushions, writhing in pain as he tore off his shirt. "You bitch!"

Emma ran to the front of the dhow, her dress hanging in tatters from her body. She jumped up onto the prow and looked around her. Steele was rummaging in a bag at the back of the boat. The obvious way of escape was to dive overboard, but once in the water there was no way she could outswim the boat and there were no other vessels in sight. He could circle her until she tired of treading water, shoot her or run her down with the propeller. On board, she could still fight him, and she could still hurt him before he did whatever it was he was going to do to her. Her mum wouldn't have given in without a fight. All the same, she screamed into the night: "Help me!"

Sonja heard the cry as she shot past the first of the two dhows she had seen out sailing on the red-gold waters. There had been a man and a woman on board the other boat, but when they started waving to the lone kitesurfer she was fairly sure it couldn't have been Martin and Emma. As she skimmed past the wooden sailboat she confirmed it was a much older couple.

The scream had come from the only other boat in sight and she brought the kite down to maximize her speed.

The woman on board had climbed up onto the prow and Sonja saw diaphanous shrouds of white material snapping in the stiff evening breeze. "Help me!" she cried, and Sonja knew at once it was her daughter.

There was no time to think of a plan. She saw another head bobbing along the dhow's deck and recognized Martin. He reached up for Emma and she shrieked as he grabbed her by the ankle and pulled her crashing down on top of him.

"Help me!"

The cry tore into her like a bullet and she aimed amidships on a kamikaze course toward the wooden craft. As she came close enough to recognize their faces clearly she saw Martin turn to stare at her. "That's right," she said to herself, "it's me you bastard, and I've come to get you."

She saw his right hand move up, holding something, and Emma disappeared from sight. Emma was screaming, and Martin struggled for a few seconds to subdue her, but when his hand reappeared she glimpsed the telltale curved magazine of an AK-47. Sonja heard the pop of the bullets leaving the barrel, and the displaced crack of air somewhere off to her right. SAS men were crack shots who fired thousands of rounds during their training to qualify as expert marksmen. Sonja was two hundred meters out and closing fast, and soon she would be dead if she didn't do something fast.

Martin fired again and one of the two shots was close enough to almost burn her cheek. Sonja lifted the kitesurfer's steering bar quickly over her head to just past the twelve o'clock position and soared into the air. Steele raised his rifle to follow her midair flip, but his next volley sailed wide. Sonja pulled the bar down to two o'clock and dropped back to the water's surface on a path well forward of the boat, and as she transitioned back toward the dhow her sudden change of direction put him further off his aim. Martin disappeared from sight for a moment and Sonja heard him swear. She imagined Emma was fighting him, trying to spoil his aim. Good girl, Sonja thought; just be careful, my baby.

The wooden hull rushed up toward Sonja with frightening speed. "Go Emma!" Sonja yelled. "Dive overboard!"

Martin popped up above the gunwale, rifle at his shoulder. Sonja raised the bar again and lofted up into the darkening sky. As she did so she let go of the bar with one hand and reached for her pistol. She stayed attached to the kite via her harness and one-handed grip as she tried to aim at Martin. There was a splash as Emma jumped overboard.

Steele fired a three-round burst on automatic and Sonja felt the hammer blow of a bullet in her left shoulder, forcing her to let go of the bar completely, but the harness held her. The force of the hit made her body spin and the board came away from her feet and splashed into the sea. Sonja fired blindly in Steele's general direction. The wooden deck of the dhow was beneath her as she grasped the emergency harness release with her left hand and yanked on it. She screamed in pain from her shoulder wound and then dropped hard to the weathered boards three meters below as the kite sailed off into the dark sky. Steele's firing pin clicked on an empty chamber and as he dived to one side one of Sonja's bullets found its mark, hitting him in the thigh.

Steele rolled behind the brazier's sand box as Sonja dragged herself up off the deck and emptied the last rounds from her magazine. She tried to reach for the left pocket of her shorts, but her arm now refused to work. She stared at the blood pumping from her shoulder and shook her head in anger and disbelief. Steele poked his head up over the lip of top of the box and saw her pistol was locked open, smoke curling from the breech. Sonja dropped to her knees and placed the empty firearm on the deck so she could reach across her body to the pocket with the spare magazine. Steele rose and launched himself at her. He kicked the pistol across the deck before knocking her to the boards in a tackle. Sonja jabbed her fingers into the wound in Martin's leg and he rolled off her. She crawled toward her pistol, but Steele was on his feet again. He stamped his foot down on her wrist just as her fingers almost reached the barrel.

Sonja bellowed in agony. Steele stared down at her, eyes wide as he rammed a spare magazine into his AK and yanked back on the cocking lever. "Hello, Sonja."

She snatched her aching hand back and put pressure on the bullet wound in her shoulder as Martin kicked the empty pistol further out of reach, sending it sliding across the deck back toward the sand box. One-handed, he unthreaded the belt from his linen trousers and backed off a couple of paces. "Don't move or I'll kill you."

"You may . . ." Sonja gasped, " . . . may as well do it now."

He shook his head as he wrapped the belt around his thigh, threaded the tongue through the buckle and pulled it tight. The blood flowing from his wound started to slow. Sonja, meanwhile, could feel her own blood pumping from her shoulder with each heartbeat. "Call her back," Steele said.

"No."

"Emma!" Steele yelled across the darkening waters. "Emma, come back on board. I've got your mother here and I'm going to kill her if you don't show yourself."

"Swim, my girl!" Sonja yelled. "Don't listen to him."

Steele laughed. "I've fantasized about having the pair of you," he said to her, then called out, "Count of three, Emma. Then she dies. One . . . two . . ."

Sam switched to breaststroke so as not to disturb the waters as much as when he was swimming freestyle. The breeze that had propelled Sonja rippled the ocean's surface, and further masked his wake as he swam. The spear gun trailed behind him from the leg rope attached to his ankle.

He'd run after Sonja but there was nothing he could do after she stole the kiteboard at gunpoint. The African man who'd been running the beachside franchise had run off in panic as soon as the crazy white woman had taken to the water. Sam had seen the man's flippers and spear gun lying beside the folded umbrella and deckchairs and grabbed them.

He'd heard the gunfire and seen the muzzle flashes coming from the dhow, silhouetted against the crimson of the evening sky. At least he knew he was swimming toward the right boat, but it was a hell of a long way from shore and he wondered if he would find anyone still alive when he got there.

"Go to your mother," Steele said as Emma eased herself over the gunwale. Her face was white with fear and her teeth were chattering as she moved to the bow of the boat, leaving a trail of salt water dripping behind her.

"Mum!" Emma dropped to her knees and wrapped her arms around her mother, whose face shone deathly white in the dark. There was blood everywhere. "Mum . . . I'm so sorry for everything." She kissed her mother's cheek and Sonja buried her face in her daughter's hair; her lips close to her ear.

"Left pocket," Sonja whispered.

Emma moved her face away from her, but caught the stern look in her mother's eyes, so she didn't say anything else. Emma looked back at Steele. "She's bleeding to death. You've got to let me help her."

Steele shook his head. "I'm hurt too, Emma. Crawl over here like a good little girl and tie some of that pretty dress of yours around my thigh."

"No."

"OK," said Steele. He raised the AK to his shoulder and took aim at Sonja. "One . . . two . . ."

"Stop!" Emma crawled on her hands and knees across the deck toward him.

"My," Steele said, "this *is* fun, isn't it, girls?"

"You bastard," Sonja said.

"Too true, I'm afraid." Steele looked down at Emma, who was ripping a swathe of material from her stained, wet dress. "Good girl."

"What now, Martin?" Sonja asked.

"Good question. I really didn't want something like this to happen, but you were very hard to kill, Sonja. Impossible, in fact. First the Zimbabwean CIO failed to kill you at the ambush of the presidential convoy, but I was sure they'd get you at Divundu. After that I had to think long and hard about how to have you killed by the dam security guards."

"You supplied dud RPG rounds, grenades and mortar bombs to the Caprivians. Why did you let me take real explosives to the dam?" Sonja asked. Steele kept a close eye on Emma as she wrapped the makeshift bandage around his leg.

"Two reasons. First, it was such a small quantity, in the kicker and the detonating charges, that you might have been able to tell if it was fake; and secondly, I thought that, given who you are, Sonja, you might just pull off the job and destroy the dam. That way, as it happened, I still got paid by that obnoxious fool, Bernard Trench. Quite a nice bonus. Of course, if you somehow managed to blow the dam and live I knew I'd end up facing a tricky little situation like this one."

"Is it all about the money, Martin? It's the gambling, isn't it?"

He shrugged. "Go back to your mother, Emma. Go sit next to her." He shifted his attention back to Sonja as Emma crawled to her. "Yes and no. I do owe an awful lot of money to some very nasty Russian gentlemen in London who will kill me, slowly, if I don't pay them. You know, I really did love you there for a while, Sonja, but despite my repeated attempts to get back into your good books you kept rejecting me. So I started looking at this little carbon copy of you, who was growing into a woman every bit as beautiful as her mother. I knew that if I could get my hands on your money, I'd have enough to clear all my debts. I'd have bugger-all left over, but I would have lovely young you to ease my financial and emotional pain."

Emma sidled up next to Sonja and wrapped her arm around her.

"That's why you wanted the paternity test, isn't it," said Sonja. "You sick bastard."

"Sick? Not at all. That was precisely the point of the test."

Emma looked at him, and then her mother. "What paternity test?"

Steele gave an exaggerated frown. "Sorry Emma, your mum and I forgot to tell you. I'm not sure if you remember your mother swabbing your mouth once when you had braces, but we were conducting a little experiment on you. I'd always wondered if I was your father, but it turned out your dad was a low-life IRA terrorist who helped blow up a bus full of schoolkids. Bet you're relieved about that, eh?"

"What?" Emma looked at them both in confusion.

"Yes, so once I knew you *weren't* my little bastard, Emma, I thought it would be OK to get to know you better. I wouldn't want anyone to think I'd be capable of incest." Steele gave a shudder. "Yuck. Not me at all."

"You'll have to kill us both, now," Emma said. "And you're right. I don't care who my father was, as long as it's not you."

"Emma," Sonja said. "Don't goad him."

"Yes, Emma," Steele nodded. "Listen to Mum. So, Sonja, what are we going to do? Any ideas?"

"You can have all our money," Sonja said. "No strings attached. In exchange for our lives. We'll go away somewhere overseas and leave you to pay off your debts and do whatever you want."

Steele laughed out loud. "That's a good one, Sonn. You'd be after me before I even finished counting it. You're too good at killing people. Yes, Emma, that's your mum's real job. She's a very good killer. No, I'm afraid that's not an option."

Sonja narrowed her eyes. "I'm going to be dead in half an hour, Martin, if I don't get medical attention, and you're not going to be too far behind me." She looked at Emma and then Steele. "Listen to me. Both of you. Martin, I'm going to offer you my life in exchange for Emma's."

"No!" Emma cried.

"Shush," Sonja said. "Martin, you can kill us both, but if that happens my money will be so tied up you'll never get access to it. Emma, if I die then the money technically goes to you, but this creature here is your legal guardian. Sorry, baby. It's the worst decision I ever made in my life and I deserve to pay for it."

"No, Mum!"

"Shush. I want you to go with him, Emma. Let him take our money and pay off his debts. Martin, if you've got a shred of honor left in your body you'll give Emma what's left over and let her go, but I doubt you do."

"Mum!" Emma wailed. "Don't make me do a deal like this. I couldn't live with myself."

Sonja looked at Steele, who simply nodded. She reached over for Emma and held her tight against her. Emma started crying again, her tears running down her mother's face and neck. Sonja moved so that Emma's back was to Martin, blocking his view of her.

"Enough. Don't try anything, Sonja. I'm watching you."

Sonja nodded and gently pushed Emma away, back down to the deck. She raised her bloodied right hand back up to the wound at her shoulder. She managed to stand, but started to sway. Emma got up and put an arm around her waist, but Sonja shook her head. "Sit down, my girl."

Sonja took a step toward Steele, who raised the AK-47 to his shoulder. "Not too close. I don't want to get blood all over me."

Emma howled and sank to the deck. Tears rolled down her face and her body shook. "No, Mum! Don't please. I beg you, Mum. This is all my fault for letting him manipulate me. I should have known better. Don't let him do this."

Sonja looked down at Emma. "All we have is each other, Emma. This is all I can give you."

"Enough," Steele croaked.

Sonja glared at him. "You bastard. Do it. Now!"

Steele glanced downward, as if trying to summon the courage to do what she wanted. It was then that he noticed the rivulet of water running from the aft deck. He started to turn.

Sam lay on the deck, looking up at Steele's back. He had the spear gun ready and he was sure Sonja had seen him as she took the step toward Steele. He guessed she was talking to him, when she said, "Do it."

He curled his finger around the trigger and squeezed. The spear flew from the launcher just as Steele started to turn. Sam had aimed for the back of where he guessed Steele's heart would be—if the animal had one—but by turning his torso Steele moved and the spear pierced his left upper arm.

Steele roared and flailed and raised his gun hand again. Sam saw Sonja staggering toward the Englishman and was worried Steele would still be able to turn and aim the AK-47 at her. Sam reefed back on the spear gun, which was still attached to its projectile by a nylon lanyard. Steele yelled in pain again and was hauled off balance. As he fell he pulled the trigger and fired a wild burst of rounds from the AK. Some bullets went into the air while two others hit the deck between Sonja and Emma.

Sonja lunged toward Steele, but he dropped to his knees and swung the empty rifle up and away from his body, catching Sonja under the chin with the barrel. Her head snapped back and she fell to the deck, unconscious. Emma screamed and fell down beside her mother, cradling her head in her hands.

Sam rushed Steele and sent him sprawling onto the deck. He grabbed the rifle and smashed it into the planking, bashing Steele's fingers until he let go. Steele threw a heavy blow that caught the American square on the side of the chin and rolled him to one side. Sam was unprepared for the power behind the punch and it dazed him. Steele got to his knees, reached across his body and grabbed the pointed end of the spear. He gritted his teeth, gave a war cry of pain and rage, and pulled the spear all the way through. He reversed the metal shaft, stood and kicked Sam viciously in the ribs. Sam doubled and tried to roll away, but Steele was on top of him, straddling him, before he could get away. Steele raised the spear high, aimed it at Sam's eye and prepared to deliver the killing thrust.

Emma saw the fight as if it was happening in slow motion. Martin bellowed like a wounded animal as he ripped the spear through his arm, dragging the nylon rope with it like a giant sewing needle.

She saw the rage and murderous bloodlust on his face. Her fingers closed around the hard metal magazine of bullets she'd pulled from her mother's shorts when she'd held her close. Her mum had put her body between Emma and Martin to give her the chance to find what was in her left pocket.

Her mum was unconscious—maybe already dead—and Sam Chapman, a man Emma had only ever seen on television, was lying on his back. The madman Steele was about to kill him and then that would be the end of them all.

Emma saw her mother's empty pistol on the deck where Martin had kicked it away. It was at the base of the sand box that held the charcoal brazier. Emma was petrified and wanted to curl up into a ball and cry, but then she looked down at her mother's still, blood-covered body. Her mum had been ready to die for her.

Emma rose like she was on the starting blocks at the school athletics track. She wasn't the fastest runner, but one of the teachers said she was good off the blocks and had good reflexes. Her toes gripped the coarse grain of the wood decking and she launched herself forward.

Steele must have seen the movement in his peripheral vision, because he turned as he raised the spear above his head. He paused, tilted back his head and laughed. "Run, little Emma! I'll have plenty of time for you!"

She dropped to the deck beside the warm tin that held the fire box together. She saw him raise the spear high again, and Sam raised his hand in a futile attempt to ward off the strike.

Emma had never fired a gun in her life but the pistol felt oddly familiar as soon as she picked it up. She'd known boys who played computer games and seen enough movies to know the basics. But there was something else. As she slid the boxlike magazine into the butt she must have accidentally or instinctively knocked or pressed something, because the top bit flew forward and she knew, right then, that it was ready.

Emma pointed at Steele as his arm started to flash downward and when the point of the spear was just inches from Sam's head she pulled the trigger.

36

Sonja opened her eyes and the whiteness temporarily blinded her. She blinked and winced as she moved and felt the pain in her shoulder. She smelled flowers.

"Here, let me help you sit up," Sam said.

She looked across and saw him standing there. Bits and pieces of a dream flashed across her mind. Martin's body; flashing blue lights; Emma crouching on the deck of the boat with a pistol in her hand; the sound of gunshots; thinking she was dead.

Sam leaned over her and she felt strong arms around her, sliding her along white sheets that smelled of starch. That smell always reminded her of the army. "Where . . ."

"You're in hospital, in Mombasa."

"Uh. OK." Sonja closed her eyes and had a sudden dizzying panic attack. "Emma!"

The door to the private room burst open and Emma came racing in. She wore a green T-shirt and khaki shorts. "Mum!"

Emma hugged her and kissed her and Sonja ignored the pain and wrapped her good arm around her girl and hugged her tight, not wanting to let her go. Emma started crying and Sonja sniffed back a tear. With Emma still sitting on the bed Sonja looked over at Sam and held out her hand. He took it. "What happened to Steele?"

"Emma saved our lives, Sonja," Sam said. "A fisherman came up to us after hearing the gunfire and pointed the way to the hospital, here on the main island. We didn't have a radio or phone or anything so Emma and I got the engine started and came straight here. You lost a lot of blood and needed a couple of transfusions. We were scared sick."

"And Steele?" Sonja repeated.

Sam looked at Emma, who nodded, and then looked back into Sonja's eyes. "We tossed his body overboard and made sure it wouldn't float and sank the boat."

Sonja squeezed his hand. "Good job. Both of you."

"The Caprivi Strip was on the news this morning," Sam said. "The Namibian government agreed to sit down with the United Democratic Party at talks in Johannesburg, sponsored by the United Nations. They're going to be discussing plans for increased autonomy and maybe even a future referendum. Parts of the Okavango Delta are flooded, but local environmentalists are saying the damage is no worse than if they'd had really heavy rains. Miraculously, no one was hurt or killed by the water escaping the dam. There was lovely video of the water running down a dry channel and elephants sucking it all up."

Sonja blinked as she thought of her father, and of Miriam and little Frederick. She hoped they were safe. Sonja turned to Emma. "I'm so sorry, my girl, that I put you through all this. I'm so sorry you had to see such terrible things, and I'm sorry for being such a crap mother." She coughed.

"It's OK, Mum." Emma laid her head down on the pillow next to Sonja's and kissed her on the cheek. "I'm sorry for being such a bitch to you lately, and for letting that man get to me. I feel like a fool. One thing's for sure, though, I'm never touching a gun again as long as I live."

Sonja tugged on Sam's hand so that he could be closer to her and Emma. "Neither am I."

Emma got up off the bed. "I was just going to get a drink when you woke up. Would you like something from the shop? How about you, Sam?"

"I'm good," said Sam.

"Same here," Sonja said. "Thanks for asking, love."

Emma backed toward the door of the room. She blew a kiss and Sonja smiled back at her daughter as she pushed open the door with her bum and went out into the corridor.

Sonja kissed Sam on the lips, then said: "We won't be safe until we're on a plane out of here. There are too many loose ends."

"I think we're going to be OK," Sam said, sitting on the bed beside her. "Chipchase called the hospital and I spoke to him while you were out of it. Somehow he knew you were here. He says his people here in Mombasa have taken care of the body of the guy you killed in the dinghy, and the security guards you roughed up in Steele's house have been paid off. The guy with the bullet in his leg is in a private clinic working out how to spend his new-found fortune."

Sonja frowned. "I should have killed the pair of them. I still won't feel safe until we're out of Kenya. I don't suppose you kept a gun?"

Sam looked up at the ceiling, not saying anything about the promise Sonja had just made to her daughter. "I'll be glad to get back to the normality of television." He walked over to a wooden closet in the corner of the room, opened it and dragged out Martin Steele's green army dive bag. He hefted it up on the bed and unzipped it. Inside was the AK-47, two spare magazines of ammunition and a pair of hand grenades.

"Good," Sonja said. "I feel better already."

Sam sighed. "You're going to love America."

Emma paused in the corridor, reached behind her and pulled down the T-shirt, just in case her pistol was showing.

Acknowledgments

This book is a work of fiction, but some of the issues in it are based on fact.

There *was* a proposal, several years ago, developed by the Namibian and Angolan governments to dam the Okavango River at the same place where my fictional structure is located. The dam was meant to supply hydroelectric power to local communities. The project faced intense opposition from environmental groups and the Botswana government and was subsequently shelved.

There *is* a United Democratic Party, which supports greater autonomy for the Caprivi region. There *was* (and for all I know still is) a Caprivi Liberation Army whose armed members attacked the police station at Katima Mulilo in 1999. The brief but armed insurrection was put down by Namibian security forces and a number of people were arrested. The region has been at peace since.

There *are* several thousand Lozi people living in Botswana in self-imposed exile. A conversation with a Lozi man outside the Spar supermarket in Maun (where my fictional Sonja meets the equally fictional Gideon Sitali) provided a good deal of inspiration for the part of my story involving the CLA.

All this aside, it was never my intention to promote or further the cause of those people of the Caprivi region who wish to create an autonomous homeland. Namibia is a stunning country and one of the safest and friendliest African nations I have ever visited. I certainly hope that war never returns to this place.

There *is* a Xakanaxa Camp, and it was my very great pleasure to stay there while researching this book, courtesy of Wayne Hamilton from the Africa Safari Co in Sydney, and Steve Ellis, of Personal Africa in South Africa. Several other locations in *The Delta* are real, including Drotsky's and Ngepi camps on the Okavango River in Botswana and Namibia, respectively. Thanks also to Mack Air for flying Nicola and me into and out of the Moremi Game Reserve. There are so many beautiful locations in this part of Africa that it's impossible for me to cram them all into one book, but I hope I've done the real places I've mentioned justice.

Several generous people paid good money to worthy causes to have their names (or the names of their friends and relatives) used as characters in this book. I'd like to publicly express my thanks to everyone who bid for names at fund-raising auctions in support of Painted Dog Conservation Inc., an Australian-based charity which supports research and conservation of the endangered African Painted Dog; The SAVE Foundation (NSW), which is involved in relocation of black rhino from South Africa to the Okavango Delta and other rhino conservation projects; and The Gray Man, an Australian organization which rescues child prostitutes from a life of hell in Southeast Asian countries. I hope Sydney Chipchase, Stirling Smith, Cheryl-Ann Smith (née Daffen), John Lemon and John Little all enjoy their fictional alter egos.

Thanks, too, to the following friends who helped me with my research: former army engineer John Roberts, for his advice on constructing and blowing things up; Neil Johns for his tips on riding and caring for horses in the African bush; and Are Berentsen, of Fort Collins, Colorado, who studied coyotes in the wild for real. For factual information on the Okavango Delta I referred on a number of occasions to an excellent book: *Okavango: Jewel of the Kalahari* (Struik, 2003), by Karen Ross.

Several people read the manuscript of the *The Delta* and provided invaluable feedback. Namibian journalist Desiewaar N Heita checked my references to his country's political, cultural and environmental situation, and South African "Lion Whisperer" and film maker, Kevin Richardson, whose biography *Part of the Pride* I co-wrote, vetted my scenes involving the filming of wildlife documentaries. As always, my wife Nicola, mum Kathy, and mother-in-law Sheila did a fantastic job as my unpaid editors.

Seven books on and I'm more grateful than ever to my friends at Pan Macmillan Australia for continuing to let me live the life I've always dreamed of. Thank you, Publishing Director Cate Paterson (first, as always), Publisher James Fraser (not least of all for showing me around Mombasa), Senior Editor Emma Rafferty, Copy Editor Julia Stiles, and my Publicist, Louise Cornegé. I love you all.

Thanks, too, to my new agent, Isobel Dixon, of Blake Friedmann Literary Agency in London, for taking me on and promoting me outside of Australia.

And last, but most definitely not least, thank you.